1001 Dark Nights Compilation Nine

Four Novellas By:

Carrie Ann Ryan
Heather Graham
Jennifer Probst
Christopher Rice

1001 Dark Nights

EVIL EYE
CONCEPTS

Sign up for the 1001 Dark Nights Newsletter
and be entered to win a Tiffany Key necklace.

There's a contest every month!

Go to www.1001DarkNights.com to subscribe.

As a bonus, all subscribers will receive a free
1001 Dark Nights story
The First Night
by Lexi Blake & M.J. Rose

Table Of Contents

One Thousand And One Dark Nights

Once upon a time, in the future…

I was a student fascinated with stories and learning. I studied philosophy, poetry, history, the occult, and the art and science of love and magic. I had a vast library at my father's home and collected thousands of volumes of fantastic tales.

I learned all about ancient races and bygone times. About myths and legends and dreams of all people through the millennium. And the more I read the stronger my imagination grew until I discovered that I was able to travel into the stories... to actually become part of them.

I wish I could say that I listened to my teacher and respected my gift, as I ought to have. If I had, I would not be telling you this tale now.
But I was foolhardy and confused, showing off with bravery.

One afternoon, curious about the myth of the Arabian Nights, I traveled back to ancient Persia to see for myself if it was true that every day Shahryar (Persian: شهريار, "king") married a new virgin, and then sent yesterday's wife to be beheaded. It was written and I had read, that by the time he met Scheherazade, the vizier's daughter, he'd killed one thousand women.

Something went wrong with my efforts. I arrived in the midst of the story and somehow exchanged places with Scheherazade – a phenomena that had never occurred before and that still to this day, I cannot explain.

Now I am trapped in that ancient past. I have taken on Scheherazade's life and the only way I can protect myself and stay alive is to do what she did to protect herself and stay alive.

Every night the King calls for me and listens as I spin tales. And when the evening ends and dawn breaks, I stop at a point that leaves him breathless and yearning for more. And so the King spares my life for one more day, so that he might hear the rest of my dark tale.

As soon as I finish a story... I begin a new one... like the one that you, dear reader, have before you now.

Hidden Ink

A Montgomery Ink Novella

By Carrie Ann Ryan

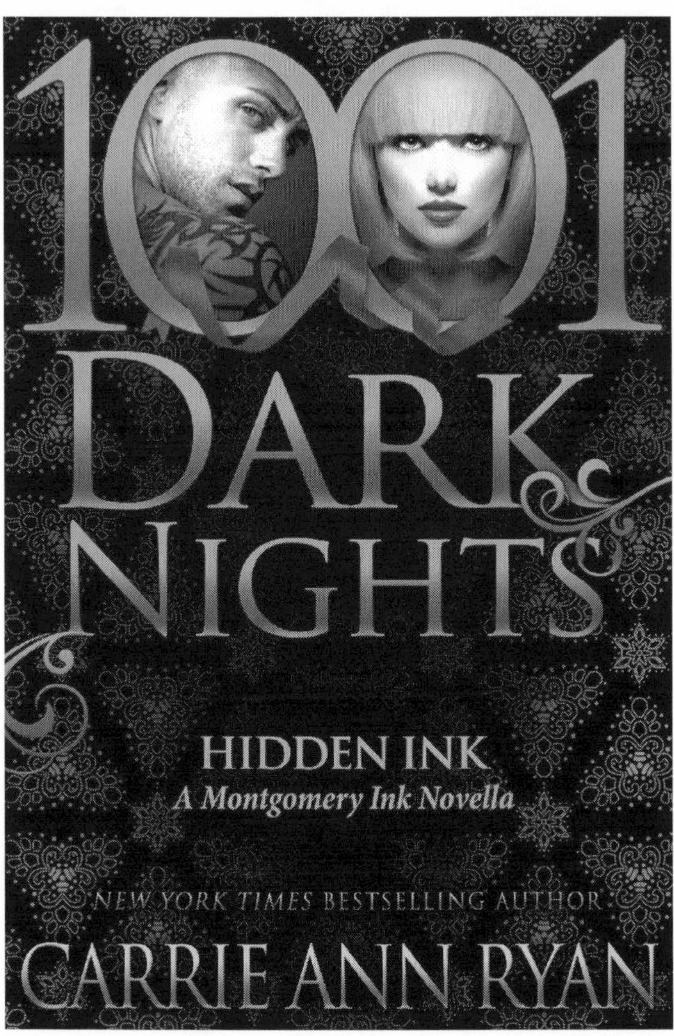

Acknowledgments

I am so grateful to be able to write the worlds I love and work with 1001 Dark Nights again. Thank you Liz Berry, MJ Rose, Kim, and Jillian, as well as the rest of the 1001 Dark Nights team!

This book and the characters inside hold a special place in my heart. I had hoped to write Hailey and Sloane's story almost two years ago, but the timing never truly worked out. Now it's finally time for them to find their HEA as well as for you readers to be able to see what secrets Hailey and Sloane hold.

Diving into Hailey's, as well as Sloane's, past made me look into myself more than I was ready for, but I am truly blessed that everyone will be able to read their story.

I want to thank Kennedy Layne, Shayla Blake, Carly Phillips, Lexi Blake, Angel Payne, and Julie Kenner for helping me along with this book. Writing it broke me ever so slightly.

And as always, thank you readers, for being with me for each step of my journey. You guys rock!

Chapter One

Hailey Monroe bit into her lip, closed her eyes, and moaned. Loudly. Dear gods and goddesses that was…heavenly. Earth shattering. World changing. Orgasm inducing.

That was the best damn cream cheese turtle brownie she'd ever baked in her life.

She may have baked pies, cakes, tortes, cookies, muffins, biscotti, and other kinds of decadence in her past. But right now, with this beautiful, mouthwatering cream cheese turtle brownie in hand, she knew she'd never achieve such greatness again.

At that depressing thought, she ate the last of her treat and frowned.

Seriously? The pinnacle of her success in life, the greatness she had hoped to achieve lay in a brownie.

A brownie sent from heaven, mind you, but a brownie nonetheless.

She quickly wiped up any spare crumbs then went to the sink to wash her hands. It was kind of upsetting that in her twenty-seven years of living, this baking achievement was *it* for her. Most people would think finding a cure for the common cold, painting something that reaffirmed beauty and life for others, or building homes for the unfortunate would be something that made a pinnacle a pinnacle. Instead, Hailey had dessert. This divine brownie.

It probably didn't help her thoughts that she kept calling the damn thing heaven-sent and divine. It was just a baked good, one that crumbled when roughly handled, like the rest of them. It would be consumed wholly and forgotten in the next moment, never to be heard from again.

At least Hailey herself was stronger than that. Some days.

She cracked her knuckles, wincing at the pain in her joints—a *wonderful* side effect of all the drugs and treatments she'd poured into her system over the years—and rolled her neck. Today was a new day, a new adventure. It was the same mantra she repeated to herself every morning.

Hailey owned and operated Taboo, a café and bakery in the middle of downtown Denver. She had prime placement right off the 16th Street Mall and the business district. During prime hours, she had men and women in suits and neatly pressed clothes, begging for coffee and leaving with something sweet and delicious. No one could rightly say no to Hailey and her baked goods if she were really trying.

Her shop catered to more than just those in a hurry on their way to a meeting or working on a very important case. Families came in on late afternoons or on non-school days with children in tow. Her hot cocoa and cookies went quickly when school holidays met cold Denver weather days.

People in all shapes and sizes ventured into her shop, and she loved it. There was never a dull moment. Even when the place was only filled with a customer or two, they were *hers*. After thinking she'd never see the middle of her twenties, she was now looking at the back end of those years and owned her own business besides. She was a caretaker, a businesswoman, a baker…a survivor.

She pressed her lips together at the last word.

A survivor.

If she kept telling herself that, kept letting the news and random websites tell her more of the same, then one day she might believe it. However, she hated that word and everything that came with it. She'd fought and won, but at what cost?

Hailey shook her head. There was no time for those kinds of thoughts this early February morning. Today, she had to make sure she was at least competing with the chain coffee shops around her—the Mega Starbucks two blocks over on each side of Taboo. Seriously, Denver had a Starbucks on every other corner, and where there wasn't a Starbucks, there was a Caribou Coffee or something else of the like. It wasn't as if she'd ever make as much money as them, but she did well. Her goal wasn't to become a millionaire or turn her small shop into a chain—she just wanted to *live*.

That's all she ever wanted to do.

So she'd compete in her own little way and make sure her shop looked ready for the next holiday. Valentine's Day. It was almost here. Actually, the clock calendar had just changed to February at midnight. Her decorated cookies and cupcakes would have hearts and pink all over them, and that morning, she'd put out her best festive Valentine's Day decorations. It wasn't overboard or cheesy, but just enough pink to remind her of happiness and love—not the pink that became an overbearing reminder in October.

Hell. Twice in one morning. She needed to stop being depressed about the past and look to her future with the same wide-eyed wonder she had as a teenager. Her aching bones and muscles could use the happiness.

Hailey rolled her shoulders back and finished up her morning prep. She'd been at it since four thirty that morning. Baker's hours were evil, but she didn't have to wake up as early as others, she knew. Her store opened at six a.m., and it was almost that time now. She had two people who worked for her, but Hailey was the one who did the baking and most of the cooking. The others worked the register and served while they were here. They also helped build the sandwiches or paninis—depending on the special on any given day—and heated the soups. Hailey made sure there was never a dull moment in Taboo.

The door between her shop and the one next door opened, and she pressed a hand to her stomach.

"I smelled coffee," Callie said as she walked in, her red-streaked black hair looking shiny that morning. In fact, the woman herself glowed. Her ink stood out on pale brown skin, and she smiled as if she had the best news in the world.

Considering Callie was six weeks pregnant, Hailey supposed she did.

"You scared the crap out of me," Hailey said with a laugh and rubbed her stomach again. She remembered the time when she used to rub the space over her heart if she was nervous or freaked out, but that was a long time ago.

Callie winced and bit into her dark ruby lip. "Sorry about that.

I got to Montgomery Ink early to work on a sketch and needed coffee."

Hailey frowned and went to the coffee pot that she'd turned on only a few moments before. "I'm only giving you decaf. I don't want your very sexy, silver fox of a husband getting all growly with me. While you might like it when he gets growly with you because you get a spanking and orgasm out of it, I do not."

Callie pouted. "Fine. Decaf. Maybe I can trick my body into thinking it's real so I can pep up."

Hailey raised a brow as Callie bounced from foot to foot. "Honey, if you're any more pepped, you'll pep the heck out of Maya and Austin when they get into the shop."

Callie rolled her eyes before looking around Taboo. "Oh, I love when you decorate for a new season and holiday. You know how to do it so it's not all crepe paper and hearts dangling from the ceiling."

Hailey started the pot of decaf and held back a yawn. Maybe she needed some caffeine herself. With a sigh, she poured herself a cup of the regular coffee and set to work adding creamer, whipped cream, and chocolate shavings. It might not be an espresso since she didn't want to bother making that from scratch just then, but she could still have fun with the toppings.

"I don't mind the crepe paper and dangling hearts," Hailey said as she started work on Callie's decaf. With a little caramel and whipped cream, the sugar would help Callie feel like she was drinking the real thing. Plus, everything Hailey made was all-natural, so there wouldn't be any extra chemicals messing with the baby.

Callie took the offered cup with a smile. "My precious."

Hailey rolled her eyes. "Okay, Gollum. Drink up. And take a seat, okay? You're way too wired this morning, and yet you wanted caffeine. What's up?"

Callie sat and licked at her whipped cream. "I'm just happy, you know? This time two years ago I was just starting to work for Austin and the rest of the Montgomerys. Austin and Maya took a chance on me. And my sketches. Now I get to tattoo for a living. Plus, my Morgan was my first piece all on my own once Austin promoted me from apprentice to full-time artist. I not only got to ink the best phoenix in the world—because oh my God, have you seen his back? Heck, yeah—but I fell in love with him, too. And he loves me back, even though we're totally not the same age, and I say totally way too much. Now we're married and having a baby! It's unreal." Callie smiled big, her eyes bright. "Sometimes I feel like I don't deserve it. Like one day I'll wake up and everything will be just a dream and I'll be back working four jobs to pay rent on my ramshackle home. And Morgan won't be beside me every morning. He's my everything, and yet he shows me how to be *more* than that somehow."

Tears filled Callie's eyes and Hailey quickly handed over a few napkins. Her heart ached for some reason when it should have been only happy for the other woman. She and Callie were close in age, yet they had gone down such different paths that some days Hailey felt years older. The two of them and Miranda—Austin and Maya's youngest sister—were the youngest of the crew that hung out together. The Montgomerys and their circle ranged in age from mid-twenties to early forties, and most days, the age differences didn't matter. Hell, Morgan was in his forties and having a baby with Callie.

Age was just a number.

It was the heart and experience of a person that made things work.

Hailey didn't have her soul mate, didn't have that person who would help her find the better Hailey. She only had herself and her drive to keep going. That had to count for something. And she would *not* be jealous of Callie.

Just because Callie had met the man she was meant to be with and the man actually felt the same way about it didn't mean that Hailey wouldn't.

Of course, Hailey felt like she had already met that man, but that was neither here nor there. That man didn't want her so it was all water under the bridge anyway. What mattered at the moment was Callie and her tears, not whatever the hell was going on in Hailey's head.

Hailey pushed thoughts of sexy tattooed men who didn't want her out of her mind and went around the counter to put her arms around Callie.

"Honey, what's wrong?"

"I'm happy," Callie hiccupped. "Oh, God. I'm only in my first trimester and the hormones are getting me. How is that possible? I thought the tears and mood swings came in the third trimester and then right after the baby came."

Hailey kissed the top of Callie's dark hair and sighed. "I think it depends on the person. I've never been pregnant before so I don't know. You can ask Sierra or Meghan, though." Sierra was Austin's wife and Meghan was his sister. The two women were also part of Hailey's and Callie's inner circle. "They've been through all of this before. Meghan twice in fact. And who knows, with the way she and Luc are trying, she could get pregnant any day now and only be a couple months behind you."

"That would be nice," Callie said as she sniffed. The other woman wiped her face with the extra napkins Hailey had handed her and sighed. "This is crazy. I came in here because I love you and because, hello, coffee, and now I'm all weepy."

"Welcome to being pregnant." Hailey may not have firsthand experience with pregnancy, but the treatments she'd had in the past caused similar hormonal fluctuations. One minute she'd be happy, smiling away, the next, sobbing uncontrollably before moving on to a rage she'd never felt before. The drugs might technically be out of her system, but if she wasn't careful, sometimes, she still went through those mood swings.

Hailey had kept her previous diagnosis and past hidden, so she couldn't tell Callie any of that. She didn't know why she hadn't spoken of it before. Well, she knew a little bit. Once someone said the word *cancer*, she would be stuck with the label for the rest of her life.

She wouldn't be Hailey, the woman with the platinum-blonde bob and red lips.

She wouldn't be Hailey, café owner and businesswoman.

She wouldn't be Hailey, the woman with secrets who had a connection to the sexy man next door, which no one spoke of but everyone knew existed.

She would become Hailey, breast cancer survivor.

Hailey, not whole.

Hailey, not fully a woman.

She mentally slapped herself. It had been how long, and she was still feeling this way? It had been years since the surgeries, the treatments. She was cancer free. Enough time had passed that she *was* cancer free, not just in remission.

Hailey wasn't the same woman she was before, but in all honesty, who was the same person they were at age twenty?

She needed to push that aside and worry about Callie right then. One day soon, she would tell the girls about her cancer. She hadn't known them when she was sick, but keeping secrets like this wore on her. Plus, she wanted to make sure the girls were taking care of themselves. She'd been young when she was diagnosed, way too young for that type of illness, and yet she'd had to go through everything that came with it. She didn't want her friends to face the same things she had.

No one deserved that.

"I'm happy," Callie said again, this time her eyes clear of tears. "And Morgan is going to freak when he finds out that I cried today. Because even if you don't say anything. He'll know. He's just that good."

Hailey kissed her friend's cheek and let out a laugh. "It's because he loves you."

Oh, to be loved like that. Unconditionally. To know that someone could see deep inside and know every emotion, and take the time—and care enough—to cradle that feeling…

Hailey was indeed jealous, but it didn't matter. Callie deserved all of that and more.

All of her friends did.

"He does love me, doesn't he?" Callie said with a smile. "Okay, now that I've gotten coffee out of you and cried on your shoulder, I'm going back to the shop to work like I said I would." She let out a sigh. "Another reason I'm in here early is that Morgan had a super early appointment. The call was with someone in another time zone. I hate being at home alone. So thank you for being you and letting me ramble. The guys and Maya should be into the shop a bit later. I'll send them over since those brownies look to die for."

Hailey grinned. "They *are* absolutely amazing. I taste-tested one this morning. For business purposes, of course."

"How you keep your curves looking like a fifties pinup *and* taste all of your sweets is beyond me."

Hailey snorted. "It takes a lot of yoga and running to keep me in the shape I am, thank you very much. And you're like the size of one of my legs, so shut up."

Callie rolled her eyes then bounced toward Montgomery Ink. Hailey loved the fact that there was a door between the two shops. When Hailey had first opened her shop four years ago, she'd been intimidated by the very broody, bearded, tattooed men next door. And then there was Maya.

The tattoo artist and middle Montgomery girl was a force to be reckoned with—all ink, piercings, and attitude. So, of course, Hailey became friends with her right away. Contrary to her feelings about being next door to people she hadn't quite understood at first, she fell in love with their connections, attitudes, and sense of family. They were loud when they wanted to be, quiet and respectful at other times. They partied when they felt like it and threw small gatherings other times. They weren't rough and tough to the point where she ever felt scared to be around them. Others might be assholes and judge the Montgomerys on their ink—and yes, their kink—but Hailey had found her soulmates. Her family.

She didn't have a family of her own so it was nice to be adopted into theirs, welcomed into their open arms. Though the door between the shops had been there before she bought the place, the Montgomerys hadn't used it with the prior owner— a prim and proper older woman who had no time for tattoos and ruffians.

Seriously. Her words.

Now the door was never locked, and the Montgomerys and their crew could come in and out of Taboo when they wanted food and caffeine. Hailey went over there often, as well, with trays of goodies and sometimes empty-handed just to see the beautiful artwork.

She was still a blank canvas, but knew she eventually wanted ink of her own.

One day she would be brave enough to ask for it.

It wasn't the ink she was afraid of, wasn't the needles. God knew she'd seen enough of those in her life thanks to chemo, radiation, and the countless tests and treatments.

No, it was the person she wanted to do her ink.

While Maya, Austin, and Callie would bend over backward to help her with her tattoo and the nerves that came with it, she didn't want them to do it. She had someone else in mind.

Someone she was afraid to talk to for fear of what would spill out.

Someone who didn't care for her as she cared for him.

Hailey's phone buzzed and she sighed. Today was a day for melancholy thoughts, apparently. She turned off the timer on her phone then went to the front of the café to flip the sign to *Open* while unlocking the door. Two of her morning regulars, men in business suits, who had the courtesy to get off their phones before they walked into the shop, smiled at her.

"Good morning, gentlemen," she said with a smile. "Your usuals?"

"You know it," one said.

"Of course," the other one added in.

She smiled widely then went back to her counter to get their drinks and pastries. Soon her help would be there to work the register so she wouldn't be alone. The crisp morning air had filtered in with the brief opening and closing of the door, and as she worked quickly, she knew today would be a good day.

Any day she could do what she loved would be a better day than the last.

By the time Corrine came in and took over the front station, Hailey was already buzzing with the adrenaline of a morning rush. There was nothing like earning a living doing something she loved. The brownies were a hit, and the first batch she'd set out was soon gone. Normally, she would have saved them for the afternoon crowd so customers would eat her bagels and other morning delights, but she didn't have the heart to hide them in the back. Nor did she have the will.

She'd have eaten the whole batch and gained all that weight Callie had joked about. Lying on the kitchen floor in a sugar coma wasn't the best way to run a bakery.

The morning passed by quickly, and soon, Hailey found

herself in a slight lull. After talking to Corrine, she made a tray of pastries and to-go cups of coffee—each one individualized for someone special. She wasn't sure exactly who was working today over at Montgomery Ink, but she knew at least the main people would be there, and she was familiar with their drink of choice. Even if she made extra, nothing would go to waste. Austin and Maya would make sure of that.

Hailey made her way through the door and held back a sigh at the sound of needles buzzing and the deep voices of those speaking. She loved Montgomery Ink. It was part of her home.

"Caffeine! I want to have your babies. Can I have your babies, sexy momma?" Maya asked as she cradled her coffee and cheese pastry.

Hailey snorted. "Are you talking to me or the coffee?"

Maya blinked up at her, the ring in her brow glittering under the lights. "Yes."

Hailey just shook her head and handed off a drink to Austin, who bussed a kiss on her cheek. His beard tickled her, and once again, she wanted to bow down at Sierra's feet in jealousy. Seriously, the man was hot. All the Montgomerys were.

Soon she found herself with only one drink on her tray along with a single cherry and cream cheese pastry.

His favorite.

Behind Maya's work area sat another station.

Sloane Gordon's.

All six-foot-four, two hundred something pounds of muscle covered in ink, his light brown skin accented perfectly by the designs. The man was sex. All sex. Sloane had shaved his head years ago. She was convinced he kept it shaved just to turn her on. He kept his beard trimmed, but that and the bald head apparently jump-started a new kink in her.

Who knew?

He was a decade older than Hailey, and though he didn't speak of it, she knew he'd been through war, battle, and heartbreak.

And she loved him.

Only he didn't *see* her. He never took a step toward her. He also looked as if he were ready to growl at her presence most of the time.

Much like he did now.

"Thought you'd forgotten me," he said, his voice low and gruff.

She shook her head then raised her chin. "No, I have yours here." After she had handed him his drink and pastry, careful not to brush her fingers along his, she glanced down at his client, who was in the middle of getting his back done.

While Sloane looked dangerous and battle worn, this guy looked gentler, but not soft in the slightest. His hair was longer on top and flopped down over his forehead and into his eyes, but the sides had been clipped short. He had a short beard and a smile that looked as if it came easily. His green eyes sparkled, and Hailey could only smile back.

"Hello there," he drawled.

Oh, my. A southern accent—just a hint of drawl but not too much. If she hadn't been in the presence of the one man her body and soul had chosen for her, she might have gone weak in the knees at the sound of it.

"Hi," she said back, well aware that Sloane was staring daggers at her.

"What's your name?" the stranger asked. "I'm Brody."

"Hi, Brody. I'm Hailey. I own Taboo next door."

His smile widened, showing a bit of dimple. "I've walked by there a few times, but now I know I need to go inside."

She shook her head on a laugh. "I see. You scent my baked goods and now you'll come inside."

"It wasn't your baked goods that made me want to step inside."

What was she doing? Flirting with another man in front of Sloane like this? And why did she care? He wasn't hers. He never would be. She would never have Sloane Gordon in her life beyond a few curt words and grunts of thanks. She was young, healthy, and *alive*. She should be able to flirt whenever she wanted.

Determined not to look at Sloane, or notice how quiet it had gotten within Montgomery Ink, she tilted her head and put her hand on her hip.

"Really?" she asked.

"Really. How about I come over after I get this done and have a bit of sugar to keep me going?"

She laughed, throwing her head back. "Oh, honey, that was a terrible line, but you are welcome to come over. I'll give you a bit of…sugar." She winked then turned toward the door, adding a little sway to her hips as she left.

She might not be able to have the man she wanted, but she could still be *free.*

She wasn't the same woman she'd been before the cancer destroyed her body and soul, but she was still Hailey Monroe.

Strong.

Alive.

And annoyingly single.

Maybe it was time to do something about that. Sloane or no Sloane.

Chapter Two

Sloane Gordon forced his foot off the pedal and carefully, oh-so-carefully, set the tattoo gun on his counter. Permanently maiming the little fucker in his chair was bad for business. Plus, he didn't feel like going to jail for harming the shit. Sloane already looked like someone who had spent a few years behind bars—even if he hadn't. He didn't need to perpetuate the image.

But the man in front of him was *this* close to getting his ass kicked.

Who the fuck wore their hair like that? This kid looked like he was in a boy band and should be bouncing around on stage as teenage girls screamed his name. Sure, Brody looked to be around Hailey's age and was a *little* bigger in muscle than the kids who sang about lost loves and being theirs forever, but it was the principle of the matter.

No man should hit on a woman while she was working. Especially not when said woman was Hailey Monroe.

Sloane's Hailey.

Only she wasn't his. Contrary to popular belief, he'd never been with Hailey—though he'd thought about it. Often. He'd never held her in his arms, never cupped her cheek and felt the softness of her skin—because damn it, it would be soft. It just looked it. Soft and warm and perfect.

Hailey Monroe wasn't Sloane's, and he needed to get control of himself.

The two of them had a connection from the very first time they saw each other, but he'd never claimed her. Not that she was his to claim and all, but he'd stayed back. He knew she wasn't for him, or rather, *he* wasn't for *her*. So he'd done the best thing possible and stayed away.

That didn't mean he was okay with some new guy with too much product in his hair hitting on her. Of course, Sloane hadn't missed the way Hailey had flirted right back. She'd even moved her hips just enough while walking away to let them all know she was aware of being watched.

What the hell was up with that?

In the few years they'd been circling each other yet never moving closer, he hadn't once seen her go on a date, hadn't seen her flirt with another man beyond a wink or two. Those winks, he knew, were just her personality. But he wanted them all.

He was a selfish bastard and he didn't want her flirting with Brody. He didn't want to see her with another man period, especially not one she'd flirted with right in front of him.

What kind of man did that make Sloane?

He wanted her, but he couldn't be with her so he wouldn't let others be with her either.

He wasn't sure he liked that man, but hell, he couldn't stop himself. He could say he'd always been this way, but that would be a lie. He'd never reacted this way to another man around Hailey. But she'd never flirted back either. Sure, Griffin had joked about things with Hailey and she'd smiled in the past, but Griffin would never have crossed the line. Now he was with Autumn and no longer a concern when it came to Hailey.

There was an unwritten rule that Hailey was *his,* and he needed to figure out what he was going to do about it. He knew he didn't have the right to do anything about it, but that didn't stop him from dreaming, from wondering.

He looked up from his hands and into Austin Montgomery's eyes. His boss raised a brow and looked worried. Sloane couldn't blame the other man. *He* wasn't quite sure what he was going to do. It wasn't Brody's fault that he'd stepped into something even Sloane didn't understand. That didn't mean Sloane was going to make it easy on the kid.

Sloane and Hailey had a dance of sorts that had been going on since day one. They'd get slightly closer, but then one or the other would back away. They'd talk about everything and nothing at the same time. She always left him the best cookies and made sure he was fed and taken care of no matter what. He always made sure she was safe, never letting her walk to her car out in the back parking lot alone. At social functions where they were together in a large group, they usually sat next to or near one another. They never touched, but they made sure they were always in the vicinity of each other.

The others knew that there was *something* between him and Hailey. Hell, the guys and Maya razzed him about it more often than not. It wasn't that Sloane was never going to make a move; it was that he wanted to make sure it was the right time for that move.

He blinked. Well, hell, that idea was new. Apparently, he *would* be making a move. He was barely in the right headspace most days, let alone in the right place for him to be with Hailey. He'd moved slow, wanting to ensure that he didn't spook her, didn't fuck himself over. Because when he did move—if that happened at all—there would be no turning back. He wanted to be her everything, much like she already was for him. She'd be his in body and truth, and he'd make sure he gave her what he could. There was no partway when it came to the ownership of his heart, his soul. But some darkness would have to remain his and his alone.

And until he could know for sure that the darkness within him wouldn't touch Hailey, he had to hold himself back. He'd known he was playing with fire by waiting, by watching for years and never doing more. But she'd held back, too. She'd known it wasn't the right time yet.

Or maybe he was wrong? Maybe he'd screwed up and now he was about to lose it all. Lose it to someone closer to her age, someone who made her laugh and her eyes sparkle.

Sloane wanted to be the man that made her throw her head back and laugh like that. He wanted to be all of those things and more. But he couldn't. Not yet. It wasn't the time, and now it might not ever be the time.

Jesus, his head hurt from going back and forth. He wanted her, he ached for her, but he wasn't good enough for her. He'd never be pure for her. But at some point he may have to let that go. Realize that while he wasn't light—instead, darkness—he was still *hers*. And that would have to be sufficient.

Sloane might not be good enough for Hailey, but damn it, nobody was. This Brody, with his too-gelled hair, wasn't even close to being what she needed.

"Are we taking a break?" Brody asked as he looked over his shoulder. "Everything looking good back there?"

Maya cleared her throat, and Sloane forced his attention away from Brody and toward the other tattoo station. His other boss and friend pressed her lips together, surprising him. He'd have thought Maya would have a sarcastic quip or something to say about what the hell had just happened. Even Callie stood by Maya's side, wide-eyed and a little surprised. He didn't blame the younger woman. For as long as he'd known her, she'd been trying to figure out why he wasn't with Hailey.

How was he supposed to tell them he wasn't worthy of the blonde bombshell with secrets of her own? That if he was with her, he'd taint the beauty of her soul, the exquisiteness of her smile. That's what he did. He brought in the shadows, carved deep inside, and rotted the core of someone because of what he'd done, what he'd seen.

But he was a selfish bastard. He knew that. Sloane knew it might be time for him to stand up and actually do something about what he'd been hiding from for years. To do that, however, he needed to make sure this kid knew his place.

"Shit," Brody mumbled under his breath. "I stepped in it, didn't I?" The younger man turned slightly in his chair and grimaced. "I didn't know she was yours, bro. I just saw a pretty girl with no ring on her finger and thought she was fair game. I'm sorry. I didn't know she was taken."

Sloane let out a breath, his rage over this kid backing down slightly, though the swirl of self-pity was well on the rise. Lovely.

"She's not…"

Brody shook his head. "Yeah, she is. I saw the way you looked at her, and I know you're about this close to knocking my head right off my shoulders. So you might not be dating her officially, but I stepped in it. I'll go in there and then back off. I'd just leave, but that wouldn't be right, and I don't want to hurt her feelings. You know?" He shrugged. "If you don't want to finish my ink, I get it."

Sloane was aware that the others were staring at him, waiting for him to confirm or deny his so-called relationship with Hailey. They were waiting for him to say something. Anything.

"I'm not going to fuck up your ink, kid."

Brody raised a brow. "I know I'm taking my life in my hands, but I'm not that much younger than you. No need to call me kid."

Maya muttered something under her breath about insolent fools while Austin groaned.

"You're asking for me to punch you in the face, aren't you?" Sloane growled out, his voice low and deep. Though in reality, his voice was always low and deep.

"Not really. I just figured if you're calling *me* kid and Hailey looked to be about the same age as me, then maybe you're calling *her* kid, as well."

"Jesus Christ," Austin growled. The man also coughed out what suspiciously sounded like a chuckle.

"How about you shut up and let me finish your ink?" Sloane asked casually, though he felt anything but casual. "Then you can head on out of here and we'll call it a day."

Brody sighed then turned so Sloane could work on the last shading of the tattoo. "Whatever, Sloane. But I've got to say, if Hailey smiled at me like that, maybe you need to step up your game and actually do something about her. Because if you're saying that you're not with her but act like no one else can be with her either, that might cause problems. Just saying."

"Brody, for the love of God, stop talking," Maya snapped. "He has a tattoo gun like two inches from your skin. Do you really want to piss him off?"

"He's not going to mess up my ink," Brody said back slowly. "He already said that."

"I might change my mind," Sloane said. He wouldn't. None of the crew at Montgomery Ink would. Even pissed off, they wouldn't fuck up ink. That was their income, their passion, their life. Fucking up ink was not an option.

"You wouldn't," Brody said calmly. "You like me, even if you want to punch me in the face right now."

Sloane chuckled slowly and he saw Austin's shoulders relax at the sound. "Hell, kid, you have an ego on you."

"Helps with the ladies. Though not your lady. I won't poach."

If Sloane hadn't wanted to kick this kid's ass for daring to come near Hailey, he might have become friends with the idiot. As it was, he was withholding judgment on that until he could figure out what the hell he was going to do about Hailey at all. He couldn't keep doing this, couldn't keep freaking out if another man came near her. Of course, he hadn't actually freaked out physically before. This was a first.

She'd smiled at Brody.

She'd given him one of *Sloane's* smiles.

Hell. He needed to get his head out of his ass.

He finished up Brody's work in silence then stretched his back as the other guy stood up and ran a hand through his hair.

"Okay, I'm going to go tell Hailey I won't be by later. That way I don't make her feel like shit or something, you know?"

Sloane just raised an eyebrow. "You told her you were going to stop by after you were done with your ink. It's after your ink, so you stopping by to go in there to tell her you won't be stopping by seems kind of idiotic."

Brody just shrugged. "You not doing anything about a woman you clearly have feelings for seems idiotic."

"Oh, dear God," Maya mumbled, and Austin let out a rough chuckle.

"Shut it, Montgomerys," Sloane bit out. Freaking Montgomery clan, always getting in his business.

"The kid's not wrong," Austin said quietly. "You've been circling around that girl for years. If you're not going to do something about it, maybe it's time to back off."

Sloane let out a low growl and narrowed his eyes at his one-time friend. Austin stared back, unrepentant. Sloane flipped him off then brought his attention back to Brody.

"Why don't you just go and I'll deal with Hailey?"

Brody's brows rose. "And if I choose to go in there so she doesn't think I'm an asshole?"

Sloane snarled, and Brody raised his hands in surrender. "Hell, Sloane. Fine, but you better go in there and make sure she doesn't feel like I didn't come in because of her. You get me? Because that's a shitty thing to do."

"I'll make sure she understands." Not that he understood. What the hell was he doing anyway? Now he was pushing men out of Hailey's way and acting like a complete idiot. He'd have to go over there and talk to her about feelings and shit. Sure, they talked about everything under the sun that had nothing to do with what was important usually, but he had a feeling this would be important.

Why the hell was he changing things?

Why the hell had she said yes to Brody?

Brody tilted his head. "You know what, screw it. I'm going over there to tell her I won't be by for sugar. I'm not going to be the asshole here. You are."

Sloane wanted to reach out and grab the kid by the neck, but he restrained himself. The other man walked through the door connecting Montgomery Ink and Taboo, leaving Sloane feeling like an idiot of epic proportions.

"I can't believe you just did that," Callie said softly. "I know you and Hailey have this…thing or whatever, but you seriously just stepped in it."

"Don't start with me, Callie."

"Don't get mad at the pregnant chick," Maya snapped.

This time, it was Sloane who held up his hands in surrender. "Jesus. What the hell is wrong with everyone today?"

Maya stalked toward him, her eyebrow ring glittering under the lights. "Oh, I don't know, maybe it's because we're watching you act like a douche and yet you don't seem to see it."

He ran his tongue over his teeth. Oh, he knew he was being a douche, but he didn't know how to stop it. He hadn't been able to stop many things recently, and yet he just kept making mistakes. Kept getting closer and closer to Hailey, knowing he'd be the one to hurt her eventually. He'd stayed away from her for a reason at first, then made sure to keep his feelings in check when he hadn't been able to be away anymore.

Now he'd put himself in the center of something that was rightly none of his business. A small part of him didn't care, and that part wanted her to be his until the end of days. But the rational part of his mind knew he needed to stay away. It would be better for everyone if he just kept to himself and kept Hailey on her side of the wall.

But he'd fucked that up.

Truly.

"You're not going to say anything?" Maya asked. She searched his face, and this time, he didn't see anger, he saw disappointment. Nothing cut him quicker than seeing that in the eyes of his friends. "I want you happy, Sloane. Why can't you see that?"

"I could say the same about you," he said without thinking.

Her eyes widened for a moment, her face paling. "You know what? The hell with it. I'm done. Hurt yourself, block off any emotion you think you could have, but if you hurt Hailey any more than you already have, I'll kick you in the balls."

With that, she stormed off, and he closed his eyes, cursing himself. Maya had her own issues and he shouldn't have brought it up, even in the vaguest of senses. Friends didn't do that, didn't dig the knife deeper when they knew the other was hurting.

Yet Sloane kept messing things up.

"Why don't you go for a walk or go sketch?" Austin asked quietly. "Take a breather."

Sloane let out a breath and gave a tight nod. Montgomery Ink was his family, and he had to remember that. He'd been dancing around what Hailey meant to him, what he wanted her to mean to him, for far too long, and now he had to deal with the consequences. The others had always known there might be something brewing between the two of them, but now he'd done something blatant about that…connection.

And as soon as Hailey found out about what he'd done, he'd be in for it.

He closed the office door behind him and let out a sigh, running a hand over his face. Then he sat down at the main desk and traced his finger over the edge of his sketchbook. He'd been an artist for as long as he could remember, though he'd never thought of himself as such. He'd been good with a pencil since he'd been a kid and yet had always held it close to the vest. He hadn't wanted the others to know what he could do. Not when a weakness such as art could mean a fist.

He'd learned long ago that his fingers were better for triggers than graphite and ink.

Or so his father had told him.

His skin tightened and he clenched his jaw, forcing his breath to come in even pants rather than the shallow ones his lungs seemed to want to do. His chest constricted and he rubbed his fist over his heart.

He stuck his ear buds in his ears and turned on some alt-rock that didn't have too much bass and had the lead singer's soothing croons instead of lyrical whining about lost hearts and lack of empathy. Sloane needed to calm down before he had another anxiety attack. He'd never had one in the middle of the shop, but he'd been damn close before. It'd been a decade since he'd been in the service, and yet he could still hear the yells, the shots that never seemed to go away. If he took deep breaths and focused on drawing, he could calm himself enough that he wouldn't break out in a cold sweat. If he beat back the pain, he wouldn't vomit on the floor, wouldn't smash his hand into the drywall because he didn't know another form of release.

Sloane nodded to the beat as he forced his eyes open. His hands once again traced the sketchbook before he opened it, pencil in hand. He had a few drawings to finish so they were ready for clients, as well as things on his mind he could just draw for relaxation, but his mind wouldn't focus.

Couldn't focus.

A hand touched his shoulder and he whirled around, standing in one breath, his hand raised, the pencil poised as a weapon. The beat of the music increased, as did the sound of his heart.

Hailey stood in front of him, her eyes wide, one hand on her chest, the other out in front of her.

Protecting herself.

From him.

This was why he wasn't for her.

This was why he'd stayed away.

He'd only hurt her. Only lose her to the demons that plagued him.

"What?" he bit out, pulling the ear buds from his ears.

She took a step back at the sound of his voice.

Sloane let out a breath. "Shit. I didn't mean to scare you. You just startled me."

Her throat worked as she swallowed hard. "I can see that." She licked her lips and put her hands down, fisting them at her sides. "What the hell is wrong with you?"

He froze, not knowing what to say. Had she seen the panic in his gaze? Seen the fact that he wasn't whole? That he was damaged goods…far too broken for a woman like her?

"Why did Brody tell me to 'take it up with Sloane' when he said he wasn't interested in me?" she continued.

He swallowed hard, the short burst of relief that she hadn't seen the truth of him quickly replaced with the damning feeling he'd messed up.

"He wasn't good enough for you," he said simply.

Her eyes narrowed, her cheeks pinking with color. He loved the way her face carried emotion. Most of the time she kept her smile on, as if she had to be happy and bubbly for her clients, adding "sugars" to her drawl when she felt like it. But sometimes he saw beneath that, saw the woman he wanted in his life but knew he couldn't have.

"Fuck you, Sloane."

His brows rose. Hailey didn't normally curse at him.

"Don't look at me like that, you asshole. In fact, don't look at me at all. Who do you think you are? Who the hell do you think you are, Sloane? I thought you were my friend, but maybe I was wrong. What kind of man steps in and tells another to back off? It wasn't your place, that's for sure. I smiled at *one* man. That's it. I said I'd be over at my shop when he was through with his ink. That's it. And yet, that somehow triggered your alpha complex and you had to scare him away. How dare you say he's not good enough for me? You don't know him. And, apparently, you sure as hell don't know me."

Tears filled her eyes and she blinked them back quickly, raising her chin.

Damn it. He was an ass. A prick. A loser. A douche.

"Why did you do it?" she asked, her voice low. "You've stayed away from me for *years*. We've been friends but never got too close. Why did you change the rules?"

She'd changed them first by flirting with a man in front of

him, but he didn't bring that up. He'd already hurt her, hurt himself in the process.

He needed to man up, he knew it, but he also knew he really wasn't good enough for her—wasn't what she needed.

"I'll take you out," he said, surprising himself.

Her jaw dropped. "What?"

"Go out to dinner with me." What the hell was he doing? He'd pushed Brody away because he thought the guy wasn't good enough for her—or so he told himself—but that didn't mean Sloane *was* good enough for her. In fact, he knew he wasn't.

"You told Brody to go away because you wanted to go out with me?" she asked, her voice rising.

"You said I changed the rules, so let's change them more. Go out with me."

She blinked rapidly then nodded. "Fine."

Not the best response, but he'd screwed the asking up royally. He couldn't blame her. "I'll pick you up at seven."

"Tonight? You want to go out tonight?"

"You have a problem with that?" Could he be more of an ass?

"You know what? I don't know anymore, Sloane. I have no idea what's going on, but fine. I'll see you at seven." She let out a breath, closed her eyes for a beat, and then met his gaze. "I hope we figure out what we're doing before it's too late." She whispered the last part before walking out of the office, leaving him alone.

He hoped for their sake they figured it out as well. Because he'd just crashed through the wall they'd carefully erected between the two of them, and now they'd have to deal with the consequences.

And while his mind whirled and he tried to figure out what the next step would be, that small part of him that always held out hope, the part he knew he buried deep daily, pulsated.

He was going out with Hailey.

Finally.

And he was going to mess it all up. Again. It was what he did. He just prayed he didn't break Hailey in the process.

Chapter Three

Hailey had lost her damn mind. That was the only explanation for why she was standing in front of her mirror in her robe with her hands wringing in front of her. It all seemed like a dream, but from the way her heart beat in her chest, she knew it was real.

Far too real.

One minute she'd been making coffee, trying to figure out how she'd get out of drinks or whatever with Brody, and the next she was standing in Sloane's office saying yes to a date. With *him.*

It didn't make sense.

The moment she'd stepped back into her café, she'd known she made a mistake flirting with Brody. While she'd wanted to stand up and take a step in a direction that didn't include her waiting for a man who would never truly want her, she hadn't meant to take a leap that fast. It wasn't that Brody wasn't attractive. And he'd been sweet to her. It was more that he wasn't *for* her. And while, at the time, she'd thought Sloane would never be for her either, she knew she didn't want Brody like that. It had been a lapse in judgment and one she would have had to fix right away.

Only Brody had shown up all apologetic smiles, saying he wouldn't be staying. While she should have felt hurt that he would back out so quickly, she could only feel relief. He seemed like a nice guy—with perhaps a dangerous edge—but she didn't want him the way she should. Even for a cup of coffee with a bit of flirtation. She'd smiled back and said she understood—though she hadn't truly understood his quick change of mind, even if she'd been relieved. When she'd asked him if there was anything wrong, he'd told her to ask Sloane about it, and she'd had to clutch the sides of the counter, hard.

After dropping that bomb, the damn man had just walked out of her café, hands in his pockets with a smile on his face.

It didn't make sense. Why would Sloane have anything to do with Brody backing out of their almost-date? So, when she'd stormed over to Montgomery Ink, angry and hurt that Sloane would dare to interfere, especially when he hadn't done anything when it came to her and him—at all—she'd been ready to tear him a new one.

No one had been more surprised than her when he'd asked her out.

Or rather, when he'd told her they were going out.

She wasn't quite sure how it had happened, only that she'd raised her chin and said yes. She shouldn't have, she knew. The man hadn't wanted her until someone else had taken a chance. That wasn't how relationships were supposed to start. He wasn't supposed to keep her at arm's length, waiting for him to make up his mind. That wasn't fair to her, wasn't fair to him.

And yet she'd been weak.

She'd said *yes*.

She closed her eyes as she gripped the edges of her robe. There was no way Hailey could back out now. He'd be there to pick her up soon, and then she'd take another chance at life.

She'd taken that chance before—had the scars to prove it—so maybe she could do this. Maybe she could be with someone and remember that it wasn't the wholeness of her body that made her who she was, but the strength of what was inside. Only, she'd proven she was weak by saying yes in the first place, hadn't she? She'd given in to his actions to get them where they were too easily.

She was so damn confused, and the fact that she was *excited* at the same time didn't help. She'd wanted Sloane for years, and now they were getting their chance. Maybe she should just push aside the *how* and go with the *now*.

Hailey opened her eyes and met her gaze in the mirror. She could live in the now—she'd been doing it since that fateful day when she'd faced her mortality with a fragile strength she hadn't known she possessed. Oh, she and Sloane would have to discuss how it had come to be, if only for a few moments, but she could move on.

She fingered the edge of the robe before letting the fabric fall to the floor. She stood naked in front of her mirror, relying on a strength she had long since honed in the darkness.

Her surgeon had done a wonderful job, but there was only so much anyone could do with a bilateral mastectomy that dug deep into the tissues. It had taken six surgeries for her reconstructive surgeon to find the right balance. Each time, she'd cried in pain, threw up from the meds, and ached in places so deep she never thought she'd be able to get up and breathe again.

Her breasts were gone.

What remained was thanks to the skill of her surgeon. A large scar—slightly faded over time but there nonetheless—slashed through each new breast. Other scars from surgeries, ports, and treatments covered her upper chest, her belly, and between her breasts. It wasn't pretty, and sometimes she knew it was downright horrific.

When she'd first taken off the bindings and pads from the initial surgery, she'd sobbed—gut wrenching sobs that wracked her whole body…or at least the body that remained. They hadn't been able to start the reconstructive process until her second surgery due to the depth of her cancer cells. It shouldn't have hurt her as much as it had. She was *alive*. Breasts were just breasts.

But that was all a fucking lie.

She was a *woman*. Her breasts had been part of her. She'd loved her body, even as a twenty-year-old. Sure, she might have wanted slightly more curves where it mattered when she'd been that young, but it hadn't happened. Instead of coming into her own out of her teens, she'd faced her own mortality in a way no woman should have to.

So, yes, to the outside world she had a normal body—if normal was even a word these days. Her surgeon had been brilliant, and after all these years, Hailey knew how to wear the right clothes to ensure no one would guess what scars lay beneath.

But she wasn't the same woman she'd once been.

One thing she'd done differently than most women was her nipples. She'd opted to not have them kept in any sense of the word, as some women do. It hadn't been the right surgery for her, and she'd wanted to move on. Her nipples weren't part of who she was—or at least that's what she'd thought at first. She'd also decided not to do anything about tattooing fake ones on. At least not yet. She'd warred with herself over it and had even almost asked Maya to do it for her…but it wasn't what she wanted. She'd had implants put in during one of the later surgeries, though they weren't perfectly even. She'd missed her curves, and though at the time the new ones hadn't felt like *hers*, she'd grown to see them differently.

In the years since her diagnosis and recovery, she'd formulated a plan. She wanted a certain kind of tattoo over what were once her breasts, and in her heart, she knew whom she wanted to do it. While Maya, Austin, or Callie would take great care of her, she wanted the one person she knew carried a darkness, a scar along his soul as deep, if not deeper, than her physical ones.

She wanted Sloane.

She let out a shuddered breath.

She'd never had the courage to ask him…maybe it was time. After all, if he saw her naked, he'd know about her breasts. And if she took this date—this relationship—further, he'd see it all.

It was a step she hadn't been willing to take before, but maybe, just maybe, Brody's interference would help her not only heal the remaining scars on her body, her *soul*, but show Sloane what he could have with her—what she could have with him.

She wasn't the woman she once was, she reminded herself, but then again, no one truly was.

With a roll of her shoulders, she donned her dark leggings and tunic top. It clung just right to her curves but didn't showcase any unevenness in her chest. No matter how many surgeries she had, she'd never have perfect globes. Then again, she hadn't when they'd been real anyway. Bras and holding her shoulders back helped with those issues. Once she was naked…well, that was another form of trust, one that she'd tried to give before but failed.

A year or so after her last surgery, she'd slept with a man she'd been seeing. He'd known she had cancer, but hadn't known the depth of her…newness. He hadn't made her come during the encounter, and had stayed away from her upper chest to the point she felt like a pariah. She couldn't get the sensations she'd once had with nipple play since she didn't have them anymore, but completely ignoring where they once had been by not even glancing at them when she'd had her shirt off had quickly ruined any tingling she might have felt for the man. Part of that may have been her fault as she hadn't communicated her feelings, but damn it, he should have tried to make things better for her.

She hadn't slept with a man since.

The fact that it took her longer with a vibrator to come than it had before the chemo and radiation didn't make things any easier. But if she were patient—and honest about thinking about Sloane while getting herself off—she could come eventually. And while she missed hot sex, she missed the intimacy of being with another even more. She'd had a few boyfriends during high school and the start of college, so she hadn't been that inexperienced. She also hadn't had a boyfriend during the ordeal, so she'd gone from who she'd been to this new version of her without someone to see the progress.

Going out with Sloane tonight was a hurdle of trust she'd never faced before…at least a different type of one. If and when she told him about her cancer, told him of her body, she'd be giving a part of herself to him—an intimate part—before she even let him touch her.

She trusted Sloane more than she trusted almost anyone—just from the way he'd treated her since they met. The chemistry between them had only burned brighter as time moved on.

They both had their reasons for keeping away until now.

She would tell him hers because there would be no hiding it if things progressed.

She just hoped he'd tell her his.

"Enough of that," she mumbled to herself. She'd spent the past twenty minutes staring in the mirror, trying to figure out how she'd gotten herself into this situation, and now she was going to be late if she didn't get a move on.

As fast as she could, she finished straightening her hair, the sleek threads forming a perfect bob. Her post chemo hair wasn't as straight as it used to be so she had to iron out the wave if she wanted her hairstyle to work. Her thick bangs rocked in her opinion, and she was grateful her hair hadn't thinned like so many others' had. This hairstyle, actually, came from one of the wigs she'd had during her treatments. She'd loved the way it framed her face so much, she'd let her hair grow out into the style.

She quickly did her makeup, making sure her lips were stained a deep red. If she pressed a glass to her lips or even kissed Sloane later, the stain wouldn't come off. She loved this brand and prayed her shop continued to do well so she could afford it.

The knock on the door came precisely on time, and she grinned. Sloane was known for his promptness. And knowing him and his military mindset, he had probably been outside for five minutes waiting for her because being right on time was actually late to him. She wasn't usually late for things, but she sometimes came in by the skin of her teeth.

Hailey ran her hands down her long tunic again before opening the door, her heart beating loudly in her ears.

Damn she loved the look of this man.

He wore an old leather jacket that fit firmly to his shoulders and made her want to peel it right off him. His legs were encased in faded denim, but the jeans weren't too old with holes or anything—just perfectly fit to his legs in the ideal blue. The black boots he wore only accentuated the sexy bad-boy image that made her heart beat even faster.

He'd put a knitted beanie on his bald head since it was still a bit cold outside despite the fact that it had warmed up some that day. Of course, with Denver weather, it could drop below freezing tomorrow and then be almost shorts weather the next day.

"Wow," she whispered, and he grinned at her.

"You're pretty wow yourself." He stuck his hands in his pockets and rocked back on his heels. His eyes were bright, as if he wasn't sure how he'd ended up here either. Of course, she was probably just projecting.

"So…you want to come in?" She bit her lip. Why was this so awkward? This was *Sloane*. They saw each other practically every day. He was in her shop more often than not just to talk. Or in Sloane's case, to grunt and mumble unless something was truly important to him. They knew each other…so why did this feel different?

Because it *was* different.

He tilted his head, studying her face. "If that's what you want. I have reservations at Illusion in a bit, but I can move that if you want to do something different." He grinned again. "I didn't actually ask you what you wanted to do after all."

She let out a breath. "We did this a little backward, didn't we?"

He shrugged. "So what? We're doing this, whatever this is, our way. That's all that matters. So, why don't you go put a jacket on and we'll head to Illusion. We'll figure the rest out when we do."

She nodded, oddly warming at his words. She liked the use of the word *our*. She hadn't been an *our* in far too long. As soon as she got her jacket and purse, she locked the door behind her and stood on the front porch with Sloane. He slid his large, calloused hand over hers and she licked her lips.

He'd touched her in the past, of course; slight caresses or a small pat on the back.

But he'd never held her hand.

This was *happening*.

"Ready?" he asked, his voice low, deep.

Was she ready? She wasn't sure she'd ever be ready, but here she was, with Sloane, as whole as she could be and about to take a leap.

"Yeah," she whispered. "Yes, I am," she said a little more clearly.

He met her gaze and gave her a nod. "Good." With that, he led her to his truck, a very sexy extended cab with thick tires for the winter. She knew he also had a bike he used whenever it was warm, and she'd always imagined riding behind him, her thighs wrapped around his body as they rode.

She blushed, annoyed with herself for even blushing in the first place, and pushed those thoughts from her mind.

Date first.

Sex later.

As soon as Sloane got into the cab, he raised a brow at her. "Either you're cold from standing outside too long with me or you're thinking dirty thoughts."

She snorted and waved her hand. "I forget you know me so well."

He licked his lips. "Does that mean you're thinking dirty thoughts?"

This was Sloane, she told herself once more. She could be herself.

"So what if I was? You're sexy, and I was thinking of your bike."

He smiled then, his teeth white against the tan of his skin. "When the weather gets warmer, I'll take you for a ride."

Of course, her mind immediately went to the thought of riding *him*. And then the idea of her riding on his bike in general. Did he mean that he wanted her with him, as in *with* him, on that bike or was it just a friend thing?

And why the hell was she thinking so hard.

"Stop thinking so hard."

She gave him a side-eye as he drove. "Stop reading my mind."

"I can't help it. It's just what we do."

"True," she mumbled. "What *are* we doing, Sloane?" She hadn't meant for that last part to come out, but she apparently couldn't hold it in.

He let out a sigh and gripped the steering wheel a little tighter, as evidenced from the whiteness of his knuckles.

"I'm taking you out. We're going to eat, talk a bit, then we'll figure it out."

She pressed her lips together. "And? And what then? I mean why now? Why did you wait until Brody asked me out to do anything?"

He let out a little growl then pulled over to the side of the road. Her eyes widened as he put on his flashers and turned to her.

"Okay, let's get this straight. You and I? We've been circling each other for a while now. I know it. You know it. So let's just say it."

She nodded. "Yeah, you're right about that, but—"

"I'm not done."

She snorted but waved for him to continue. She kind of liked him all growly and broody—God help her.

"I liked the dance we had even though I hated it. I've wanted you, Hailey, but…well, for reasons of my own, I stayed away. I know I'm not good enough for you, but I don't damn well seem to care right now. I love what we have, love that we talk and I watch you bake, but I want more." He paused for a moment. "I don't know as I deserve it, but I want it. And for the record? You could have asked me out anytime before now. You're not one to back away. You have your secrets, but you say what you want most times."

She swallowed hard, her mind whirling. "I guess I could have asked you out before. And you're right. I *do* have secrets, and that's why I didn't do anything about it."

He studied her face once more. "Well, we're doing something about it now. So let's move on from why we didn't before and figure out what we're going to do next. I know those secrets of ours are going to come out, but—"

This time, she interrupted him. "But if we keep going in circles, we'll only end up hurting each other."

"Exactly. So, does Illusion sound good to you still? Or do you want something different? I know you work with food every day, so you choose."

Illusion was a hipster place that had popped up in downtown Denver a few months ago. It wasn't as pretentious as many of the new hipster places tended to be, and they had fantastic food. They were a hole-in-the-wall that tended to be busy—hence the reservations for dinner. But everything was organic and tasty. Since Hailey only ate organic thanks to the chemicals she'd pumped her body full of in her effort to get healthy, it worked for her.

"Let's go," she said softly and took a breath.

Sloane reached out and cupped her cheek. Without thinking, she leaned into his touch. "Okay, then, Hails. Let's get some food."

He let her go, turned off the hazards, and pulled out onto the road again. All the while, Hailey sat back, her cheek still warm from his touch. She had no idea what she was doing, but damn it, she couldn't wait to figure it out.

"Do you want to come in?" Hailey asked a couple of hours later, her belly full and her cheeks aching from laughing all night.

Dinner with Sloane had been memorable to say the least. He was all big, bearded, broody, and inked. And oh so hers for the evening. He'd laughed with her, touched her when he could—a casual brush of fingers along silk. He would lean in close to tell her a joke and then smile wide when she laughed.

Sloane didn't smile enough.

The fact that he would in her presence warmed her.

Sloane stood next to her on her porch, his large body towering over her but not scaring her in the least. He was the largest man she knew, and yet she knew, without a doubt, he'd never physically hurt her.

"I could get warm," he answered.

She swallowed hard, unlocked her front door and stepped inside, feeling his warm body behind her. He helped her slide off her coat, his fingers brushing along her ribs. She shuddered out a breath.

When he pulled her to face him, she tilted her head up and licked her lips.

"I've wanted to kiss you for a long while," Sloane said softly. "Should have done it before."

"Then do it now," she whispered.

When he lowered his head, pressing his lips to hers, she surrendered to him. She wrapped her arms around his neck and pressed her body to his, aware she was doing something she had not done since the diagnosis

Willingly allowing another to know the feel of her body.

It had taken years for her to allow herself to think of her body as beautiful. As brave. And with this kiss, she would take it one step further.

She would allow another to hopefully think the same.

His tongue slid along hers, and she moaned, loving his taste, the feel of him…everything.

When he pulled away, they were both breathless, a fundamental part of their relationship forever changed.

She met his gaze and knew there was something she had to do before she took the next step. It wouldn't be fair if she didn't.

"I…I've wanted to do that for far too long," she finally said.

Sloane grinned, though she saw an emotion pass through his eyes she couldn't quite name. Secrets, she thought again, they both had secrets. So, perhaps it was time she shared hers. She'd hidden them for so long, she almost didn't know the words.

When she pulled away, he frowned. But he let her go, his fingers lingering on her hips as she moved.

"I'm glad we did it, then. How about we do it again?" he asked.

She licked her lips but held up her hand as he took a step forward. "I need to tell you something first."

He tilted his head. "Okay."

She let out a little laugh. "You're always like that. You say okay and you *listen.* That's what I've always liked about you, Sloane."

He shrugged. "No use in being here if I'm not going to listen. You want to sit down?"

She shook her head. "No, but let's go into the living room anyway. I don't want to be so close to the windows."

His brows raised, but he took her hand and walked with her into the living room. Her heart beat hard and her blood pounded in her ears once more, but this time, it wasn't in breathless anticipation.

"So…you know how we were talking about secrets? Well, I think I should tell you mine…you know…before we do anything else."

He shook his head. "You don't have to tell me anything you're not ready for. I know we started off tonight, hell *today*, on an odd note, but if we're going to do this, let's do it our way. Remember?"

"I want to do this." She closed her eyes. "It's so much harder to date someone you know," she mumbled.

He let out a snort. "The 'get to know you' part is out of the way. You know my favorite drink, and I know the faces you make when you're tired or annoyed. So yeah, we can't hide things like that from each other. But I know you hold something back from everyone, from me. I don't fault you for that. We all need our secrets."

She nodded. "I know. And I should have told everyone long ago. I didn't mean to keep it to myself for so long. It's not that I'm ashamed..." She paused. "I'm not ashamed. But it's…it's not an easy subject. And all of us—the Montgomerys and crew—have been through so much. And since my…thing is in the past, it was hard to bring up."

Sloane took a step forward but didn't touch her. "Tell me, Hailey. You know you can tell me anything. What happened?"

She raised her chin, knowing it was all or nothing. "I had cancer. Breast cancer. In the course of my treatment, I had a bilateral mastectomy. The shape you see now isn't who I was, but it is who I am now. I'm a survivor, Sloane, but no one knows."

Chapter Four

Sloane quit breathing. Just quit breathing, his mind going in a thousand directions yet not moving at all.

"Cancer," he breathed. "Breast cancer."

Jesus. He still couldn't breathe.

"Yep. The big C. I'm cancer free now, by the way. I didn't say that before. I'm actually surprised I said as much as I did. I mean, I practiced saying it in the mirror, but as I haven't told anyone in years, it was hard. Different. You know?"

She kept rambling, and he took two steps toward her, gripped her upper arms, and crushed his mouth to hers. Emotion poured through him and his body shook. She gasped into his mouth before kissing him back.

When he pulled away, he rested his forehead on hers and let out a shuddered breath. "I almost lost you before I met you. I don't know what I'd have done if I'd never had you in my life, Hailey."

Her hands went to his stomach, just resting there. He relaxed at her touch, even as his belly leapt at the feel of her hands on him.

"Sloane."

He moved to cup her face and used his thumb to brush away the single tear that had fallen. "Fuck, Hailey. I knew you were hiding something, but I had no idea it was this. You had *cancer* and didn't tell anybody." He thought about what he knew of her past and frowned. "Wait, how old were you? Did you have anyone?"

She shook her head between his hands, and he let her go but did his best to keep his touch on her.

"I was twenty when I was diagnosed. It took two weeks from the results to my surgery. Since I was Stage 1B, I had a great chance, but they wanted to work fast before it spread to other parts of my body. The tumor was small, thank God, but it was just at the edge of being large enough where they'd been worried. I opted for them to take off both breasts rather than just the right one." Her hand went up to her chest and he looked down, his mind still whirling.

"But you were alone. Weren't you?"

She nodded. "You know my dad left when I was a kid, and my mom died when I was eighteen. I wasn't able to afford college full-time, so I was taking night classes while working at a bakery. I thank that place every day for what they gave me. Not only did they teach me how to do what I love now, but the job gave me benefits so I could afford the treatments."

She continued, and he kept silent, not knowing what to say. What was there to say when the woman he *loved* had almost died and he hadn't known?

"I went through chemo and radiation, but both treatments were relatively short because it hadn't spread. I was lucky. I know that sounds weird to say since it was cancer, but I was lucky."

"Hails."

She gave him a sad smile. "It took six surgeries for them to reconstruct my chest. I'm not the same. Not even a little bit, but I'm me."

He ran a hand down her arm and gripped her hand. She squeezed it. Hard. "You're beautiful, Hailey. Inside and out. I've always known that. But that you have the strength you do, the courage you have after all of that? I am in awe of you."

She pressed her lips together and her eyes filled with tears.

"Shit. I didn't mean to make you cry."

She shook her head and smiled. "It's a good cry. I wasn't sure what you would say. You're a man of few words, after all."

She was not the first person to say that. "I speak when it's important. And you're important."

Far too important for him. Hell, he was dirt, tainted compared to her. And he was so fucking big. He could break her with one careless move. How could he ever think he was good enough for her? At the same time, he knew if he walked away right then, he'd not only regret it forever, but she'd think it was because of her.

She wrung her hands together and bit her lip.

"What is it?"

"I've wanted to tell you for a long while. Not because it was a huge weight on me, even though it was, but more so because..." She let out a breath. "I don't have nipples anymore. I mean, they took them away when they did the first surgery. I will never have the kind of sensation I once had. It's impossible. But I've always wanted to do...something."

He froze. Austin and Maya had done a few nipple tattoos at the shop where they made the ink almost realistic. It was hard, but a tattoo that Sloane knew took courage beyond what others thought. All of those at Montgomery Ink had tattooed over and through scars in their line of work. Hell, it was how Austin had met his wife, Sierra.

But he wasn't sure he could deal with Maya or Austin doing Hailey's ink. He knew he had no right to be possessive, but he wanted to be the one to help her...if that was what she wanted.

"I don't want nipple tattoos. I just don't think they're for me. But I do want something. I've been toying with the idea of art across my chest for a while. I've just needed the courage to tell my story and then do something about it."

He took a deep breath. "I think you have far more courage than you give yourself credit for."

She smiled at him, breaking his heart all over again. "I've always thought..." She stopped, frowned. "I've always thought I should have you do it. I don't know why. I mean, I know we've wanted each other, we've said so tonight. But this is different. I always thought you could help me. But I've been scared."

He leaned forward again and kissed her softly, his heart beating rapidly in his chest. "I would be honored to help you. You can trust me, Hails. I'll take care of you."

She put her hands on his chest and moved forward. "I *do* trust you. That's why I told you. Why I want you to do my ink."

Sloane kissed her again. "I'll do anything you need me to do. And when you're ready for me to start it, I'll be by your side, making sure it's exactly what you need. For you to ask me this..." he shook his head. "You blow me away, Hailey. You fucking blow me away."

She smiled at him then, and he was lost.

He loved this woman, loved everything about her, and now he had fallen that much deeper. He just prayed he could keep her.

The bomb blast hit his Humvee hard, and his brain rattled. Sloane gasped for breath, the fire burning around him all but searing his skin. He reached for his brother, but couldn't feel him. Couldn't feel much of anything.

Just the pain.

Sloane sat up in bed, sweat pouring from his skin as he tried to swallow. Only he couldn't breathe, and he had to keep his heart from pounding right out of his chest.

Fuck.

He hadn't had one of those nightmares in years. He knew he'd never rightly forget that day, but he thought he'd move past the night terrors that kept him up, that kept his hands unsteady and his eyes red-rimmed.

Sloane grunted as he pulled his legs to the side of the bed and rested his head in his hands. He just needed to take a few deep breaths and then he'd be fine. He'd done this countless times before. PTSD didn't go away with happy thoughts and willpower alone. He knew it might never go away, but at least he wasn't struggling on a day-to-day basis. He was doing far better than some of his friends from the service. Hell, at least he'd come home whole. Or even come home at all. His body might be covered in scars, but he'd kept his limbs and his sight.

That had to count for something.

The thought of loss and coming through made him think of Hailey and he sobered rapidly. He'd only been to war. Only fought and lived, coming out mostly whole.

She'd lost far more than he had.

And yet he felt like she was doing so much better than him. She'd fought with grace, or at least he figured she had. She'd even told him about the tattoo she wanted *him* to give her. When he thought of his situation, all he'd done was live—when so many hadn't.

No one else in that truck had lived through that roadside bomb.

Only him.

How was it *he* deserved to be here? How did he deserve to come home and be with a woman who made him feel like everything would be okay?

He didn't deserve it.

But he was just selfish enough to go through with it. Somehow, he'd have to figure out how to live with that.

After he'd kissed her again the night before, he'd told himself he needed to leave. There had been a lot said that day, and they both needed time to let it all sink in before they took the next step. As they'd both said the night before, they were past some of the initial awkwardness that came with getting to know someone on a date. They were already friends, already close. Now they would be closer. He didn't know when they would sleep together, but he knew it would happen once she was ready.

He frowned. She'd said she had no nipple sensation, but did she lose anything else?

Sloane would have to ask her that outright. There was no way he'd hurt her if he had the chance to make things easier for her in the long run. Maybe he'd do some research on what others dealt with so he knew the right questions to ask. Considering he knew from his own therapy with PTSD that everyone's treatments and aftermaths were unique, Hailey wouldn't be textbook. But at least he'd be somewhat prepared when and if they went to bed together.

They weren't young, well, he wasn't anyway, so he wasn't going to be some nervous kid when it came to sex. He'd make sure she got what she needed and do his best not to screw it up by hurting her in some way. It wasn't that she was different from other women he'd been with—though she was because she was *Hailey*—it was just that he was so fucking scared. He wanted to make sure he didn't mess up.

Somehow, in the course of a day, he'd gone from standing to the side, being near her but not with her, to dating her. He didn't know if they had a label, but it was at least a new step in a direction he wasn't sure he'd ever be ready for.

Sloane stood up and ran a hand over his head, noting he'd need to shave again soon. He liked the feel of the air on his bald head, so he kept it shaved. He'd done it in basic training and hadn't stopped since. It didn't seem to bother Hailey, so he'd keep it.

Today, he had to go to work and act like nothing happened in front of the others. Sure, they'd heard her storm into his section, but they'd at least pretended not to listen. He didn't want them to give Hailey or him shit. All the while, he'd want to ask her what was going on and scream that he'd kissed her at the top of his lungs.

If he weren't sure of his age, and the fact that he was nearing forty, he would have thought he was some damn teenage boy getting to kiss his first crush.

Hailey was his first for a lot of things, though, so maybe that made sense.

His first friend he'd fallen for. The first woman that he knew would be nothing but serious after getting out of the service.

His first…just his first chance at Hailey.

By the time he made it to Montgomery Ink, his head ached from too many thoughts and lack of coffee. He hadn't made any at home, and he wasn't sure if he should go into Taboo and get some from Hailey. Seriously, it was like he was a teenager again.

When he had the time, he should just go over there for coffee and see her.

Things had changed, but *they* hadn't. And once he remembered that, everything would be okay. At least he hoped so.

Sloane stretched his back as he took a seat at his station. He had three appointments that day—two smaller ones that he could get done in less than an hour each—and another one that would take most of the afternoon. That one he knew had to be perfect. Not that any of his work was less than perfect, but the one that afternoon had to be better than the rest.

While each of the artists at Montgomery Ink did all kinds of work, they each had some specialties they were known for. Sloane had become known for his remembrance pieces. Those who had lost someone in the service came to him. He'd done ink remembering fallen soldiers—men, women, and dogs—as well as those who wanted to remember their branch in general.

Today he was doing an eagle for someone and wanted to make sure he got the feathers just right. The bird would look as if it were taking off; its wings stretched back, legs bent.

He hated and loved doing these all at the same time.

Maybe, just maybe, if he could help others, he'd rid himself of the stain of blood on his hands. Only he knew that wasn't an option. He'd be tainted until the day he died—and he refused to let that time be short. The men who had fallen by his side deserved far more than what they'd received, and Sloane refused to give up when they hadn't had a chance.

He let out a shuddering breath, pushing the memories back. It usually wasn't this bad, but for some reason, he couldn't quite get out of this funk.

Of course, he knew the reason, and she was just a wall away, working and probably smiling. Giving in to temptation had done something to him, broken down the barriers that had held the panic at bay.

"So…what happened last night?" Maya asked. He lifted his head to see her leaning against the table in his station, her pierced brow raised.

He leaned back and folded his arms over his chest. Rather than answer, he just stared at her.

She narrowed her eyes. "You're not going to answer me, are you?"

He remained silent.

She threw up her hands. "Fine. But if you hurt her, I'll kick your ass. Oh, and if she hurts you, I'll kick her ass. I'm an equal opportunity ass kicker."

Sloane smiled then. "I've always admired that about you."

Maya flipped him off then went back to her station, leaving Sloane alone with his thoughts. When he had the time, he should just go over there for coffee and see her. He didn't like not knowing what to say—hence why most people thought he was the silent type. He only spoke when it was important and he knew the words. *This* was important. But he didn't know the words.

So, instead of going next door and seeing her like he wanted to, he stayed put and waited for his first client. He'd go over there eventually. He couldn't hide from her.

And that's what scared him.

The day thankfully passed quickly, and he stood up, rolling his neck to try and get the crick out. His stomach grumbled and he cursed himself. Somehow, he'd gone through most of the day without eating anything except the protein bar he'd found in his desk. Who knew how old that thing was. In the past, Callie might have gone and gotten the crew lunch, but now that she was a full-time artist and not an apprentice, she was just far too busy. Autumn, Griffin Montgomery's woman, worked up front most days, but today had been her day off. That meant he'd been forced to get his own food and hadn't had the time between clients.

"Go get food or go home," Austin said from his station.

Sloane looked over at his friend. "What?"

"You haven't eaten today, and that's fucking stupid in our line of work. You don't have any clients on the docket and the walk-ins aren't that bad today. Maya, Callie, and I can handle the influx."

Sloane ran a hand down the back of his neck. "We need more artists."

Austin nodded. "I'm putting out my feelers for someone who can be here for as many hours as we are. Or maybe I can get another apprentice."

There were four other artists that worked there on partial shifts, but they weren't full time since they either lived too far away or had other jobs. What they needed was another full timer.

"If I hear anything, I'll let you know," Sloane added.

"Good. Now go next door, see your woman, and get some food. Head home and take her with you. Or at least make her go home. She's been here as long as you have I bet."

His woman.

He sure loved the sound of that. But was it the truth? Was she his? They hadn't truly discussed what they were doing, other than that they were taking it one moment at a time. The fact she'd bared her secrets to him had meant more than anything.

Sloane nodded at his boss, then the others, before cleaning up his station. After, he headed into Taboo through the side door and stopped two feet in.

She was magnificent.

Her teeth bit into her lip as she fought not to laugh at whatever Sierra, Austin's wife, had said. She had flour on her apron, but other than that, she looked pristine—not like a woman who had probably been on her feet for a full shift.

He'd always known she was strong, but now that he knew the truth, he saw the depth of that strength. He was a big man—big hands, large chest—just *big*. He could break her if he weren't careful.

He could break her with more than his strength, he knew. The fragility that slid under the surface of her skin wasn't easy to see, but he saw it. She could be the strongest woman in the world and still carry that.

He couldn't hurt her.

But he just might.

She turned to him then and smiled, though there was wariness in her eyes. It made sense, after all. He hadn't come by for coffee and this was the first time they'd seen each other since he'd left her house the night before. He wasn't sure if he should go to her, kiss her senseless, then carry her out of the building over his shoulder, or stay here and watch her from afar.

He stuck his hands in his pockets and let his smile rise just a little so she would know he liked seeing her.

Sierra looked between them and smiled like the Grinch at Christmas. She all but rubbed her hands together in glee. Of course, he only saw this out of the corner of his eye, as the rest of his attention was on the blonde in front of him—the blonde he wanted in his arms.

"Hey," he said.

"Hey."

Sierra clapped her hands together, this time in truth, and slid off her stool. "Hi, Sloane. I'm going to head to Harry and Marie's to pick up the kids." She grinned. "They wanted time with the grandbabies today. Hailey was just telling me she was done for the day since her closing crew is here. Perfect timing."

She waved and said her good-byes before she headed through the door to Montgomery Ink, presumably to kiss her husband on her way out.

That left Sloane and Hailey awkwardly standing in front of one another in silence.

Hailey cleared her throat. "Uh, yeah, I was about to get off."

He wanted to get her off.

Jesus, his mind needed to stay out of the gutter.

From the way her cheeks blushed, her mind had gone there, too. Interesting.

"Want to get something to eat?" he asked. His stomach rumbled then. Loudly. He winced. "Apparently, I really need to eat."

She smiled then and waved at the counter. "Let me get you some stew. It's the kind you like. I'll get a bowl, too."

He met her gaze. "Can we take it to go?"

She studied his face for a moment then nodded. "That I can do. Where are we going?" She bit her lip again, this time her gaze traveling down his body, slowly.

"Your place," he whispered, and she sucked in a shaky breath.

"Oh. Okay." She looked up again and licked her lips. "We can do that." She turned back to the kitchen, and he swallowed hard.

He didn't know what they would do once they got there, but he couldn't wait to find out. She came back quickly, her jacket on and a large bag in her hands. He took it from her, their hands brushing.

They both sucked in a breath, and he had to smile. "I'll follow you," he said softly before leaning down to brush a kiss against her lips.

She pressed closer and he had to hold back a groan. They were in public—her shop and place of business. It wouldn't do to have him pick her up by the waist and place her on the counter so he could get a better angle at her mouth.

He'd have to wait for them to be alone for that.

When he pulled back, she licked her lips again. "See you at

my place," she breathed, then took his hand and led them to the parking lot.

The relief that hit him was heady. He'd been afraid they'd have to hide this since things were so new, but that wasn't the case. He hadn't thought twice about leaning down to kiss her once he'd seen her, and he was damn lucky she hadn't pulled back too quickly.

They needed to talk, but first…first he needed her taste.

As soon as they entered her home, she locked the door behind them and pressed her back against the hard wood.

"Hungry?" she asked.

He nodded but set the bag down on the entry table. "Yeah, I am. But I think food can wait."

She smiled then. "Good."

He cupped her face then crushed his mouth to hers. Her lips parted for him, and he tangled his tongue with hers, both of their resounding moans going straight to his dick. She put both hands on his back, her fingernails digging into his beat-up leather jacket.

That wouldn't do.

He wanted to *feel*. He pulled away then tugged off his jacket and threw it on the floor before doing the same to hers.

"You want this, Hails?" he asked, his voice ragged. He needed to know before he moved on.

She reached up and bit his chin, sending a shock down his back. "Yes. I want you. I've wanted you for years. I wanted you to come over today and kiss me good morning, but I'm glad you didn't. Because if you had, then I'd have taken you to my office and had you right there on my desk. Probably not the best way to try and get work done."

He stared at her a moment, then threw his head back and laughed. "Jesus, I'm so fucking glad I'm not alone. I tried to keep you off my mind like I have for so long, but it didn't work. When I wasn't thinking about if I should come over to your side or not, I was thinking about what I wanted to do to you as soon as I saw you. It's bad, Hails. I want you so much that I don't know if I can be gentle."

"Sloane…"

He ran his hands up her rib cage and stopped right under her breasts. "You need to tell me what to do, Hails. I don't want to hurt you."

"You can't hurt me," she whispered, though they both knew that wasn't quite the truth. But they didn't talk about that. Couldn't talk about that.

When he moved to cup her breast, she sucked in a breath. "Tell me what to do." She didn't feel any different than what he'd thought she'd feel like, but damn if he'd hurt her.

"You're doing it. I'm not made of glass, Sloane."

He leaned down and pressed his mouth to her temple. "You're far stronger than glass, but I want to make this good for you."

"I'm pretty sure it's impossible for you not to."

He kissed down her neck, and she tilted her head to give him better access. "I'm not going to make love to you for the first time against a door. The first time we'll be in your bed." He kissed her again. "Next time we can be against the door. Or on the table. Or in the shower."

She let out a shuddering breath. "I take it you have this all planned out."

"Not quite that, but I've thought about all of it."

She tilted her head up to meet his gaze. "Me, too."

He pressed his mouth to hers and pulled his hand away from her breast. As she wrapped her arms around his neck, he reached around to cup her ass in his hands and lifted her off the ground. She let out a little squeak along his mouth, and he kissed her harder. When he moved toward her bedroom, she wrapped her legs around his waist, her heat pressed hard against him.

Fuck. He wasn't going to last long.

As soon as he got to her bedroom, he set her down and pulled away so he could study her face.

She bit her lip then tugged on the bottom of her shirt. "I…I've only been with one other person since the surgeries. I know you don't want to hear about other men, but I wanted to make sure you know that you won't be the first to see my scars other than my doctor." She pressed her lips together. "You'll be the second, actually."

He ground his teeth together at the thought of her with

another man but pushed it away as fast as he could. She was telling him this for a reason and he got it, but it didn't mean he had to like it. From the hesitant way she moved, he had a feeling the asshole before him hadn't done his job. Sloane would be damned if he'd allow that to happen again.

"Like I said, tell me what to do."

"Just make love to me," she whispered. With that, she pulled her shirt over her head and let out a breath. He could see the scars on her stomach, the port scars on her chest. The bra she wore covered most of her, but he could tell she'd had surgery.

He moved closer then put one hand around her back to the clasp of her bra. He leaned down and kissed her softly. When he undid the clasp, she moved her arms so the bra fell on the floor between them, tangling with their feet.

"It's not pretty," she said, her voice stronger than before. "But it took me a long time to realize I'm beautiful despite the scars."

Sloane pulled away and looked into her eyes before dropping his gaze to her chest. His heart constricted at the sight of what had almost taken her from him.

"You're beautiful *with* the scars, Hailey." And that was true. Her surgeon had done a fantastic job, but even if they hadn't been as precise as they obviously were, she'd have been beautiful.

Long scars bisected each breast and smaller ones marred the undersides. Parts of her skin had dimpled or scrunched together as the tissue and muscles underneath had been moved around during her healing.

"I don't look like I once did."

He tilted his head at her and nodded. "No one does. You look like a fucking survivor, Hailey. That's all that matters to me. You get that? You're *here*. You're here to be with me and that's what I know. You're alive, breathing, fucking *thriving*. What more can I ask for? So you don't have nipples? So what? You're *here*."

Tears filled her eyes and she reached up to wipe them away. He took her hand quickly before wiping her tears away himself.

"I'm not going to lie to you, Hailey. I won't do that. I know you don't look like you once did, but fuck, I don't either." He pulled back and took off his shirt. Scars covered his back and sides, as well as most of his chest. Surgical scars, scars from cuts and abrasions, as well as a few burn scars dotted his skin.

"Oh, Sloane..." She reached out and brushed her fingers along the largest one—a mix of burn and jagged lines. "I didn't know."

He shrugged but put his hand over hers before pulling her palm so it rested over his heart. "I hid them like you hid yours. No reason for others to know and not know what to say, to feel. But you're not anyone. You're Hailey. We're both scarred, but we're *here*."

And those he'd left behind weren't.

But he wouldn't think about that now.

Not when he had Hailey in front of him, bared in body and soul.

"Will you tell me about them?" she asked.

At first he thought she was talking about the men he'd lost, but then he knew she was speaking of the scars. Of course, they went together in a way, and he knew he'd have to tell her everything eventually.

"Not right now. Let me love you first."

"Okay," she said. "I'll hold you to that."

"Just let me hold you."

Sloane kissed her again, running his lips along her neck before kneeling in front of her. Hailey's body shook, but she placed her hands on his shoulders. When he kissed her left breast and the scar that resided there, he felt the first tear drop on his head. He kept going, kissing each scar, each mark that had cost her, but in the end, had saved her. Without the pain, without the scars, he would have lost her before he'd had her. And he'd never forget that.

While Hailey might not be able to feel his touch here the same way she once might have, he wanted to love her in every way he could. They both would come tonight, would make love until they were spent, but first, he needed to love her body.

All of her body.

He might be too large, too jagged, too haunted, but he'd make this special for her.

He couldn't suck on her, play with her the way he might have with another woman, but there were still things he could do. By the time he moved his lips across her chest, and then down her belly, she had her hands on his head, pressing him closer.

He pulled back and grinned. "Bet you wish I had hair for you to pull right about now."

She sniffed, though her eyes were dark with desire. "I…I *felt* that, Sloane. It wasn't…it wasn't like before, but you kissing me…"

He quickly moved to his feet and crushed his mouth to hers. She gasped and pressed her body to his. His hard cock rocked against her belly and he groaned.

When he pulled away, he moved them both to the bed then pulled her pants down in a quick move. She gasped and laughed when they caught on her shoes.

He snorted, then undid her shoes and threw her pants across the room. "Next time we take our shoes off at the door."

She met his gaze. "Deal."

He quickly pulled off his clothes—shoes first—and climbed into bed with her. They kissed again, their hands roaming over each other's bodies until they were both left breathless. When she went to grip his cock, he stilled her.

"If you touch me right now, I'll come and ruin the rest of our night." He groaned when she slid her foot up his calf. "I'm not as young as I once was."

"I forgot I'm dating such an older man."

He let her go, only to reach around and smack her ass. "Sassy."

"You know it."

Sloane licked his lips then cursed before getting up and searching for his wallet and the condom he'd left in there.

"That thing still good?" she asked.

"Yep," he said and came back to her while rolling the condom on his length. "I put it there this morning."

"Feeling cocky?" she teased.

He covered her body before he pressed the tip of his cock to her entrance. "You're about to feel my cock."

She groaned. "Bad joke, Sloane."

"True, but you'll still feel it. All of it." With that, he kissed her again, thrusting his hips and filling her in one move. They both groaned, their bodies shaking.

"You're...bigger than I thought."

He couldn't help but grin. "Thank you." He kissed her. "And you're fucking tight as hell."

"Thank you," she teased then gasped as he moved.

He tangled their fingers together and kept his gaze on hers. Her eyes darkened and her mouth parted as they made love, slowly, eternally. They'd be different another time, be harder, hotter, or whatever they needed. But for now, for that moment, they were *them*.

He wasn't a poet, wasn't someone in touch with his feelings, but with Hailey under him, her trust and body in his arms—literally—he felt like he could die right then and find heaven.

Though he didn't want to leave her, didn't want to lose her.

As he thrust once more, her pussy clenching around him like a vise, he came with her, their hearts beating as one, their breaths coming in pants.

She was his, if only for the moment.

And if he tried hard enough, he might not fuck it up. But he knew himself, knew his past.

He wanted her, wanted *this* until the end of his days, but he was Sloane Gordon, and he didn't get happy endings.

He never had...and he never would.

Chapter Five

Hailey was sore in all the best places and out of her damn mind. She and Sloane had made love two more times the night before—despite Sloane saying he wasn't a young man anymore. He might be a full decade older than her, but there was nothing old about those moves of his.

While she'd always known they'd be explosive in bed—there was no way a man built like Sloane, a man so good with his hands, would be anything but amazing—she hadn't known it would be *that*…hot.

He'd been so slow and careful at first—each kiss, each breath pleasure-filled and achingly tender. And as they explored one another, their heat ramped up and turned…molten.

Her heart hurt at the thought of how sweet and sexy he'd been.

And now she had no idea what the hell she was going to do.

They hadn't talked about what this meant, what their future would hold because that would be too important. They were taking things slow. Well, as slow as they could since they'd already slept together. But she had to remember, they'd been dancing around one another for years.

Falling into bed with one another was inevitable.

Falling in love with him was as well.

If only she knew if he could fall for her.

It hadn't escaped her notice that while she'd told him her secrets, he hadn't done the same for her. She had a feeling it had to do with the scars that marred his body—the depravity of which surprised her. He'd been hurt. Badly. And she hadn't known the depth of that pain. She wanted to, and she prayed that he would tell her what had happened.

But that wouldn't happen unless and until he was ready.

Just because she'd been ready to finally tell him of her past didn't mean he was ready as well. It wasn't fair of her to put her own timeline on his needs. If they kept going as they were, sure and steady, hopefully he'd feel ready to reveal.

Hopefully, he'd open up more and more and be the man she knew he could be beneath the gruff edges.

Still, she didn't know if they had a true future because they hadn't *talked* about it. And that annoyed her to no end. She was a pile of nerves, so unlike herself, that she wasn't sure what the heck she was doing.

"Okay, girl, if you're going to stand in the corner looking like a lost puppy, I'm going to have to kick your ass," Maya said with a grin.

Hailey snorted, then shook out her arms. "Sorry, doll, I'm a little off tonight."

"No shit," Maya said simply and held out a margarita glass filled to the brim. "You're driving so you get a virgin one. In fact, I *only* made virgin frozen strawberry margaritas tonight. Boy, how things have changed."

Sierra rolled her eyes as she drank her frilly, pink, non-alcoholic drink. "We all need to go home and get ready for work tomorrow and spend time with our families. Or we have a thousand other things to do."

Hailey took her drink and went to sit next to Miranda.

"Pretty much," Miranda added. "Decker and I may not have kids, but I still like to see him nightly."

"And you like practicing making those kids," Callie teased.

"I don't need to think about Miranda practicing making babies," Meghan said with a smile. "Though Luc and I *are* practicing as much as we can."

"Bitches," Maya mumbled.

"You're just jealous we're getting laid," Autumn said with a sweet smile.

Maya threw a pillow at her, barely missing Autumn's drink.

"Watch it, doll, you're about to stain your couch," Hailey said.

"I hate you, too," Maya said with narrowed eyes. "I know

that blush on your cheeks and the swagger in Sloane's walk. You got laid. It's about time."

Hailey raised her chin. "Yes, I did. There's no point in hiding it. I had hot, dirty, sweaty sex, and I plan to have it again." That much about her relationship she knew.

The girls squealed and did little booty shakes in their chairs.

"All hail Hailey and Sloane!" Maya called out. "To their glorious sex, even though I'm not having any."

"Whoo!" the others chimed in.

Hailey rolled her eyes but took a sip of her drink, wishing it had alcohol in it. "You know, Maya, you could be getting laid. Just saying."

Maya gave her a smile that didn't quite reach her eyes and Hailey wanted to curse. She did her best not to look at the woman currently sitting next to Maya.

Holly was Jake's girlfriend. Serious girlfriend it seemed. Maya and Jake were best friends, though the whole world thought they were something more. Apparently, everybody was wrong, and Maya was doing her best to bring Holly into the fold. Only, sweet and adorable Holly didn't quite fit in—not that they'd let her feel like that. The Montgomerys and crew weren't assholes.

Though Hailey wanted to know more about what was going on in that corner, she knew she had to think about something else. She'd asked the girls—Sierra, Callie, Maya, Holly, Miranda, Meghan, Autumn, and Tabby—to meet up so she could tell them what she should have told them long ago. Autumn was new to her circle, as she'd just recently found love with Griffin Montgomery, and Holly had sort of just shown up since she'd been hanging out with Maya at the time, but Hailey didn't mind that they were there. They'd all gathered at Maya's since that was where they usually met—there or at Taboo. Maya didn't have children, and she had a large living room with tons of space to sit. Plus, she had a kick-ass blender.

"Okay, now that we've made Maya feel bad about the sad state of her sex life, why don't you tell us why you wanted us to meet?" Callie asked.

Hailey let out a breath. "It's like you read my mind. I already told Sloane this, but I wanted to tell you as well. All of you. It's something I should have told you way before this."

Miranda leaned close. "What is it?"

"Seven years ago I was diagnosed with breast cancer." She told them the story as she'd told Sloane, straight and to the point. Yet this time it didn't seem as hard, as if once she'd said it aloud it became easier.

The others cried and moved to hold her close. She let the tears fall as well, the women in this room her family by choice, not by blood. She'd lost everyone else close to her, but at least she had these women—and the men who loved them.

She had Sloane as well, and she had to remember that. As long as they didn't mess up the friendship they had, she could do this. She *could.*

When Meghan cupped her face and kissed her cheek, it brought Hailey out of her thoughts of Sloane and into the present.

"Why didn't you tell us before?" the other woman asked. "Why did you carry this burden yourself?"

Hailey pressed her lips together. "I don't know. At first I was getting to know all of you, and then it was hard to bring up. But I didn't want to hide it anymore." She blew out a breath when Meghan stepped away. "But since I'm talking about it, do your self-exams, ladies. It saved my life. If you feel a lump, you get it biopsied. You do something. Your doctors might not know everything right away, so you ask the hard questions. Get me?"

The others nodded then did a group hug that brought Hailey peace.

"I love you ladies. Just saying." Hailey hiccupped a laugh then stood back to wipe her tears. "And on that note, I think I'm going to go home and take a long, hot bath. I really just wanted you all in one place to tell you. I know you all have families and work to go home to. But, yeah…"

She said her good-byes as the group broke up and wiped their tears. It had been harder, a hell of a lot harder, to tell Sloane, but she was glad she'd told the others. They would tell their men, tell the Montgomerys, and then she wouldn't have those secrets anymore.

She was free.

Free to go home alone and figure out what the hell she was

going to do with Sloane. Ten minutes later, she stepped inside her house and stood in her living room, a little too lost for comfort. What if she messed everything up? What if he did? Why was she so scared of what could happen with him. He liked her for *her*, but what if they made a mistake. What if this ruined what she had with him before…with the Montgomerys. What if…

She cursed at herself.

She was putting herself in a corner when she didn't need to be. This was so unlike her that she hated it.

The knock on her door surprised her, and she looked through the peephole. As soon as she saw Sloane's large form she relaxed, even as her body warmed at the thought of him.

"Hey," she said once she'd opened the door.

He had a six-pack of beer in one hand, a pizza in the other, and a smile on his face. "I heard your girls' night ended early. What do you say about a movie?"

She stepped back and ran her hand down the hardness of his stomach as he passed. "Okay," she said simply.

Okay. They would be okay. If she didn't think so hard, they would be okay.

They had to be.

* * * *

The heat from the bomb flayed his skin and he screamed. He couldn't move, couldn't breathe. The weight of part of the Humvee pushed at his chest and he placed his hands on the edges, growling as it burned his flesh.

He turned to the side, his body going still at the sight of what shouldn't have been.

The five other men at his side stared at him with dead eyes, their mouths hanging open, their jaws unhinging as they screamed a soundless scream. They reached for him, clawing at his body as he tried to break free.

But he could never be free.

The chains of memory, of guilt for living and finding the happiness he was never supposed to find, tightened around his chest, his neck, his gut. He started to suffocate. The five bodies shifted back to their whole forms, young men with no hope in their gazes, only death. They'd been too young to drink but old enough to die in his arms.

Sloane woke up again, his body shaking.

Thank God he'd slept at his own home that night. He'd yet to sleep at Hailey's even though they'd been together more than a few nights already. He knew his dreams well enough that he couldn't predict when they appeared. He didn't want Hailey to have to experience them, or rather him when he had them. And God forbid if he ever woke up swinging, he wouldn't be able to deal with the consequences.

It'd been a couple of years since he'd talked to a professional, but it might be time to do that again. He wasn't afraid of shrinks, but sometimes the ones who hadn't been over there just didn't get it. They said the right things, nodded at the appropriate times, but until they saw their friends dying or a little kid being shot in the head because he'd crossed the street at the wrong time, they just didn't know.

He was fine most days. In fact, he was much better than he used to be. He could sit in busy rooms, deal with loud noises. His symptoms came later, in dreams. He didn't have it as bad as other guys, but he knew the nightmares and the fact that sometimes he broke out into a cold sweat, even during the day, may not ever go away. He'd never been violent, other than needing to box for stress relief sometimes, but he was like that before he'd seen what he'd seen, done what he'd done. Before he'd had Hailey and had opened up a part of himself he wasn't ready to face—let alone let Hailey see.

He didn't usually wake up swinging, but it could happen if he weren't careful. Things weren't rainbows and unicorns. Things didn't just get better. And even if he had the ability to self-reflect and knew he was in pain and knew he had to move on, it wasn't going to happen overnight. It might not ever happen.

And that was something he had to live with.

But it wasn't something he had to force on the woman he loved.

He had brothers who had gone through worse. He knew others had gone through hell. PTSD wasn't something someone could wear a ribbon for and call themselves a fucking ally. It was something that afflicted way too many people, and yet others who didn't understand said to just get over it.

He wouldn't get over it.

And hell, if he got over it, what would happen then? Would he forget his brothers? Forget the ones he'd lost?

He growled to himself, frustrated with the path his thoughts had taken.

Fuck this.

He pulled himself out of bed and made his way to the shower. He pulled the lever to as hot as he could take it, and let it steam up the room when he took care of his business and brushed his teeth. Then he stomped into the stall and tried to wash away the guilt and sin covering him.

If only he had Hailey with him. She'd help. Whenever he was deep inside her, he forgot the pain and only thought of her. At the thought of her, his dick filled and throbbed. He fisted it, his mind going in a thousand different directions, but Hailey was at the forefront. He thought of her warm heat, the way she gasped as she came, the way she raked her nails down his back. He placed one hand on the shower wall and pumped into his hand, squeezing at the base and twisting up in rapid motions.

As he pictured her arching her back, her fingers in her pussy as she looked at him, he came.

Hard.

Spurts of come hit the shower wall then slid down in the now cooling water.

He took a shaky step back then roared. He punched the damn wall, his fist sliding through the poorly made tiles. Pain ricocheted up his arm, and he wasn't sure if he'd broken his hand or not, but he didn't care. He didn't care about anything. He was dirty, stained. Scarred in more ways than one. He'd just fucked his hand, thinking of a woman far too good for him.

He wasn't worth anything. Just a man who should have died with his men instead of living to see another day…living to love her.

It wasn't fair to those who had been lost.

It wasn't fair to her.

As he pulled his hand out of the tile, he winced. Blood dripped down his skin and to the drain below. He flexed his hand, but he didn't feel any burning pain so he figured he'd been fucking lucky. He was a tattoo artist, damn it. He worked with his hands daily, and he could have easily just ruined *everything* in a blind rage.

And what would happen if he ruined it again with Hailey, huh?

He should break it off before they got too close. If he broke it off sooner rather than later, there might still be pieces to pick up so they could keep some semblance of friendship.

But first, he'd help her with her ink. He'd do it because he was an asshole and selfish enough to want it to be *him* to mark her body…even though he couldn't mark her soul.

Not in the way they both needed.

He wasn't good enough for that. And once Hailey realized that, it would all be lost.

And Sloane would be alone.

Where he deserved.

Again.

Chapter Six

There was something wrong with Sloane, but Hailey couldn't figure it out. She ran her hands over her pants, keeping her eyes on him as he stared at his sketchbooks. He might have said all the right things, done the right ones, too, but there was something off with his eyes—as if he truly didn't believe what he was saying.

Or maybe she was just thinking too hard. She did that all the time.

But there was a tension in his shoulders that hadn't been there before.

There was a gruffness to his voice that scared her.

Not in a way that meant pain, but in a way that meant…brokenness. She'd never heard it before, not even in the days when he'd lock himself in the Montgomery Ink office and focus on his sketches rather than the world. He'd do that for hours at a time when he didn't have clients, then come over to Taboo with a need for coffee and food. She'd take care of him and make sure he had enough in him to make it home, but even then, the darkness in his eyes hadn't been like it was now.

She didn't understand it.

It couldn't have been something she did, because, damn it, she hadn't done anything. And she wasn't the type of person to immediately blame herself for every little thing. But he was scaring her enough that she began to wonder if maybe she *had* done something.

And that worried her.

"There a reason you're standing next to me hovering like you want something?" Sloane asked, though there was a smile in his voice. Perhaps not as bright as it had been only days before, but it was something. He set down his pencil and turned to her. He held open his arms, and she slid into them, wrapping her own around his neck.

"I didn't know what to do with my hands," she answered. Her gaze met his and she did her best to try and figure out what was wrong, but that wouldn't happen until she asked him.

And knowing Sloane, he wouldn't tell her.

Sloane's mouth quirked into a grin and he lowered his hands to cup her ass. "I know what I can do with *my* hands, Hails. Why don't you explore with your own and figure out what you need to do with them."

She rolled her eyes but kissed him anyway, a soft kiss that turned into something much hotter, much deeper. Sloane's hand molded her butt, bringing her even closer as they kissed. When she broke away, she had to catch her breath. Then she wiped the lipstick off his lips.

"Sorry about that," she said when she showed him her thumb.

He shrugged and kissed her thumb anyway. "I think it makes my lips pop, don't you?"

She threw back her head and laughed, aware his hands were still on her ass. "It accentuates your skin tone for sure. But really, sorry it's all over your lips. I didn't wear the stain today since I like to try different things, but I guess I'm not used to having to worry about rubbing it off on another person's body."

He licked his lips, his eyes on her own. "Oh, really…what part of my body are you thinking of putting your lips on?"

She lowered her head so she could run her teeth along his earlobe. When he shuddered against her, she bit down slightly. "Where do you want my lips?"

His grip on her tightened, and she let out a happy sigh. "Anywhere you want them, Hails. Anywhere you want them." He squeezed her again but didn't move her closer. "Before we get naked and show each other exactly where we want to put our lips, though, I want to work on your ink. I have a few ideas sketched, but I can't do much more without your input and without tracing your outline."

She gulped but nodded. Her body cooled somewhat—not that it ever completely cooled in Sloane's presence. They were in his home office because he'd wanted to do the outlining in private. Eventually, when he did the actual ink, he'd close off part of the shop so it would just be the two of them and no one would see if she didn't want them to. While that was standard practice for intimate tattoos, she still loved the fact that he took care of her.

She also hadn't been to Sloane's that often, so it was nice to see where he lived, be among his things. It wasn't a large place, and frankly a little stark, but it smelled of him. And except for the construction work in the bathroom where it looked like he was redoing tiles, everything seemed to be in order.

And if she thought about tiling a bathroom, she wouldn't have to think about the fact that they were about to outline her chest so she could get the tattoo she'd wanted for years.

Sloane moved his hands to cup her face. "Hails."

She blinked at him.

"We don't have to do this now. We don't have to do this ever. The ink you get is for *you.* Yeah, I might see it when your shirt is off, but anything we do from here on out is for you."

The way he said that made her pause. *Might*? Did that mean he might *not* see her once it was done?

She forced those thoughts from her head and focused on him. "I want to. It's just a lot. You know?"

He brushed her cheek with his thumb. "I know. And we don't have to do anything today. We can just make out."

She winked, some of the tension going out of her shoulders. "Can we make out after?"

"It's a deal." He kissed her softly then turned her around so she sat in his lap. She could feel his erection under her, but neither of them said anything about it. Not yet.

"So you already did some sketches?" she asked. She didn't reach out and trace the leather-bound book in front of her, but she wanted to. This was *his,* so she would restrain herself.

He fisted his hand in her hair and she melted on his lap. When he pushed her hair to the side and kissed behind her ear, she melted more, causing both of them to moan.

"Hails, baby, don't squirm or I'm going to fuck you right here and we're never going to get your ink done."

"You're the one fisting my hair and kissing my neck."

He pulled on her hair, and she moaned.

She didn't move, but she *did* bite into her lip. "So." She cleared her throat. "Sketches."

He let her hair down and kissed her temple. "I didn't know what you wanted since we hadn't gotten that far. I don't know if you want flowers or symbols or anything. But I was up late and had an idea. You don't have to use this. In fact, I suggest you don't. And though I know your body quite well now that my hands and mouth have been on every inch of you, I don't know it to the detail I'd need for a tattoo. So things would have to change anyway depending on angles and shit. But, if you like it as a base, then sure. I just couldn't get it out of my head. You know?"

"I know." She leaned into him. The fact that he'd thought of something for her, as if he couldn't *stop* from sketching it, brought a warmth to her chest she didn't want to think about just then. "Show me."

Sloane reached around her and opened the book, his hands steady, but she could feel the tension in his body. This was important to him. Not just the ink he would eventually place on her skin, but what he was going to show her. It was important to her, as well.

She sucked in a breath at the first drawing. "Sloane."

He didn't say anything, but she let her shaky hand reach out and trace the edge of the paper. "How…how did you know?"

"What do you mean?"

"It's…it's almost exactly what I had in my head. How…how did you know?"

He swallowed hard; she could feel it. "I guess I know you better than I thought I did."

She let the tears fall then and studied the drawing. She loved this man, loved everything about him. He *knew* her. She may not know everything about him yet, but she'd find out.

She had to.

Her hand shook once more as she put her finger on the edge of the paper and pressed her lips together. He'd captured almost exactly what she wanted, at least most of it, without even having to ask. Long branches reached out from her right side and across her chest. The trunk of the leafless tree would go down her side, with the roots wrapping around her hips. The bark wouldn't be brown, but a mix of Gaelic symbols in dark black with shadows in between. She might ask him to add splashes of reds and pink in the white parts if it would look good. She wasn't sure. As for the branches, they would tangle together over her breasts with a single hot pink ribbon wrapping itself around them, the edge dangling off the end of a branch. Cherry blossom petals fell down from the tree and added a splash of color to the imagery. At the base of the tree, a rose bush lay with vivid red roses wrapping up her belly and over her scar.

"It's…"

"Your strength and beauty in one. If you don't like the ribbon, we can take it away. Or we can put an octopus or a cake or something on your side."

She snorted. "Really? An octopus? A cake?"

"You're a baker. And people like putting octopuses on their bodies these days. No idea why. Probably because of all the legs."

She wiggled so she sat sideways on his lap. "It's…perfect. I mean, we could add things to it or something, but it's what I wanted. I wanted a tree, I wanted symbols, I wanted pink and red. You *got* me, Sloane. You get me."

He tugged her close and kissed her jaw. "I like to think I get you, Hails. I'll have to sketch your body to make sure I can do this, but you have just the right curves that it won't look like a hunk of bark on your side, you know?"

She grinned. "I trust you, Sloane."

He met her gaze, and something passed over his eyes she couldn't read. "You honor me, Hailey. Fucking honor me."

"I don't think I'd be able to trust anyone else to do this." She hadn't meant to say that, though she'd stated something similar in the past. She felt so raw right now, so open. She trusted him with her ink, but for some reason, she was scared to trust him fully with her heart.

But it was far too late for that fear.

She'd already given it to him.

She had to pray he wouldn't break it.

"I'm selfish enough not to want anyone else to do this," he

said, his voice low and gruff. He cleared his throat then, breaking the moment. She didn't blame him. It was so serious, and yet, if she didn't remember to breathe, she'd forget.

"Let's get that trace done," he said after a moment of almost-awkward silence. He helped her off his lap then got the paper ready while she stripped off her shirt and bra. She felt bare, exposed. She'd been far more naked than this, but for some reason, the way he traced her body multiple times reminded her of the hospital. Maybe it was the clinical way he was working with her. While she appreciated it, she wanted her Sloane back.

He paused and frowned. "I'm fucking up."

She shook her head, her eyes clear of tears. She was pulling herself in so there wouldn't be tears. No emotion. Just a raw ache that would never go away.

"You're not."

He let out a sigh and placed the paper and pencil on his table before bringing her into his arms. Her bare chest pressed against his clothed one and she sank into his hold.

"I wanted to keep it professional and not scare you, yet I didn't think about *why* you wanted me to do your ink."

"I wanted you to do my tattoo because I trust you."

"Yeah, to know what you want, to do what you want, but I didn't do what you *need.* You needed me to be a mix of the artist and the boyfriend. And I fucked it up."

She shrugged. "I didn't know that's what I needed."

"Well, I won't fuck it up again." He mumbled something else under his breath, but she didn't quite catch it. "Let's finish up, and I want you standing between my legs as I do it. You feel scared at all, you just touch me." He licked his lips. "Or you could just touch anyway." He leaned back and stripped off his shirt, the sight of his tanned skin, ink, and scars almost too much for her.

She placed her hands on his chest. "Will this hurt with the angle?"

He shook his head. "Nope. If I need you to move a certain way, I'll ask."

He kissed her softly then got to work, this time not clinical at all. It helped her body relax and keep her mind focused on him rather than the odd scenario of being traced for a tattoo that would take multiple sessions and be painful as hell. But she'd made it through the worst pain of her life; she could make it through this.

When he finished, he put his hands on her butt again and brought her closer to him. His lips brushed hers, and she sighed into him, loving his taste. It was a mix of the coffee they'd shared earlier and that unique flavor that was all Sloane.

The kiss started slow, sweet, and oh-so-perfect for what she needed. Then she made a sound in the back of her throat that always seemed to push Sloane right to the edge, and he growled right back.

Perfect.

His hands on her ass tightened and he deepened the kiss, his tongue taking control of hers. He set the pace and she didn't mind it. Not when the outcome was him inside her and her nails raking down his back.

When he pushed her back slightly and stood in front of her, she let her hands run down his chest and hooked them into his belt loops.

"I want my mouth on you, Hails. Think you can stand when I do that?"

She shook her head. "No. The last time you put one of my legs on your shoulder while you had your mouth on my pussy, my knees gave out. Remember?" Her knees about buckled then just thinking about it.

Sloane ran a hand over his beard. "You're right. Okay. I have an idea." He quickly gathered her up, eliciting a squeak from her throat, and moved to the kitchen where he set her down on the island in the middle of his kitchen. It wasn't that big of a kitchen, but the island fit. Barely.

And now her ass was on it.

Nice.

"Isn't this where you cook?" she asked, tilting her head to the side so he could nibble at her neck.

"I've never put food on this. I don't cook all that often. Now stop thinking and let me love you."

She squeezed her eyes shut at his words but let him kiss her, then let him take off her pants. Hailey leaned back on her arms as he knelt in front of her, placing her legs on his shoulders. At the first lick of his tongue on her cunt, she let her head fall back, his name a whisper on her lips.

He devoured her. There wasn't another word for it. The feel of his beard scraping the inside of her thighs made her even wetter—something she hadn't thought possible before Sloane. He hummed along her clit and her legs shook as she came, his name that much louder from her lips.

"Sloane. I need you inside me."

She looked up and he already had his pants off and the condom on his cock. Without a word, he gripped her hips and tugged her to the edge of the island. She sat up to put her hands on his shoulders as he sank into her. He was so freaking big that he stretched her, but it was a good stretch, the kind that led to orgasms and fucking rainbows and unicorns.

When he started to move, she let her head fall back once more. She couldn't breathe, not when her heart raced and her body felt warm, tingly, and on fire all at once. He put his hand on her back and she looked at him.

"I need a better angle," he growled. "Can't feel all of you. Need you to be able to move with me."

With that, he pulled out and carried her over to the living room, one hand fucking her with his fingers, the other keeping her steady. She gripped him tightly, loving this side of him. When he sat on the couch and placed her on top of him, she slid right back on his cock and they both froze. At this angle, he was deep. *So deep*. She had to breathe a moment so she could accommodate all of him.

"You okay, Hails? This good for you?" His voice was low, his eyes dark.

"Yeah," she gasped as she started to rock her hips. "Better than okay. Fuck me, Sloane."

"Then move, darling. *Move*." He gripped her hips and lifted her up before slamming her back down on his cock. She dug her nails into his shoulders and rode him, their bodies sweat-slick and her pussy clenching him as she neared the edge.

"Come for me, Hails. Come on my cock."

She met his eyes and came, his voice so low it vibrated deep within her. He crushed his mouth to hers as he came with her, his seed hot inside the condom. Her body shook, but she kept moving, not wanting this moment, any moment with him to end.

Because she may have just had another bout of the best sex of her life, but she knew something was still off. There was something wrong with her Sloane.

Something that told her if she didn't figure out what it was, he wouldn't be *her* Sloane for much longer.

Chapter Seven

Sloane stood in the office of Montgomery Ink and tried to figure out what he was going to do next. His back hurt from bending over too long with the last client, on top of not being able to sleep that much the night before.

He hadn't let Hailey spend the night, making sure he took her out to dinner before dropping her off at her place. But he knew she'd caught on that she hadn't woken up in his arms. He'd never woken up with her pressed against him.

There was something wrong with him and he knew it. He had to talk with someone because not doing so would only make things worse. For Hailey.

There wasn't much he could do about how he felt about himself at this point. As soon as he finished her ink, he'd find a way to let her go so she wouldn't end up hurt because of him. Once she knew how he'd come to be, how he'd ended up in Montgomery Ink, she'd see. It wasn't fair to keep at it, to keep having her in his arms. He'd already told himself that he wouldn't sleep with her again—even if his body ached for it. It made him an asshole to keep having her with him, knowing he couldn't keep her. Yes, it was better for Hailey in the long run not to be with a man such as him, but it didn't make it any easier.

"Sloane?" Callie came up to him, her hand on the barely noticeable bump at her center. "There's a man outside asking for you." She bit her lip. "I don't think he wants to come inside, but I was out there trying to get some fresh air and saw him."

Sloane's senses went on alert. "Who was it? Are you okay? Should you be going outside alone in your condition?"

Callie shook her head, a smile tugging at her lips. "You sound like Morgan. I'm fine going outside in the daylight. I promise. But

I don't know his name. He only said he wanted to talk to you." She took a deep breath. "He's wearing a uniform, Sloane. But it's old and dirty. He also looks strung out, but I don't exactly know. It could be that he's homeless and tired, but it seemed a bit more than that."

Sloane froze at her description then cursed. "Don't go outside, Callie. Stay here with Austin and Maya. Okay?"

She frowned at him. "Who is it, Sloane? What has you so worried?"

He lowered his head and kissed her temple. "Just be safe, Callie. I'll go outside and see what it is. If it's a drugged-out guy, though, I don't want you anywhere near him." Nor did he want Hailey anywhere near him, but he couldn't say that without drawing attention to the issue. If Callie were worried about him, she'd bring Hailey over and then he wouldn't be able to hide his past anymore.

And he needed to in order to keep Hailey untainted.

He left a confused Callie in the office and made his way to the front of the store, aware that Maya and Austin were watching him. He ignored them and walked outside in just his Henley, picking up his leather jacket from the hook at the front of the store on his way.

The hauntingly slender man in front of him was a blast from the past. The guy was a few years younger than Sloane, but looked at least fifteen years older. It didn't look like he'd shaved in over a year, nor did it appear as if he'd cut his hair. Normally a buzz cut, it brushed the top of his shoulders and hadn't been washed in far too long.

He wore an old uniform, as well as a threadbare jacket that hadn't belonged to him in the past. He shifted from foot to foot, his attention on the sky above them.

"Jason." Sloane's voice was gruff, but firm. He didn't know why the man was here today, but damn it, it tore at him that Jason was like this.

If it weren't for luck and some determination, he'd be right by Jason's side, living on the street, strung out and in pain.

"Ever wonder what it feels like to fly?" Jason asked, his eyes still on the clouds.

Dread filled Sloane's belly and he did his best to keep his voice calm. "I used to, but I found I like my feet firmly planted on the ground."

Jason met his gaze and Sloane wanted to break down. The man wasn't high, far from it. Instead, his old friend, the man he would have died for, the man he'd almost died for, felt *everything*. There weren't enough drugs in the world to hide the pain of what Jason was feeling—of what Sloane felt every day. Callie had been right in thinking it could be a lack of sleep that led to the look of him, and now Sloane knew that was true. Jason may have used in the past, but it had never been something he constantly did.

"If my feet are on the ground, then I know theirs aren't."

Sloane held back a curse as bile rose in his throat. "They might not have boots on the ground, but we're here, Jason."

"And they aren't. You still dream of them? Still dream of the burning. Because I do. That's why I don't sleep, you see. Because if I sleep, they're louder. Now they're just whispers, telling me I should move on. Telling me I should stay. It doesn't make sense, Sloane. Why doesn't it make any sense?"

Sloane moved forward and slid his leather jacket over Jason's shoulders. It was old enough that Jason might be able to keep it for a bit before it was stolen by someone else on the street. He didn't dare give him something better in case someone thought it was worth Jason's life. He'd done that before and hated seeing the cuts on Jason's lip from the fight. He also could take Jason in or force him off the streets. He'd tried that and had only ended up watching Jason walk away again. His friend *needed* to stay where he was and Sloane could only help so much.

"You need to stay warm, Jason. Have you eaten today? Let me get you something to eat." He wouldn't take him to Taboo, though it was the closest. He didn't want to bring Hailey into this. Or bring this to Hailey. She'd see the darkness beneath his skin and know the truth.

"I can still hear them screaming." Jason faced Sloane fully. "Why did we live? Why did I have to be in the truck behind you guys? I should have been in your truck like normal. But I got in the other one when we ran out of that last building. I got into the wrong one. And now they're dead and I'm here and it doesn't make sense."

Sloane clenched his jaw and put his hand on Jason's shoulder. "Let's get you something to eat, Jason."

The other man shook his head. "I'm okay."

He wasn't. But then again, neither was Sloane. "Let me give you some money for later, then." He pulled out his wallet and took out the rest of the bills he had in there. It wasn't much, but it was something. He stuffed them into the pocket of the jacket he'd given Jason and squeezed the man's shoulder. "Be safe, Jason. Please." Tears pricked at his eyes and he forced them away. He didn't have a right to cry. Not anymore.

"I always am, Sloane. That's the problem. Isn't it?" With that, Jason shuffled off, his hands in his new pockets.

Sloane stood there for another few minutes, watching Jason walk away and knowing he hadn't done enough. He never did.

"Sloane?"

He closed his eyes and took a deep breath, breaking inside once more. Hailey's voice broke him into a thousand pieces, and yet he knew he couldn't show her that. Wouldn't. She'd seen it. What had she heard? What would she do?

"Go inside, Hailey."

He heard her move toward him, but he kept his attention focused on the direction where Jason had disappeared.

"No. I won't. You're cold out here."

"Then you're cold, too. So go inside."

"Sloane." So much depth, so much emotion in that one word.

He wasn't good enough for her. He was too dirty. Too unclean. He'd let the others die. He hadn't been enough. Their deaths slid over his skin as if it owned him. He wasn't what she needed. Regardless that he loved her. He was too rough, too on edge. Too full of guilt and sin.

She wouldn't leave him, not unless he pushed. And if he didn't push, he'd shatter her more. He'd have to break her right then.

"It's over, Hailey. I can't do this anymore. We had our time and it was fun, but I can't do it. We're just too different."

"Look at my face when you say that. Look at my face when you try to end it without telling me anything at all."

He turned then to face her. They stood in the middle of the sidewalk, though it was too cold outside for many people to be out and about. The others in the shop stood at the windows, staring, but he had to get this over with. He had to protect her from him.

"We had what we had, but I'm not made for long term. You're made for so much more than me. So it's over."

She pushed at his chest and growled. "Stop it. Stop acting like this. This isn't who you are."

"I'm exactly this, Hailey." He gripped her wrists and pushed her back. "I'm nothing. Don't you get that? You don't know me at all and that's my fault, but fuck, everything's my fault. So just walk away now."

"You're the one walking away. Not me."

"Then let me walk."

With that, he turned on his heel and headed to the alley that would lead him to the parking lot. He had his wallet and keys and didn't need anything else from the shop. He'd just broken the one woman he'd promised to never hurt, but he hadn't had a choice. If he'd have stayed, she'd have been marred.

He'd let those close to him down before, let them burn and die and scream.

He couldn't do the same to her.

* * * *

Hailey watched him walk away and wondered what the hell had just happened. How could he do that? How could he leave her standing in the middle of the sidewalk as if nothing had happened?

Oh, she'd known he'd do something like this soon, she'd felt it, but she hadn't known it would hurt this much. It shouldn't hurt this much. Right? She rubbed her breastbone and tried to keep the tears from falling. She would not cry. If she did, then it would be final, he'd really be gone and she'd have done nothing about it.

For a moment, an agonizing moment, she thought him leaving was truly about her. Maybe it was about her scars, maybe it was about what he'd seen when he'd traced her. But then she mentally hit herself upside the head and pushed those thoughts away.

Sloane hadn't lied to her about what he felt about her body. He couldn't fake that. And damn it, she'd spent years learning to love herself for who she was and what she'd overcome. She'd be damned if she let herself tear all that away.

He'd left because of something within himself he hadn't been able to run from, hadn't been able to bury deep enough. She knew he'd kept secrets for far too long, had hidden who he was, but she'd thought they'd have longer to figure it all out.

This Jason had been the catalyst for Sloane cutting his ties. She didn't know exactly what had happened, but she'd figure it out…if she could.

From what she could tell, Sloane saw a man within himself that he thought wasn't for her. He'd put her on a damn pedestal and thrown himself into the depths of hell.

She saw a man that was worthy. A man that had fought and come out ahead. He put everything he could into his life and who he was, even if he'd tried to keep his past firmly in the past. Yet the man didn't believe in himself.

"You need to come inside," Maya said from behind her. "It's fucking cold out here, and watching him walk away isn't going to help."

Hailey turned on her heel and wrapped her arms around herself. "He left," she breathed, her voice slightly cracking. "How could he just leave?"

Maya held her arms open, and Hailey moved toward the other woman but not close enough to take the hug.

"If you hug me right now, I'll cry. Be the bitch I know you can be and get ragey with me."

Maya grimaced and tugged on Hailey's arm before dragging her into the shop. "I'll be a bitch in a minute. Let me make sure you don't have freaking frostbite or something."

Callie had a mug in her hand and a frown on her face. "I made you hot cocoa, but it's not as good as when you make it. And I can never get the chocolate shavings right."

Hailey smiled despite herself and took the mug from Callie's hands. "I'm sure it's wonderful. Thank you, Callie." She took a sip and let out a breath. "Sugary," she mumbled. She twisted her mouth. "How many people saw him walk away from me?"

Austin pressed her shoulders and forced her to sit in the front chair. He crouched in front of her, his eyes full of knowing. "Not that many." His voice was deep and reminded her of Sloane's.

She would not cry.

Not now.

Maybe not ever.

If she cried, then she'd break; she'd show she'd given up. And she couldn't do that. Not yet.

"Enough, though," she whispered.

Autumn squeezed in between Austin and the front desk, her eyes wet. "No one's really outside since it's so cold, and no one in Taboo would have been able to see at that angle. So it was just us in the shop. The two clients were in their chairs so they couldn't see either. They're over at Taboo getting a much-needed food break."

"It was just us, Hailey," Callie said softly. "And we're here for you."

Hailey took a sip of the cocoa Callie must have made over at Taboo. Normally, Hailey didn't allow those at Montgomery Ink to work behind the counter, but she didn't have the energy to care about that right then.

"He's an asshole, Hailey," Maya said. "He's an asshole for leaving like he did, but he's *our* asshole. Just think about it, okay? He pushed you away for a reason."

Hailey took another sip. "I know he left for a reason. I know he pushed me away for that same reason. He's just kept that so close to the vest for all these years, it's hard to break through it. I know I shouldn't put him on the same timetable for revealing his secrets as I put myself, but when he does this? Maybe I should have pushed."

Austin let out a breath then squeezed her knee. "Maybe you should have. Maybe *we* should have. Fuck. I've known Sloane for longer than you have, and I still don't know about his past. I don't know the reasons he sometimes takes a week or two off and needs to be alone. I tried to ask once, and he shut me down. I *let* him shut me down. Friends don't do that shit. So you're not alone in this, Hailey."

But she felt alone. She couldn't help it. He hadn't pushed the others away as he had her. She *loved* him, and yet she hadn't been enough to chase away the darkness. If that was even her job to begin with was another story altogether. In fact, she didn't need to chase away all of it, but to function, she needed to *know* of it. That was the difference.

Resolved, she took a deep breath.

"I'm not going to let him go that easily," she said simply. "I'm not that kind of person. Even if we weren't dating, we're friends. I…I can't see him hurting and not want to do something."

"We're here if you need us," Autumn said softly.

"And if you need us to hold him down for you, we can do that, too," Maya added, bringing a smile to Hailey's face.

"I might take you up on that."

"Make sure you make him grovel, though," Maya said with a sad smile. "I mean, after you talk and you're on the right path, make him grovel. Because he hurt you. He might have done it for a reason, but you're hurt and that's not okay."

Hailey pressed her lips together and nodded, tears once again threatening. "You can count on it," she whispered.

Sloane was *hers,* and she'd be damned if anyone took him away from her.

Even him.

Chapter Eight

Sloane wanted a fucking drink but wasn't about to use that to cope. He'd done his best not to when he came home from the desert, and he'd be damned if he did it now. But it was tempting. Damn tempting.

He'd known it was going to hurt like hell when he finally let Hailey go, but he hadn't known it would be this bad. It had only been a day, and yet the agonizing minutes had gone by way too slowly.

He was such a fucking idiot, but there was nothing he could do about it now. He just prayed she'd be okay eventually, and hell, that he hadn't lost his job at Montgomery Ink for leaving like he had.

Seeing Jason like that had ripped him open. He'd bled with that man and had almost died with him. Yet what right did Sloane have to be happier than him? Choices had brought him to the place where he was, but did that mean he deserved the outcome of those choices?

Hailey was far too good for him. She'd survived and thrived. He'd made it through his life, and that wasn't the same. If she were with him, she'd know the truth.

That he was stained with the blood of his fallen men. That he'd killed to protect them, but hadn't done a good enough job. He'd killed to protect himself and his men, yet how could he live with that? He hadn't been enough for the others and yet somehow he'd lived.

He wasn't going to end it—that wasn't the kind of man he was—but he also couldn't consciously bring another down with him.

Hailey deserved better than that. Deserved better than him.

The knock on the door surprised him, but it shouldn't have. It was probably Austin here to kick his ass for leaving not only Hailey but also the shop. The big man could probably take him, and that was saying something.

Without bothering to look out the peephole, he opened the door and froze.

"Hailey," he said, his voice a broken growl.

She had her hands folded over her chest and a glare on her face. She looked hot as hell and even madder.

"If you shut the door in my face, I'll just keep knocking, so you better let me in."

Caught off guard and a little turned on, he moved to the side so she could storm past. And storm she did. She let out a small growl and turned on her heel.

"Well? Close the door, Sloane. We have to talk."

He'd done his talking in front of Montgomery Ink. If he did it again, he wasn't sure what he'd say.

"I already said what I needed to."

"Well fuck you, Sloane Gordon. You need to let *me* talk, then. And when I'm done, you better be ready to talk or I'm going to kick your ass."

His eyes widened, but he didn't say anything. He'd never seen her like this, but damn if he didn't like it. He'd loved her passion before, but hell, this was something more.

He finally closed the door, and she lifted her chin. Before he could take a step toward her—or away from her since his mind couldn't figure it out—she stripped off her top so he could see her scars. He froze, unable to speak, to think. Her face was one of fury, but her stance that of strength.

"You see this? This is all of me. I'm not going anywhere. You think I'm less of a woman because of what happened to me? You think I'm less of a person? I sure as hell don't think you're any less of a man because you have PTSD, are scarred, or had to go through hell. You need to talk to me. You got it? You need to tell me what is going on in that head of yours and know I'm going to be there. I was your friend before this and I'm not going away."

Sloane opened his mouth to speak but couldn't formulate words.

"I don't know what happened over there because you won't tell me. If you don't want to go into the details, that's fine. For now. Because you need to talk about it, Sloane. Hiding away from it clearly isn't helping. I love you, Sloane, and you're in pain. I hate to see it and yet there's nothing I can do if you keep hiding. So, yeah, I'm standing here topless so you can see every inch of my pain, of my past. I'm not hiding anymore. Please don't hide from me."

Shame covered him and Sloane took a step forward. He didn't touch her, couldn't if he wanted to think, but he let out a shuddering breath.

He hadn't missed that she'd told him she loved him. But could she love him without knowing the truth? He walked past her to the couch and heard the telltale sign of a sob. Fuck. He was messing this up.

When he pulled the throw off the couch and wrapped it around her shoulders, she frowned at him. "I don't want you to get cold."

"I don't feel much of anything, Sloane."

He closed his eyes and took a deep breath. She was here. Here and waiting. If he didn't open himself up, she'd leave for good, and he'd always know he'd hurt her, scared her. Yet once he told her everything, she might leave anyway.

But what way would hurt her less?

"I've killed, Hailey." He cleared his throat. "I've killed and hurt. I've watched the life drain out of someone's eyes because I was ordered to. Because if I didn't, they'd kill my men or me. I didn't want to, never did, but I did it anyway."

She pressed her lips together. "I figured you had, Sloane. That doesn't change what I think of you."

"It should, damn it." He paced, running a hand over his head. Hair was just starting to scrape his palm and he knew he needed to shave again. That didn't matter, though. The only thing that mattered was making sure Hailey understood what he was saying, understood *why* he'd left her standing on the street like he had.

"I'm dirty, Hailey. I have blood on my hands that I'll never wash off. No matter how many times I told the shrinks after I got out, they didn't understand. The only ones that do are the ones that were over there with me." He stopped pacing and met her gaze. "But out of all the men I went over there with, the only one that came back was Jason. And you saw him. He's what I should be."

"Don't say that. You know you're not supposed to be that shadow."

He shook his head and let out a shout. "I damn well should. I lost *everyone* but Jason over there, and fuck it, I lost Jason there, too. He didn't come back whole, no one did, but for some reason I came back with more than I should. How could I? That roadside bomb wiped out my unit. Fucking burned them to a crisp and I was forced to listen to it, to watch it. I almost bled out and burned with them, but I didn't. Instead, I have to walk in this world every damn day knowing I'm not good enough. No matter what I do, I'll never be worth it. I'll have never earned my life. Jason didn't die that day either, yet he left more on the field than I did."

"Sloane." Tears slid down her cheeks, but he didn't wipe them away like he normally would have. If he did, he'd break, and he was already shattered as it was.

"Yes, I have PTSD. That doesn't go away with the love of a good woman, with the ability to *see* that I have it. It's never going to go away, Hailey. I might be able to look like I'm normal on most days, but sometimes I'm going to freak the fuck out. Sometimes I'm going to have nightmares. Sometimes I'm not going to be okay. How is that good enough for you? How can you stand to be with me knowing I'm not whole? I came home. Others didn't. My friends had to die for me to be able to stand here in front of you. They were the ones that didn't make it and yet because they died, I lived. I was able to make it out and yet their families will never know how much they meant to me."

She choked out a sob. "I'm not normal, Sloane. I'm sure as hell not whole. You said yourself I was more than my scars, and yet you don't think you are as well? Scars aren't just the ones on our skin, aren't just what we can see when we look in the mirror. I *know* I have them inside, on my heart, on my soul. I *know* you have them, too. And I'm fine with it. I love the man in front of me, scars and all. Can't you love him, too?"

"I'll taint you," he whispered.

"You can't, Sloane. Just love me. Love is enough to get us started. We can talk to someone if we need to, but love *is* enough. It doesn't heal all wounds, doesn't make the past go away. It doesn't heal our scars, doesn't erase the pain, but it *does* make it worth it. With you, I know I'm okay. I know I'm loved. Even if you haven't said it."

He let out a breath then stepped toward her. She cupped his face with one hand, the other on the blanket before he cupped her face instead. When she wiped the tears from his face he hadn't known had fallen, he closed his eyes.

"I love you, Hailey. I love all of you, every breath of you, every ounce of your soul. But I'm not worthy of you."

"You're a fool, but I love you, too, Sloane. And you don't get to decide if you're worthy of me. That's not how love works. You don't get to walk away from me, leave me bleeding and in agony because you're afraid to hurt me. You *hurt* me anyway, trying to protect me, and I'm not going to let you do that again. You hear me? If you want to leave me, then you do it without lying to me. You do it by saying you don't love me and you don't want me."

He opened his eyes and cursed. "I love you, Hailey. I just damn well said it. Of course, I want you. I can't breathe with wanting you."

"Then let that be enough. We can do anything, Sloane. But we have to be together to persevere. You're a good man, Sloane Gordon. I saw you with Jason. I saw you try to help and know you could only do so much. Don't become him, Sloane. Help him, but don't let his pain take away what you have. Don't fade into the shadows because you feel you should. Step into the light *because* of those you lost. Show them that their loss was worth it. Show the world that you made it and you live for them, not in spite of them."

Jesus, he loved this woman. She saw into the heart of him and yet he'd almost lost it all because he was so scared.

"I love you, Hails. I pushed you away before I had you, then did again because I was scared."

"Don't do it again," she whispered, tears sliding down her cheeks in earnest. He wiped them away with his thumbs.

"I fucked up."

"Yeah, you did," she said honestly.

He snorted.

"Don't do it again. You don't get to push me away because you're scared."

He kissed her then, softly, with everything he had within himself. She kissed him back, and he fell that much more in love with her.

He pulled away and traced one finger down her side and under her breast. "Don't hide from me either. I know you haven't, but…"

"But I might. Because it's scary. I know." She kissed his chest. "I promise to be open."

"I'll never leave you again," he said softly.

"I want to believe that," she whispered. "So prove it to me, Sloane. Every day. Prove it to me."

"Be with me. We've hidden everything else in the past, but I'm all me now. You're all you. We're bare. You got it? You're mine. I fucked up, but I'm not doing it again. I'm going to have you every way I can and I'm not letting go."

She smiled softly and nodded. "We've wasted too many years because we were scared. I'm not going to waste any more."

He kissed her then, this time deeper. "I love you, Hails."

"I love you, too. Oh, and happy Valentine's Day."

He frowned and thought about the day before letting out a rough chuckle. "Happy Valentine's Day, baby."

She let the blanket fall from her fingers and he let out a groan. He hadn't allowed himself to look at her fully before, but now he took her all in. When she licked her lips, he had to have her.

He crushed his mouth to hers even as she tugged on his shirt. Soon they were stripped down, pressing their bodies together as tightly as possible, hands roaming and grasping. He pulled out a condom from his discarded pants pocket and let her slide it over him. The act almost made him come, but he held strong. Barely. He moved her toward the front door and gripped her thighs.

"I've wanted to fuck you hard against a door since the first time," he growled.

She bit his lip and opened for him. When he slid inside oh-so-slowly, they both moaned.

"Is it still fucking when we love each other? Or is it making love?" Her nails dug into his shoulder and he slowly pumped in and out of her.

"I know it's making love when it's slow." He sped up. "When it's going fast,"—he pounded into her—"when it's me fucking you hard. It's fucking, loving, and everything in between."

She bit into her lip and rode him even as he fucked her into the door, their bodies sweat-slick and their moans rising. When her cunt clamped around him and her eyes darkened, he slammed into her, coming hard with her. He kissed her lips, his body shaking. She kissed him back.

"Love you, Hails. All of you." He wrapped his arms around her, knowing he'd have to take them down to the floor soon before his legs gave out.

She nipped at his chin, her hands lazily skimming his back. "Love you, too, Sloane. You're my broody, bearded, inked man. What more could I want?"

With her in his arms, in his heart, he knew the answer. Life. And she was it. He wouldn't run from her anymore. He couldn't. She'd seen the heart of him and hadn't run, hadn't shied away.

He'd been wrong before, but now he was all too right.

He had his life, his future in his arms.

He didn't need anything else.

He'd found his future in the one person he'd hidden from.

He'd found his Hailey.

Epilogue

Hailey winced as the needle dug into her skin, but she didn't call out. Tattoos were not for wimps, that was for sure. Yeah, the nice adrenaline rush that came from long-term sessions under the needle were nice, but hell, it *hurt.*

But it would be worth it in the end.

Plus, her tattoo artist was sexy as hell and pretty damn gentle, all things considered.

They were on the final session for her ink and she had the routine down by now. Sloane had curtained off his station so it was only the two of them, though she'd allowed Autumn, Maya, Callie, and even Austin to come in and look. The latter hadn't made Sloane happy at first, but he'd relented. They'd wanted to make sure she had support during not only the long and painful sessions but also during the emotional waves that came with it.

Sloane wasn't tattooing nipples on her skin.

He was tattooing memories.

With each new detail, she saw the strength she'd needed, saw the pain and agony she'd faced, saw the tears she'd let fall. It wasn't easy to let the others see what had become of her chest, but they hadn't treated her any differently. She wasn't made of glass, but of hardcore power and woman.

And that she was okay with.

They'd embarked on a journey she hadn't thought possible. She'd hidden her scars, her past from him, from the world, and yet now, everything was out in the open and she didn't feel any less.

In fact, she felt like she had *more.*

Every time she looked in the mirror now, she wouldn't see a survivor—but a woman with a future, a woman with a past, a woman with a man she loved who'd inked her skin with such tender care, she knew he'd put part of himself into each stroke.

"It's magnificent," Maya said softly, unlike how the other woman usually spoke. Of course, Maya was going through her own hell right then—not that she'd talk about it with Hailey. Now that Hailey had found her future, though, she knew she was steady enough to help Maya. If and when the other woman let her in, she'd be there for her.

"I do good ink," Sloane said simply as he finished up part of the color shading on the inside of the trunk.

She winced when he went over the same area for the fourth time, but didn't call out. She was getting the hang of this tattoo thing. Maybe next time she'd go a bit smaller, though.

"You do better than good ink," Maya said. "It's a fucking masterpiece. I have to say I was a bit jealous at first that he was the one to do this for you, but hell, I don't think I could have done this justice. Not in the way he's doing it."

Hailey let a single tear fall. "He's amazing."

"I am," Sloane said with a smile.

Maya snorted. "He's putting his love for you in the ink, so yeah, it's perfect. I can't wait to see it when it's all healed." She leaned down and brushed a kiss to Hailey's temple, surprising them both. "I'll leave you two alone for the last bit. Thanks for letting me watch."

Hailey frowned as the other woman left them, but Sloane clucked his tongue. "When Maya is ready to talk, she will." He wiped down Hailey's side, then patted her thigh. "I'm all done, baby. I don't want you to stand yet since I want you to drink some juice first, but I can bring the mirror over."

She smiled and held out her hand. "Kiss me before you do. I want your lips on mine before I look."

Sloane moved around to the front of the bench then lowered his head to hers. She kept her eyes open so she could watch his face.

"I love you, Sloane. Every inch of you."

"Same goes, Hails. Same goes. Love you, baby."

She'd look at her new tattoo in full later when she could breathe, but first she'd look at the man she'd fallen for, the man who had fallen for her.

Hailey had been so scared to move forward with him, so scared to do more than survive, but now, with Sloane in her life and her own head on straight, she had more than she could ever hope for.

The two of them had been through their own hells and had come out the other side stronger than ever—scarred, broken, but *alive.*

They'd hidden their pasts, yet opened up to one another to ensure that they'd move on together. Her ink would be hidden from most, but not from him, not from the man she loved.

He was inked on her skin, on her soul, on her heart.

He was hers.

Forever.

* * * *

Also from 1001 Dark Nights and Carrie Ann Ryan, discover Wicked Wolf: A Redwood Pack Novella, and Adoring Ink.

About Carrie Ann Ryan

New York Times and USA Today Bestselling Author Carrie Ann Ryan never thought she'd be a writer. Not really. No, she loved math and science and even went on to graduate school in chemistry. Yes, she read as a kid and devoured teen fiction and Harry Potter, but it wasn't until someone handed her a romance book in her late teens that she realized that there was something out there just for her. When another author suggested she use the voices in her head for good and not evil, The Redwood Pack and all her other stories were born.

Carrie Ann is a bestselling author of over twenty novels and novellas and has so much more on her mind (and on her spreadsheets *grins*) that she isn't planning on giving up her dream anytime soon.

www.CarrieAnnRyan.com

Also from Carrie Ann Ryan

Redwood Pack Series
Book 1: *An Alpha's Path*
Book 2: *A Taste for a Mate*
Book 3: *Trinity Bound*
Book 3.5: *A Night Away*
Book 4: *Enforcer's Redemption*
Book 4.5: *Blurred Expectations*
Book 4.7: *Forgiveness*
Book 5: *Shattered Emotions*
Book 6: *Hidden Destiny*
Book 6.5: *A Beta's Haven*
Book 7: *Fighting Fate*
Book 7.5: *Loving the Omega*
Book 7.7: *The Hunted Heart*
Book 8: *Wicked Wolf*

The Talon Pack (Following the Redwood Pack)
Book 1: *Tattered Loyalties*
Book 2: *An Alpha's Choice*
Book 3: *Mated in Mist*

The Redwood Pack Volumes
Redwood Pack Vol 1
Redwood Pack Vol 2
Redwood Pack Vol 3
Redwood Pack Vol 4
Redwood Pack Vol 5
Redwood Pack Vol 6

Montgomery Ink
Book 0.5: *Ink Inspired*
Book 0.6: *Ink Reunited*
Book 1: *Delicate Ink*

The Montgomery Ink Box Set #1 (Contains Books 0.5, 0.6, 1)
Book 1.5: *Forever Ink (also found in Hot Ink)*
Book 2: *Tempting Boundaries*
Book 4: *Harder than Words*
Book 4: *Written in Ink*
Book 4.5: *Hidden Ink*
Book 5: Ink Enduring (Coming Jun 2016)

Dante's Circle Series
Book 1: *Dust of My Wings*
Book 2: *Her Warriors' Three Wishes*
Book 3: *An Unlucky Moon*
The Dante's Circle Box Set (Contains Books 1-3)
Book 3.5: *His Choice*
Book 4: *Tangled Innocence*
Book 5: *Fierce Enchantment*
Book 6: *An Immortal's Song (Coming April 2016)*
Book 7: *Prowled Darkness (Coming May 2016)*

Branded Packs (Written with Alexandra Ivy)
Book 1: *Stolen and Forgiven*
Book 2: *Abandoned and Unseen*
Book 3: *Buried and Shadowed (Coming July 2016)*

Holiday, Montana Series
Book 1: *Charmed Spirits*
Book 2: *Santa's Executive*
Book 3: *Finding Abigail*
The Holiday Montana Box Set (Contains Books 1-3)
Book 4: *Her Lucky Love*
Book 5: *Dreams of Ivory*

A Stand Alone Contemporary Romance
Finally Found You

Wicked Wolf

A Redwood Pack Novella
By Carrie Ann Ryan
Now Available

The war between the Redwood Pack and the Centrals is one of wolf legend. Gina Eaton lost both of her parents when a member of their Pack betrayed them. Adopted by the Alpha of the Pack as a child, Gina grew up within the royal family to become an enforcer and protector of her den. She's always known fate can be a tricky and deceitful entity, but when she finds the one man that could be her mate, she might throw caution to the wind and follow the path set out for her, rather than forging one of her own.

Quinn Weston's mate walked out on him five years ago, severing their bond in the most brutal fashion. She not only left him a shattered shadow of himself, but their newborn son as well. Now, as the lieutenant of the Talon Pack's Alpha, he puts his whole being into two things: the safety of his Pack and his son.

When the two Alphas put Gina and Quinn together to find a way to ensure their treaties remain strong, fate has a plan of its own. Neither knows what will come of the Pack's alliance, let alone one between the two of them. The past paved their paths in blood and heartache, but it will take the strength of a promise and iron will to find their future.

* * * *

There were times to drool over a sexy wolf.

Sitting in the middle of a war room disguised as a board meeting was not one of those times.

Gina Jamenson did her best not to stare at the dark-haired, dark-eyed man across the room. The hint of ink peeking out from under his shirt made her want to pant. She *loved* ink and this wolf clearly had a lot of it. Her own wolf within nudged at her, a soft brush beneath her skin, but she ignored her. When her wolf whimpered, Gina promised herself that she'd go on a long run in the forest later. She didn't understand why her wolf was acting like this, but she'd deal with it when she was in a better place. She just couldn't let her wolf have control right then—even for a man such as the gorgeous specimen a mere ten feet from her.

Today was more important than the wants and feelings of a half wolf, half witch hybrid.

Today was the start of a new beginning.

At least that's what her dad had told her.

Considering her father was also the Alpha of the Redwood Pack, he would be in the know. She'd been adopted into the family when she'd been a young girl. A rogue wolf during the war had killed her parents, setting off a long line of events that had changed her life.

As it was, Gina wasn't quite sure how she'd ended up in the meeting between the two Packs, the Redwoods and the Talons. Sure, the Packs had met before over the past fifteen years of their treaty, but this meeting seemed different.

This one seemed more important somehow.

And they'd invited—more like *demanded*—Gina to attend.

At twenty-six, she knew she was the youngest wolf in the room by far. Most of the wolves were around her father's age, somewhere in the hundreds. The dark-eyed wolf might have been slightly younger than that, but only slightly if the power radiating off of him was any indication.

Wolves lived a long, long time. She'd heard stories of her people living into their thousands, but she'd never met any of the wolves who had. The oldest wolf she'd met was a friend of the family, Emeline, who was over five hundred. That number boggled her mind even though she'd grown up knowing the things that went bump in the night were real.

Actually, she *was* one of the things that went bump in the night.

"Are we ready to begin?" Gideon, the Talon Alpha, asked, his voice low. It held that dangerous edge that spoke of power and authority.

Her wolf didn't react the way most wolves would, head and

eyes down, shoulders dropped. Maybe if she'd been a weaker wolf, she'd have bowed to his power, but as it was, her wolf was firmly entrenched within the Redwoods. Plus, it wasn't as if Gideon was *trying* to make her bow just then. No, those words had simply been spoken in his own voice.

Commanding without even trying.

Then again, he *was* an Alpha.

Kade, her father, looked around the room at each of his wolves and nodded. "Yes. It is time."

Their formality intrigued her. Yes, they were two Alphas who held a treaty and worked together in times of war, but she had thought they were also friends.

Maybe today was even more important than she'd realized.

Gideon released a sigh that spoke of years of angst and worries. She didn't know the history of the Talons as well as she probably should have, so she didn't know exactly why there was always an air of sadness and pain around the Alpha.

Maybe after this meeting, she'd be able to find out more.

Of course, in doing so, she'd have to *not* look at a certain wolf in the corner. His gaze was so intense she was sure he was studying her. She felt it down in her bones, like a fiery caress that promised something more.

Or maybe she was just going crazy and needed to find a wolf to scratch the itch.

She might not be looking for a mate, but she wouldn't say no to something else. Wolves were tactile creatures after all.

"Gina?"

She blinked at the sound of Kade's voice and turned to him.

She was the only one standing other than the two wolves in charge of security—her uncle Adam, the Enforcer, and the dark-eyed wolf.

Well, *that* was embarrassing.

Blood on the Bayou

A Cafferty & Quinn Novella

By Heather Graham

Dear Reader,

I have an absolute love for the City of New Orleans and a great deal of Southern Louisiana. I'm not from there—I am a Floridian from start to finish. But, when I was very young, I went on a business trip to the city with my dad. No, we did not walk down Bourbon Street. He took me to the zoo, showed me the beautiful architecture and the eerie beauty of the cemeteries. I was smitten.

Every year since Katrina, friends have helped me put on Writers for New Orleans—a writers' conference at cost; at first, it was just to bring people back into an empty city.

Now, it's because we can't seem to stop!

Being in love with the city, it's where I chose a shop for Danni Cafferty. The first Cafferty and Quinn book, *Let the Dead Sleep*, 2013, introduces Cafferty and Quinn and the Cheshire Cat, her shop on Royal Street. In that first book, Danni loses her father, a fascinating old Highlander she has adored. (Shades of author intrusion there!)

And she finds out just what kind of legacy he has left her.

Let the Dead Sleep was followed by *Waking the Dead.* (Hey! They slept long enough.) And, next, *Let the Dead Play On.* (All available through Mira Books!)

The books are near and dear to me, like the City of New Orleans. I can walk down Royal Street and see my imaginary shop there—right around the Rodrique studios (I love the Blue Dog!) and one of my favorite places ever to shop—Fifi Mahoney's. They have a salon, and they also sell some of the most artistic and amazing wigs to be found anywhere, along with funky jewelry and cool cosmetics.

I can imagine Danni and Quinn moving about the city; I know how they feel about tourists, and what they really like to do with their down time.

This year, I'll be coming out with a new series in Spring, straight suspense, revolving around a New York City FBI agent and a young woman working with criminal psychology—who also happens to be part owner of a pre-Civil War Irish pub. Kieran's family has a checkered past—toeing the line between her brothers and the law is often a tricky task, and despite herself, she's suddenly involved in diamond heists about the city that suddenly begin to end with murder.

But, that's for the future.

Now, I hope you'll enjoy this Cafferty and Quinn novella—they're like old friends to me now, so I know I'll be working with them again.

Prologue

So far David Fagin was pleased.

"We have a few legends around here," he said to the group. "The Honey Swamp monster being one. It's said that he lives side by side with the *rougarou*."

He smiled at two of the young women in front of the group who were clad in heavy coats and huddling together.

"Every good swamp has a monster," he said. "Any of you seen *The Creature from the Black Lagoon*? Maybe not. It's a classic. But, hey, there's always Netflix. Anyway, it was a 1954 black and white film. Horrible special effects compared to what we see today, but kind of cool when you think about the poor stunt man in that rubber suit. It's your typical swamp monster. Big, scaly, out to kidnap beautiful young women and do in the handsome young men out to save them. The *rougarou*, he's different, and he's partial to this area."

"What's that word again?" someone asked.

"*Rougarou.*" And he was careful to sound it out phonetically. Ru-ga-ru. "Some say he's French. Others make him part Native American. He's the size of a man, but stronger. Some compare him to the Wendigo of certain local tribes. Now the Wendigo's name has been translated to mean *cannibal,* and by some to mean *the evil spirit that devours mankind.* Most agree the name derives from the French, *loup-garou,* wolf-man. The creature is usually seen as bipedal, with the head of a wolf. Sometimes, he's seen with other monstrous heads."

Though he and Julian Henri had been in business for several years, this was their first time doing the Bayou Night Myth and Legends Tour. Even Mother Nature had cooperated. No snow on the ground, or even in the air, but the night still brisk. Southern

Louisiana seldom received snow, and when it did fall it didn't stay long on the ground. Out on the water, though, the cold rose like a mist, embracing the bayou and making everything seem all the more dark, chilling, and menacing.

Insects serenaded the gathering. An owl hooted beneath a full moon. Every now and then came the splash of a gator sliding down a mud bank into the water. Even the sounds of Highway 90 in the distance added to the eerie feel.

Julian's family had long owned property and few people knew the swamp better. Both of his parents had passed away during the years he'd been at college. Once he returned, everyone had urged him to sell. Byron Grayson, the realtor, had advised keeping swampland was ridiculous. He'd be happy to take it off Julian's hands. Victoria Miller, owner of another tour business, had offered Julian even more money for the property. Victoria's significant other, Gene Andre, the son of an old Cajun family himself, had urged her to buy both the land and the business. But Julian had determined that he and David could make a real success of it.

Now David was convinced that they could.

So far, on their first outing, not a hitch, and people seemed to be loving it.

David, like Julian, also hailed from the low country, which added a bit of authenticity to everything they planned to do on this tour. Though they often faked their Cajun accents. Four years at Harvard had nearly caused David to "pahk his kah." And Julian's stint at NYU in the theater department had seen to it that he could switch into a Bronx drawl just as quickly as he could spit out his hometown *patois*.

They'd returned home from their respective universities four years ago, had a chance meeting at a favorite café on Magazine Street, then two years ago ventured into the tourist business. They'd started out doing history tours in the French Quarter, then added plantation visits. A day on the bayou had been next, and now they'd moved to the Night Myths and Legends Tour by lamplight.

As always, when they started a new tour, they led the first few themselves and played up their Cajun heritage. Thanks to reality

TV, people pretty much expected them to be toothless and illiterate. But breaking stereotypes was fun.

Their pontoon boat afforded a seat for the captain and the tour guide. Tonight Julian served as captain and David the guide.

"This swamp has often been a hideout place for pirates, smugglers, and outlaws," David said. "The unwary who seek shelter here. Those who don't respect the dangers because they're in trouble. Legend has it that, from time to time, the *rougarou* has happened upon those who hid in the swamp. You have to be real careful here."

A nearby alligator slid into the water.

One of the young women in front let out a short scream and jumped in her seat.

"That's probably old Meg," he said. "She's an irritable bag. Been around a long time and just isn't fond of tourists."

"Is a gator as scary as that *rougarou* thing?" a man in back called out.

"Few things are as scary as the *rougarou*," David said. "Remember, this region was largely French and the French were good Catholics. You know how it goes that if you're bitten by a werewolf in the light of the full moon, you become one."

Nervous giggling greeted his words.

"Down here, we've always mixed our monsters with religion. Part of the legend has it that the *rougarou* could enter the soul of a man who didn't follow the traditions of Lent. That was a time of trying hard to be good and behave, with kindness and brotherhood toward your fellow man. Bad guys have bad things happen. Good guys get good. And, you see, if such a man had his soul stolen by the *rougarou*, he would kill all the decent men."

"So the bad guy became badder and the good guys paid?" a teenager asked him. "Maybe it's cool being the *rougarou*."

"Not really. Because the good guys would hunt down the *rougarou*, bash his head and slice his throat," David said. "Then they cut off his head and chop out his heart." He smiled. "So, *rougarou*, watch out."

He allowed his story to sink in before telling them more about their surroundings.

"A swamp is defined as low-lying, uncultivated ground where

water collects. A bayou is a body of water lying in flat lowland, an offshoot of a slow moving river or marshy lake or wetland. It's low water with all kinds of creatures and trees, with civilization far away. But not so far anymore, as you can almost see the lights of the highway from here."

He grinned.

"1756 to 1763 are the important years. The English and French are fighting. The French from Acadia, in what is now Canada, came south to escape persecution from the English. Cajun culture comes from that time. French fur traders first came to this area in the late 1690s, and it was the French who founded New Orleans in 1718. *Nouvelle Orleans*."

"*Viva la France*," one of the teens shouted.

David smiled. "Absolutely. However, the city and surrounding areas were ceded to the Spanish as a secret provision of the Treaty of Fontainebleau after the Seven Years' War. It took a long time for the Spanish to gain any kind of control, and the flavor of the city remained French, though slowly mixing with Spanish. Then fires ravaged the city. When the area was rebuilt it all became Spanish."

"Bravo Spain!" another said.

"Again, absolutely," David said. "But in 1801, another treaty gave it all back to the French. By then the Americans had arrived with permission to use the ports. I'm telling you all this to explain the mix of cultures and culture clash. The French had their *rougarou*. When the Americans came, they added the Anglo church, and though the fear of witches had died out, it was resurrected here. We already had our African-Caribbean voodoo thing going. So we just added all the new stuff in to our own legends."

He pointed out in the dark.

"Just to the right, ahead, is the site where the Good Witch of Honey Swamp lived in the early 1800s. Her father had been a Scottish sailor, her mother a voodoo queen. She cured people, and it was claimed she could control the weather."

He shifted everyone's attention in another direction with a hand gesture.

"Back over there you'll see some old houses built up by the bayou. They look close, but they're about a mile apart. They've been there all these years, owned first by the rich, and now by us working stiffs. Our good captain, Julian Henri, lives up there."

"A working stiff, I assure you," Julian called out.

Laughter rose among the passengers.

Julian pointed far to the left. "Right over there, friends, that old shack on the water is my place. I grew up around here as an only child. Alligators were my pets."

Of course, not a word of it was true. But it sounded great.

David started to speak, then paused, a bit puzzled. He could have sworn he saw lights flashing by Julian's place. Though he owned it, Julian did not live there. He stayed in the French Quarter, where they kept their offices. He did keep a few lights on in the place, but they didn't flash. Maybe it had been a trick of the moon.

"Alligator for a pet," someone said. "Really?"

"Not much to cuddle with at night," Julian teased.

"It's so creepy out here," one of the young women in front said. "Weren't you always scared?"

"When you grow up out here, you don't think about it," Julian explained. "It's just home."

"Even with old *rougarous* and witches and voodoo and whatever else?" someone asked.

"Now that's the thing. When you're from here, you're protected."

Then Julian shrugged at David, turning the group back over to him.

David took the cue and said, "Some say that the Good Witch of Honey Swamp offended a powerful slaveholder who called himself Count D'Oro. He owned one of the houses, like Julian's, on the water. The Good Witch had no interest in becoming his mistress or performing her magic for him. So one night the Good Witch of Honey Swamp was dragged from her home, tied to a tree, and burned alive. She made it rain, and the rain kept putting out the fire. But finally, the flames consumed her. As she died she cursed the count and all who knew him. It's said that her curse backfired. Count D'Oro turned into a *rougarou* and slaughtered dozens of people before he was caught, before he had his head bashed in and his throat ripped out, before being tied to a stake and burned to nothing but ash. They still say if the witch's curse is repeated, the soul of D'Oro will come back. And the *rougarou* will roam the swamp once again."

"What were the witch's words?" a teen asked.

A shrill scream pierced the night.

From one of the young women toward the front of the boat.

For a moment, it seemed that David's heart stopped. Had they been moving too close to shore? Was another alligator aiming toward the pontoon boat?

"The *rougarou,*" the young woman screeched, moving from her seat.

"Careful," he warned.

The pontoon boat shouldn't flip, but with such a sudden shift of weight he wasn't sure. "Please, please. What is it? If you saw something in the trees—"

"No," the young woman cried, looking over at him with huge eyes. "Blood. There's blood on the bayou and a man. He's dead."

David carefully moved to her side of the boat.

They were close to the shore.

And he saw it.

A dead man.

Feet still tangled in the grass, head battered, blood dripping.

"*Rougarou,*" someone else shouted. "They're moving in the trees."

And there was someone out there.

Gone in a flash, racing away, thrashing through the underbrush.

Rougarou? No way. They weren't real.

Not like the corpse.

And the blood on the bayou.

Chapter 1

Michael Quinn heard the hysterical crying the minute he entered the police station. The young woman creating the commotion was inside Detective Jake Larue's office. Someone else was trying to soothe her while not becoming hysterical herself.

"This one is right up your alley," Larue told him as he approached.

"My alley?"

"That young woman is certain she saw a *rougarou*. She was on a bayou tour in Honey Swamp last night."

He smiled. No kid grew up in Southern Louisiana without hearing about the *rougarou*. Every region of the world had their own particular brand of monster. The *rougarou* belonged to the Cajun region of Southern Louisiana, stretching right into the city.

"Honey Swamp?" he asked. "Doesn't a problem in that area go to the Pearl River police?"

"Yep," Larue said. "But she's here because she believes the *rougarou* followed her home, showing up in the window of her hotel last night."

He arched a brow at the ridiculousness of the statement. "I'm assuming there's more."

"A dead man in the swamp. Head bashed in, throat ripped."

Which grabbed his attention.

"I want you to talk to them," Larue said. "I told them that you're a *rougarou* expert and that you'll get to the bottom of things. They were out on some night ghost tour in the bayou and their boat came upon the dead man. Right now, she's so hysterical that she's not making sense. But you *rougarou* experts are used to dealing with that."

He shook his head at Larue's sarcasm. He was no more a

rougarou expert than someone was a ghost expert. Once upon a time, he'd worked with Larue as partners in the NYPD. Before that, Quinn's life had been anything but normal. He'd actually been a pretty horrible person, not as in deadly or criminal, but as in vain and egotistical. His prowess in sports had led to excess, which eventually led to him being declared legally dead.

Which changed everything.

While clinically dead, he'd seen a strange personage, who told him it was time to turn around. An angel? Maybe. But the experience had led him to the military, then the police—and then to Angus Cafferty. When Angus died, neglecting to tell his own child, Danni, what he really did on and during many of his buying trips, Quinn had brought her up to speed. It hadn't been easy. She'd not believed anything he'd said, nor had she much liked him.

In fact, she'd loathed him.

He'd never imagined how hard it would be to make her believe that all things in life were not what they seemed. But most legends had their roots in truth. She'd both grown up with Angus and wanted to believe that the world was filled with good. She was, however, her father's daughter. So when she finally came around to realizing what they were sometimes up against, she'd been brilliant.

And still exquisite.

Five-feet-nine-inches of willowy perfection, vitality, and intelligence. A mane of sleek auburn hair and the kind of blue eyes that seemed endless and could steal a man's soul. He always smiled when he thought of their rocky beginning.

She was both stubborn and opinionated.

But he couldn't imagine life without her.

His smile widened before noticing his friend's stare. Larue was studying him. When they'd been partners, Larue had known Quinn had something of an extra sense, and Larue wasn't the kind to fight, deny, or question it. In fact, Larue didn't want to know what lurked beneath the surface. He just wanted whatever bad was happening to stop. So he tended to bring Quinn in on the unusual stuff, which allowed Quinn to be both a private investigator and have the police on his side.

"You can help?" Larue asked.

"How long have we both lived around here?" he asked Larue.

"Lifetimes."

"And have you ever seen a *rougarou*?"

"Look, I'm not you," Larue said. "I don't have the gift, or whatever it is. Anyway, the Pearl River guys are working the murder. Two fellows I know fairly well, Hayden Beauchamp and Dirk Deerfield. Good detectives. Beauchamp called me this morning. The tour directors and the guests on the boat were all out of New Orleans. I've got a car ready to head out so you can meet with them and see the murder site, if you think you can help."

He pointed at his old friend. "Say what you will, but we've heard the legends for years on a *rougarou*."

"I get it. That's why you're going to need to be on this," Larue softly said. "Did you hear what I said? Head bashed in, throat ripped out. That's only happened once before that I know about, and, of course, you know about it too."

Quinn winced and nodded.

He didn't believe that a *rougarou* had wandered into the French Quarter to jump around the guests' windows. But he did remember the murders that had taken place out at Honey Swamp when they'd been kids.

"There's more," Larue said.

He waited.

Larue pointed to the two women in his office. "There were drops of blood on the balcony where they're staying. So far, we know it's human and that's about it. We have it as a top priority, but we don't have any DNA results back yet. It all sounded like a prank when they walked in here. I don't have your ability with the strange or whatever, but I do have a cop's sixth sense. And something tells me that this is going to get worse, and weirder, before it's all over. Will you talk to these women for me, please, Quinn? God help us, we might have been kids back then, and it's not like we don't still have our fair share of pretty awful crime, but this could be like last time."

And he knew what that meant.

Serial killings.

"We have to jump on this," Larue said. "Or the whole damned bayou, and maybe this town itself, will run red with blood again."

* * * *

"I'm opening up," Danni Cafferty called to her friend Billie McDougal.

She walked across the first floor of the old house at the corner of Royal Street that she'd inherited from her father, unlocking the door of the shop portion and flipping over the OPEN sign.

She was smiling.

It was going to be an exceptionally good Friday because she couldn't wait for the night.

They, meaning herself, Quinn, Bo Ray Thompkins, Billie, Father Ryan and Natasha, also know as Mistress LaBelle, were going to get together as soon as they all closed up for the day. Also, it was going to be a night when they could bundle up a bit. New Orleans was actually chilly in January. Even the mules drawing the carriages filled with tourists seemed to enjoy the respite from the heat, clopping down the streets with what seemed like a hop in their steps.

They were planning an evening of great food and music. Not necessarily an all-nighter, which was easily possible in a city that never slept. Her shop, the Cheshire Cat, would be open tomorrow, a Saturday, but not until eleven. And Quinn, a might-have-been-guitar-player, was scheduled to sit in with friends down at a bar on Chartres Street. She loved when he played. He wasn't quite as good as many of their friends, who spent just about all of their waking hours playing their guitars. But he could have been if that'd been his goal. He was a natural and he loved it.

And she loved Quinn.

Go figure. When he first strutted into her life she'd thought him an arrogant hunk. She'd hated the fact that Angus Cafferty working with Quinn had been a secret her father had kept from her.

But things were different now.

And it wasn't just physical, though he was near the perfect man, lean of muscle, all six-four of him. It was that she knew that even when he'd been hero-worshipped by kids as a star athlete, he might have been oblivious but never cruel. She'd thought him the biggest ass the world had ever known when they first met. But eventually, she learned, after her father's death and through a difficult and deadly case involving the theft of a special statue, that he was far from it. He'd changed and become a man with a dedication to the world and those around them.

A person even her father had trusted.

Sure, the beginning hadn't been easy, and life still made things a challenge between them. But there was something that made the challenges worth it, and sleeping with him every night certainly helped ease away the day's dilemmas.

"I'm ready," Billie called to her, grinning.

His words trilled.

Billie had come to America with her father from Scotland. And though he'd been in the States for years, his rich Scottish burr hadn't faded. Tall and gaunt with a thick thatch of white hair, Billie could have easily stood in for Riff Raff in a performance of *The Rocky Horror Picture Show*. He was as dear to her as a man could be, her self-appointed guardian after her father's death, and the one who, with Quinn, had finally allowed her to see just what her father had really *collected* through the years.

"I'll be bringing me pipes," Billie assured. "And don't roll your eyes at me, lass. I'll just see if I can't be part of one or two songs."

"I love it when you play your pipes," Danni said. "It's just that the bar is small and bagpipes are loud. But it's great to have them."

Billie laughed. "Hey, now. I just want you to know, Miss Danni Cafferty, I made good money in me younger years standing on the streets with me hat out. You should have seen the folks throwing bills in it when I played."

"Maybe they were paying you to stop," Danni teased.

"Ah, lass."

"Kidding, Billie. I love it when you play."

"Here's hoping Quinn does make it back," he said, "and that he's not starting into some fresh trouble with Detective Larue. I'm looking forward to some fun times this evening."

"Don't worry. Quinn said he'd be back in plenty of time, and we'll head right out at closing."

The front door opened quickly and a tall man entered.

Who she recognized.

David Fagin.

She greeted him, curious because of his anxious manner.

David was an old friend. They'd gone to high school together, one of those magnet schools for the arts. She'd been in visual art and David had focused on theater. They'd bumped into each other a few times over the last three or four years, and he'd come to her father's funeral. They'd talked about the changes in their lives, their plans and dreams, and she recalled how he'd been excited about his business ventures. She'd told him that she was happy too, still working as an artist, running her father's shop.

David had dropped by a dozen times, but today he seemed to not be on a buying excursion.

"Danni, I need your help."

Billie stepped up beside her, ready to listen to whatever it was their visitor was about to say. She noticed how David shifted on his feet and kept looking around, as if someone were after him.

"Danni, I've heard… There are rumors. We're talking a life or death situation." His eyes focused on hers. "My life."

She swallowed hard and felt a sense of dread. She wanted to push David back out the door and pretend he'd never come. Every once in a while it was still difficult to reconcile all that had happened in the last several years. She'd thought her father the most wonderful man in the world. Tall, sturdy, and gruff, the perfect Highlander with his rich accent, booming voice, strength, and kindness. He'd traveled the world. On buying trips. Only after his death had she learned that they had been anything but.

Oh yes, Angus Cafferty had been a collector.

At the Cheshire Cat they sold local art, jewelry, clothing, and some more unusual items. Angus had especially loved unique pieces, one-of-a-kind carved masks, Egyptian trinkets, religious artifacts, custom items. One of the display cases had been created from an authentic Egyptian sarcophagus. A display in the left window featured a Victorian coffin, a turn-of-the-century mannequin, and a 19th century vampire hunting kit. The right window held local lore. A stunning display from the so-called Count D'Oro, an 18th century aristocrat who murdered numerous young women and dumped their bodies in the swamp. Among them, a beautiful, young witch who had cursed him at her death. Legend noted that he'd been a cruel man whose soul had been consumed by the devil, and only when he'd been caught by vigilantes and then burned alive in the swamp himself had his evil been laid to rest.

But Angus had also acquired the *dangerous.*

Items best described as having evil upon them.

And as the inheritor of the business, she now was their owner.

"Okay, David, let's have a chat," she said.

A nod to Billie and he understood to cover the store. She led David through the shop, past her studio, and opened the kitchen door where Wolf, Quinn's giant mixed breed dog, bounded toward her, then let out a loud woof at the sight of a stranger.

"He's a friend," she told the dog, then turned to David. "Don't be afraid of Wolf. He's a good dog. If he thought Quinn or I were in danger he'd rip into someone like hell on wheels, but as soon as he knows you're a friend he's like a puppy."

"Hey, Wolf," David said. It seemed like there was a catch in his throat when he said the dog's name.

"Sit, please." She motioned to the small breakfast nook. "Coffee?"

"In lieu of a morning shot of whiskey? Sure."

He took a seat as indicated but still looked jittery enough to shoot through the ceiling.

Danni poured coffee as David surveyed the kitchen.

"I got a note," he said.

She laid two cups of coffee on the kitchen table and sat to join him.

His fingers drummed nervously. He looked at her, his dark eyes haunted and serious. "From the *rougarou.*"

She studied him and could tell he was serious. Quinn was a

licensed private investigator. And, apparently, during the years she'd been blissfully naïve, her father, and the shop, had gained a certain hush-hush following, a place where people turned when they needed help with strange, life-threatening events. She wished Quinn was here now. But Detective Larue had called him that morning and he'd gone in to help with whatever Jake wanted. He wouldn't be back until early evening.

"The *rougarou* killed a man last night, Danni. Killed him horribly, about a minute before we reached him. There was still blood in the water. His head was bashed in, skull cracked like an egg, throat torn out." He drew a deep breath. "Bitten out. By savage teeth."

Her heart skipped a beat at the horror, and she could only imagine the sight he'd seen.

"The *rougarou*?" she asked.

Her window display dealt with the *rougarou*, a monster said to consume the souls of the evil and turn them into killing machines.

David curled his hands around his mug, seemingly baffled and defeated. "I just heard myself. I can't believe what I said. And I'm from that damned swamp. I grew up along the Pearl River. Yeah, we base the business here in the city, and my apartment now is just off Esplanade on Bourbon, but I know that swamp. I've trapped gators, caught catfish as a summer job, worked crawfish nets. I know the bayou."

She'd always liked David. He'd majored in theater, but she'd always thought he might have turned into a playwright. He loved to tell stories. Had a flair for the dramatic, which he'd used to make a good living with the tour company he'd started with Julian Henri. There, his love of local lore and dramatic talents had combined perfectly. She knew that he and Julian had accumulated raves from almost every online travel site.

"*Rougarou*. I think the thing is real," he muttered. "I didn't at first. I mean, it was all going so well. The *rougarou* was a legend told to scare kids, to make us be safe, to make us behave. All the stories about the Good Witch and Count D'Oro. They're just that. Stories. Last night, the tour boat was full and we were going to make some serious money. We're booked for weeks to come. But I don't know now. I've put the tours on hold and returned the fees paid. We were telling the tales, talking about the area, working the group, and then we found a dead man."

She'd not seen nor heard any of the local news for the day. Most of the time Billie or Bo Ray managed the shop. She was there often, but thanks to them she could focus more on her studio and be with Quinn. More time to deal with problems just like this one since, after all, she had inherited the Cheshire Cat and all that came with it. Now she realized that Jake Larue had probably called Quinn because of the murder—even if it had occurred way out in Honey Swamp.

"David, you do understand that whoever killed this man may have been aware of our local legends and just used one to their advantage."

She could barely remember the details of when the last bayou murders had taken place. Understandable, given she was only six. But it was as if history was repeating itself. History from long ago.

And from not so long ago.

He looked at her, his thoughts apparently running parallel with hers. "You remember, don't you? It was the same thing. Those young women out in the swamp. Three of them. And they never did catch the killer. They blamed it on the *rougarou.* The local people did, anyway. The press dubbed him the Wolfman Killer because of what happened to the throats. That was twenty years ago. Then the killing stopped. And now?" His voice carried anguish. "What else could it be?"

"There are still many logical reasons why this happened, David. Even in the way it did. There are still the normal motives for murder. Someone was furious. Someone wanted to get even. Jealousy, hatred, greed. And this someone knows the legend, as we do, and thought that killing like that would cause everyone to get scared and shake the police off the right track. Yes, this is truly horrible, but I'm still confused. You said that the *rougarou* sent you a note?" She tried to smile and ease his sense of fear. "This is the first time I've ever heard that the *rougarou* liked to write."

David's fear wasn't eased, nor was he amused, and he glared at her. "In the mud, Danni. He wrote in the mud. Near the dock. Julian brought the people and our boat back in. I went with the police. But when they brought me back in I saw it by the floodlights we keep burning by the dock. There were letters, weird letters, like a kid had written them."

"What did they say?"

"'I'm coming for you.'"

David's voice was just a sliver of sound on the air.

"The area had been pretty trampled by then. People were really freaked out. They couldn't wait to get back on the bus. The police had to interview them all." He tightened his hold and dropped his gaze to his mug. "The cops didn't see what I saw, Danni. And before I could tell them to stop, they walked all over the letters, erasing every last one."

"David, that message could have been for anyone. You said there were twenty or so people on the tour. And it might have been innocent, like someone's friend trying to say that they'd be there to pick them up instead of them coming back into town."

"You don't get it, Danni."

He thrust a finger into his chest.

"My name was there. In the mud. It said, 'David, I'm coming for you.'"

Chapter 2

"I know it was a monster."

Jane Eagle appeared to be the younger of the two women seated in Larue's office—and the most hysterical.

"Okay," Quinn said gravely, not disputing her. He turned to her friend and travel companion, Lana Adair, and asked, "Did you see the monster?"

Lana tossed Jane a guilty expression, as if she hated telling the truth. "I didn't see him. Not in the swamp. But I did see the dead man. His head was…there was blood in the water and…white stuff. I mean the poor fellow's brains. Oh, God."

"Did you see the monster at your balcony window?" Quinn asked.

Lana shook her head, glancing sadly at Jane again. "I did see what looked like bloody prints of some kind. We didn't even call the police. We left and got a cab because we didn't know where we were going and asked for the closest police station. Detective Larue sent some men out right away, and he told us it was blood."

"The guy on the boat wasn't lying," Jane said. "It was a monster. A *rougarou*. That's what he was talking about. And he was so good, so knowledgeable. He was great. Until—"

"The body in the bayou. And for all that blood and stuff to be in the water, it had to just have happened," Lana said.

"The guide didn't freak out. I think his friend did a little. Or his partner. The captain. His name was Julian. After the lady saw the body and yelled, he turned white. Then the guide—"

"David," Jane said. "Cute. Nice."

"He was pretty competent," Lana said. "He got on some kind of radio and called the police. They came in a boat. David, yeah. David, that's his name. Anyway, he got on the cop boat and the captain brought us back to the dock to be questioned."

"We were all freaked out on the bus back to the city," Jane said. "We had drinks."

"Lots of them," Lana added.

"Oh, we don't usually," Jane said. "I mean, yeah, it's New Orleans, but we're not big drinkers. I just love the city in winter. Kinda cold, but not too cold. Nice to walk around." She hesitated. "It was there. We're at that cool place on Dauphine. It's only two stories and every room has a balcony, either looking over the courtyard or the street, and every balcony has a window and a door. The *rougarou* was in the window. I saw him. And he saw me. He knows I saw him in the swamp and I think he's after me because I did."

She was close to hysterics and Quinn knew he needed to calm things down. "We can start by moving your room."

"You really think there was a *rougarou* and that it followed these young ladies to their hotel?" Larue asked, obviously trying hard not to sound so incredulous that he offended the young women.

Quinn looked at Larue, who quickly read his expression. No, he didn't think a monster had followed them. But changing rooms could appease the young women, or at the least make them feel better, as if the police were trying to do something.

His friend nodded in agreement.

"We'll get a police escort and have you out of your hotel and into one that is right on Bourbon Street," he said. "It'll be a room over one of the hottest night spots where there are always cops and security guards. Detective Larue and I will go with you so that we can personally make an inspection. Now, bear in mind, we don't doubt what you saw. We're just not sure what you saw is really a *rougarou*." He lifted a hand as Jane was about to protest. "People in this area all know the legends about the *rougarou*. Someone out there might be using the legend. In this day and age, it's quite possible to fake a monster."

They both looked at him with huge eyes, seemingly wanting to trust in him.

"Sound like a plan?" Quinn asked Larue.

The detective nodded. "Let's move, though. We have to get

out to Honey Swamp. We're going to help the task force with the investigation."

Ten minutes later they were at the hotel where the young women were staying. Quinn inspected the balcony while they gathered their belongings together. The room sat on the second floor, but the balcony might have been easily accessed from the street. There was a heavy pipe near enough for someone to crawl up and gain a grip on one of the wrought iron rails. "How did someone walk through the French Quarter all dressed up without being noticed?"

"This is New Orleans," Larue said. "Not far from Bourbon Street. Think about it, Quinn. Does anyone really notice *crazy* around here? I mean, there's a lot of crazy."

"Something like the *rougarou*? A giant man with a wolf's head?"

"Somebody walked stark naked down Bourbon Street about two days ago, and it took that long for anyone to report it to the police," Larue told him.

"That's not a *rougarou*."

Larue shrugged. "Okay. I'll give you that."

"To put a spin of logic on this, I'd say that it was more than possible for a man to dress up, then crawl up here to scare Jane and Lana. It's also possible that whoever was here had nothing to do with the murder in the swamp, or maybe someone got wind of the situation and knew that the two young women had been on the tour and decided to scare them. They're visitors, yes, but they know the city and they might have met a young man anxious to scare them. Then he comes along and offers his presence as protection against whatever has them frightened."

Larue did not argue.

"At any rate," Quinn said. "Let's go meet your friends from Pearl River."

* * * *

"I remember the murders," David said, looking into space as if he could see across the years. "My dad was so worried about my mom. He didn't want her going out at all. They found the one young woman, Genevieve LaCoste, almost where we were last night. I don't know why I remember her name so clearly. She was a mess. The medical examiner said that she'd been ripped up by animals after death. But Danni, her throat was ripped out, too. Just like the guy last night. The cops never found the killer. They insisted that there was a killer, but old Selena Duarte told them that it was the *rougarou.* She said that the young women had behaved badly. They ignored the rules of Lent and spent their nights drinking and meeting up with young men at bars."

"They never caught the killer," Danni said, "but that doesn't mean that there was a *rougarou.* Have you offended anyone, David? You or Julian? Do you know if anyone is angry with you? Someone who would do something so horrible, just to ruin your tours?"

He laughed. "There's old Selena Duarte. But she's five-foot-two and pretty fragile."

"Why is Selena upset with you?"

"She considers the swamp her personal property."

"But other companies do swamp tours there."

"Apparently, according to Selena, our night tours have awakened the spirit of the *rougarou.* We're not being respectful."

"Anyone else?" Danni asked.

She wished that Quinn was here. She wasn't sure how to help David or where to go from there. She'd learned that objects could be evil. Either within themselves or by making others believe in evil.

The *rougarou* of legend was not a thing, not inanimate. It was a beast, a creature, a monster.

"Julian is one of the nicest guys in the world. He's never offended anyone," David said. "Except for that one guy. He wanted a job with us, but Julian didn't like him. He said that he came in for the interview either stoned or drunk. And when Julian said something, the guy told him that he should be cool, 'it was like, New Orleans, and you know, we're all laid back here.' In fact, he thought that we should serve absinthe on our swamp tours, and that the captain and the guide ought to drink with everyone. You know Julian. He's a safety first kind of guy. Partying is fine on your off hours, but never when you have a responsibility. He told the guy to get out. The guy told Julian that he was going to rot in hell."

"You still have his application?" Danni asked.

"Sure. But whether people tell the truth on an application or not is another matter," David reminded her.

"Let's head over to the office. Is Julian there?"

"He should be. It's right on Chartres Street. Are we walking?"

"Yep. And we'll take Wolf with us," she told David.

Though he couldn't protect them from everything, the dog's presence might make David feel better. She hurried into the shop to tell Billie that she'd be with David and to give Quinn a heads-up if he called. Billie had Bo Ray down working with him. She left the shop with David.

As they walked down Royal Street to the corner, then to Chartres, they passed her shop window. Count D'Oro stood there, his mannequin eyes fantastically evil, his white shirt and gold vest impeccable despite the pool of fabric "blood" at his feet and the display of "*Rougarou* Repellent," voodoo-doll-like charms on the small three-pronged stool by his side. The mannequin had an evil twist to its lips and he gripped his cane with its silver wolf's head with casual ease, as if ready to move at any moment. David stopped walking and stared. It was clear that he hadn't noticed the window when he'd visited the shop in the past.

"Count D'Oro, known to have awakened the demon of the *rougarou* before his murder spree," he said.

"The man was a sick murderer long before he believed he had the power of the *rougarou*, and long before he claimed that it was the *rougarou* doing the killing," she told him.

David continued to stare at the display, then he turned to Danni. "He claimed that the *rougarou* did the killing. Others claimed that he turned into the *rougarou*, that his head became the head of a vicious wolf-like monster with mammoth, ripping teeth. Supposedly, he used that cane to bash heads in."

"That cane is plastic, David. It's just a display."

"Of course," he murmured, laying his hand on Wolf's head. "Let's go talk to Julian about the weird guy who applied for a job. But from what he said, the guy wasn't much of a *rougarou*. More like an idiot."

He started walking.

She followed him, glancing back at her own display.

Strange.

It seemed like the smile on the mannequin of Count D'Oro had widened.

Ever so slightly.

* * * *

The two cops from Pearl River seemed like solid guys. Hayden Beauchamp was young, fairly new to the force, slim, fit, and a bit in awe of the older Dirk Deerfield.

Deerfield was a twenty-five-year vet with the force. Larue had told Quinn that he was planning his retirement in another five years. Before being with the Pearl River force, he'd spent five years with the LAPD. He was weathered, easy, and confident, and he'd heard about Quinn.

In fact, he'd seen him play football.

"There was a professional career out there for you," he told Quinn after shaking his hand. "Can't say as that I'd not have chosen football over police work or investigation."

Quinn shook his head. "Football honestly wasn't that kind to me. I think I'm where I'm supposed to be now."

They'd met at the station and gone through the medical examiner's initial notes. Then they looked at the crime scene photos.

"Thing is, the bayou isn't kind," Deerfield said. "We had police and forensic crews out to the site within the hour. But all the blood and other matter had dispersed. A few creatures were already nibbling on the corpse. We're lucky a hungry gator didn't just take it down."

"Shall we see the site?" Larue asked.

Deerfield nodded. "You can, but there's nothing to find. Crews went over the area. Not a single piece of evidence. Not even litter thrown out by a passersby. But, sure, we can head to the site. All this harkens back to some bad stuff about twenty years ago."

"I remember," Quinn said.

"I even remember," Beauchamp added. "I was just a kid back then, but I remember. I can't believe that I'm working with a cop who was on that case. Sad and amazing. All that, and the killer got away."

"Still haunts me," Deerfield said. "We never caught that guy. From what I understand, though, it wouldn't make much sense for this to be the same perpetrator. From the classes they send us to, I understand that such a killer either gets worse, gets caught, or gets dead. He just doesn't stop for twenty years. And that *rougarou* bull that goes around? What? Some wolf-headed, old Cajun legend hides out for twenty years without anyone catching sight of it? I don't think so."

"You're thinking some kind of a copycat killer?" Larue asked Deerfield.

"Could be. Regardless, he needs to be caught. Three young women. Lovely, sweet girls. And we had nothing. Boyfriend of one was seen by dozens of people working. We checked out the local tours, the neighbors, you name it. We had no forensic evidence. It was a nightmare."

"Just like here," Quinn asked. "The same. Down to the details?"

"Same method of murder," Deerfield said wearily. "But this time the victim was a man. Someone has been studying the past."

"Autopsy was first thing this morning," Beauchamp said. "Rush on everything, and since so much of his skull was cracked in, throat all ripped up, and him in the water, the ID became a challenge. We can't just put a picture of him out in the papers. No fingerprints matched anything we have, but we do have some dental charts in our missing persons report."

"Bring up the autopsy report, will you, Hayden?" Deerfield asked Beauchamp.

Quinn lowered his head to hide a small smile. Deerfield was key in that partnership. Older, more experienced, aware of the pitfalls. Beauchamp pulled his weight in their partnership with tech expertise, his phone the size of a notepad, and he had the report up as Deerfield finished speaking.

"White male between the age of twenty-eight and thirty-four. Five-feet-ten-inches tall. One-hundred and seventy-five pounds.

Last meal—crawfish etouffee, grits, and asparagus. He'd eaten somewhere in the hour and a half before his death, and Doc Melloni has been around a while. He knew right away, which is good. Thing is, most places out here do serve crawfish etouffee."

"We're still checking out local restaurants and cafes, and at least they're a little sparser out in this area than they are in the city. Of course, he could have been in the city and made it out here just in time to have his head bashed in and throat ripped out." Deerfield shook his head. "Anyway, as you can see, the man was in excellent health, fit and sound before his demise."

"He might have lived to a hundred," Beauchamp said sadly.

Twenty minutes later, the four of them headed out with a young officer in a police boat, straight to the spot where the body had been found.

Deerfield did the talking, pointing to the shore.

"Body was there, right at the edge of the water, mostly head first, or what was left of the head. Feet were caught up on the high grasses. As you can see, the trees are pretty heavy around here. You've got a fair distance to the road. Course, you've got a few businesses dotting the shoreline, not too close. And you're a football field from here out to the highway. Locals come around, as do the tour boats. But it's pretty isolated. That's what's hard to figure. What was a guy in a business suit and Gucci loafers doing out in this part of the swamp?"

"We're expecting to get an ID on him soon," Beauchamp said. "No wallet on him, but pretty damned weird for a robbery. I mean, it was overkill."

"Can you get me in a little closer?" Quinn asked the captain.

The man nodded and eased the boat toward the muddy shoreline.

Quinn jumped out.

The grasses and mud were heavy right where the corpse had been found. Thick trees sprouted from the more solid ground further in. As Deerfield had pointed out, they weren't that far from the highway. He could hear the traffic in the distance.

"The victim was killed right here, right on the shoreline. The blow to the back of his head was first?" Quinn asked.

"That's what the medical examiner concluded," Deerfield

said. "The victim had to have been standing near the water. He was then twisted around for the attack on the throat."

"And human teeth could have done the damage?" Quinn asked skeptically.

Deerfield shrugged. "Enhanced human teeth, maybe? People do all kinds of crazy things. We got one of those whacky vampire cults out here, you know. Heaven help us. They use pig's blood in their rituals, keeping it legal and all, but I've seen some of them with their teeth all filed to points. But was there some other kind of creature involved? We don't know, as yet. And I'm not so sure testing will get us the answers."

"Okay, so the killer could have parked up on the road. Possibly came in from the city. I know I go into the French Quarter often. Easy enough," Beauchamp said.

"Ah, easy when you're young and good-looking," Deerfield said lightly. "But, sure, simple enough to get into the city and out."

"Maybe he went into the city and lured the guy out here somehow," Beauchamp said. "The victim trusted him, thinking they were coming out here for something else."

"It's possible," Deerfield said, smiling at his young protégé.

"Could have arrived via some kind of boat?" Quinn asked. "Anyone on the tour report seeing any other boats in the area?"

"No," Deerfield said, "but, yeah, they could have come by boat. Thing is, we haven't found any unknown cars parked in the area."

"The car could be down in Honey Swamp somewhere," Quinn said, pointing to the road. "Easy enough for someone to escape that way. The young women this morning reported that something was moving through the trees. The killer, I'd say. So he went back to the road, jumped in a car, and drove away."

"Unless it was a *rougarou*," Beauchamp suggested, shrugging. "In which case, it's still hiding out there in the woods. Waiting."

Or it ran back to New Orleans to watch young women in their hotel rooms, Quinn thought.

"I have to apologize," Deerfield said. "Hayden has really studied the old case."

"It's kind of like Jack the Ripper. You can't help coming up with theories. And a lot of the locals do believe in the *rougarou*," Beauchamp said.

Deerfield shook his head. "I don't believe in the *rougarou* or in witches, good or bad. I do believe that there was a killer before who was clever. And now we have a new one. Anyway, we're glad for your help. We don't want to fail again. Ready to head back in?"

Quinn nodded and climbed back in the boat.

They drifted away from the shoreline and the engine roared to life.

"Stop," Quinn shouted.

"What?" Larue demanded, startled. "Quinn—"

"You see something?" Deerfield asked, perplexed. "We looked all over last night and into the morning. They didn't find—"

"Over there. Bring the boat closer to shore again." Quinn pointed. "There."

The others stared for a moment and he understood why. He wasn't sure how he'd seen the body floating himself. The victim's hair was as dark as the water beneath the shade of the trees, her clothing a mottled green.

"Oh, no," Beauchamp breathed.

"Another victim," Larue said, reaching over the hull of the police cruiser and turning the body.

The left portion of her head and face were obliterated, her throat slashed to the bone.

"Oh, my God," Beauchamp whispered.

* * * *

Danni and David reached the tour company's booking office on Chartres Street. David introduced their reservationist, a grave young woman with beautiful golden mahogany skin, big hazel eyes, and dark hair. Her name was Sandy Richardson. She attempted a smile for Danni.

"I can guarantee you that whatever tour you take with us, you'll be informed and entertained. We're truly one of the best companies you'll ever find."

"Danni is an old friend, Sandy," David said.

"Oh," Sandy said. "In that case, I should tell you that people are furious. They don't want you canceling the bayou night tour. One guy told me that he'd be out there with his shotgun, and no *rougarou* or swamp thing or any other creature would get his hands on anyone."

"Unfortunately, this kind of thing draws all the weekend warriors out," David said wearily. "Did you say that we were closing the tour only temporarily?"

"I did. Your weekend warrior wants to head out with a boat anyway," Sandy said.

"Best of luck to him," David murmured. "Is Julian back in the office?"

She followed David down a narrow hallway to a half open door. Julian Henri, a slim young man with a shock of dark hair and serious eyes, was seated at a desk, shoulders slumped as he stared at his computer.

He looked up as they entered the room, his eyes flickering with recognition. "Danni Cafferty? You look great. How are you?"

She smiled. "Good. Thanks, Julian. Glad to see you. Sorry about the circumstances."

"Yeah, thanks." Then he frowned, looking at David. "Oh, no. You went to Danni's because of the rumors when we were young? That her father collected things that were haunted or evil. Danni, I'm so sorry."

"No problem, Julian, really," she said. "I'm not sure what we can do, but—"

"Yeah, that's right. I've heard. You're with Michael Quinn."

"You know Quinn?" Danni asked.

"I know of him," Julian said. "And it sounds good. I'm happy for you both. This thing with the tour is horrible and scary. There could be more. And you can't believe the e-mails we're getting. I'll read you one of my favorites." He tapped the keyboard on his desk. "'You irresponsible asses. A few years up north and you forget who you are and what you came from. Money hungry asses. You've awakened the *rougarou.* Death is on your hands. You're murderers.' Here's another one, really concise. 'Fuck you, monster men.'" He shook his head and looked up. "Do you believe this crap?"

"Why not?" David asked wearily. "There are television shows dedicated to chasing the yeti or abominable snowman. People love legends more than the truth."

"And," Danni said, "some people are just superstitious, and really stupid, cruel, rude, and horrible. It'll go away when the police find the killer."

Julian looked up at her. He was about her age, still not thirty, but looked younger with thin dark hair and wide eyes. Usually quick to smile, today he looked as if he was simply beaten down.

"They didn't catch the guy when we were kids," he said. "Could that same murderer have waited for twenty years to start over again? Or did we somehow really awaken the soul of Count D'Oro and let him run around as a *rougarou* again?"

"Someone is obviously playing on legend," Danni said. "Julian, did you see anything?"

He shook his head with disgust. "I was just maneuvering through the swamp, like I've done most of my life. We had a good group on board. They listened, joked around, laughing. It was good. Then I heard the scream and saw the body."

"What about the young man you didn't hire? David said that you don't have any enemies, but that you didn't hire a guy who was being a jerk."

"That guy? He didn't seem smart enough to kill anyone. Maybe you don't have to be smart. His name was—" He paused and hit a few keys on his computer again. "Jim Novak. Thirty-three. No college. But somehow graduated high school. He claimed that he'd been a tour guide in Savannah. I never tried to verify his résumé since I knew we weren't hiring him."

"Address?" Danni asked.

Julian drew a notepad toward him, checked the computer screen, and scribbled down the address. He handed the paper to her.

"Can you think of anyone else who might not want you guys to make a success of this tour? Or anyone who might want to somehow use the two of you as scapegoats?"

Julian looked at David. "What's her face? The woman who owns that other tour company. Victoria—"

"Miller," David added.

"She was ticked-off about us doing this tour," Julian said.

"I think she was madder because her boyfriend, that Gene Andre guy, thought it was a great idea. And then there's the realtor, your dad's old friend, Julian," David said.

"He wanted to buy the property with the docks," Julian said. "Guess they're pretty worthless now."

"What's the guy's name?" she asked. "There are lots of realtors around."

"Byron Grayson. Old, smart-looking dude," Julian said. "Always in a gray suit."

"To be honest," David said. "I can't even imagine him in the swamp."

Danni nodded. "I'm going to head back and start doing some research. Here's the thing, whoever killed that man knew the legends. I'll see what I can find."

"I'll walk back with you," David said. "Julian, I'll be back—"

"I'm going home to my apartment, not out to any of the shacks by Honey Swamp," Julian said. "I'm going to duck and cover for a while."

"We will figure this out," Danni said,

But what if they couldn't? They were talking about the swamp.

A great place to hide a million sins.

She said good-bye to Julian and Sandy, then she and David walked the few blocks from the Legends office back to the Cheshire Cat. They came through the shop and spoke briefly with Billie and Bo Ray. They'd both seen the news and knew what was going on.

Back in the kitchen with David, she drew out her laptop and began searching for all the information she could find about the *rougarou*, Honey Swamp, and the murders that had taken place there.

"Julian's family owns that property," David said. "They've owned it since before the Civil War. If I understand it, they bought it from the parish after Count D'Oro met with vigilante justice. That's why Julian is afraid people will blame this on him."

"David, the legend of the *rougarou* was around long before

Count D'Oro," Danni reminded him. "Julian can't really believe that this is his fault in any way."

"But he does."

"He blames himself because you two are doing tours? Come on. Many companies do bayou tours."

She heard a key twist in the courtyard door that led straight into the kitchen and looked up to see Quinn enter. He walked in looking weary, his dark hair tousled, eyes grave. And he immediately noted David in the chair.

Quinn had grown up in the Garden District. He was older than Danni and David by several years. He glanced at David, then at Danni, and she realized that they'd never met.

"Quinn, this is David Fagin," she said, rising.

David rose to shake hands. "So you're the 'Mighty Quinn.'"

"I am Quinn. Not sure about mighty." He visibly relaxed with the handshake. "Does you being here have anything to do with the bodies in the bayou?"

"Yes. Wait. Bodies? I only knew about the one," David said.

"Count is up to two," Quinn replied. "We found a second victim, a young woman, this afternoon."

He was quiet a minute and then looked over at Danni.

"Actually, *I* found her."

Chapter 3

The basement wasn't really a basement. The rest of the house was built up, allowing for a basement in an area that could flood. The first French fur trappers had chosen wisely when they had settled in the French Quarter. It was the highest ground around. Which wasn't saying much since most of New Orleans was below sea level. The Cheshire Cat's basement had been Danni's father's office, the place where he'd housed his private collection and *The Book of Truth*. Quinn knew that Danni had not known of the existence of the book until the day her father died. Angus had talked about the book, but Quinn himself hadn't seen it until he and Danni had been forced to seek its guidance.

Called *The Book of Truth,* it might have been better labeled *The Book of Fantasy and Legend.* It noted creatures from every culture and society, from vampires and werewolves to "fairy folk" and beyond. When, exactly, it had been written they didn't know. It appeared to be medieval, coming from a time when the world was filled with superstition and feared darkness and the devil. But the book was also filled with curious bits of history that often helped. Like how to kill vampire, which they'd not as yet studied, though they had made use of other parts in curious ways.

Quinn perched on Angus's desk, glancing at the various objects that were piled here and there. Some Greek, Egyptian, medieval, and Victorian era pieces. Crates and boxes littered the room, some labeled DO NOT OPEN.

Danni sat reading.

David had gone, headed to his own apartment in the city to hide out. Danni had told Quinn everything David and Julian had said. Many people in New Orleans were transient, most had come to the city, fallen in love with it, and stayed. Others had been there forever and would never leave. It was possible that all the hate e-mails were just superstitious locals.

"'*Rougarou*,'" Danni read from one of the books. "'French, cultural, regional, similar to other creatures born of evil, caught in the web of sin, sometimes, the sins of others. Eater of men's souls. Silver does not slayeth this beast, only the cleansing of fire will lay it to rest.'"

"That's it?" Quinn asked.

"That I can find," she said. "Quinn, what about the murders twenty years ago? You probably remember more than I do."

"I remember that my parents wouldn't let me anywhere near Honey Swamp. It was only young women who were killed, but it was as if a monster suddenly arose out of the earth. They never found a single clue as to who had murdered those women. The thing is, when you find a body in a swamp, even now, it's hard to find any kind of evidence."

He paused, thinking.

"David said that his name was written in the mud and the police didn't see it. What if David imagined what was written? Maybe this has nothing to do with them. Then again, maybe it does. I say we check out the guy who applied for the job. Then, the realtor and the tour group lady."

"Jim Novak, Byron Grayson, and Victoria Miller. They mentioned her boyfriend or partner, too, a guy named Gene Andre. Andre apparently approved of their tour, which pissed off Victoria Miller. Quinn," she asked, blue eyes wide and somber, "shouldn't we be looking into the past? Or calling on Natasha, maybe."

"You want to suggest this has to do with voodoo?"

"Certainly not. But Natasha has connections on the street, and she'll remember the past better than we do." She winced, looking at him sadly. "We could definitely get together with her and Father Ryan. At the very least, they're older and both have excellent memories."

Quinn nodded. Father Ryan was a most unusual priest. Excellent at what was expected of him in his calling, capable of much more. He'd been there with Quinn's parents when he'd flatlined. He'd been there when stranger things had happened and hadn't even blinked. Maybe his faith allowed him to see beyond what others were willing to accept.

Natasha Laroche—Mistress LaBelle—owned a voodoo shop just down the street. She was one of the most regal women Quinn had ever known. She sold the usual, gris-gris, statues, herbs, and all the customary voodoo paraphernalia, and read tealeaves, palms, tarot cards and more. But she was also a priestess with a devout following. She and Father Ryan, despite their passions to their own religions, seemed to have everything in common and worked exceptionally well together. Part of an odd assembly of strange crime fighters, and also great friends.

"You go and see Natasha," Quinn said. "I'll check out this address and pick up Father Ryan."

He stood. Wolf, who had been sleeping at his feet, hopped up too.

"You stay and watch over Danni," Quinn told the dog.

"I could swear he heard you mention Father Ryan," Danni said. "Take Wolf with you. I'm fine. I'm nowhere near Honey Swamp and Natasha is just down the street. They should both be ready for whatever. We had intended to go out tonight, remember?"

Quinn nodded and paused to kiss the top of her head. For a moment, he didn't want to leave her, not even for a second. Her hair always smelled so clean and yet so evocative. He wanted to forget all about *rougarous* and dead bodies in the swamp. He even wanted to forget about a night out with music and friends. Lock the world away. Play out a scene from *Gone with the Wind* and sweep Danni off her feet, carry her up the stairs, dive into the comfort of their bed and the sensuality of her bare flesh.

"Quinn?"

He snapped back to reality. "Yeah, I'm going."

He headed for the door.

The phone rang.

It was Jake Larue.

"I'm sure as hell not saying that there was a *rougarou* out there last night," he told Quinn.

He heard the "but" in Larue's voice.

"But the guy did follow those young women back to the city.

The blood on their balcony matched that of the first victim. The man found last night in the bayou."

* * * *

Jez, Natasha's unbelievably handsome, mixed-race assistant, had apparently been told that Danni was coming. Natasha always seemed to know these things, exuding an air of mystery in her manner and demeanor. Jez informed her that Natasha was waiting in the courtyard.

Natasha was wearing a colorful dress and a turban to match, all in shades of orange and gold that enhanced the dusky quality of her skin. She sat at one of her wrought iron tables, a pile of books at her side. She rose and enveloped Danni in a hug, and then indicated they should both sit.

"No music tonight?" Natasha asked.

Danni shook her head. "Tell me what you know?"

"Quite a bit, actually. I went and looked up the old murders as soon as I heard what happened."

"The young women killed twenty years ago?" Danni asked.

"No, I went way further back, all the way to Melissa DeVane."

"I don't remember the name. Was she one of the victims?"

"She was, but not twenty years ago. When the French lost this area to the Spanish, Spain didn't even send a governor right away. The French more or less refused to acknowledge what was going on. I know you've heard of Count D'Oro."

"He wanted the Good Witch of Honey Swamp—"

"Melissa DeVane."

She connected the dots.

"Count Otto D'Oro was a horrible man. Richer than can be imagined. He had many mistresses, and many of them disappeared. Nothing could be proven against the man. He was very powerful. It was said that he had his own army of enforcers. He was into everything. Prostitution, gambling, piracy, you name it. But Melissa lived out in Honey Swamp. She was reputed to be able to cure the sick, to make crops grow, even to bring the rain. She never did anything evil. And she was beautiful. Naturally,

D'Oro wanted her."

"And she didn't want a thing to do with him." Danni could tell where the story was going.

"But he kept insisting. The story goes that she caused rain and a flood, leaving him trapped with some of his minions in the swamp. He was furious, so he waited for the floodwaters to recede, then sent his minions to get her. He tied her to a tree and threatened to burn her alive. She said that she'd rather kiss flames than him. Supposed eyewitness accounts claim that the rains came again when he tried to burn her. In the end, though, it couldn't rain enough to dampen his enthusiasm. Eventually, he got a fire going. And that was when she cursed him. People say that he then turned into the *rougarou*—because his soul had been consumed by evil. And, as you've heard, he was eventually hunted down. Even his own people turned on him. And, he, too, was finally burned alive and the murders in Honey Swamp came to an end. Here's the thing. He carried a cane with a silver wolf's head. Like the cane of the mannequin in your window."

"I need to get that display down," Danni said. "What about the cane?"

"Apparently, D'Oro had some kind of an evil magician, or warlock, or whatever one chooses to call such a man in his employ, nowhere near as gifted as the white witch and certainly nowhere near as beautiful. The silver wolf's head on the cane absorbed the brunt of the curse, and that's what made D'Oro become a *rougarou* rather than falling victim to one himself."

"You think that the cane causes the evil?" Danni asked. "But it's not in any museum that I've ever heard about. And D'Oro wasn't buried. His ashes were left to disperse into Honey Swamp, along with whatever was left of his bones."

"That would make one assume that, somewhere in Honey Swamp are the remnants of that cane," Natasha said. "Unless, of course, someone found it."

"That's a long shot," Danni said.

Natasha was thoughtful. "It brings us back to the question of what evil *is*. Greed, lust? Hatred?"

"The world and the human mind are complex, Natasha. People kill for a lot of reasons. They torture and commit atrocities for their own goals and agendas. And then again, is someone with a totally fractured mind evil or just broken?"

"I don't know about every circumstance," Natasha said. "But what's going on here is evil, by any definition." She paused. "The mind is powerful. We all know that. If you believe that you have an incredible power granted to you by the devil, or simple evil, can you make it so? Perception can be a form of truth."

"You're right about that," Danni murmured. "So what do we do? Search the swamp. Search the streets for someone with a silver wolf's head cane? Or look to the reasons people become evil? Natasha, two young women were on the tour boat that came upon the first victim. The one young lady was convinced that she saw a *rougarou* on her hotel balcony."

"We can believe we see many things," Natasha said.

"But there was blood on the balcony that matched the blood of the first victim. Detective Jake Larue just called Quinn. Whoever killed that first victim came into the French Quarter as a *rougarou*."

Natasha sat in silence for a minute. Then she lifted one of the books from the stack at her side.

"This is on the murders from twenty years ago. There was one young lady named Genevieve LaCoste. She was a shopkeeper in the Garden District. She'd been out with a boyfriend to Honey Swamp the day she was killed. She'd come back to the city, but was found the next day, dead, in the swamp. Maybe, just maybe, this *rougarou* sees what he wants and comes after it. Your young lady was very lucky to escape him."

"She wasn't alone. She was with a friend."

"Maybe the *rougarou* expected her to be alone. Or maybe whoever was pretending to be a *rougarou* was startled away by her screams or something from the street," Natasha suggested. "Read more of the book. Twenty years ago wasn't the first time people were found ripped apart in the swamp. It happened eighty years and about a hundred and fifty years ago, too. There was nothing about it with rhyme or reason, just every twenty or fifty years, that kind of thing. But it happened first with Count D'Oro, and it's happened again and again through the years."

"No rhyme or reason," Danni mused. "Except that, there has

to be a reason. We just don't know what it is yet."

"Evil."

"And evil is usually personified. There's an evil man out there. We have to find out who he is." Danni rose. "I think I'm going to check on the value of my property."

"What?" Natasha asked.

"Pay a visit to a realtor," Danni said. "Meet me back at my place in about two hours?"

"I'll be there."

* * * *

Father John Ryan lived in the rectory by the church.

He stood to almost Quinn's height, leanly muscled, bald, and equipped with sharp gray eyes that seemed to quickly assess people and problems. Born in Ireland, he'd served in the heart of Africa and various other places where he'd acquired knowledge about many cultures, peoples, and religions. Not a man to judge, instead more one to evaluate and appreciate.

"I was expecting you," the priest told Quinn. "And Wolf, of course." Father Ryan greeted the mammoth dog with affection. "I assumed there would be no music tonight. So what do you know so far? I'm assuming you're here because of the murders in the swamps? They just announced that a second body was found."

Quinn nodded.

But before he could speak, Father Ryan said, "Now I get it. You found the second victim."

He nodded. "What do you know about the Wolfman murders twenty years ago? Were you here then?"

"I'd just arrived in New Orleans," Ryan said. "And yes, I do remember. It was all horrible. One of the young women killed was local. I presided at her funeral."

"Tell me about her."

"Genevieve. I'd met her only briefly. She was such a beautiful young lady. Striking in every way. She ran a shop in the Garden District and grew up here. She went all the way through Loyola, a stellar student in the business school. Her shop was wonderful and she was eager to take more classes. To do good things. Her death was tragic, and the police were determined. But it was one of those cases where the swamp consumed all the evidence. After her death, the murders stopped."

"But there were other victims," Quinn said.

"Both lovely young women." Father Ryan paused, deep in memory. "Patricia Ahern and Sonia Gavin. The one was from New York City. The other a Texan, I think. They'd been in New Orleans on vacation. I know the police investigated all the tour operators at the time since both girls had been on tours. Of course, Genevieve hadn't been on a tour, but she'd been out in the swamp with her boyfriend the day before. He was a suspect, but was cleared. He'd been back at work in his father's bar all through the night."

"I heard a little on the past this morning. Detective Deerfield was working back then, too. Those murders fell to the Pearl River department. Those guys seem to think that someone definitely knows about the past murders and all the local lore. Which, I suppose, would point to a local. Only this time we have a male victim. Years ago they were all beautiful young women. I keep thinking, why? What was happening then, and can it have anything to do with what's happening now? Seldom does a savage killer wait around twenty years to start all over again."

"Unless he was in prison," Ryan said. "But the cops are good. Larue and the Pearl River men will be checking for anyone who might have gotten back out. I still think that we'd have heard about a killer brought in who'd done anything like this. There's a connection with the past murders. There's probably a connection back to the D'Oro and the Good Witch and the *rougarou* story. One murder last night, another today. This killer is on a spree. We have to move on this."

"What do you suggest?"

"Meeting at the house tonight. But we may have something."

Quinn went on to tell Father Ryan about David Fagin and Julian Henri, their new swamp tour, and the e-mails they received.

"Rival tour group?" Father Ryan said doubtfully. "That's pretty drastic, brutally murdering people as a means of getting rid of competition."

Quinn's phone buzzed.

He checked the display.

Danni had sent him a text.

Back at the Cheshire Cat at 7:00?

He hit the *O* and *K* keys and sent his message, then looked at Father Ryan. "Want to check out the local competition?"

"Sounds like a plan. That is, of course, as long as we're sending someone out for dinner once we get there."

Quinn pulled out his phone again. Victoria Miller owned Crescent City Sites. The reservation office was on Decatur Street, about a block from Jackson Square.

"We taking Wolf with us?" Father Ryan asked.

"Hell, yeah," Quinn said. "Wolf is always up for a good swamp tour, aren't you, boy?"

The dog barked his agreement.

They headed out to Quinn's car. It wasn't much of a drive, but the evening had turned cold. The streets of the French Quarter were heavy with pedestrian traffic and finding a place to park on the riverfront took some time. From there it took them only a matter of minutes to reach the tour offices. The doors were closed against the cold. Quinn pushed them open. Wolf followed first, then Father Ryan. The woman behind the counter was probably in her early forties, the kind though who would be a beauty at any stage of life. Her features were delicate, her body slim. She was dressed in a tight red sweater that enhanced the platinum color of her hair and the brilliant shade of her green eyes. She smiled at first in welcome, then seemed to shrink back as she noted Wolf.

"Sorry," Quinn said quickly. "I'll have him wait outside."

"No, it's all right. He just startled me. Your dog is the size of a pony. Come in, please. What are you looking for? Actually, I should tell you we really can't allow the dog on the swamp or plantation tours. Though honestly, for a walking tour, if you wanted to hang in the back, I suppose it would be okay. I'm getting ahead of myself. What kind of a tour are you looking to take? I'm Victoria Miller."

"Michael Quinn, and this is my dog, Wolf. And the tall gentleman behind me is Father John Ryan."

"Nice to meet you," she said, frowning. "You're an unlikely

tour group."

"Honestly, we're here because of the murders in Honey Swamp," Quinn said.

"Oh." Her fine features grew taut. "We don't do murder site tours."

"I'm a private investigator, working with the police," Quinn said.

She shook her head, as if baffled. "Why are you here? Legends is the company that was involved. It was one of the Legends boats that came upon the body of that poor man."

"Yes, but you have boats out there all the time, don't you?" Quinn asked.

"We don't do anything like a ridiculous monster tour." The tone of her voice indicated that it was offensive that anyone might even think such a thing.

Quinn picked up one of the brochures advertising a vampire tour. "But these are okay?"

"That's different. We do vampire tours that include facts about Anne Rice, the craze that went around because of her books, the people in the city who practice 'spiritual' vampirism, and the cults who drink animal blood. We try hard to keep facts and history in our tours."

"Sounds enterprising," Quinn said, offering her his best smile. "We were hoping you might have some clue as to what's going on in the swamp. If there have been strangers hanging out around any of the docks. If you've seen anything unusual. You do own a big tour group, known for blending fact with fun."

That mollified her ego.

"I have to admit," she said. "I thought it was ridiculous that David and Julian wanted to start their own thing. I wanted to buy Julian's property. It could have helped us. I mean, he was already running tours in the city and out to the plantations. There are a zillion tour groups working around here. We didn't need another one. And as far as the swamp goes, I'd check it all out with some of the realtors who keep trying to buy property."

"Are you from this area?"

She tossed back her long blond mane. "I'm from New England. But don't go thinking that doesn't make me every bit as good as the Legends guys. Those of us who aren't from here love the area with a greater passion. We research whatever everyone else thinks that they know. We're good. No. We're excellent. But the two little college brats wanted to usurp my business."

"Did you threaten them?" He smiled as he added, "Or send them a few e-mails?"

"I wouldn't stoop so low," Victoria said. "Now, you gentlemen are not the police. And if you were, I couldn't help you anyway. If you don't mind, I'm busy."

He glanced around at the empty office. "I can see that you are."

He, Father Ryan, and Wolf headed for the door. But before they left, the priest nudged him. A door was ajar to a back office. Inside, a young man sat, watching, listening. He saw that Quinn and Father Ryan had spotted him. He nodded, as if he was aware they needed answers that could not be provided then.

Quinn lowered his head in acknowledgement.

Message received.

And they left.

* * * *

A receptionist told Danni that Byron Grayson would be right with her, but after twenty minutes she still sat in the waiting room. His offices were down in the Central Business District, near the convention center. He must have been doing well enough as the offices were elegant. Plush sofas and a wide screen television adorned the waiting room, along with a pod coffee maker. A visitor could also grab a power bar or read any one of a number of high-end magazines.

She rose and approached the receptionist's desk. "Excuse me. Is Mr. Grayson available this evening? If not, perhaps—"

"I sent him a message ages ago that you were here," the receptionist said. "Let me buzz through to his office. He's usually out as soon as I let him know we have a new client."

Another buzz, but no answer.

"I thought he was back there," the receptionist said. "I had a list of items that needed to be attended to on my desk this morning."

"You mean you haven't seen him all day?" Danni asked.

"I don't disturb Mr. Grayson," she said. "If you'll just wait a minute, I'll see what's keeping him."

The receptionist started down a hallway. Danni held back, and then followed behind her. A knock on a closed door went unanswered so the woman opened it.

And screamed.

Danni ran up behind her and looked in, expecting to see a dead man.

But there was no one there.

Only a massive pool of blood spilled over Grayson's desk, dripping onto the rich beige carpet in little crimson waves.

Chapter 4

Quinn and Larue arrived at the offices of Byron Grayson at about the same time. Larue was accompanied by sirens blazing and Quinn with Father Ryan and Wolf. He left the priest and the dog on the street and hurried into the realtor's office. Danni sat in the waiting area, her arms around the shoulders of a young woman, shaking with fear. Larue was hunkering down to talk to her as the forensic people worked in Grayson's office.

"All day, I was sitting there. All day," the woman said. "And something like this was happening." She turned wide eyes to ask a question, but not to Larue. Instead, to Danni. "Oh, my God, the *rougarou.* It's real and came into the city. It rushed by me when I wasn't looking and ate poor Mr. Grayson while I was sitting right out at the reception area."

"There's a lot of blood in there," Danni told the girl. "But that doesn't mean that a *rougarou* went by you—"

"Oh, but it had to have gone by me. Oh, my God, it could have eaten me. Do you think that it came in through a window? Can a *rougarou* crawl on walls? Maybe it was in here all night? But it had to have waited to eat him. He left instructions on my desk. You see, I never bother him. What he needs he tells me, and I announce clients, and they come out. Don't think he's a mean man. He isn't mean at all. He's a great boss. He just works best that way. Says he's like a really old computer, though he still doesn't understand computers completely. And he only likes to have one window open at a time. He has to be dead. Mr. Grayson. Eaten. Oh, oh, how horrible."

She began to sob.

Quinn walked over to the waiting room sofa and hunkered down by Larue. "Miss—"

"Jensen, Belinda Jensen," the woman murmured.

"When did you last see your boss?" Quinn asked.

"Last night, closing time. But I know he was here this morning. He left paperwork for some closings on my desk."

"But you didn't see him all day?" Larue asked.

Belinda shook her head. "But that's not unusual. Mr. Grayson stays in his office, sometimes without me seeing him. I just announce things to him through the intercom. He comes out as soon as he can when we have clients. Every once in a while he comes out and says let's go to lunch. He's a good boss. But when he's working, he's working."

One of the forensic techs stepped back into the waiting room and grabbed Larue's attention. The detective stepped over to the young man. Quinn rose too and walked toward the tech and Larue.

"It's all right. Mr. Quinn is working this with us," Larue said to the tech. "What is it?"

They were all thinking that Byron Grayson, a realtor, frequently in a suit, might be their first victim. But Grayson couldn't be the body they'd found in the swamp. Grayson was an older man. Their corpse had been that of a man in his thirties. So neither victim had yet to be identified.

"It's not human blood," the tech said. "We're not sure what it is, but it's not human blood."

"Not sure what it is? Paint or something like that?" Larue asked.

"No, it's blood, all right. Just not human."

"Animal?"

"Has to be. We're just not sure what kind of animal."

* * * *

"I'll see that Natasha gets down the block," Billie told Quinn, standing.

They'd finally all met at Danni's house on Royal Street. Father Ryan, Natasha, Danni, and Quinn, along with Bo Ray and Billie McDougal. Everything they all knew had been exchanged. Danni would keep researching the past murders and more about

Byron Grayson's business. Bo Ray and Billie would hold down the shop and keep their eyes and ears open. Father Ryan and Quinn were going to head back to Honey Swamp and speak to the owners of the shacks and homes around the area. First up, of course, would be Julian Henri's old place. Easy enough—they had Julian's permission to tear it apart, top to bottom.

"Maybe there are some secret places where the *rougarou* has been hiding all these years," Bo Ray said.

"I don't think that there is a *rougarou*," Danni said.

They all looked at her.

"You know we've all discovered that strange things happen in this world," Father Ryan said.

"They find new critters all the time, animals we thought were extinct," Billie pointed out. "Maybe such beasts have existed for years. Maybe there is something like an abominable snowman or the Loch Ness monster."

"We do tend to believe in only what we see," Father Ryan said. "And since my life is based on a belief in what I don't see, I never deny the possibilities."

"I think there's something more than a creature that just pops up at certain times," Danni said. "I mean, we don't know what went on years and years ago, and people have disappeared in swamps and never been seen again many times." She stood and gathered up a few of the paper plates they'd used for the pizza they'd ordered for dinner. "This time, I think there is a more logical answer. There's something that we just haven't discovered yet."

"The two young ladies on the boat said that a *rougarou* was outside their window," Natasha said. "They found blood on the balcony, the blood of the first victim. And now, there's a man who is missing with an unidentifiable blood left all over his office."

"I know," Danni said. "And I don't dispute the fact that there might be some kind of living creature that science hasn't discovered, captured, or realized yet. I just still keep thinking back to Count D'Oro."

"And a curse?" Father Ryan asked.

"I'm not thinking curse so much as bad human behavior,"

Danni said. "Count D'Oro was a horrid person, a sick killer. He wanted Melissa DeVane. By historic accounts, she was young, beautiful, filled with vitality."

"I get it," Bo Ray said. "She thought he was like dung on a shoe, and that made him want to have her all the more. And she turned him down."

"Did she make it rain? Or did it rain because it was Southern Louisiana?" Danni nodded. "The thing is, yes, all the *rougarou* killing came about. But the count wanted something."

Billie frowned. "One of the victims killed is male. Another female. And, unless I don't know everything, there was no sexual assault."

"Not everyone is after sex," Danni said.

"Most people," Bo Ray assured her. "I mean, you two, you and Quinn, you're at it—sorry, sorry. Together all the time, so you don't realize—"

"Bo Ray," Quinn said.

"Sorry, sorry."

"He's a Texan." Father Ryan lowered his head to hide a small smile. "Texans can't help themselves. They just say it like it is."

Danni wagged a plastic fork at them all. "David believes that he was personally threatened with the writing in the mud. Someone wants something. Julian Henri owns some great property, if you're into swamp tours and history. I think we're all supposed to believe what's happening is a throwback, and that it all has to do with a *rougarou*. But I don't buy it."

"Okay, in the morning everyone is on it," Quinn said. "Let's all get some sleep.

"I'll see to Natasha," Father Ryan said. "You all just hunker in for the night."

Danni went to walk Father Ryan and Natasha out through the front of the shop and lock up. Bo Ray and Billie finished cleaning up and headed for the stairs to the third floor attic where they had their apartments. Quinn put through a call to Larue. With what they'd heard about the previous murders, he wanted to make sure that the two young women who'd received the balcony visit were safe. Larue assured him that he had a man on guard at the new hotel where they'd been taken.

"Inside room," Larue told him. "No balcony, hotel security, cameras everywhere. If a *rougarou* does make it up there somehow, we'll make history."

Quinn thanked Larue and they said goodnight.

Danni still hadn't come back.

He walked out to the shop and saw that she was staring at her front window from the back. Her displays were always excellent. She knew where to shop and where to find the right pieces that made everything perfect. He slipped his arms around her waist and rested his chin on the top of her head.

"We'll find out what's going on," he told her.

"The cane," she murmured. "The story goes that Count D'Oro had his own wizard, and the silver grip wolf's head on his cane was magical. That it gave him the power to deflect Melissa DeVane's curse and become the *rougarou*."

"We talked about that. I don't think we can find the old cane in the swamp, Danni."

She shook her head. "I don't think the cane is in the swamp. I think someone had it hidden away. And maybe someone else has found it, believing they have the power of the *rougarou*."

"That's a lot of maybes. For now, it's kind of late. Bed?"

She turned in his arms with a smile, then checked the door and called to Wolf. "Hey, boy. Time to guard the hallway."

The dog barked his approval.

Danni hurried ahead and Quinn followed her up the stairs. Wolf curled up on his bed in the hallway. When Quinn entered the room, he found that Danni had laid a trail of her clothing from the doorway to the shower.

He smiled.

And he followed.

The curtain was drawn. Steam filled the bathroom. She stood in the shower. He couldn't help thinking that she could have been a mermaid, or a siren, smiling with the kind of light in her eyes that was sure to drive a man mad. He allowed his gaze to fall upon her.

"Did you need a written invitation?" she asked.

He stripped, stepped into the shower, and drew her into his arms. Warm water beats pulsated on his skin. The surge of steam was both relaxing and invigorating, the feel of her body crushing against his overwhelming. He would never tire of feeling her against him. The wonder in her eyes always seemed so fresh, her smiles evocative. The taste of her lips part of a fantasy, and every time he kissed her he felt a rush of arousal.

Her fingers slid down his back, then moved to his chest.

He reached behind her, cupping her buttocks, and lifting her to him, their every point of contact now an erogenous zone.

He kissed her again.

This time more passionate.

"Shampoo in the tub," she whispered to him.

The words made no sense.

"Slip, fall, break body parts," Danni whispered. "Not as much fun."

Now he understood, and he lifted her over the rim of the tub, following her out quickly himself. Not to lose the moment, he kissed her again, and they became engaged in twined lips and stroking hands.

"Towel rack," Quinn said.

"What?"

"Towel rack. Big bruise on the back, maybe your head against the wall. A concussion. Not as much fun."

They both laughed.

Danni threw open the bedroom door and they made a beeline for the sheets, shivering.

"It's cold out here," she said.

Quinn landed on the bed at her side. "Not to add more bad and trite lines to the wonderful foreplay I've initiated," he kissed her shoulder. "But give me a chance and I'll warm you up."

Safe from falling, tripping, or breaking bones, he wrapped his arms around her, covered her with the length of his body, and eased himself slowly down. She quickly rose against him, seeking the same, kissing his flesh, teasing him, light brushes, far more serious touches that escalated him to a place where the world existed in the physical sense of the two of them, and nothing else.

Later, lying beside her, Quinn thought that life could be strange indeed. He thought about the wasted years gone before. He hadn't deserved a second chance, but had gotten one anyway.

Danni was a part of that second chance. They might not ever really understand their role in the world as it had fallen to them. Maybe Angus had never really understood himself. But Danni was his lifeline now.

Whatever happened, they had one another.

He smiled.

Trite and a bad pickup line. But true.

As long as he had her, the world could send him anything.

Wolf began to bark, then the dog slammed himself against the bedroom door.

Quinn jumped from the bed, drew on his jeans, and reached to the bedside table for the SIG Sauer P226 that Jake Larue had given him last Christmas.

Danni was leaping out of bed, scrambling for clothing too.

"Stay here," he told her. "My old Glock is in the top drawer. Get it."

He hurried out of the room.

Wolf waited in the hall. Bo Ray and Billie were running down the stairs.

"Hold off," Quinn said.

"Following you," Billie said. "Bo Ray, get in with Danni."

The look he tossed Quinn was to remind him that Billie had worked with Angus for years before a young upstart like Quinn had come along.

Wolf led the way to the ground floor and the courtyard entrance. Quinn opened the door and Wolf rushed out, barking furiously. Quinn stood perfectly still. Whoever had been there was gone. And whoever had been there had been blessed with the capability of jumping high fences, as the gate that led out to Royal Street was still latched tightly.

"Quinn," Billie said. "Over here."

He walked to the courtyard entry for the kitchen. There, by the door, were what appeared to be footprints of some large bipedal creature.

Billie hunkered down and touched the substance creating the prints, then looked up at Quinn.

They both knew what it was.

Blood.

* * * *

Danni poured coffee as she listened to Quinn.

It had been just a few minutes after 6:00 a.m. when Wolf, Billie, and Quinn came back into the house, too late to bother trying to get back to sleep.

Quinn called Larue.

No, he didn't want a major investigation. No, he didn't believe that the Royal Street house had been besieged by a league of *rougarous*. He didn't want a big deal made out of it. No sirens blazing.

"But I want to know what that blood substance is, so send a tech over," he told Larue. "Whatever is going on, they think they're going to scare Danni and me away. That's what that was all about. *Rougarou* or not—whatever, whoever, they didn't want to mess with Wolf. We're in good shape here, and whoever came by didn't actually try to get in. Just get me a tech to look at the substance."

He listened, thanked Larue, hung up, and came for the coffee pot.

"They'll have somebody here in a few minutes."

"They have anything yet on Byron Grayson?" Danni asked.

Quinn shook his head. "Go figure. A major office building in the Central Business District and no one saw a thing. I'm heading out to the swamp today. I want you—"

"Quinn, you can't worry about me all the time. That's not the way this works." She stood on her toes to plant a quick kiss on his lips. "However, today, you don't have to worry about me. Natasha and I are heading to the library. We're going to find out what's happened over the years." She was quiet a minute and then said, "There are dozens of theories but in Salem, Massachusetts, during the witch hysteria, a strong theory was that people let their hatred take hold, and a lot of that hatred had to do with people wanting prime land. Accuse a neighbor and the land was taken and then it went up for sale. None of that came about this time until David and Julian opened their business. I'm going to see who is doing what."

"Byron Grayson wanted the land," Quinn told her. "And Grayson has gone missing."

"Be careful," she said.

He gave her what should have been a quick kiss good-bye for the day.

She caught the anguish in his eyes and the kiss became something deeper.

A loud "ahem" made them break apart and laugh.

Bo Ray had apparently followed Billie in, because he said, "See, when life is good, you just don't think the way some others might. That came out wrong. That doesn't mean that all single people are sex fiends. I just…okay. Bo Ray, time to just shut up and get your foot out of your mouth."

Quinn looked at Bo Ray and shook his head with amusement. "Keep in touch all day, everyone."

Billie nodded.

"Go," Danni told Quinn. "You two have coffee. Enjoy your breakfast. I'm going to take that display down before I take off with Natasha."

Quinn exited out the kitchen door to the courtyard and the garage. He paused there, looking back at her. She smiled. He nodded and kept going. Danni headed down the hallway and into the store. Moving a few props, she reached the store side of her left facing display window. The mannequin wasn't heavy, just a little awkward. She picked it up first and set it down, staring at the creation. It was damned good. She'd bought it from a friend in Louisiana's booming film business.

The eyes almost seemed to follow her.

She wagged a finger at the mannequin. "Sick murderer, playing on legend. How could you kill that beautiful young woman who never hurt a soul? Or kill anyone. Look at the legacy you've left."

Crawling back into the window, she hurriedly gathered the rest of the items that had made up the display, tossing them into the shop. Then she looked around, trying to decide what she was going to put up in place of the display on Count D'Oro and the *rougarou.*

Billie came into the shop.

"Egyptian," she announced. "We have that mannequin of Cleopatra. We can add a lot of the local jewelry. There's a really beautiful ankh and then, to the side, we can add in a display of those fleur-de-lis pendants. Not Egyptian per se, but for now it will do."

"Aye, lass, got it. I'll need Bo Ray to help."

He turned and left her, heading back down the hallway.

The mannequin of Count D'Oro suddenly fell over.

The cane rolled across the floor and landed at Danni's feet, the silver wolf's head seeming to stare up at her. For a moment, she froze. The way the mannequin had landed, it seemed to be staring at her too. She trembled despite herself, then walked over and glared down at the mannequin, kicking the cane to the side.

"We will end this," she said with determination.

And it almost seemed like the mannequin disagreed.

Challenging her to do so.

Chapter 5

Quinn met up with Detectives Beauchamp and Deerfield and they headed out on a police boat, stopping by properties in Honey Swamp, briefly speaking to those they found along the way. Everyone seemed to think that the *rougarou* had awakened, so they were all staying armed and close to home.

"I'm going to have a bunch of shot-up tourists on my hands soon enough," Deerfield said, looking a bit like a disgruntled bulldog.

They saved Selena Duarte for the next to the last and planned on visiting Julian Henri's property last. Quinn hopped up on the dock at Selena Duarte's rustic wood home on the water. He knocked at the door several times, peered in the window, and knocked again.

No answer.

He headed back down to the dock to speak with Beauchamp and Deerfield.

"She's not there," he said.

"Selena's there," Deerfield said. "She's just being an old pain in the ass."

Deerfield hopped to the dock and left Beauchamp and Quinn to tie up the boat.

"Selena, you ornery cuss. It's Detective Deerfield. Open the damned door."

To Quinn's surprise, the door opened.

Selena Duarte was white haired and wrinkled to the nines, and she appeared to be older than the earth itself.

"What the hell you doing out here, bothering an old woman? You know damned well I ain't guilty of a damned thing. What, you think I could even wield some kind of a weapon hard enough to do in a big man or a woman for that matter? And you think I got good teeth all of a sudden? My dentures barely bite through butter."

"Not out here to accuse you of anything, Selena. We came here to find out if you might have seen anything," Beauchamp told her.

She pointed at Quinn. "What you doing out here, football-blow-it-all boy? Heard you went military, cop, and then P.I. in New Orleans. You're a far cry from the city, Quinn. You know nothing about these swamps."

"I did grow up in the area, Mrs. Duarte. I've been out here often enough," Quinn said.

She sniffed. "So they called you in, huh? Thinking that you could catch the *rougarou.* They're wrong. The *rougarou* belongs to the swamp. When the *rougarou* is hungry, people are going to die. That's all there is to it. When the *rougarou* has had his share of killing, then it will all stop. And that's the way it is. You go work your mumbo-jumbo in the city, young man." She pointed a long, bony finger at Quinn. "You watch your step. The *rougarou* knows about you."

"Is that a threat, Mrs. Duarte?" Quinn asked. "If so, the *rougarou* will have to get in line."

She sniffed loudly and looked at Dirk Deerfield. "We both know, don't we, Dirk? They didn't catch no one last time, and they're not going to catch anyone this time. The *rougarou* will do what the *rougarou* wants."

"Just like the honey badger," Beauchamp murmured.

Selena turned her sharp gaze on Beauchamp. "That some kind of a joke, boy?"

"No, ma'am."

"Selena," Deerfield said. "All I want to know is have you seen anything?"

"Yeah, I seen something. I seen it moving through the thick trees. It's big. Can't say as I saw the face clearly, but seems to me I kind of saw it in my eyes. Teeth like you wouldn't believe. Ugly face, ugly as sin. I heard something in the back, looked out there, and saw it running through the trees. I shut my door and lit a few candles on my altar. I got out my poor dead husband's shotgun and I sat there with it all night, though I knew if the *rougarou* wanted me, the shotgun wouldn't matter none. But, like last time, the *rougarou* isn't after an old woman who spent her life working and just wants to be left alone." Selena looked at Deerfield. "The *rougarou* is after the innocent and the sinners. None of us in between folk. You mark my words, you'll find out those people you ain't identified yet were sinners, or maybe a priest and a nun. Don't know which. But there will be somethin' about them."

"Selena, which way was the *rougarou* running?" Quinn asked her.

"Away from my place, heading for the highway. Maybe he hitchhiked his way into New Orleans. What do you think? Maybe he can fly. Don't know, don't care. I intend to keep to myself, like always."

"Selena, if you see or hear anything, anything at all," Deerfield began.

"What? I'm going to call you? I ain't got no phone out here, Dirk. No cell phone, no house phone. Maybe I can send up some smoke signals."

And she laughed.

"I'll be back by," Deerfield promised.

"You be careful, Dirk Deerfield. You're just the kind of man the *rougarou* may want."

"Mrs. Duarte," Beauchamp said politely, "you really are mean as dirt."

"You go on now. All of you. Ain't nothing here for you. You're spinning wheels, just spinning wheels. The *rougarou* will take what it wants, and if you leave it alone, the damned thing will go back to sleep and by the time it comes back again, I'll be dust and ash in the cemetery. Go on. Git."

Quinn was certain that if she'd been holding a shotgun, she would have pointed it at them. He turned and headed down the dock with the other two men.

But Beauchamp couldn't let it go and turned back. "You're sad, Selena Duarte. A sad old sack of a woman. Sorry to say, I'll probably be the one picking up your bones when you die, holed up in your shack all alone, without anyone to give a damn."

Selena stared after them, startled and in silence.

"Unless the *rougarou* gets you first," Beauchamp muttered.

They continued to the boat.

Little else to do.

* * * *

"Danni?"

She was down in the "basement" of the shop, in her father's office, sifting through page after page in his book, hoping for another reference to the *rougarou.*

The voice was Jake Larue's.

"I'm down here," she called out.

Larue descended the stairs and said, "You're not alone down here, are you?"

"Hardly."

Wolf lay at her feet.

"Someone is playing tricks on us," he said. "Those footprints at your place, the substance. It's blood. Human. It came from the second victim, the young woman Quinn found in the swamp. I'm beginning to wonder if there is a *rougarou* running around."

"A very athletic *rougaro*u," Danni said. "How does the creature make its way into the city? Does it have a chauffeur? In which case, we're still looking for a living, breathing man. Has forensics determined the type of blood that was found in Byron Grayson's office?"

"They're still trying, coming up with gator, raccoon, fox, and wild boar."

"A mixture?"

"Hard to analyze, or so I've been told."

"Has anyone found Byron Grayson?"

"No sign of him."

"But," she asked, her words slow, "no more bodies, right?"

"No more bodies. I tried to get Quinn. He must be out of phone range. I just wanted to tell you to make sure that you were careful. Someone, or something, was in your courtyard."

"I have Wolf," she said. "But I promise, I'll be careful."

He said good-bye and she returned her attention to the book. But no answers were there. She closed the cover, called to Wolf, and locked up the basement. Heading up to the shop, she told Billie she was going to the library. Wolf would have to stay at the house.

She also shared what Larue had told her with Billie.

"I'll be on the lookout. And Wolf is the best alarm system in the world. He's got an instinct that puts you and Quinn to shame," he added with a grin.

"Yes, he does. Anything from Natasha or Father Ryan?"

"Natasha called a bit ago. She's put some feelers out among her community. People are scared. Most believe that there is a monster out there, *rougarou* or other."

"And Father Ryan?"

"He said that he's checking into local records. No word among his parishioners that anyone knows anything about what's been happening."

"I'll be at the library on Loyola," she said.

She headed into the courtyard and across to the garage. Twenty minutes later, she was sitting in the public library. The librarian had been a tremendous help, supplying her with stack upon stack of information dealing with the Wolfman murders of twenty years ago. She was deep into her reading when she jumped, startled to see that someone had taken a seat in front of her.

Father Ryan.

She let out a sigh and sat back, smiling. "You startled me."

"What have you found?" he asked her.

"Did you ever hear of or know a man named Jacob Devereaux?"

"Sure. He was a realtor in town. Died years ago, though."

"Did you know that he was interviewed about the murder of Genevieve LaCoste?"

"I did. He was a frequent visitor to her shop, if I recall. The supposition at the time was that he had a crush on her. But he also had an alibi. There was nothing that suggested he'd pulled off the crime. The police were looking everywhere. I think the belief at the time was that the murderer had been transient, and that he'd moved on. Either that, or he was a *rougarou,* and his appetite for blood had been sated."

"This guy didn't happen to be a parishioner of yours, did

he?" Danni asked hopefully.

He shook his head.

"They haven't found Byron Grayson," she told him. "All they found was a pool of mixed up blood in his office. What if he's out in the swamp? What if he's gone a little crazy, wanting to buy property, determined to make it so bad for David and Julian that they have to sell?"

"Danni, if you brought this theory into a court of law, they'd laugh at you."

"I know, but you said Jacob Devereaux was dead. Here's the thing. Go back to the beginning. Count D'Oro brutally killed Melissa DeVane because he wanted her and her magic. More powerful than the magic his own wizard possessed, even though the magic of his supposed wizard was strong enough to keep him alive as a monster. Let's say that twenty years ago, this Jacob Devereaux was in love with Genevieve LaCoste, and she wanted nothing to do with him. He knew about the legend, maybe he even knew about the power that was supposed to be in Count D'Oro's cane. Somehow he knew where the cane could be found. Once he had the cane, he thought he was all-powerful. So he killed the young women and then he died."

Father Ryan rose and walked over to the counter and the helpful librarian. A few minutes later, the librarian produced an old book. Father Ryan didn't come back to the table. He flipped through the book, returned it to the librarian, then came over to where Danni was sitting.

"Jacob Devereaux died twenty years ago. A month after the last murder," he said. "Now, I warn you, that doesn't prove anything."

"I still think we should call Quinn and Larue. Someone who was in love with that young woman, who was found in the swamp, might be worth investigating."

"Danni, they haven't identified her. How are they going to find someone who might have been in love with her? And the first person killed was a man."

"Yeah, I know," Danni said, frustrated.

Her phone rang. She glanced at the caller ID.

Quinn.

"You're all right," she said, answering.

"Yeah, and you?"

"I'm with Father Ryan." She smiled across the table at the priest.

"I thought I should check in," Quinn said. "Also, we have an ID on the man whose body was discovered first. Abel Denham. New Englander. A realtor, planning on relocating to Southern Louisiana."

"Realtor?" She looked at Father Ryan. "Quinn, I think that's it. He might have been out there looking at property. Byron Grayson remains missing, but he might be out there too. In that swamp." She gripped the phone tighter. "Killing people."

"We're at Julian's property now, by the boat slip. It's the departure point for their tours. I'll call you back if I find anything. What's up on your end?"

"Realtors. Lots of realtors," Danni said firmly. "Are you with the Pearl River police? Ask Detective Deerfield if he remembers interviewing a man named Jacob Devereaux. He was suspected to have had a crush, some kind of longing, for Genevieve LaCoste. If so, this could all tie in."

"Will do," Quinn said. "Stay safe, okay?"

"Absolutely," she promised, ending the call.

She repeated the conversation to Father Ryan, who stood. "I'll head up to the Garden District and see what people can remember about Genevieve."

"How are you going to do that?"

"Public record. I'll find out who's still in the same area and then I'll knock on some doors."

"And they'll just let you in?"

He smiled and shrugged. "This collar can open a lot of doors. Keep in contact."

She promised that she would and he left. For several seconds, Danni drummed her fingers on the table. Then she picked up her phone and called Larue.

He answered her second ring.

"I was just thinking," she said. "Does anyone know yet why Abel Denham was relocating to New Orleans?"

"I guess he fell in love with the city. People do," Larue said.

"We need to find out why he was relocating, Jake." She hesitated. "I believe it was because of a young woman. He was coming here to be with someone, because she'd moved to New Orleans. Maybe his girlfriend was a student or a teacher. Maybe she was coming down to work at or go to one of the colleges. I don't know. But I think that's a possibility."

"Okay, we'll move in that direction," he said. "We'd figured the victims had been random."

"Twenty years ago, only young women were killed. And look into anything you can find about Jacob Devereaux."

"He's been dead for years."

"Humor me."

"I'll do my best."

They hung up and Danni stood. Quinn and Father Ryan had been by Victoria Miller's tour company headquarters, but she hadn't. She didn't know Victoria Miller. Maybe it was time to check her out.

She thanked the librarian, headed to her car, then back to the French Quarter. She didn't want to be seen at the shop, so she parked at the public lot by the river, then headed to Crescent City Sites, intent on meeting Victoria Miller herself. The woman wasn't a realtor, but she had tried to buy Julian Henri's property on the swamp.

The front doors were open to the street, as were those of many businesses in the area. The tour desk was just about eight feet back from the entry, but there wasn't anyone manning it. Danni wandered in. There was an office in the back. Perhaps the woman was there. Before she could go in, she heard a voice whispering with anger.

"You were supposed to be gone. I paid you good money. You were supposed to be gone."

"Hey, I like the city. No one but that idiot knows who I am."

As Danni stood there, another man came in from the street. He had an air of authority about him, as if he belonged there. He paused, aware of the whispered conversation too.

"Can I help you?" he asked her.

"Yes, I'm actually living in the city," she said. "But there's so much I haven't seen and so much I don't know. I was thinking of taking some tours."

She spoke softly, hoping to hear more of the conversation going on in the office, but that wasn't to be the case.

A man emerged from the back.

He appeared to be about thirty with shaggy, unkempt hair, wearing dungarees and a faded plaid shirt. He looked at Danni, caught her eye, smiled, and then exited the front doors.

"I'm Gene Andre," the man who had first come in said, stepping behind the desk. "I'd be delighted to help you. What are you thinking? French Quarter, Garden District, ghost tour, vampire tour. You name it, we do it all. And, of course, all our guides are completely licensed. We're good here in New Orleans. Lots of stories that may or may not be true, but the city asks that we have our facts right."

Before she could reply, a woman came bursting out of the office.

Attractive, smartly dressed, and furious.

"Don't talk to her, Andre. I know who she is. That's Danielle Cafferty. She's with that bull-sized P.I., Quinn. She's here to try and make it look like we're guilty in all this somehow. Get out, Cafferty. Get out now, before I call the police and issue a restraining order against you and Quinn for harassment."

"I was really interested in your tours." Danni lifted her hands. "But that's okay. I'm gone."

She left the office quickly, thinking that her ruse hadn't gone well. On the street, she paused for a minute. A prickling sensation seemed to rip along her spine. She turned quickly and saw that the man who'd been arguing with Victoria was just across the street, by the old Jax Brewery.

He was studying her.

He realized that she saw him, then hurried off.

* * * *

Julian Henri met Quinn and the Pearl River detectives at his property.

A new wooden sign with the words *Legends Tours* rose high on a pair of wooden piles at the side of the property, visible from the swamp and from the old gravel road that led in from the main highway.

"This is it," Julian said. "And why the hell anyone would want it, I'm not sure."

He opened the front door and led them in.

There was a large living area filled with comfortable chairs and a sofa. Just beyond, a counter with an open area led into a functional kitchen where there was a large coffee pot and a bowl with offerings of various kinds of snack bars.

"We thought we had it just right," Julian said. "A bus to bring people out here, and then they could mill around a bit while we gave them some history and allowed for anyone who wanted to head here by their own transportation to arrive. We tried to make it homey and comfortable. We wanted it to be like you were on an adventure with friends."

"Nice," Quinn murmured. "And back there?" he asked, pointing down a hall.

"Two bedrooms. If we had to, or needed to, for any reason, we could stay out here." He shrugged. "I grew up in this house. My parents had the left room. I had the one on the right. The back door leads to the docks."

"I'll look at the rooms," Beauchamp said.

"I'll take the dock," Deerfield said.

"I'll just look at everything," Quinn said.

"Please, anywhere, anything," Julian told them.

While Beauchamp was in the one bedroom, Quinn headed to the next, which must have been Julian Henri's parents' room. The walls were covered with bookcases and hundreds of books. He looked them over. Classics, manuals, and a lot of contemporary novels. Staring at the shelves, he saw that the older Henri had kept order too. Hunting, fishing, and how-to books in one area. Dickens, Poe, Lovecraft, Thoreau, and more together in another. There was also a shelf for authors associated with Louisiana in one way or another. Eudora Welty, Truman Capote, Tennessee Williams, and more. But oddly, stuck between *In Cold Blood* and *A Streetcar Named Desire* was a book with no title and a worn leather cover.

He reached for the book and quickly realized that it was

Julian Henri's father's journal.

He flipped through the pages, seeing all kinds of entries. Bass-fishing tournament, Julian's grade school play. Mardi Gras notations. Years of a father's plans for his wife and child and himself. He decided to concentrate on entries that had been written twenty years ago.

I told the bastard I wouldn't sell. He kept insisting that I could have a better life elsewhere. I told him I'm a swamp man. He said it was no life for a child. I told him my child was brilliant and would do what he wanted, when he wanted. Bad taste left in my mouth.

Quinn flipped through a few more pages.

They found her today in the swamp. That beautiful, beautiful girl. I told them that they needed to check out Jacob Devereaux. He was the most insistent son-of-a-bitch I've ever met. I was in the city, in her shop one day, and I caught him doing the same thing with her, insisting that her boyfriend was a louse and that she needed to be with him.

A day later another entry was also about the murder and Jacob Devereaux.

He was here again. Told me that if the murders continued, my place would be worthless. I should sell now. I threw him out. Then, later in the day, I wanted to take a stroll. Went to get the old cane with the beautiful silver wolf's head grip. It was gone. I'll be damned if the bastard didn't steal it. I kept it right by the door.

* * * *

As Danni headed to her car, her phone rang.

She glanced at the caller ID and saw that it was Natasha and answered. "You've got something?"

"Maybe, maybe not. I talked to Father Ryan about your conversation in the library. He told me that you were curious about that long ago realtor, Jacob Devereaux. An old-timer friend of mine came in the store and we started talking. He's convinced there is a *rougarou*, by the way, but here's the thing. He knew Devereaux. Said the man was slimy as motor oil. Had money, and thought that meant he could buy any woman he wanted. Said he slept with who he wanted, when he wanted. And get this, Danni, he was sure that Devereaux had a child out of wedlock. Didn't know with who or what the kid's name might have been, but he's convinced that the child existed."

Danni quickly filled in the gaps, then added, "Let's say that Jacob Devereaux wasn't just a slimy dick, he was also a murderer. How better to get rid of people than to kill them in the swamps as a *rougarou.* He dies, the murders stop. But his child would now be about twenty."

"Or older," Natasha said.

Danni let out her breath. "I know it's nothing but theory. But it's not a bad one. Devereaux is a human monster. A killer. He has a child out of wedlock, murders the women he can't get, like beautiful Genevieve. He has a child who comes back—"

Her phone signaled that another call was coming through.

"Hang on," she said to Natasha. "Larue is calling. I've got to go. I'll call you later."

She switched lines, still walking back to the car park by the river.

"Danni, you're psychic," Larue told her. "I checked into our first victim. He did come here because of his girlfriend. She's due to start a teaching position at the end of the month and hasn't been seen in the last few days. They haven't been reported missing because they were both moving. We're working on finding out if our second victim *is* Mandy Matheson, Abel Denham's girlfriend. I'll call as soon as I have anything else. I'm working on getting the information to Quinn right now."

"Thanks, Jake. Also, I saw a suspicious looking character at Crescent City Sites arguing with Victoria Miller, just before she threw me out. I'm not sure if it's relevant to the case but wanted to let you know." Something about the fight bothered her, though she knew better than to get stuck on any one thing when dealing with a case, so she changed course. "We've been looking for a connection between the murders twenty years ago and the murders now. There was a man back then named Jacob Devereaux. Natasha just told me that Devereaux very likely had a child out of wedlock. Count D'Oro was in love with the Good Witch of Honey Swamp. She died, along with others. Devereaux had a thing for Genevieve LaCoste, and she was the last to die on the next go-around."

"We'll look into it all, Danni," Larue said. "I'll get with Quinn and the Pearl River detectives."

"Thanks."

She ended the call and slipped her key into the lock of her car. Movement from behind caught her attention. She whirled to see the unkempt man from Crescent City Sites. The very one she'd just mentioned to Jake. But that thought was short lived.

Something hard slammed into the side of her head.

And the world went dark.

* * * *

Quinn brought the journal to Dirk Deerfield and showed him the entries.

"You remember this man Devereaux?" he asked.

"Of course, I remember him. We never had anything on him, though. At the time when Genevieve would have been killed, he had an alibi. A prostitute in the Quarter swore that he'd been with her. Weak alibi, but an alibi. I couldn't charge the bastard, then he up and died. The murders stopped about a month before his death. Peter Henri, Julian's dad, had a thing for Devereaux. Hated him long before any of the murders in the swamp started. Everyone here was accusing everyone else. Old Selena claimed that the *rougarou* did it. And when it came up again, how the hell do you blame a man who is dead for murdering people?"

"Someone has the cane," Quinn said. "Someone sick enough to kill a lot of people. I want to check out what's going on in the city."

He put a call through to Larue.

As soon as he had the detective on the line, he told him what he had found.

"Danni just called me about Devereaux," Larue told him. "How do I connect a realtor who has been dead for twenty years with a realtor who was moving down to New Orleans? None of this really makes any sense." Quinn couldn't help but have the same thoughts. "There was also a mystery man at the Crescent City Sites tour office, not happy with Victoria. Danni heard them arguing before she was thrown out. She's also convinced that it somehow goes back to men who can't get the women they want."

In other words, they had a mess on their hands.

"Hey," Beauchamp called out. "Get down here."

"I'll call you back," Quinn said and ended the call.

He'd been in the house with Julian. Beauchamp and Deerfield were down at the docks. Julian looked at him with alarm. Quinn brushed past him and hurried to the docks. Beauchamp had walked into the high grasses at the shoreline.

"Third victim," Beauchamp shouted. "Might be Byron Grayson."

Quinn walked to the water. There was a body in the swamp. The head was bashed in, the throat was gone. He'd been there for a while as the crabs had been busy.

He suspected Beauchamp was right.

And Byron Grayson wasn't under suspicion anymore.

"Get Doc Melloni out here," Deerfield said.

* * * *

The first thing Danni became aware of when she came to was the blinding pain in her head. She was going to have a lump the size of Texas on her skull. The next thing she realized was that she was tied and gagged, lying in the trunk of a moving car. Quinn's training came to her quickly. Kick out the back lights. She struggled and twisted and finally got her legs in position.

She kicked hard.

And was rewarded with the sound of broken glass.

She'd done it.

The car jerked to a stop.

The trunk opened.

"Clever little witch, aren't you. Doesn't matter much. We're here."

He reached into the car and with a startling strength, lifted her out.

She saw nothing but trees and bushes, but smelled the air.

They were at a swamp.

Honey Swamp, she imagined.

She struggled like crazy against the man carrying her. They

were leaving the dirt road, moving closer to the water.

"Stop it," he said. "I'm not trying to hurt you."

Really?

He had a strange way of showing it.

"You are the witch," he said. "The Good Witch of Honey Swamp. They said that you were dangerous. I didn't understand until I saw you. But it's you. All good and noble, tempting men as if you were a naked siren on the high seas. Oh, no, I don't want to hurt you. The *rougarou* has a very special plan for you."

The *rougarou?*

He carried her to an old, dilapidated shack close to the water, hidden in a thicket of trees. He shoved open the door with a foot. There was a cot on the floor and he eased her down to it.

"The *rougarou* is coming," he told her.

And he left, closing the door behind him.

Then she saw it.

Leaning against one wall.

A cane.

With a silver wolf's head for the grip.

Chapter 6

Quinn called Larue back as Doc Melloni supervised the initial assessment of the body and had it fished from the water.

"The poor bastard," Larue said over the phone. "I guess I'll get on out there. I've got people working on all the angles we discussed. Hey, by the way, I've been trying to get Danni back on the phone. Do you know where she is?"

Quinn frowned. "When did you last speak with her?"

"About an hour ago. Maybe a little more."

"I'm hanging up and going to try to reach her."

He did and Danni didn't answer. He tried the shop, then Natasha and Father Ryan. Naturally, he sent them all into a panic. Something he too was beginning to feel.

He thought back to the events of the day, searching for any red flags, and called Larue. "Get to Crescent City Sites." It was probably nothing, but it was all they had. "Find out who that mystery man was. Drag Victoria in for questioning if you have to, but get some answers." Fear sank in his stomach. "I can't find Danni."

"I'm on it," Larue told him.

Quinn jumped down to the docks. Fear gripped him like a vise.

Deerfield came over to him.

"I can't find Danni Cafferty," he told the cop. "And I've got a bad feeling."

"You don't have to stay here. Get back to the city."

Quinn stood. "No. If he's got her, he's going to bring her out here, somewhere."

"Maybe you're panicking unnecessarily."

He shook his head. "Danni wouldn't be unreachable if she

were all right." She carried her phone at all times. "He's got her and she's out here. And I'm going to find her."

"This swamp is enormous. We'll have to call out every officer we have."

Quinn looked at the police cruiser. "I need your boat."

"You got it. What are you going to do? I'll go with you."

"You stay here. I'll take the boat."

"I'll get Beauchamp out searching, too."

"There's one person I have to talk to, and I will get answers from her," Quinn said.

He left Deerfield and the commotion with the body and headed out. Selena Duarte must have heard the boat returning. She stuck her head out and then disappeared, slamming the door.

Quinn's phone rang as he jumped up on the dock.

It was Larue.

"Found her car, Quinn, parked by the river. Her cell phone was on the asphalt by the driver's side." Only years of training kept him from total panic.

"What about Victoria Miller and that boyfriend of hers?" Quinn asked.

Larue seemed to hesitate a moment.

"We can't find them, Quinn. The business is all locked up. I've got every cop in the city looking for them."

Quinn raced toward Selena Duarte's front door and banged on it. "You can answer the door or I'll break it down."

"They'll fire you," she called back.

"I'm not a cop, and I don't give a damn if they arrest me. You will let me in right now. And you will tell me what's going on out here."

No reply.

He slammed his shoulder hard against the door.

Wood reverberated.

Two more times and he'd have the damn thing open.

"Stop," Selena called out from inside.

The door opened and she stood there with a shotgun in her hand.

"Put that damned gun down," Quinn said.

She stared at him a moment and then lowered the weapon.

"Ain't no shells in it anyway. Or maybe I would've shot ya."

"I need your help," he told her.

"I'm not the *rougarou*," she said.

His phone rang.

Larue.

No choice, he had to answer.

"Where are you?" Larue asked.

"Getting answers," Quinn said.

"I spoke to those two young girls again, the ones who saw the *rougarou* on their balcony. Jane Eagle and Lana Adair. I asked them about men being inappropriate, urging them to go out. Seems some young guy at a bar on Bourbon Street got really obnoxious. He insisted that they come with him. The bouncer at the bar is a huge guy, a friend of the cops in the Quarter. The girls came to him, but before he could do anything the guy disappeared."

"Thanks," Quinn said. "Gotta go. Doesn't matter too much who it is now. I've just got to find Danni."

"We've got officers streaming into the swamp, Quinn."

"They won't be in time. I've got to go."

He hung up. "Selena, talk to me. Time is running out."

"I don't help the *rougarou.* I just know that it's out there."

"Whoever, whatever it is, it has a friend of mine. And I will kill or die in the process, but I will do everything I can to find her. Now, are you going to help me?"

* * * *

Danni worked as hard as she could at the ropes that were binding her. She managed to free the gag from her mouth, but doubted screaming was going to do her any good. She had to stay calm and collected, which was difficult. At any moment, someone could walk in, bash her head in, then rip her throat out. Quinn was out here, but Honey Swamp was twenty miles long and seven miles wide, one of the most pristine river swamps in the country. Lots of isolated places. It was so crazy. The man who'd taken her was definitely crazy. But he wasn't the *rougarou.* Instead, someone else was coming. And why had her captor seen her as Melissa DeVane? Because of the shop? Because of what she and Quinn did, searching down objects? And there was the cane across the shack. Refurbished, certainly. Its length appeared to be ebony, making the silver of the wolf's head all the more shiny. She winced, thinking that the head of the cane might have been the object used to smash in the victims' heads.

She kept struggling, while thoughts raced through her mind. Who could have done all this? Was the man who'd kidnapped her the bastard child of Jacob Devereaux? If so, why isn't he the *rougarou*? Wouldn't he have taken on that role, rather than leaving it to someone else?

There was always a reason for murder.

Jacob Devereaux had obviously been a sick narcissist, determined to kill Genevieve LaCoste because she wanted nothing to do with him. But this time it had been a man who'd been killed first, then his girlfriend. Had someone been in love and killed his rival, then the woman who'd turned him down?

She kept working on her bindings.

Her hands came free.

She sat up and drew her legs close, working desperately on the knots at her ankles, which were tight. But she was determined. She leapt to her feet, ready to reach for the cane and run.

The door to the shack blew open.

And there it stood.

The *rougarou.*

Immense, covered in some kind of pelt, with a giant wolf's head.

Before she could move, it picked up the cane.

And came toward her.

* * * *

"What is it that you've seen, Selena? Damn it, you have to tell me," Quinn demanded.

"I told you, I'm not the *rougarou.* And if I say anything, the *rougarou* will kill me. I may be old, but I don't want to go that way."

"Selena, I'm going to hurt you worse than any *rougarou*."

"You wouldn't."

"Try me. And why do you think that the *rougarou* will kill you for talking? How will the *rougarou* know that you even talked to me?"

She was silent for an unbearable moment, gnawing on her lip. "He left me a message. In the mud. I came out to hang laundry and it was there, in the yard. A big dug-out sign that said *Silence is golden. Silence is life*. I know it was from the *rougarou*."

The same kind of message that had threatened David Fagin.

He decided to try kindness and softened his tone. "You tell me what you know and I'll see to it that you're safe from the *rougarou* forever."

"I wish I believed you," she said.

"Believe me. The *rougarou* dies today."

"I know just about where he lives," Selena said. "Or where I think he lives."

"Near here?"

She hesitated. "I've seen him come and go. When I've looked through the trees, I've seen him. Come out with me, in back. I'll show you where."

"Let's go," Quinn said.

* * * *

The *rougarou* picked up the cane and pointed it toward Danni.

She stayed dead still. There was no way to escape. And the thing didn't speak. It just stood there, impossibly tall with its giant wolf's head, neck, and ears. A mask, of course. A man beneath.

"You will be dead," she said. "I swear it."

The man who'd taken her captive appeared from behind the *rougarou*. "You think you can curse the *rougarou*. I knew that you were the reincarnation of the witch. I knew it."

"I don't curse people and I'm not a witch," she said. "But I can tell you that Michael Quinn will be looking for me, and when he finds me, you two are going to pay."

She was sure that she heard the *rougarou* speak beneath his mask, and he seemed angry with the man who'd seized her. Seemed like threatening had bought her time, though how anyone would find her in the swamp, she didn't know.

She pointed at the man who'd seized her, deciding to play a hunch. "You're the illegitimate son of a man named Jacob Devereaux, aren't you?" Her guess got their attention, so she continued. "Why you would want to follow in the footsteps of a father who didn't even recognize your existence, I don't know. And why you would be subservient to another, when you're the son of the last *rougarou,* that's mind boggling."

"You are a witch, definitely a witch!" the man cried. "But I will be the next *rougarou,* whether your idiot friends hire me or not."

One more piece of the puzzle clicked. And with her only goal to keep him talking, she threw another accusation their way. "So is the *rougarou* Victoria? Did she get you to apply for a job with David and Julian so that you could find out more about what they were doing? Were you supposed to try to sabotage their tours? Guess what? You didn't even impress them enough to remember your name."

"Shut up, witch! My name is Jim Novak and they damn well know it. You're just stupid! You're a stupid witch," he said.

The *rougarou* slammed the cane against the man and whispered something that Danni didn't catch.

Novak stepped toward her. She leapt at him, striking, clawing, screaming, using all of her strength. To no avail. He gave her a head-ringing pop atop her head and the world began to spin.

He tossed her over his shoulder and headed outside.

She struggled as he set her down and reached for ropes.

She was being tied to a tree.

In the time that he'd left her before the arrival of the *rougarou,* Jim Novak had been preparing for her death.

She wasn't going to be beaten or ripped to death.

She was going to be burned alive.

* * * *

Selena Duarte brought Quinn out back, to the land side of her Honey Swamp shack, and pointed far to the west.

"Through all those trees," she said. "When I see him, it's in that direction. I've seen him there many times. I don't know what's back there. It's overgrown and dense. And there are potholes and swampy land in between. All kinds of critters. Gators, snakes. They leave the *rougarou* alone. But you may not make it through."

"I'll make it," Quinn told her. "And Selena. Thank you."

He headed in the direction she'd pointed. By his reckoning, there was a lot of marshy land between Selena's, the main swamp, and the road. But there had to be something out there. Some kind of old camp or shack. As he walked, he called Larue and told him where he was and where he was going.

"Find out," he said. "There has to be something around these coordinates. Get some techs on it. Maybe there's a way for cops to get there by a road of some kind before I can make it."

Larue promised he was on it.

Quinn kept walking. Grass tangled around his feet. The mud was ankle-deep. He came upon a patch of bare land by a little pool. A gator, six or seven feet long, lay half in and out of the water.

"Brother, leave me alone and I'll leave you alone," Quinn said.

He skirted the alligator and kept going. Luckily, the beast continued bathing in what remained of the sunlight. He paused, looking ahead. For a moment, he thought that he saw smoke.

Which quickly dissipated.

He blinked but kept going, with a landmark now.

Toward the smoke.

* * * *

"You can't kill me," Danni said. "I'm the Good Witch of Honey Swamp, remember? I can make it rain."

She so startled Jim Novak that, for a moment, he paused and looked up at the sky.

"I call upon the rain," she yelled, feeling ridiculous.

But she had given him pause.

The *rougarou* let out some impatient sound and Novak stepped forward again and lit the dried branches around Danni's feet.

She inhaled an odd smell.

Gasoline.

On the wood.

"I call upon the rain," she shouted again.

And to her amazement, it began to rain.

* * * *

Quinn ran, tripping and stumbling.

To make matters worse, it had begun to rain. Heavy. Almost blinding him. His phone rang. It nearly slipped from his fingers as he answered, still making his way through the mud and muck.

Larue.

"There's an old shack out there. It's been there for years and years. You're not going to believe who originally held the property rights around it."

"Count D'Oro?" Quinn said.

"Bingo. We've got a team heading there as quickly as possible."

"I'm almost there."

"Quinn, we found Victoria Miller and Gene Andre. I had them brought in. They did hire that guy, Jim Novak is his name, to harass David Fagin and Julian Henri. But they swear that's all they did. They said that he found them and instigated it. He promised he'd find out what David and Julian were up to and that he'd do his best to make their new company miserable. Victoria paid him, but then he wanted more money. Of course, Gene says he was against it from the get-go and wanted to tell us." The doubt was clear in Larue's voice.

"You have both of them?" Quinn asked.

"In custody."

"Thanks. Gotta keep moving."

"Police are on the way."

"They may not be in time."

He hung up and renewed his efforts with a burst of speed. He was pretty sure he knew just who the *rougarou* might be.

And he'd given him plenty of time.

To set a trap.

* * * *

The rain doused the fire, despite the gasoline. But as the sudden deluge eased, Novak stepped forward to light it again.

"I control the wind and the rain," she yelled, praying that the Louisiana weather would not let her down. And, to her relief, it did not. The rain fell harder.

Novak let out a cry of terror.

The *rougarou* seemed undaunted and stepped forward. Tied to the tree, Danni could do nothing. The "creature" drew out a knife. But instead of planting it in her, he severed the ties binding her and drew her from the tree.

Rain kept falling.

The heavy wolf's head cane was raised, ready to smash it down on her head. But a mammoth mud creature burst from the swamp and tackled the *rougarou.*

She blinked away the rain.

The mud creature was Quinn.

Quinn straddled the costumed man, pinning him down, wrenching the cane from him and throwing it away. The *rougarou* struggled for the knife. Quinn backhanded him across the face so hard that his arms fell flat. Danni dived for the knife. She heard a howl. It was Novak, racing for her.

She braced herself, ready to use the knife.

An explosion pierced the air.

Gunfire.

From Quinn's weapon.

Novak was hit in the kneecap. He let out a howl of pain that seemed to tear through the swamp as if a beast had been brought down.

"Get up," Quinn shouted at the *rougarou.*

As he did, the rain eased.

Quinn ripped the mask off.

To reveal Detective Hayden Beauchamp.

Epilogue

Detective Dirk Deerfield was the most stunned that the "*rougarou*" had been his own partner.

He shook his head over and over again.

Quinn felt badly for him. He'd thought his young partner an upright fellow and had been completely duped.

"He asked me about the old case a lot," Deerfield said. "I thought that sometimes it was just to remind me that while I might be the veteran and him the rookie, things had gotten by me. It never occurred to me that he was planning murders in the same way. Murders with the same details."

"How did Beauchamp and Jim Novak meet?" Father Ryan asked. "That has to be one of the most unlikely duos ever."

"It wasn't surprising to me that Jim Novak is slightly crazy," Natasha said. "Ignored by a father who died when he was a child. Not even given his name. His mother didn't want him. He bounced through the system, went through all kinds of foster homes, unwanted. I guess a legacy as a *rougarou* was better than none."

They were all there, Natasha, Father Ryan, Billie, Bo Ray, Danni, Quinn, along with Jake Larue and Dirk Deerfield, gathered at a place called Wicked Times. Beauchamp and Novak had both been arraigned on murder charges. Danni had been cleared from the hospital, since Quinn had insisted she have the knot on her head looked at. Communication between all of them had been somewhat choppy, and they were all still trying to put the pieces together.

It was also supposed to be a social night at Wicked Times. The place was new. It had just opened on Magazine Street, and in an hour or so, Quinn was going to play with the band and he was excited. They had a guy on rhythm guitar named Fats McGinnis, odd name since Fats was a tall, lean, twig of a man, one of the best in the city on guitar.

Danni liked to compare the situation to that of Sherlock Holmes with his violin. But Quinn always assured her he was no Sherlock Holmes.

As if she'd just read his mind, Danni asked, "How did you know? I mean, before you came after him, you knew that the *rougarou* was Hayden Beauchamp."

"Process of elimination, my dear Watson. It was the pieces all of you gave me. Larue was keeping in constant contact. I figured that Jim Novak had something to do with it. But, of course, I could see Novak when I came through the trees. We knew it wasn't Byron Grayson, he was dead in the swamp. When Larue checked with Jane and Lana and found out that, yes, they'd been harassed in a bar on Bourbon, but the guy had disappeared, I figured it had to be Beauchamp. Someone young enough to head out into the bar scene and someone close to the investigation. He knew all the little details of the previous murders that the public might not have known. He'd seen all the crime scene pictures. He knew how the '*rougarou*' had been killing. When we found Byron Grayson in the swamp, Deerfield had us all split up. Naturally, Beauchamp knew that Danni was missing. He knew about my communications with Larue. He had to figure then that Novak had taken Danni for him and that Novak would think that he had scored the win of the world. Apparently, Beauchamp found the silver wolf's head cane years ago and had become obsessed with the story and its possibilities."

He paused.

"We believe that he actually killed his first victim, an unknown young woman we found buried in the front of the shack, after he found the old property. As you surmised, Danni, people can be sick and cruel and perpetuate heinous crimes without props or legend. But he had the cane. And when he met Novak, he was able to convince him that he was the *rougarou*, and that a *rougarou* always had a man in training, ready to step up to the task. When Beauchamp wanted to get rid of someone or take revenge, he called on Novak, who brought him his victims, and, we believe, did most of the killing. Beauchamp met Mandy Matheson and Abel Denham somewhere in the city when they first arrived. I'm assuming that Beauchamp immediately had a thing for Mandy. When she didn't respond, she was with another man, for God's sake, Beauchamp decided they both deserved to die. But he thought he'd also have a little fun. He knew Victoria Miller. She'd been running tours for a long time. He knew she was furious with David Fagin and Julian Henri. So he sent Novak to befriend them, and then actually got them to pay him to torment Julian Henri.

"When they talked, both Beauchamp and Novak decided that Julian's father had been the bastard who'd somehow caused Jacob Devereaux's death. Devereaux had tried and tried to get ahold of Julian's property, but never did. He'd stolen the cane from Peter Henri, but he'd never managed to dislodge him. Making sure that David and Julian stumbled on the first victim, and then writing a threat in the mud, pretty much ruined their intended business. Though now, knowing that people do tend to like the gruesome, they may be able to start up again."

"We know a lot," Deerfield added, "because Novak is talking a blue streak. He's still convinced that he'll be the *rougarou* one day."

"It's still absolutely amazing that you found me in the middle of a swamp," Danni said.

"More amazing is that you made it rain." Larue grinned.

Father Ryan cleared his throat. "God made it rain. But who knows? Maybe, as the Good Witch that Danni can prove to be, her words went to God's ear."

"It is Southern Louisiana," Danni noted. "It rains all the time."

Everyone at the table turned toward Danni. She did have some powers. Sometimes it was in drawings she made while doodling or when she sleepwalked. This time?

Rain.

"Maybe the legend of the *rougarou* is a little bit true, and maybe the legend of the Good Witch is entirely true," Quinn said.

"Glad I'm on her side," Bo Ray said, and they all laughed.

"As far as finding you, I knew that Selena Duarte knew more

than she was saying. I don't think she was even being all that elusive on purpose, even though she was scared and believed that the *rougarou* would leave her alone as long as she kept quiet." He shook his head. "Beauchamp actually made me really like him when we were with Selena. He reminded her that she'd die alone if she kept being so mean. I thought he cared about her. Now I realize that everything about his personality was a mask, just like the wolf's head mask he wore."

"How did he manage to rip out throats the way that he did?" Bo Ray asked.

"Novak did the throat ripping," Deerfield said. "He's had all his back teeth filed to a point. Beauchamp couldn't do it. There were a few times when he had to be in uniform quickly. So being covered in blood wouldn't work. Beauchamp told Jim Novak that honing his teeth was a way of preparing to be the *rougarou* himself."

They all sat in silence for a moment.

"Something scared the '*rougarou*' off the balcony when he came into the city. I'm sure he meant to take Jane Eagle and Lana Adair," Deerfield said.

"Probably someone in the street, or the fact that a scream would have drawn attention," Larue said. "Those girls don't know how lucky they are."

"But which one came into the city as a *rougarou*?" Natasha asked.

"It was actually Hayden Beauchamp that night," Larue said. "Which is probably why the girls are still alive. Beauchamp didn't want to get caught. Novak saw himself as a *rougarou* in training. I don't think he would have been scared away."

"Let's hope that they're both locked up forever," Natasha said.

"They could get the death penalty," Father Ryan said, which brought everyone there to look at him.

He lifted his hands. "Judgment isn't mine. I'm just referring to the law in the state of Louisiana."

A moment later, Quinn was asked up to play with the group, which he did. And it felt wonderful. It reminded him that he was alive. That they were alive.

Good times were what made up for the bad times. Now and then, Quinn glanced at the table. He was glad to see Danni smile at him. She was having fun. And she seemed to enjoy the fact that he was happy too. There was just something about a guitar, something soothing, even when his playing was really anything but. But he loved who he was playing with, loved the night. And loved that he had kept his word to Selena Duarte and the *rougarou* had been caught.

It was late when they all parted. Since Dirk Deerfield was still reeling, he was going to head out on vacation. That night, he was staying at Quinn's family home in the Garden District. The next morning he was flying off for a long awaited trip to London. They bid one another goodnight. Larue headed off in his car, as did Father Ryan and Deerfield. The rest of them piled into Quinn's car. They dropped Natasha off first, then parked in the garage at Danni's house on Royal Street.

Billie and Bo Ray headed up.

Danni and Quinn greeted Wolf and gave him treats.

Then Danni headed up.

Quinn checked the door to the basement. The items there had no power over anyone anymore, but Quinn still kept the basement door locked. He called to Wolf and they headed upstairs. The dog curled up in his bed. Quinn walked into the bedroom he shared with Danni.

She was waiting for him.

He smiled. "Maybe you are a witch. A temptress, driving men to madness, seducing them."

She frowned, rising to meet him. "Quinn, I've never been like that."

He laughed, taking her into his arms, loving the sensation of holding her, feeling her against him, especially with the image of her in the power of the "*rougarou*" still lurking in the back of his mind. For a moment, he held her tenderly. Then he caught her chin with his forefinger and lifted it.

"I mean nothing evil in that. Just teasing, my love. The cane is put away, far from the hands of those who might see it as an evil power. But your strength is entirely different and can't be shut away. You are a witch, of course, of the best kind. You have the kind of magic that seduced my heart and soul. With your laughter, your vitality, your concern for others in the world around you, and then of course—"

He paused.

"I love you for your—"

And he whispered in her ear.

"Ah," she said, drawing a finger gently down his cheek. "Let's make use of all that you love."

Her fingers then slid down the length of his back.

A good night lay ahead.

But he did want to know one thing. "Just how did you make it rain?"

"Magic," she said. "How else?"

* * * *

Also from 1001 Dark Nights and Heather Graham, discover Crimson Twilight, When Irish Eyes Are Haunting, All Hallows Eve and Hallow Be The Haunt.

About Heather Graham

Heather Graham has been writing for many years and actually has published nearly 200 titles. So, for this page, we'll concentrate on the Krewe of Hunters.

They include:

Phantom Evil
Heart of Evil
Sacred Evil
The Evil Inside
The Unseen
The Unholy
The Unspoken
The Uninvited
The Night is Watching
The Night is Alive
The Night is Forever
The Cursed
The Hexed
The Betrayed
The Silenced
The Forgotten
The Hidden

Actually, though, Adam Harrison—responsible for putting the Krewe together, first appeared in a book called Haunted. He also appeared in Nightwalker and has walk-ons in a few other books. For more ghostly novels, readers might enjoy the Flynn Brothers Trilogy—Deadly Night, Deadly Harvest, and Deadly Gift, or the Key West Trilogy—Ghost Moon, Ghost Shadow, and Ghost Night.

The Vampire Series (now under Heather Graham/ previously

Shannon Drake) Beneath a Blood Red Moon, When Darkness Falls, Deep Midnight, Realm of Shadows, The Awakening, Dead by Dusk, Blood Red, Kiss of Darkness, and From Dust to Dust.

For more info, please visit her web page, http://www.theoriginalheathergraham.com or stop by on Facebook.

Discover more from Heather Graham

Crimson Twilight: A Krewe of Hunters Novella

It's a happy time for Sloan Trent and Jane Everett. What could be happier than the event of their wedding? Their Krewe friends will all be there and the event will take place in a medieval castle transported brick by brick to the New England coast. Everyone is festive and thrilled . . . until the priest turns up dead just hours before the nuptials. Jane and Sloan must find the truth behind the man and the murder--the secrets of the living and the dead--before they find themselves bound for eternity--not in wedded bliss but in the darkness of an historical wrong and their own brutal deaths.

When Irish Eyes Are Haunting: A Krewe of Hunters Novella

Devin Lyle and Craig Rockwell are back, this time to a haunted castle in Ireland where a banshee may have gone wild—or maybe there's a much more rational explanation—one that involves a disgruntled heir, murder, and mayhem, all with that sexy light touch Heather Graham has turned into her trademark style.

All Hallows Eve: A Krewe of Hunters Novella

Salem was a place near and dear to Jenny Duffy and Samuel Hall -- it was where they'd met on a strange and sinister case. They never dreamed that they'd be called back. That history could repeat itself in a most macabre and terrifying fashion. But, then again, it was Salem at Halloween. Seasoned Krewe members, they still find themselves facing the unspeakable horrors in a desperate race to save each other-and perhaps even their very souls.

Searching for Mine

A Searching For Novella

By Jennifer Probst

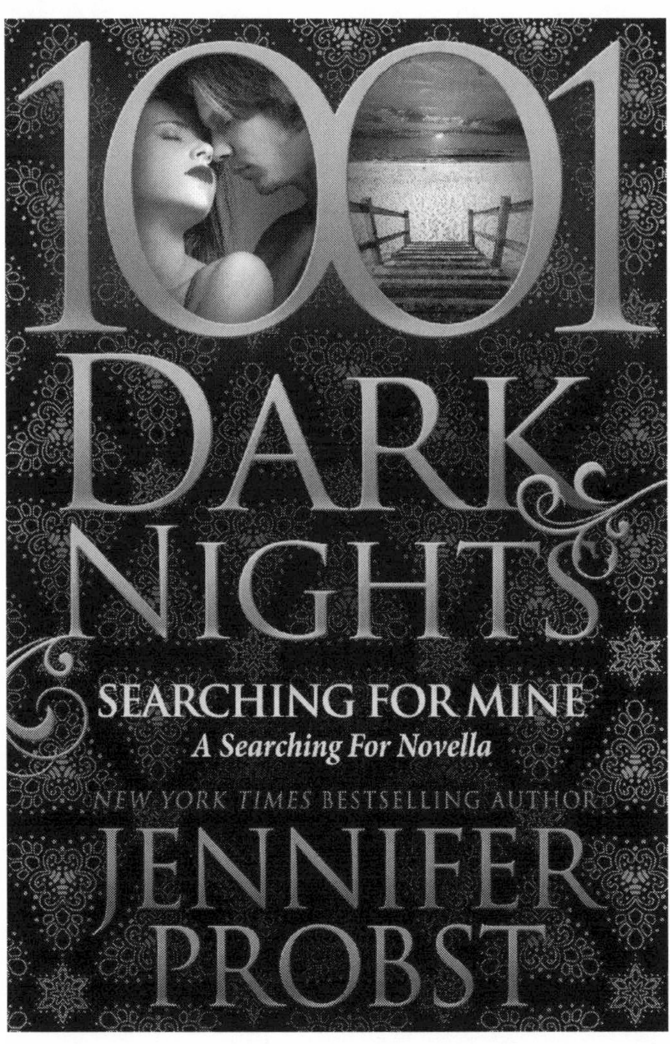

Acknowledgments

Ah, so many people to thank!

Smooches to the amazing 1001 Dark Nights team – Liz Berry and M.J. Rose. I'm so honored to be asked to participate in this series, and humbled to stand beside my talented fellow authors. I love this world you created!

Special shout-out to my street team, The Probst Posse. You guys helped me create Connor's story and it was a beautiful team effort. I love brainstorming with you guys! Here's a few specific names to thank for their specific suggestions I incorporated into the book!

Marlene Brown, Elizabeth Clinton, Stephanie Flowers Newman, Maybelline Smith, Katherine Thompson Allen, Tina Hobbs and Ada Frost

Chapter One

"A woman must have money and a room of her own if she is to write fiction"—Virginia Woolf

Connor Adam Dunkle stared at the paper. The circled letter mocked him in bright red, and with a false merriness that his professor probably relished.

A big fat F.

Impossible.

His gaze scanned the bleeding type scrawl filled with unknown marks, initials, and cross outs. At the end, two sentences were written in elegant cursive they didn't teach in school any longer.

Deduction of two letter grades for lateness. Overall, a poorly thought, shallow type paper with nothing to back up the opinion via the text.

Connor Dunkle studied the woman who was his last obstacle blocking him from getting his needed degree.

Professor Ella Blake.

If he'd ever created an image of a spinster librarian, this woman would have been his inspiration. From her drab, baggy fitting clothes, to the black glasses hiding most of her features, she practically faded into the background. Her hair was twisted up into a tight bun, giving her face a bit of a pinched look. Her gray sweater and black trousers did nothing for her figure, or her skin tone. The only brightness in her entire collage was a slash of red-orange lipstick, which became so garish with her olive skin, it literally made an onlooker jerk back.

"Many of you disappointed me with your papers. I suggest better preparation is in order to pass this class. Our first exam is Friday and there will be another paper due shortly. Please make sure you refer to the syllabus for due dates. I do not appreciate or reward lateness."

Did she shoot him a look or was that his imagination?

Unbelievable. He'd deliberately approached her last week and explained his grueling schedule. With his demanding workload and ambitious course work, he'd specifically asked Professor Blake for an extension on the paper.

Hadn't she agreed?

It had taken him a lot to register for college at thirty-eight years old, but he had his eye on a management position at Bilkins Construction, and he was determined to change his life. He'd taken extra courses and jammed in a four-year degree into two. Finally, graduation loomed before him, but he'd put off fulfilling his last course requirement of Composition 102. Of course, now he ended up with a sexually frustrated teacher focused on feminist literature to make excuses for her own lack of a love life.

"We'll be diving more into short stories and examining the female writer and what she brought to society in comparison to men at the time. I'd like to hear thoughts on *The Yellow Wallpaper*. What do you think made the story so popular? What was the writer really trying to tell us?"

Connor hid a bored sigh and tuned out of the discussion. He'd fix it. He'd be extra nice and charming and give her some needed male attention. Maybe she'd forgotten, and he'd just remind her, they'd laugh about it, and he'd get a damn C.

Professor Blake paced the front of the room in her usual black boots that made no sound. He wondered if she ever wore stilettos. Probably didn't know what they were. She preferred shoes with no sex appeal, no heel, and no sense of fun. What type of underwear did she wear to match those awful outfits? Probably cotton. Maybe even granny panties in plain white.

"Mr. Dunkle?"

His head shot up in pure surprise. She was staring at him with a focused expression that almost made him blush. Almost. Of course, she had no clue he'd been wondering about the look of her panties. He gave her an easy grin that usually charmed women within a few seconds. "Yes?"

"I'm interested in your opinion of the story."

Shit. He hadn't understood the end. Hell, he hadn't understood much of it and daydreaming in class wasn't helping him. He kept the grin and nodded. "I thought it was a brave way of portraying the character."

There. Sounded good. She tapped her finger against her orange-red lips and leaned against the side of the desk. "Interesting. Tell me more."

Shit.

He tried not to sweat and frowned, as if thinking hard, and tried to buy time. "Well, the writer struggled with identity."

Connor had heard that line in many classes and felt it was a solid portrayal of the ridiculous story he'd hated. He waited for her to move on to someone else, but instead she actually walked up the aisle to his seat. Sweat pricked his forehead. He hadn't felt this put on the spot since high school.

"So, the writer was brave and struggled with identity. Why don't you tell me exactly what you feel the story is about?"

And that's when Connor realized she knew. Up close, her dull brown eyes glinted with flecks of gold-green, pulling an observer in. Her face seemed expressionless but Connor caught the challenge in her gaze—the knowledge he had no clue what he was talking about, and she was going in for the kill.

Who would've thought a drab English professor could be so ruthless?

He regrouped and assessed the situation. Tilting his head, he stared right back, refusing to back down. "I think the story was ridiculous and contrived. It was a big whine fest of a character trapped in a room, obsessed with the wallpaper but not enough guts to get herself out of the situation. That's what I thought about the story."

The class tittered. He waited for her attack, knowing he'd challenged her in class, which was her natural terrain. Still, Connor didn't care. That story sucked and it was a relief to admit it.

A small smile touched her lips. "A fair and honest assessment," she concluded.

He grinned.

"By a reader who has no idea what he's reading. By a reader who has no desire to try and follow the writer or do more than lazily lay back and wait for the car wrecks, or sex scene, or shootout. We've become a society who wants so badly to be entertained, without using a brain cell, and refuses to do the work to engage and follow greatness. Frankly, Mr. Dunkle, you disappoint me. I had expected much more of you."

His grin disappeared.

She walked away on soundless shoes and pointed to the blackboard. "Maybe we can salvage it for the rest of the class. Let's begin."

Connor held back a groan.

This was going to be a bitch of a semester.

Chapter Two

"I thought how unpleasant it is to be locked out; and I thought how it is worse, perhaps, to be locked in"—Virginia Woolf

Ella watched her students file out of class but her attention was focused on one particular individual.

Connor Dunkle.

She sensed a play coming on, and she was actually going to enjoy it. Teaching provided her a sick sense of satisfaction when she got to take an egotist, smug person and knock them down a few notches. It also offered a perfect conduit to change the thinking and view of the world one student at a time. Sure, sometimes she felt as if she made no difference with her classes. But once in a while, she lasered in on a student who needed to be challenged.

"Professor Blake? Can I talk to you a moment?"

She turned, and right on cue, there he was. Ella hid her smile and wondered how the first round would fare. She'd pegged him from the first day, but sometimes a student surprised her.

"Yes, Mr. Dunkle?" She peered over her thick-framed glasses. She could've picked trendy or delicate frames, but she liked the way these intimidated her students. "What can I do for you?"

His charming grin could've short-circuited the light bulbs or rendered one speechless. Had she ever seen such perfect white teeth? The man was a walking delectable treat for the female vision, but Ella had prepared. She checked in with her body and was quite pleased. Other than a recognizable hum between her thighs, she was completely in control. Of course, he didn't know that. Ella judged there weren't many offers Connor made that were turned down. The reason was all six foot five inches that towered over her desk with lean, cut muscles evident beneath his casual clothes. Dirty blond hair lay messily over his brow. He wore it long, and the thick strands curled around the edge of his ears. His face was sculpted quite beautifully, from the high cheekbones, full lips, and perfect dimples. He reminded her briefly of a young Robert Redford from her favorite movie, *The Way We Were.* Sure, Redford was old now, but Ella believed the greats like Newman and Redford and Brando paved the way for Pitt and Hemsworth. And damned if her fingers didn't itch just once to brush those gold streaked strands from his forehead.

His eyes delivered the final one-two punch. Crystal blue swirled with a touch of green, clear as glass and deep as the sea. Eyes like that could mesmerize prey, but Ella had tons of practice restraining messy desires. She met his gaze, ignoring the tiny tumble in her belly, and kept her gaze on the prize.

"Yes?" she asked with a bit of impatience. He blinked, somewhat confused she hadn't ducked her head or stuttered. Oh, this one needed a reality check. Had he ever been rejected? Or was he one of the lucky ones who slid through life unscathed by others? Huh. Another similarity to Redford's character. She was going to have to re-rent that movie again.

"I think there was a misunderstanding," he began. His body language reeked of open friendliness with just a touch of sex. His navy blue T-shirt stretched tight across his chest, and his jeans were worn low on his hips, which were now cocked in a very appealing angle. He tilted his head to ensure intimacy, and damned if his dimples hadn't popped out. Oh, he was good.

He held out the paper. "I got an F. I apologize again for turning it in late. See, I'm about to graduate with a business management degree. I need to pass this course." His smile held well. "When we last spoke, I assumed you understood my position and told me it was acceptable to turn it in a few days late."

Oh, she remembered that conversation perfectly. He'd given her excuse after excuse for why he deserved more time, and she just nodded and didn't have to say a word. The man was probably so used to women giving him everything he wanted, he hadn't even bothered to wait for her verbal assent. Just walked away with a smile and a wink. He'd actually winked at her like this was 1970 and calling women in authority by *honey* and *babe* was fine.

"It was acceptable," she said calmly. "But if you'd read your syllabus carefully, you'd see each day it comes in late one full letter grade is taken off. I gave you a break though, Mr. Dunkle. I didn't count the weekend because I was feeling quite generous. Is that it?"

He blinked. Confusion flickered over his face and she had to tamp down a chuckle. He leaned in just a few inches and dropped his voice to a concerned level. "Professor Blake, I need to get a C in this class. My job right now depends on my graduation this June."

Her eyes glinted behind her glasses with pure intention. "Did you read *The Story of an Hour* by Kate Chopin? Or did you scan the Internet for analysis and summaries and stick them into your paper to make it look like you read it?"

Oh, she knew that look well. Ella waited to see if he'd lie straight to her face. A tiny crease in his brow gave him away. She was the one surprised when he finally answered. "No."

"No, what, Mr. Dunkle?"

"No, I didn't read the story. I tried. But I got bored and stopped."

She nodded. "I'd suggest if you want to pass my class you begin taking it seriously and doing the assignments. On time."

His aura simmered with frustration. "I understand. I'll be sure to read the next short stories thoroughly. Who's the next author we're studying?"

"Virginia Woolf."

He looked like he'd rather stick needles in his eye than read Woolf, but she gave him credit. He kept his expression open and understanding. "Fascinating. Hey, maybe we can get some coffee after class? Discuss some of your viewpoints. Get to know one another better? I feel like we may have gotten off on the wrong foot."

Unbelievable. The man just kept digging the crater larger and larger. He'd be lucky to graduate. She switched to her disapproving teacher voice: hard, controlled, and full of ice. "I dislike clichés, Mr. Dunkle. In both speech and company."

"Huh?"

"Gotten off on the wrong foot," she pointed out. "It's called a cliché. Look it up. Now, do you have any issues regarding the next assignment?"

He cleared his throat. "I'm just surprised we're reading another woman writer. This was never explained as a feminist course. I assumed we'd be reading Hemmingway, or Fitzgerald, or Poe. Getting more of the male perspective in society, too, you know?"

Once again, he realized he'd misspoken too late. Her gaze flicked over him, then slid away in dismissal.

"You know what they say about the word assume, Mr. Dunkle?"

"No."

Her smile was mean. "It makes an ASS out of you and me. Now if you'll excuse me, I need to get ready for my next class."

She focused on the stack of papers in front of her and began to read. His stunned silence seethed with unspoken emotions, but finally he walked away with his failing paper clutched in his hand. She risked a peek.

His stride owned pure grace and swagger. His tight, perfect ass made women want to weep. Or cop a feel.

She tamped down the flare of guilt from ogling a student, but the man was her age and ready to graduate, so it wasn't all that terrible. Besides, she'd never date the man. If he thought their little chat meant she was going to forgive lateness or inane answers in her class, Connor Dunkle would learn quickly enough.

Sighing, she began prepping for her next class. God, she was tired. She loved teaching, but lately, burnout threatened. How long had it been since she spent a night out? Or did anything more exciting than grading papers and playing Wii U Super Smash Brothers? She adored her ten-year-old son, but maybe she needed more balance in her life. Ella didn't want Luke growing up thinking women didn't leave the house other than to work. But every time she thought about going out with some friends for a drink, mama guilt kicked in. They'd already been forced to move twice before she got her permanent job at Verily College, and he was still adjusting to a new neighborhood and school. How could she leave him to pursue her own fun? The divorce may have been final for a year now, but the first year was filled with pain, anger, and lawyers back and forth. Luke probably needed more time to accept his parents would never get back together. He'd probably freak at the idea of her trying to date, and Lord knows her first priority was to her son.

Ella sighed. She had no time for dating anyway. Weekends were filled with endless errands and running around. The idea of putting on something more than a pair of sweats seemed painful.

Right now, her legs resembled a porcupine. If she ever had sex again, she'd need to bribe the beautician to give her a bikini wax.

She was thirty-five years old, and an official old maid. Maybe they'd make a card in her honor one day. If children even played that game anymore. Oh, Lord, now her mind was chattering about inane things again and she needed to get herself together.

Ella bet Connor didn't have such problems. His biggest issue was probably what woman to sleep with and what type of beer to drink with dinner. Yeah, she was being judgy, but damned if she didn't feel like she had the right just this once.

She sorted folders and her fingers closed around the glossy postcard she'd found in the Verily bakery. With purple and silvery scroll, the logo of Kinnections matchmaking agency made her pause. Tapping her finger against the edge, she rotated it in her hands and pondered.

It may be a bit pricey, but imagine someone taking the time to personally screen her matches? No bars or losers or meat markets to deal with. No dreaded Internet. Maybe there'd be a nice single father out there who was perfect for her. A man who took responsibility seriously. A man who wouldn't dump his family for a newer, flashier model like her dickhead ex-husband.

The next group of students came straggling in, and Ella shoved the card back into the pile of papers. She'd think about it. Right now, she needed to concentrate on Edith Wharton.

Ella got back to work.

Chapter Three

"I would always rather be happy than dignified."—Charlotte Brontë, Jane Eyre

Connor climbed the steps to his apartment, looking forward to some good TV, his meatball parm sub, and a cold Guinness with the perfect head. The conversation with Professor Blake kept replaying over and over in his head. What had he done wrong? The damn class was ruining his perfect GPA, which he'd worked hard for. Was she really going to bust his balls on essays that meant nothing?

He muttered a few choice curse words and stopped short. A voice hit his ears along with the sound of metal dragging on concrete.

"What's a matter, new boy? You too good to hang with us? Maybe I'll teach you a lesson. Gimme that DS!"

"No! Leave me alone!"

Connor bit back a groan and turned. The same three boys—he called them the gangsters—were tormenting some poor kid who had been shoved to the ground and pinned by his bike. An open backpack spilled a variety of contents over the sidewalk. The main bully gave a satisfied sneer and held the red Nintendo DS high over his head.

Little shits. They liked to play dirty and tended to pick out kids a few years younger. Connor knew the type well. His younger brother, Nate, had fallen victim to bullying in school and it had almost destroyed his ability to concentrate on his studies. Connor made sure no one messed with him, but he felt bad for the kids who had no one to protect them.

Connor put his purchases down and walked over to the crew.

"Practicing for prison?" he drawled. He stood in front of them with his arms crossed casually, an intimidating stare on his face. Like clockwork, the three of them looked at each other, their faces reflecting wariness and a coward's fear. Yeah, the bullies were only strong together. Break them up and they were helpless. "Here. Let me help you."

The boy on the ground ignored his outstretched hand and dragged himself to his feet. No tears shone in his dark eyes, but his skin was mottled red, and his lower lip trembled slightly. Still, pure rebellion reflected in his face and attitude. His dark hair was cut too short, emphasizing a wicked cowlick in the front, and he was skinny and all legs. A thin trickle of blood dripped down his arm. Probably a scraped elbow. He wore a red sweatshirt with the Captain America logo, athletic pants, and some type of expensive looking sneakers. Connor respected him wanting to handle the situation himself, especially at his age. What was he, about nine? Ten?

"We weren't doing nothing," the lead gangster replied. "He fell off his bike."

The boy didn't deny it. He stared at the bullies with a fierce resentment that shimmered in the air. His hands clenched into tight fists, but he didn't move, just shifted back and forth on his feet.

"Convenient. Give me the DS."

"It's mine!" lead gangster whined.

Connor looked at the kid but he didn't claim the DS. Keeping a stubborn silence, he met the gangster's gaze and refused to back down.

Connor shook his head. "Tough. I'm claiming the DS. I've been dying to try out some games so it's now mine."

The boys looked at him as if he'd gone nuts, and Connor used their shock to smoothly snatch the DS from the bully's hand. "You can't do that!" the second gangster cried. "That's stealing."

"Guess I'll be sharing a jail cell with you one day, huh? Listen up. Next time you think you're gonna have a bit of fun at some younger kid's expense, remember this. I can find each of you alone and make you regret it. Got it?"

The leader stepped back. "Whatever. Come on, guys. Let's

get out of here."

They trudged away in their ragtag group. Connor picked up the bike from the ground and thrust out the DS. "Here you go. No thanks necessary, kid."

"I didn't need your help," the boy hissed in fury. Connor jerked back at the frustration glinting from his brown eyes. "I had it handled. You screwed up everything, dude! Now they're gonna be looking for me cause they think I'm a wuss!"

Connor blinked. "Are you kidding me? You would've gotten beat up. I've seen those kids around and they don't play nice. Trust me, they won't mess with you anymore."

The boy yanked back the DS and his bike, shoving his backpack over his arm. "Whatever."

Connor rolled his eyes. "When did that word make a comeback? I mean, really?"

The kid didn't answer, just shook his head and dragged his bike toward the building next door. Huh. Guess he was a new neighbor. Connor hadn't seen any moving trucks, but he hoped the grumpy old man was finally gone. Anyone was better than a grizzled man who sat on the front stoop and bellowed at strangers on the street, drinking cheap whiskey from a brown paper bag. Even a surly kid.

Connor watched the red door shut and turned back to his own place. Maybe he should knock on the door this weekend and introduce himself. The neighborhood wasn't the best, but the location was prime for commuting to Manhattan and keeping rents low. Other than the band of bullies who haunted the streets, there weren't drugs or gangs. Just a bunch of older stone buildings with ancient plumbing, leaky windows, and pothole-ridden streets.

Still worked for him.

Connor trudged inside and reheated his dinner. The interior of his apartment didn't reflect the shabby exterior. He'd updated the original dull beige walls and carpet with a rich blue, and his brother's girlfriend, Kennedy, had transformed the bachelor pad into a home using a few feminine touches to brighten up the place. He'd moved from his old apartment he'd shared with Nate to save money, ignoring his brother's protests that he'd cover his expenses until Connor finished school.

Hell, no.

Connor had spent his life taking care of his little brother and raising him. Though Nate was now a fancy rocket scientist who used to work for NASA, Connor refused to take his charity. But he hadn't been able to afford the tuition so they'd struck a deal. Since Connor had worked three jobs to get Nate through college when he was young, Nate would front his tuition bill. Connor could live with that, knowing he'd pay back his brother every dime once he got into a management position. He'd quickly moved to this apartment to save on rent and was now able to live comfortably.

He may not have fancy granite counters or stainless steel appliances, but everything worked, including the big screen TV. The furniture was secondhand, but it was solid wood mahogany, with clean, masculine lines. The extra bedroom was a nice perk, so he used it for his workout equipment and skipped the gym membership. Photos of architectural buildings and bridges filled the walls, bringing a sense of wonder and creativity to the space. His textbooks stuffed the antique bookcase, and he'd created a small workspace in the corner of the living room, saving a spot for where he'd hang his degree.

He pulled out his sub, cracked open his beer, and ate at the sturdy pine table while he scrolled through his iPhone and updated social media. The radiator hummed and the pipes creaked in the background. The smell of sauce and meat drifted in the air. He embraced the quiet, settled in, and enjoyed the solitude. After dinner, he powered up his laptop and did a few hours of schoolwork, finally rubbing his tired eyes around nine o'clock.

To think he once had nothing to do but hang at the pub with his friends was now laughable. Most of the time, he fell asleep with his textbooks open on the table, drooling over the pages. Other than an occasional Saturday night out or hanging with his brother, his social life had dried up to an embarrassing level. He rarely saw his old friends, who were mainly into getting drunk at the bars every Friday and Saturday night, refusing to acknowledge that forty loomed dangerously close. Hell, the saddest part of all was he didn't even miss his old life.

Not even the women.

How had that happened? Not that he didn't have steady offers, but lately his sexual drive had been humming at a low level. Something seemed lacking in all of his encounters, and he couldn't seem to figure out the problem. He'd never been like his brother, craving some type of mythical connection with a woman that didn't exist. No, he believed hard in the three B's when it came to dating. They were part of his own personal Bible he'd created to keep things uncomplicated.

Beauty.

Body.

Boobs.

Marriage didn't interest him, and neither did getting tied up with all the daily routine and messiness of a long-term relationship. He'd seen firsthand how the feeling of love could turn bad and sweep everyone in its wake into a tsunami of casualties.

No, thanks. Keep it clean and everyone remained happy. He just needed to get his groove back.

He got up from the table and cleaned up. Maybe he'd spend a few minutes spacing out in front of the television. Yeah, he had to be at the job site at five a.m. for his construction job, but he needed to clear his mind from the array of numbers flashing in his head.

Dropping into the comfortable sectional, he channel surfed for a bit before he hit pay dirt. *The Fast and Furious* number—well, whatever. Nothing like some good car crashes and skimpily dressed women to soothe him. He put his feet on the coffee table and settled in.

* * * *

"How was school, honey?"

Her son dragged his fork across the chipped plate. "Fine."

Ella raised a brow. Luke slumped at the table, staring at his meatloaf with pure suffering. She didn't blame him. Lately, dinners were thrown together with little thought to gourmet taste and more to sustenance on a faster timetable. "Did you just utter the most boring, inane word on the planet that should be struck from Webster's Dictionary? The word I absolutely refuse to acknowledge in this house because I believe we have brains larger than an amoeba? Did you say the word—fine?"

He tried to look annoyed but his lip twitched. "Sorry. It was uneventful."

She grinned. "Much better." They smiled at each other and for a little while, life was just about perfect. Ella knew well about grabbing those moments in time that defined her daily routine. Her son was growing up. Every day, she felt as if he tugged another inch away from her toward the big bad world that was waiting to gobble him whole. Her gaze swept over his beloved face, with his charming pug nose, full lips, and graceful brows. His brown hair was thick and messy, with a terrible cowlick she'd never been able to tame with gel or scissors, but was such a part of who he was she hoped he'd never get rid of it. His round black glasses made him look like a young Harry Potter. Of course, he hated them and was already begging for contacts.

But his eyes were truly the window to his truth. A deep, rich chocolate brown, they reminded her so much of his father. Luke's were full of warmth, kindness, curiosity, and zeal.

His father's had been full of unfulfilled longing and too many secrets.

Ella tamped down a sigh. The last time she'd convinced Luke to sit on her lap for just a moment, his lanky legs had hung over her and hit the floor at an awkward angle. She'd spent her entire life engulfed in the magic of words and poetry, and in that moment, finally got what it felt like to grieve the passing of time. Just another one of those things you could read about or watch but didn't truly understand the flood of emotion until you experienced it. Kind of like childbirth.

"Besides uneventful, have you made any friends yet?" she asked.

His head dropped again. "Nope."

"No boys in the neighborhood? Maybe to ride bikes with or something?"

He snorted. "Let's just say there's been no welcoming committee. I'm fine, Mom. Don't worry about it."

And that's exactly why she worried. Luke was extremely

independent, and usually had no problem making friends. His wicked sense of humor won over his toughest critics, but the past months had stolen his smile.

He needed more time, and she knew he'd make friends. Pushing wasn't going to help. Attending a new school simply sucked. She'd tried everything possible not to move, but the job offer at Verily College was a gift she couldn't pass up. She hated not being home after school for Luke, but for now she had no choice. Next semester she'd have a better schedule and more flexibility, but for now, she needed to prove herself and take the unwelcome time slots leftover from the other long-term professors.

Ten years old and already he'd experienced more pain than she ever intended. He'd lost his father, his home, and his friends. As his mother, she'd only wanted to protect him and make him happy. Make him feel safe.

Fail on all counts.

She pushed away her gloomy thoughts. "I thought we'd paint your room this weekend," she offered brightly. "You pick the color—anything you want. And we can hit Target for some decorations."

"Okay."

His despondent tone cut right through her heart. "Can you do me a favor, Luke? I need the honest truth."

He looked at her with a bit of wariness. "Sure."

"On a scale of one to ten, how bad is my meatloaf?"

The faint spark of humor lit his brown eyes. "One."

"Yeah, I thought so. How does a pizza sound?"

He tilted his head and considered. "Can we eat in front of the TV, too?"

Ella laughed. "Sure, why not?"

"No History channel?"

She gave a sigh of surrender. "Fine. You pick."

He gave a small whoop and fisted his hand in the air. "Nice. I want pepperoni on mine, please."

"You got it. Luke?"

"Yeah?"

"I love you."

His face shifted to that half uncomfortable, half pleased look she recognized so well. But he gave her the words. "Love you, too, Mom."

He bounded out of the kitchen, forgetting to clean up his plate, and Ella didn't remind him. She went to order the pizza.

Chapter Four

"When the doctors came they said she had died of heart disease—of the joy that kills."—Kate Chopin, The Story of An Hour

Two weeks later, Connor realized he was in trouble.

Another F stared back at him from his last paper. As Ella lectured to the class on the limitations of creative women in society today, Connor scrolled through his iPad for the picture he'd taken of the syllabus.

Yes, it was only a month into the semester, but he'd lost too much ground. He hadn't been able to pass one lousy quiz, flunked his paper, and now his short essay she'd handed back had tanked. Even with high grades moving forward and a decent curve, he'd be hovering around a precious C-, a bit too close for comfort.

No way was he letting poetry and angry female authors beat him.

Or Ella Blake.

He made a point to read the awful assignments, though he barely kept awake. This last essay called *Death of the Moth* should've been termed Death From Boredom. Woolf was another writer he struggled to understand, and Ella seemed to think she walked on fucking water. Who watched a moth die for what seemed like hours and decided to write about it? And why on earth would anyone assign a paper on such drivel? No wonder he'd flunked.

Men didn't do shit like that.

He'd been trying to get on her good side. He was unfailingly polite and charming before and after class. He complimented her and consistently offered to help out if she needed anything. She only gave him that icy stare that froze his balls and clipped out a "no." He was getting nowhere and now he needed to do something about his grade.

Anything.

He tried to listen to her ramblings on Edith Wharton and how the author used female roles in society to exploit and push readers' emotional limits. She strolled back and forth in a relaxed, steady pace as she spoke, occasionally nibbling on her lower lip in a thought, her face half hidden by the wide, thick frames of her glasses. Today, she wore her usual brown flat boots, a long wool skirt with no shape, and a green turtleneck sweater that reached all the way up to her jaw. Did she have some type of skin infection that kept her hidden beneath so much material? Were there actual breasts under there? Her fingers were long and tapered, but the short, squared-off, unpolished nails did nothing to accentuate them. This was a woman who didn't want a man looking. Or maybe she was just lazy and wasn't into men. Maybe she spent every night reading Wharton and Brontë and lived out fantasies in her head. Hadn't he read something in the news about the power of romantic novels to give women unrealistic expectations of life? Yeah. It had been in the *New York Times*, too. So it must be true.

"Mr. Dunkle?"

Ah, crap. Here we go again.

He showed no fear and smiled warmly. "Yes, Professor Blake?"

"I'm interested to hear your thoughts on the story, *Roman Fever*."

"I liked it."

The class tittered. She never lost her smile. If she wasn't wearing the wrong color lipstick, he may have believed her lips were perfectly bow shaped and lush.

"I'm relieved. What did you think about the ending? Did you feel sympathy for Mrs. Slade when she discovered her friend was unfaithful? Or did it strike you as justice?"

He tried hard not to rub his forehead. A headache threatened. Out of all the damn stories she had to pick to discuss, this was the only one he didn't read. He'd fallen asleep at his computer and decided to skip the reading for today. Now he was in trouble.

He quickly gathered the threads of information the class had given and tried to make a rational theory. "It wasn't justice, but was it deserved? Probably. See, the problem is women are very different than men. They sink to a level of jealousy and cattiness I think is well described in this story."

Satisfaction unfurled. That was a solid answer. She couldn't torture him over his opinion.

Except the strangest expression came over her face.

Her gaze narrowed. Her lips tightened. A tightly contained energy swarmed around her like a nest of bees, humming madly before the attack. In that moment, he realized he had done something very wrong.

"I see. So you believe men don't sink to basic levels of human emotion like women?"

He swallowed. "Kind of. Men are more physical, but they see things simpler. Let's be real here. Two men would never meet in a cafe to talk endlessly for an hour before getting to the point. Women are exhausting. One man would punch the other one, they'd fight it out, and then go get a beer."

The class laughed. Some of the guys nodded in agreement and hooted their approval. Connor began to warm up to the subject. "And another thing. Society is always on the men about cheating, but if you read these pieces you keep assigning us, you'll see there was a lot of infidelity by women. They just like to intellectualize and rationalize the act to death to make it better for them to sleep at night."

Ella Blake never wavered. Pure ice dripped from her voice when she deigned to speak. "Interesting. It seems because Mr. Slade is the male, he is easily forgiven for his infidelity, though he has cheated also. Thank you for proving my point, Mr. Dunkle. Next time, please make sure you actually read the story and not use your classmates' effort to spin your own inane opinion. Class dismissed."

She marched back to her desk.

Connor's head felt as if it had gone a few rounds with the heavyweight champion. Was she kidding? How did she know he didn't read it? And who the hell was she to make fun of his opinion? If he *had* read the story, didn't he have the right to his own viewpoint?

Some of the guys came to clap him on the shoulder as they

exited the classroom. He spent some time gathering his papers and cooling down his temper. He needed his grade fixed or he'd be in some serious trouble by the midterm. It was time to have a bit of a heart-to-heart and pour on the charm. Again.

He tried not to grind his teeth as he approached. She pretended not to see him, but Connor knew she sensed his presence and was deliberately provoking him. An odd anticipation steadily built. He'd misjudged her. She wasn't as dull as he'd originally thought. He rarely dealt with women who challenged him, but he figured it was the teacher/student thing that had him intrigued now.

"Professor Blake?"

She looked up and damned if she didn't give him an almost satisfied grin. "Yes?"

"I need to talk to you about my grade. The paper. I need some help."

"I agree, Mr. Dunkle. Perhaps a tutor?"

Instead of sitting down, she grabbed her purse and seemed to be rushing out. He made sure to step right in front of her, blocking her exit. He gritted his teeth. "I don't need a tutor. I need to know what you're looking for in my papers so I can start passing this class."

"Ah, if you check your syllabus, you'll see I'm looking for creativity, original thought, and specified examples and content backed up from the text."

"I'm trying! Let's be honest for a moment. You don't like my opinions so you're punishing me. You want me to advocate these inane texts by using a lot of fancy words and lingo just so I can agree that women were mentally and emotionally tortured underneath the societal restrictions where men ruled. How is that fair?"

She tilted her head, seemingly considering her words. "Now that's an argument. Too bad there's not more of that in your papers. I have to go. I'm late for a meeting."

She strode out of the classroom, big skirt swishing, hair perfectly contained in the single, tight space of her bun. Connor took off after her, refusing to be swept aside. Not this time. "I did put that in my paper but you gave me an F."

She never broke stride, weaving in and out of the hallways amidst groups of students. "No, you didn't. You said it was about a moth, written from the point of view of a woman frustrated with her life so she decided to spend her extra time watching an insect die. You insinuated she craved a man in her life and therefore, her lack of one made her unhappy. There was no depth. Did you even listen to my lecture in class about the meaning of the essay?"

"Yes." No. He kind of drifted off in a stupor when she began lecturing. He pushed aside the guilt. "You're not being clear enough."

"You're not trying hard enough, Mr. Dunkle. You treat my class like an annoyance and with little respect. I shall treat you the same."

"I need a C- in this class or I won't graduate. I'm doing the best I can. Are you seriously going to flunk me and keep me from my degree over a moth?"

She stopped and whirled around. Her saggy sweater caught air, flew up, then settled. Her index finger jabbed the air. "Have you ever wondered what death would feel like, Mr. Dunkle? Debated life versus death? Analyzed your life to see if it was empty or just or worthwhile?"

His head spun. She was like some mad woman, fierce and way too intense over some...words. Yet, that passion connected within him for a few seconds and hit home. "Yes. Don't we all wonder what we're doing here?" he muttered.

"Good. In the beginning of the essay, the moth was joyous, even trapped between the glass with a limited view of the world. Have you ever felt happy, even when you don't know why?"

"Yes."

"But the author pitied the moth at first. Pitied its existence. The moth is destined to die. What feeling did Woolf try to explain to the reader?"

He tried to shake off his annoyance at getting into a lesson in the middle of a hallway. "The moth doesn't want to die and neither does she."

"Wrong. Yes, no one wants to die but that's not the true point of the essay. There's one guarantee in this life: death. It's part of the contract terms we get. We don't even know how much time we're going to get when we sign this contract. We're here trying to make our mark, then we're gone. Don't you ever consider what the point is?"

His gut lurched. Her slow pecking at his beliefs bothered him. Why think about all this shit when there was no real answer? Why not keep things easy? Look for happiness in the moment? Like the moth...

"Sure."

"Enough with the one word answers. '*Just as life had been strange a few minutes before, so death was not as strange.*' What do you think Woolf was feeling when that last paragraph was written? She watched the moth die in front of her, watched its struggle, watched its failure to win the ultimate battle. What do you think about that, Mr. Dunkle?"

"What do you want me to think?"

She shook her head. "We're done here."

Frustration simmered and seeped out. "The moth fought death up to the last moment. Its struggle was strange and almost beautiful to the author because we all face the same obstacles, yet no matter how bad life sucks, we still have the ability to fight to our last dying breath. Kind of like Dylan said about raging against the dying light."

Surprise flickered across her face. Slowly, she nodded. "Yes. That's what I'm looking for in your papers. You insult both of us by not giving more." Then she continued down the hallway.

Son-of-a-bitch. No, he wasn't in one of those lame movies where the teacher suddenly got the student to see the light and then he transformed his failing grade into an A. It didn't work like that. Connor caught up with her, matching her pace, and heard her deep sigh.

"Do you need something else, Mr. Dunkle?"

"How about an extra credit project? I can't base my graduation on me understanding the next few assignments."

Her snort was quite feminine and intriguing. She pushed open the double glass doors and headed upstairs. "Why should I give you such an opportunity? If you work hard enough, you should be able to pass my class."

"I can't take any chances. Please. This way, I'll know I have some cushion for my grade if I keep struggling."

Annoyance radiated around her. She reached the top of the steps, and turned to say something, but her boot caught on a piece of metal grating and she fell forward.

Connor hurriedly blocked her fall, catching her in his arms and pulling her to the side. Her body was soft and warm, and for one moment, he felt her breasts push against his chest. The clean scent of cucumber and soap drifted up to his nostrils. Low maintenance and simple, like the woman. He took a deeper breath, enjoying the natural fragrance and the way her hands closed around his shoulders for balance.

"You okay?"

Her dark eyes widened. Behind the thick lenses of her glasses, her gaze locked and held his, squeezing him as tight as her nails suddenly digging into his flesh. A bolt of heat struck his dick, and suddenly, he was hard as a rock.

WTH?

"Sorry!" She struggled and he righted her, stepping back. Her skin flushed and she scrambled toward the second level doors. "I'll think about an appropriate project for extra credit."

"Thanks."

She didn't answer, just disappeared behind the glass and got swallowed up by a swarm of students.

Shaking off the whole strange encounter, Connor headed to the library. He'd won this skirmish. With extra credit, he usually had the whole semester to turn it in and his grade would get a nice boost. As for the sudden attraction? It was proof he'd been way too long without a woman. He wasn't attracted in the least to Ella Blake. If he was smart, he'd take this Saturday night, go out with a pretty woman, and slake both of their needs.

He kept the thought firmly in his mind and refused to think of his not hot professor.

Chapter Five

"Better to be without logic than without feeling."—Charlotte Brontë

A few hours later, Ella was still replaying their encounter.

She muttered under her breath and hurried through the parking lot, ducking her head against the brisk wind tearing through the trees. She'd had students who were egotistical and arrogant. But Connor Dunkle was a whole new breed. How dare he challenge her in class? His ridiculous views on women were archaic. Lord help his wife or girlfriend. She would've taught him a few hard-learned lessons about respect. Then he dared to ask for extra credit?

The worst part was her traitorous body. When she fell into his arms, her stomach got all floaty, and her blood ran hotter in her veins. She was attracted to an idiot. Why wasn't she surprised? Her track record sucked.

Rain dripped down the back of her neck and she shivered. Spring felt a lifetime away. Of course, she'd forgotten her damn umbrella again. She had four in her trunk and never seemed to use any of them.

The well-lit parking lot cut through the dark and fog, leading to her white Honda Civic. She hit the button, slid into the seat, and turned the key.

Nothing.

Dread trickled through her. Oh, no. Please work. Please work. Please...

Keeping up her mantra, she tried the car again. And again.

It was dead.

Ella glanced at her watch. She was already running late and hated leaving Luke alone for too long. Her brain calculated through the possibilities. Triple A? No, she'd decided it was an easy expense to cut. She couldn't look under the hood because she had no idea what she'd be looking for. Frustration coiled and she pounded her fist on the steering wheel. The word hovered on her lips until she finally spit it out with passion.

"Fuck!"

God, she loved that word. Saying it was her secret vice. Even the guttural, nasty sound of it on her tongue eased some of her tension.

A hard rap on the window caused her to shriek. A huge, muscled figure towered over her car. Peering out in the dark, she lowered her window a few inches.

"You need some help?"

Ella almost closed her eyes in defeat. Connor Dunkle. Of course, he'd show up trying to be her knight in shining armor. He'd probably ask her for a few extra points on the next quiz as payment.

She refused to think of other, more interesting, forms of payment.

"My car won't start. I'll call a tow company. Thanks anyway."

A frown creased his brows. "Pop the hood. Let me take a quick look." She pressed her lips together, considering. "Professor Blake? I'm getting wet out here."

She let out an irritated breath at her hesitation. "Sorry." She was glad the dark hid her hot cheeks. Releasing the latch, he disappeared behind the hood while the rain gained fury and flung drops like a toddler in the throes of a tantrum. Finally, he returned, his thick hair wetly plastered to his head.

"It's the battery. I have jumper cables in my truck. Hang tight."

"Wait! I have an umbrella."

His smile was lopsided and full of wry humor. "Don't need it. I work construction, I'm used to bad weather."

"But—"

He'd already disappeared into the dark. A pair of headlights swung toward her as he angled his truck a few inches away from her car. She watched while he set up the cables, seemingly unaffected by the weather, and motioned for her to start the car.

The engine caught.

Relief cut through her. He gave her a thumbs-up and walked back to the window. "Keep it running a bit before you start to drive. Where are you headed?"

"Home."

Again, that grin appeared. Her heart did a slow flip-flop at the flash of strong, white teeth. Why did he have to be so damn attractive? So...viral? "I know. How long is the drive?"

"About half an hour."

"I'll follow you."

She shook her head. "That's unnecessary. I'll be fine. Thanks so much for your help."

"I'm following you," he said. "If you want to call your husband or boyfriend and let him know, that's cool. I'm not a killer or anything."

A garbled laugh escaped her lips. "I'm not worried about that. I've already felt helpless enough watching you start my car in the rain. I can get home by myself."

"It's still raining and you're keeping me here arguing. What if the battery dies again? I'll worry until I know you're safe at home. Wait for me."

His command struck her mute. She wasn't used to men wanting to do stuff for her. She'd been on her own long enough to make her own rules and was never questioned. Instead of feeling lonely and bitching about it, Ella had embraced the independence and began to like running her life. This was the first time she'd been overruled.

He was worried about her. It was kind of nice in an old-fashioned type of way.

Connor unhooked the cables and got back into his car. She hit her lights, cranked the heat to maximum, and slowly pulled out of the lot.

The commute home was slow. Cautious drivers took their time and traffic built up, but the headlights behind her stayed steady, giving her a strange type of comfort. She called Luke on her Bluetooth and told him about the delay, and he agreed to start on his homework. Finally, she pulled onto her block by her building and cut the engine. Her escort parked right behind her.

Grabbing her purse, she darted out of the car to quickly thank him, but he was already climbing out. The rain had finally slowed to a lazy drizzle.

"Thanks again for the help. I'm really sorry I took you so far from home."

He stared at her building and shook his head. "You didn't. In fact, I'm already here."

"Huh?"

His gaze narrowed and those stinging blue eyes caught and held hers. The scent of rain and the subtle spice of his cologne rose to her nostrils. His next words seemed to be a premonition of everything in the future that was about to change.

"I'm your neighbor."

"Wh-what? I haven't seen you around here. I don't even recognize your truck."

"My apartment comes with a driveway so I park over there." He jerked his head toward the back of the lot. "I think I saw your son. About nine years old? Glasses?"

Shock delayed her response. Out of all the people in the world, Connor Dunkle was her neighbor. The air shimmered around her, and the rain turned to a misty, glowing aura. She smothered the emotions running through her, screaming out she never believed in coincidence and there was a bigger reason for such a discovery. "Yes, Luke. He's ten. I-I had no idea. He didn't mention running in to anyone."

"I interrupted an encounter with some boys. He got pissed at me. Do you want me to introduce myself to your husband? I don't want him thinking I'm some stalker."

"No need. I'm divorced. What boys?"

"A group from the neighborhood. I'll keep an eye out. They get in to some trouble, but Luke seems to be able to handle himself."

She needed to talk to her son. Tell him to keep his distance from troublemakers. God, this is when she missed having his father around. "I better go. Thanks again."

"Ella?"

She stilled. It was the first time he used her first name, and it sounded oddly intimate spilling from his lips. "Yes?"

"If you need anything, just let me know."

She muttered another thank you and hurried away. She didn't want to think of Connor in any other way than a pain-in-the-butt student. Having him right next door and conversing with her son shifted the balance. She really knew nothing about him on a personal basis. Until she did, Ella better warn her son to keep his distance.

Damp, tired, and cranky, she pushed her way inside.

* * * *

Ella Blake was his neighbor.

Connor chewed over this fact for a while before deciding it could be a good thing. Hell, if he helped her out a bit, maybe she'd soften and give him a better grade. Being a single mother was tough. After his mother took off and his father checked out, taking care of Nate sapped all his effort and energy. It made more sense why she didn't take more care with her appearance. Men were probably the last thing on her mind. Still, if she ever wanted to find another relationship, she'd need some extra help.

He let himself into his apartment and wondered what it would be like to be with someone more than a few nights. Nate seemed happy, but then again, he'd always seemed to want a woman on a permanent basis. Connor was content experiencing the whole buffet, and not once had he wanted more. Was there something lacking in him? And if so, maybe it was for the best. If he was built like his mother, he may end up running out on responsibilities, and he'd rather die than hurt someone like that.

Of course, lately he'd give a monk competition. It had been so long since he'd had sex, his condoms probably had cobwebs on them.

Shaking his head at his own personal humor, he reheated some leftover pizza, opened up his laptop, and concentrated on work. He'd only been at it about an hour when his phone rang. He glanced at the ID and hesitated. Then picked it up.

"Hey, Jerry. What's up?"

The slight slur of words told him his best friend was on his way to feeling really good. "Connor, my man! Where the hell you been? Fancy college boy now and can't come out and have a few beers?"

A flare of guilt hit. When was the last time he'd seen him? Weeks. They'd been really tight working construction for a number of years and had each other's backs. Until Connor had begun wanting more. More than getting drunk every weekend. More than seducing some new woman into bed. More than blaming management for all their trouble on sites and pretending they were better than anyone else because they got their hands dirty.

The fun had begun to turn bitter. Especially when he'd made the decision to get his degree and apply for a management position.

Connor forced a laugh. "I've missed you, dude. Been dying to get out and share a pint, but I'm slammed with schoolwork."

"Didn't think you'd try and become one of them. What happened to you, man? Those books get to your brain and make you think you're something you're not?"

The words cut deep, but he kept his tone easy. "Nah, I just got a few more months and this will all be behind me. Keep my chair warm, okay?"

"Fuck the classes, man. Come and have a drink with me. There's a pretty young blonde serving me that's dying to meet you."

Half of him wanted to go. It would be so easy because it was the routine he'd followed for the majority of his life. He'd get a good buzz, bed the blonde, and be happy for a few hours.

The problem was the next morning when reality hit. When the blonde left and he had a sick stomach, lighter pockets, and the faint tang of failure in his gut. Not this time. Not anymore.

"I'll catch you next time, dude."

Jerry cursed. Then hung up.

Connor clicked off and rubbed his forehead. He felt like a traitor. Jerry and him went way back, and his friend was old school. He believed in working hard on the site and partying harder when he was done. Unfortunately, times were changing and management wanted more from their crew as things became more technological and architecturally modern. They wanted team members to grow with them, not just show up to put in time.

Connor wanted one thing: secure the lead foreman job for Bilkins Construction. He'd been lucky enough to be included on the subcontractor team for the huge project with Tappan Zee Construction, which was building the new bridge over the Hudson River, but he needed more. It was the only reason he'd spent the last two years breaking his ass to stuff four years of school into two and still make an impression at the firm. Bilkins only hired college graduates for upper management. Connor was determined to transform himself into a businessman who could straddle both worlds—the one on a working site and the one behind a fancy desk.

Finally, his efforts were working. The higher-ups noticed him and respected his work ethic and his leadership role with the crew. He'd changed his life radically to become the man he'd always wanted to be but never thought he'd deserve.

Was he betraying his friend by wanting more out of his life? An emptiness clawed up from deep within him he'd never experienced before. He wasn't sure how to feed it, so he concentrated on the only thing he could control right now.

Graduate. Get a promotion. Make more of a difference. Then maybe, the hunger would go away.

He sat at his desk for a while, then got back to work.

Chapter Six

"I don't know if I should care for a man who made life easy; I should want someone who made it interesting."—Edith Wharton

"Mom? I'm bored."

Ella slipped off her glasses and rubbed her tired eyes. Glancing at the clock, she noted it was already past five p.m., and darkness had slipped over to blanket her most precious Saturday. Not that she'd done anything great. Food shopping, cleaning, a few rounds of the Wii with her son, and then grading papers.

Now, Luke stood in front of her desk with puppy dog eyes and a young boy's leashed excess energy. Winter sucked. Sports were nonexistent, the holidays were over, and he was already bored with his new video games and stuff from Christmas. She kept waiting for him to invite some friends over, but he hadn't seemed to make any connections yet. A few times, she spotted a small bunch of boys out front talking to Luke while he waited for the bus. She didn't want to ruin anything by being his pushy, overbearing mother, so Ella kept quiet and hoped he'd make his own way.

She gave him a smile and ticked down the list of available items to entertain a ten-year-old. "Wanna see what's playing at the movies?"

"Nah. They just have lame stuff for kids."

"You are a kid," she teased. Her fingers itched to ruffle his cowlick but he was becoming a bit more standoffish with her treating him like a baby. "You too old now for Disney?"

He rolled his eyes. "Can we go to GameStop?"

She raised a brow. He gave a defeated sigh.

"Wanna bake cookies? I have some leftover holiday

ingredients. You can try to bake the biggest cookie in the world."

He seemed to consider the option, though it was obvious he wondered if it was too babyish. She upped the ante. "Then we can walk to the Chinese restaurant and get soup and eggrolls. We'll eat backward. Dessert first, then dinner."

"You still have the sprinkles and green M&M's?"

"I do. But you better be prepared. I'm going to win the cookie challenge. We each get a tray and no peeking until we're done. Deal?"

"Deal!"

She cleaned up her work and headed to the kitchen. Though their apartment wasn't huge with a big yard and fancy furniture, Ella had made it home. Using her knack for brightening up rooms with accessories and a fresh coat of paint, the two bedrooms were cozy and peaceful. The kitchen was big enough so she purchased a mobile island and topped it with mesh baskets full of bright fruit and dried herbs. Pictures crowded the walls with her favorite sayings from poets, and she'd upgraded the low utility light to a pretty Tuscan chandelier that brought pop to the room. The farm table and benches were set by the big window to get the most light. Hand towels beautifully stitched hung by the stove and dishwasher.

She tuned to one of her playlists on her iPhone and cranked the volume. Queen ground out *Another One Bites the Dust* and she slipped out two cookie sheets while Luke pulled all the ingredients out of the cupboards. They belted out the lyrics in perfect tune and began kneading dough into cool shapes in an attempt to dazzle the other.

Contentment flowed through her veins as she relaxed into her typical Saturday night. She pushed back her hair with sticky fingers and rainbow sprinkles flew up in the air, getting stuck in her sweater.

The lights went out.

Everything ground to a stop except the music, which kept blaring loud. She reached over and turned off the music, switching quickly to the flashlight app.

"Mom?"

"Don't panic, sweetheart. Probably just a brownout or

something. Let me get some extra flashlights just in case."

"This is kind of creepy."

She felt around in the dark for her famous junk drawer that contained so many weird parts she probably could've built a nuclear bomb. "It's a nighttime adventure. Remember when I used to take you on those walks when you were little?"

"The moon had to be full, you always said. Even though I worried about werewolves."

"I told you they don't exist."

"But you're afraid of vampires."

"Well, I think they *do* exist. That's why I keep tons of garlic around at all times. I read *Dracula* three times, you know."

That got her son to laugh, and Ella finally found another flashlight. She was just going to brave going into the basement to check the circuit breaker when the doorbell rang.

Her heart pounded. She didn't know anyone to drop by on them, and she'd heard of strange things happening during brownouts. Swallowing, she eased over to the window and peeked through.

Connor Dunkle stood on her doorstep.

With a rush of relief, she flung open the door and held back a gasp.

My God, he looked good.

Struck mute for a moment, she gave in to impulse and hungrily took him in. Dressed in a button down navy blue shirt that clung to his broad chest, a casual jacket, and dark-washed jeans, he simmered with delicious masculine testosterone. Usually a hint of stubble clung to his square jaw, but tonight he was clean-shaven and smelled of spicy cloves. His thick dirty blond hair fell in waves over his forehead, brushing his ears, and those sea blue eyes framed with thick lashes struck her mute for a few seconds. He towered over her in a mass of rock-hard muscle, giving her the impression of both strength and protectiveness.

He was a walking, talking specimen of everything a woman dreams of in a man. Both Hemsworth brothers mixed with Daniel Craig and a sprinkle of old-fashioned Redford. Her poor body roared into overdrive and she felt a damp rush of moisture between her thighs.

God, she was acting like a sex-starved teen. So. Embarrassing.

Finally, he spoke. Even his damn voice was gravel and satin mixed together in a symphony to the ears. "I saw your lights went out. Looks like some of the other houses on the block are affected. You okay?"

He was checking on her? To be nice or to get her to agree to extra credit? "Yes, we're fine. Thank you."

"Did you flip the breaker? Sometimes these apartments get overloaded and you need to reset it. That's what I had to do with mine."

"I haven't gone down to the basement yet."

"I'll help you out."

"Oh, you don't have to."

His gaze sharpened on her face, and his jaw clenched. Fascinated, she studied his features, noticing the air of irritation that briefly shone. "I want to, Ella. I won't stay. I just don't like the idea of you and Luke alone in the dark."

She flushed and stumbled back. "I didn't mean to be rude. I'm just used to doing things for myself. I'm sorry, come in."

He walked inside and she realized it was a mistake.

In her home, he owned the small space, filling the air with a masculine presence she wanted to sink in and savor. It had been so long since she had a man close. Even though he was only here to check her electricity. Oh, my God, she was so pathetic. He glanced around in the dark and took out his own phone, turning on the flashlight app.

Luke came out of the kitchen, highlighted in the sudden glare of light. "Mom? What's going on?"

"It's Connor Dunkle from next door," he said. "How's it going, Luke?"

Her son's voice hardened. "Fine."

"Good. I'm going to check the basement and see if I can get those lights on. Is that okay?"

Connor didn't move, as if waiting for permission from her son as the man in the house. Luke seemed to consider his words, standing up straighter in the beam of light. "Yeah, that's okay." He paused. "Can I help?"

"Absolutely. I could use a hand. Basement here?" He

motioned down the hall toward the door on the left. Ella nodded. "Same as mine. We'll yell if we need you."

They disappeared downstairs, and she tried to re-gather her composure. Why was she nervous? So silly. He was just being a friendly neighbor and helping out a single mom. Clatters rang in the air. Probably moving all the storage stuff to get to the panel. She really needed to organize better down there. Ella waited, keeping her light trained down the hall, and suddenly the electricity flickered back on.

She heard Luke's whoop and smiled. She forgot the simple things that gave children pride. He really didn't have the advantage of tinkering with tools or cars or talking sports, though she tried to keep her knowledge up to date and be both mom and dad.

They both reappeared with pleased expressions. Connor was talking to her son. "Next time, check the breaker first. Now you know which one since we tagged it."

"Got it," Luke said seriously.

"Hey, you guys were making cookies? Looks like fun."

She glanced at the mess in the kitchen and wrapped her arms across her chest. "We know how to rock a Saturday night. Thanks for helping out."

"No problem. Oh, man, I love M&M's!" His face lit up like a kid, and Ella laughed. "Can I have one?"

"You can't eat just one," Luke said. "Here." He gave him a handful. "I like the greens."

"Blue is better."

"They taste the same," Ella pointed out.

They both stared at her in disbelief. Connor rolled his eyes. "Women."

Luke grinned. "Mom, I need to check my DS. I had it charging and I don't want to lose my stuff."

"Sure, go ahead."

He bounded up the stairs, leaving them alone in a messy kitchen. Ella looked at Connor's perfect appearance and tried not to wince at the thought of her image. Dough in her hair, mismatched socks on her feet, and yoga pants. "Umm, thanks again," she offered.

"No problem. Been a long time since someone baked me

cookies. Sounds like a perfect night."

She looked at him with suspicion. Was he making fun of her? "They're easy now. Precut dough, one sheet, and an oven. Not too mysterious anymore."

Ella caught a flash of pain reflected in those gorgeous eyes before it was quickly masked. "Moms bake them the best. If I was Luke, I'd be pretty happy right now. You're a good mom."

Pleasure ran through her but she fought it off. "How do you know?"

He shrugged. "Just do."

"Thanks. You look nice. Going somewhere fun?"

"Got a date."

"Oh, that's nice." Why did she keep saying the word nice? And why were her palms suddenly sweating and her heart beating fast? She was in her own house, for goodness sakes. "I'm sure you'll have a good time."

"Yeah. Rather be here, though. Bake some cookies, hang out and watch a movie."

She laughed then. "If you had my life, that would be your routine every weekend. Somehow, I think yours is more glamorous."

That assessing gaze swung back to her, taking in her disheveled appearance. She fought a blush, refusing to apologize for being real in her own place. "Have you dated since you split up with Luke's father?"

He seemed surprised by his direct question. She was even more surprised when she answered. "No. It's hard. I wanted to make sure Luke was ready, and then I just got too busy. I wouldn't leave him alone at night anyway."

"I'd watch him for you."

She jerked back. Blinked. "You'd watch Luke for me while I went on a date?"

"Sure. We're neighbors. He seems like an easy kid. I know it must be hard, so I'd do you a favor."

It all came clear then. Her lips pursed in disapproval. "Oh, I get it. A favor for a favor, huh? I give you an extra credit assignment or a grade boost and you watch my son?"

She expected guilt or denial, but pure disgust flicked out at her in waves. "That's a crappy thing to say. Why are you so damn prickly all the time? I'm just trying to be nice."

"But you want me to give you an extra credit assignment?" she pushed.

He threw up his hands. "Hell, yes! I want to pass your class. But I'm not doing nice stuff for you just to get a better grade." He raked his fingers through his hair and she watched the strands settle right back in perfect disarray. "I may have thought that before, okay? But I swear it has nothing to do with your class. It's separate. We're neighbors, I respect you, and the offer stands."

Warmth flooded through her. He was honest. He seemed nice to her son. And even if he was screwing up with her class, he was open to do the work necessary to pass and graduate.

She had the perfect project for him.

Ella nodded. "Fair enough. I'll send you the details of the project in your e-mail on Monday."

"Really?" He stared at her with suspicion. "You're not setting me up or something, are you?"

She smiled. "No. To keep it fair, I'll offer it up to anyone else in the class who wants to bring up their grade."

He studied her face for a while. "It's going to be bad, isn't it?"

"Let's just say you'll learn a lot."

"God help me," he muttered. "But I won't look a gift horse in the mouth."

She winced. "If you want to boost your grade, stop using clichés in speech and written language. It's unnecessary."

"Yes, ma'am."

She shook her head at his mocking tone, walked to the door, and opened it. He yelled good-bye to Luke and she stepped out with him to study the block. "Looks like everyone is back on. Thanks again for—"

"Connor!"

She turned her head. A gorgeous redhead strolled down the street, her three-inch Michael Kors boots clicking on the pavement. She was wearing one of those trendy hats that made Ella look ridiculous, along with clinging leather pants, a leather jacket, and some sparkly T-shirt. Connor raised his hand in the air.

"Hi, darlin'! Be right there."

The model nodded agreeably, crossed her ankles with easy grace, and waited like a trained dog.

Connor smiled. "Sorry. That's my date."

Ella blinked. Together, they'd look more dazzling than any Ken and Barbie couple on the planet. "You didn't pick her up?"

"No. She wanted to pick me up."

Of course she did. Ella looked back and forth between them. Irritation scraped her nerve endings. "And you let her? Don't you think that's rude?"

He shrugged. "No, women like to be independent."

"She's waiting for you outside, in the cold, like a trained seal? You think that's independent?"

"Sure. I let her pick the restaurant, too."

"Is she also going to pay the bill?" Ella asked sarcastically.

Connor looked affronted. "I always pay. Look, women like to call the shots. Give them attention and some compliments and they thrive. It's simple. Not rocket science."

"Do you always date beautiful women?" she asked slowly.

"Sure. We both get what we need, and things are kept...simple."

Coldness washed over her, erasing the slight glow from seconds before. Connor Dunkle was an ass. He treated women like playthings, concentrating on the surface, rarely taking time to dive underneath. The quick pang of hurt surprised her, but she buried it and got real. Yes, he was a sexually attractive man that sent her hormones on a roller coaster ride, but he was immature, and there had never been a question of anything more between them then professor/student or neighbor to neighbor.

"Understood." She separated herself by backing into her warm, safe house, alone with her son. "Have fun."

After she shut the door, Ella couldn't help but peeking out the window. The leggy female walked toward him, pressing a kiss to his lips, laughing at something he said. They both climbed into a low-slung red sports car like the fabulous couple they were and tore off into the night for their glamorous date.

Depression threatened but she fought it back. She absolutely refused to let herself feel bad that she wasn't out on the town, pretending to be someone she wasn't with a man who couldn't care less.

She raised her voice to call her son and concentrated on cookies.

Chapter Seven

"A divorce is like an amputation: you survive it, but there's less of you."—Margaret Atwood

Connor hated Valentine's Day.

It was the only holiday structured toward the demise of men.

He muttered under his breath, pulling on his winter jacket. In the middle of the darkest month of the year, society created it for commercial reasons only. They got to jack up the price of flowers, chocolate, and dinner bills in the name of love. A complete breeding ground of discontent for women not getting what they wanted, while the poor bastards they were with scratched their head in confusion.

Another great reason not to have a relationship.

Or maybe he was just in a bad mood because he still hadn't gotten laid.

Why hadn't he slept with Tracey? The date had been perfect. Dinner, cocktails, flirting. Her offer to join him wasn't wrapped up in heavy analysis or layers of meaning. Yet, as he opened his mouth to answer, "Hell, yes!" he told her it wasn't a good night but he'd call.

His date had ended with him and his hand. Not the image he'd pictured.

Something was wrong with him. Tracey was gorgeous, and had proved to be a good lover in the past. He had a little black book that bulged with numbers and he still wasn't using it to call anyone. Maybe his overworked mental state was affecting his drive for sex? Usually, he looked at a pair of perfect boobs and was ready to go. Lately, he got lukewarm.

Except when he was around Ella. A woman he was

completely not attracted to, yet his body responded to like a switch had been flicked. A woman who barely allowed an inch of naked skin to show. That was plain scary.

He remembered what she looked like when she opened the door. A total mess. Yet, instead of focusing on the cookies in her hair or her misshapen sweater, he'd noticed her lack of glasses and hypnotic eyes. He'd noticed the scent of sugar and candy, and her pretty bare feet with pink toenails. He'd noticed the tumble of luscious dark waves that spilled over her shoulders. He'd noticed the clinging Lycra emphasizing her lean calves.

He was nuts. Around the bend. Loco. All the clichés Ella hated.

He grabbed his gloves and tried not to think of her. Since that night, she'd sent over the extra credit project, and Connor had wondered if it was worth it. It was as bad as he imagined.

Woolf. Brontë. Austen. Not separate, but all together in one big mishmash of readings and a big fat paper due at the end of the semester. She was punishing him, and he knew it. He dipped a toe in the water—another damn cliché—and began perusing *A Room of One's Own* by Woolf and was stopped cold.

Yep, more feminist fiction. More whining and "poor me, we're under men's control and we hate it" philosophy. But damned if he wasn't going to kick ass on this assignment and graduate. Even if it killed him.

Which it might. From boredom.

The air was brutally cold, warning of the storm about to roll in. Time to get the plow ready. He had a solid list of clients to make some extra money in the winter, but he'd be extra busy the next two months trying to handle the workload. He checked his watch. He was later than normal, especially if he wanted to stop for coffee on the way to Verily College. He headed out the door and heard a shout. Looking toward the driveway, he watched a bunch of boys scramble away from his truck and race down the street, whooping in loud, excited shouts of victory.

Connor ran to his truck, a curse blistering past his lips. Little shits had slashed one of his tires. The right passenger was totally flat, a jagged slice ripped through the rubber.

Hell, no. They weren't getting away with this.

He took off after them. His long legs made up time from their shorter strides. He caught a flash of red up ahead, then something flew through the air and dropped on the ground. Darting around corners, they picked up the pace, and age finally triumphed. By the time Connor got a few blocks down, they'd disappeared, their voices fading in the sharp, cold air.

Sons of bitches.

He knew it was the gang that had picked on Luke. He'd need to get some security cameras installed or set up a watch. Probably was retaliation for the DS incident. Catching his breath, he walked back, mad at himself for not pushing faster, and noticed a black object on the pavement.

He picked it up and turned it over in his gloved hands.

Glasses. Black rimmed glasses like Harry Potter.

Ah, crap. Was Ella's son now involved with their gang? He seemed like a good kid, but maybe he'd gone the other route. Join the bullies rather than be picked on. He didn't blame him. Sometimes, it felt like the easy way out, but no way was he getting away with this. Ella needed to know.

Connor headed back and inspected the damage on the tire. He had a spare, but these suckers were expensive. Pushing away his irritation, he walked next door and rang the bell.

Her face reflected the same irritation he felt. He figured she'd be friendlier after his visit, but in a way, she'd grown even colder. Her dark hair was twisted tightly back in a severe braid. Today she wore baggy tweed trousers, black waterproof boots that looked squishy soft, and a black turtleneck. The only color was her lips, which thankfully were bare from her usual orange garish color. "Hi. Is something wrong? I'm running late."

Her politeness rubbed his nerves. Even as his professor and next-door neighbor, she treated him with icy politeness. Hadn't he offered to babysit and help out? Hadn't he proved he wasn't a jerk? "I think your son vandalized my car."

She jerked back. Her mouth made a little O before her brow snapped into a frown. "That's impossible. Luke would never do anything like that. What happened?"

"My tire was slashed by the gang of boys who likes to hang out around here. I think I saw Luke running away with them."

She blew out a breath. "Trust me, you're mistaken. He still doesn't have many friends, and he's a good boy. He would never hurt someone or their property."

He lifted the evidence. "Are these his glasses?"

Ella blinked, then slowly reached out to take them. "Oh, my God. Where did you find these?"

"Scene of the crime. They were running from me and one kid dropped this. Does he wear a red jacket?"

"Yes. But-but this is impossible. Luke doesn't do things like this, I swear to you. They slashed your tire?"

He nodded. Regret flowed through him. He knew kids did bad things sometimes, it was part of life, but he had a gut feeling Luke could go down a wrong turn. His parents were divorced and he'd moved to a new school. Ella had said his dad wasn't around a lot. That was a lot of shit to deal with. "He's probably acting out. Who knows what happened. Do you want me to talk to him?"

She shook her head, dark eyes filled with grief. His heart squeezed in sympathy. "I don't know. Maybe I should handle it? I'm so sorry about this. I can call the school right now and find out what's going on."

"No, don't. Let him finish out the day and feel guilty. It's the best punishment for a kid like Luke. If it's okay, I'd like to offer him a deal to work off the tire."

"I'll pay for the damage, Connor. I feel terrible—this has never happened before."

He shifted his feet. How involved should he get with this? He didn't want to pretend he knew what she should do, but he knew Luke's behavior needed a strong hand. "I'm not worried about the tire, Ella. I've been through this stuff before. I'm not trying to tell you how to be a mom, but I had issues like this raising my brother. I'd like to tell Luke he needs to pay off the tire by working for me. It shouldn't be your responsibility, and if you pay for him, he'll figure he won."

She tilted her head in interest. "What type of work?"

"I do snow plowing with my truck in the local area. Have a list of clients. I usually shovel out their pathways manually. Luke could do that for me."

Ella nodded slowly. "Sounds fair."

"I also have some projects I'm working on in between work and school. Building my brother a shed up in Verily when the snow stops. He can help and I can teach him some stuff."

Those brown eyes narrowed as she studied him. Once again, the golden swirls around her irises intrigued him, as if trying to tell him there was something deeper about Ella Blake if he only one took the time to look.

Not that he had the time or interest.

"You have a very busy schedule," she finally said.

"I told you that in class when you agreed to give me extra time for my paper."

Surprisingly, her lips twitched in a smile. "You did. But I never agreed to more time."

"Right. That was me being an ass."

This time, she laughed. "You're learning." Curiosity lit her gaze. "You had to raise your younger brother? Did something happen to your parents?"

He always avoided talking about his past. Other than his brother, he wasn't one to share emotions or delve into painful history. But he found himself telling her anyway. "My mom took off when Nate was about ten. Dad pretty much fell apart in a drunken stupor, so there was no one around. We didn't have any other family. I just took over."

Ella stared at him for a long while. "He was Luke's age? How old were you?"

He shrugged. "Fourteen. I was able to handle it." He couldn't help the proud grin that escaped. "Nate's a genius. He worked for NASA and now he's employed by a private company working on space travel."

"He got through college with a scholarship?"

"Half of it."

"Did loans pay for the other half?"

"Nah, I didn't want him in debt. I worked a few jobs and saved so he had most of it paid."

"You worked a few jobs when you were a teenager? And paid for your brother's college on your own?"

He shifted uncomfortably. "Yeah. Honestly, it wasn't a big deal. I was working steady by sixteen. Dad had the mortgage and main bills paid at least, even though we rarely saw him. I'd never been great in school anyway, and Nate is gifted. He got the brains in the family. It made sense for him to go."

"I see," she said softly. Why was she looking at him funny? As if she was seeing him for the first time? "But you're in college now."

"I'm going for management. The company I work for won't promote anyone who doesn't have a degree."

"You decided on Verily. That's a hard school to get in to."

"They offered me credits for life experience and my current work, so I was able to chop some time off. I got lucky, too. Scored high enough on the college entry exams."

"Did you go the full four years?"

He wondered at the odd inquisition but kept answering. "Nah, I stuffed four years into two."

"Other than my class, what's your GPA?"

"3.9."

"But your brother is the one with the brains, huh?"

Her gaze stripped away the lies and got to the truth. No wonder she was a good teacher and an awesome mom. No one could hide under a stare like that, whether he wanted to or not. He'd never talked about himself this much before. Hell, the whole evening with Tracey they'd flirted, talked pop culture, and discussed her acting career. Nothing about him. Yet, here he was, spilling his guts while he stood in his neighbor's doorway.

Suddenly uneasy by everything she seemed to see, he cleared his throat, trying to get back his footing. Another cliché. Why was he noticing every simplified thought when it had never bothered him before?

He gave her a smile and fell back into his usual female mode. "Hope I didn't ruin your Valentine's Day. I know it's an important day to women."

She shuddered. "I despise Valentine's Day. I think it was created to completely torture the male species and force women to feel bad about themselves if they're not in a picture-perfect, sugar-coated, commercially driven relationship."

He lifted his brow. Who would've thought they'd actually agree on one thing? The standard words fell from his lips without thought. "I'm sure there's a line of men who are waiting to take you out tonight. You're pretty as a picture. You just have to get out there. My offer to babysit still stands."

He waited for her to blush or smile, but instead she glared. "That's the stupidest line I've ever heard in my life. We both know there's no line. I'm not pretty. And you're using those ridiculous clichés again that I hate. Why do you have to cheapen a genuine conversation with such drivel?"

His mouth fell open. "I was only trying to give you a compliment. Make you feel better about Valentine's Day."

"No, you weren't. You were trying to make yourself feel better by believing inane lines spoken to women actually make them feel good. You were being lazy because God forbid, you take the time to actually find out who someone really is. Your so-called compliments insult both of us. Don't you ever get real, Connor Dunkle?"

Shock poured through his system. How had this happened? Her son vandalized his car and suddenly she was insulting *him*? He dealt with reality every single damn day. "Hey, I'm the one being attacked for being nice. Ever consider that your adversarial ways are blocking you from getting a date?"

"I'm not looking for a pretty face to date. I'm looking for someone who's not afraid to get messy and see the pearl buried under the dirty, closed-mouthed oyster. Have you ever done something for a woman without waiting for a pat on the back? Or given a compliment on anything other than her appearance?"

"I respect a woman's brain. It's not my fault your entire gender is so obsessed with their appearance, body, and age. Women crave approval and reassurances that they're beautiful. Don't get mad at me just because I give you what you really want."

She shook her head in disgust. "Bull. You don't bother to dig deeper because you choose not to. You don't know how to relate to creative women who aren't afraid to get ugly and tell the truth. It's easier to see the surface image, isn't it? Like your date," she added with a slightly bitter tone.

Temper hit him. How dare she question his intentions? She knew nothing about him. With a low growl, he leaned forward and challenged her back. "Oh, yeah? You think you haven't judged me by my appearance? By my job or my apartment? I work construction, Ella. I have blistered, raw hands, crazy shifts, and don't own a suit. I'm thirty-eight years old without a college degree. I don't live in a fancy house and I'm not a fancy guy. Who's not being real by saying you never judged me by my appearance?"

The breath gushed out of her lungs and she took a step back. Silence descended as the angry words hung in the air between them. He shook his head in disgust. There was no reason to get upset by the truth. Women saw him as an attractive guy to have sex with but not marry. They ogled his body, not his brains. Most women he dated had no interest in a real conversation unless it was a segue to bed. Nate was the marrying kind. Stable, financially secure, wicked smart.

Not Connor.

"Forget it. This whole thing is ridiculous. I gotta go. I'll check in with you later about Luke. Happy Valentine's Day."

He stomped off without another word and refused to look back. But her words lingered in his mind for a long, long time.

* * * *

Valentine's Day was officially her nemesis.

From the moment Connor knocked on her door, things had drifted into a steep decline. Her son had committed vandalism. A crime. It was completely opposite who he was as a person and how she raised him. Her stomach curled with nausea until she wanted to just drive to the school and confront him. But she agreed having some time to deal with his guilt—hoping he had some—would be a good lesson. After all, she'd seen it a zillion times portrayed in *The Brady Bunch.*

School was a fog of battling concentration between the ridiculous hormones of college students on a national holiday for love. No one seemed interested in her lessons, preferring to talk about plans for the evening or showing off presents received from companions. The break room and cafeteria were cluttered with ridiculous stuffed animals that had no purpose, too much candy, and balloons formed in the shape of hearts. Her coworkers were just as guilty as the students. She'd caught Bernard, the history professor, trudging down the hall with two-dozen roses in his grip and a silly grin on his lips.

Awful. Just...awful.

Late morning, she looked frantically for her glasses and ended up finding them when she sat down and heard a solid crunch. When she pulled them from under her lap, the broken frame dangled limp between her fingers.

The word vibrated beneath her chest, dying to escape, but still Ella fought it back. Cursing was not a solution to the problem. The day had to end sometime, and then it would be over for a whole year.

By the time she got in her car to drive home, the roads were slippery from the snow beginning to fall. She tried to distract herself with music, but Frank Sinatra crooned on too many stations. When she punched the buttons, sappy love songs filled the speakers.

She clicked it off and drove through the snow in silence, squinting. Dammit. Her spare set of glasses was at home.

An hour later than usual, hands trembling from the slick roads and tension of not being able to properly see, Ella pulled to the curb and cut the engine. She mentally rehearsed the speech she'd been practicing for Luke. Grabbing her briefcase and purse, she tiredly pushed through the door.

And blinked.

"What's going on?"

Connor and Luke sat on the couch. Two mugs lay on the coffee table. They looked like they had been in deep conversation, and when they heard her voice, both jumped to their feet, looking almost guilty. "Sorry, we didn't hear you come in," Connor said. "How are the roads?"

"Terrible. What are you doing here?" she asked.

Connor looked down at Luke and something passed between them. Connor gave a slight nod, and her son stepped forward.

"Mom, I'm sorry. I screwed up bad."

Her heart pounded. At least he was going to confess. His beautiful dark eyes looked sad behind his glasses, and his shoulders slumped in defeat. Swallowing back the need to go comfort him, Ella dropped her bags and sat down on the leather recliner facing him. "Go ahead."

He took a shaky breath. "I slashed Connor's tire. With a group of boys from the neighborhood. I didn't want to, but I—I got mad. I got tired of being on the outside and not having any friends, and they dared me and called me a pussy, so I did it."

Emotion choked her throat. God, it was so hard to be a kid these days. But life was going to get harder, and more difficult choices had to be made. If she didn't do her job and teach him how important every decision was, she wouldn't be giving him the right tools. She kept her face impassive, letting him see her disappointment. "Connor came to me this morning and told me," she said. "He found your glasses. Are you admitting this because you got caught?"

He shook his head. "No. I felt sick all morning. I didn't know he saw me. When I got home from school, I went next door and told him what happened."

Connor spoke up. "He's telling the truth. He apologized and offered to make it right. So we came back here to wait for you, so he could tell you himself." Connor placed a hand on Luke's shoulder and squeezed in reassurance. "I told him my day was shot because I had to get a new tire, but I respected him being man enough to own up to it."

Stupid tears burned her eyes. To see the flash of satisfaction in her son's eyes for being called a man broke her heart. Yes, he'd made a big mistake, but he made it right. It was the most she could ask for, and she ached to hug him tight and not let go for a long time.

Instead, she cleared her throat and nodded. "I agree with Connor. I'm proud you took it upon yourself to tell the truth. Can you tell me who these boys are? What do you think we should do about them?"

"They're not in my school, Mom. They're older. I don't see them every day. At first, they gave me a hard time, but then they said if I proved myself, I could be part of their group."

"Do you know their names so I can contact their parents?"

"I've seen them before, Ella," Connor interrupted. "They

drift in and out of the neighborhood, looking for trouble, but I haven't been able to track down where they actually live yet."

"They said Connor needed a lesson because he's always interfering with them."

"Are they dangerous?" she asked. What if they began stalking Luke? Or tried to physically assault him? "Should I call the police?"

"They've never done anything before," Connor said. "I think this was more about Luke than me. But I've ordered some security cameras for outside my house. I picked up some for you, too, with a monitor. I'll install them tomorrow."

"You don't have too, I'll—"

"I want to." His tone warned her not to argue. "I talked to Luke about working off the tire and wanted to see if it was acceptable to you. We decided he'd help me out with shoveling on my jobs. When the weather clears, I'll also need a hand building a shed for my brother. He's agreed to both."

"I think that sounds fair," she said softly. "When do you want to start?"

"Tonight," Luke piped up. "I did my homework. Connor said he needs to go out for a few hours and I told him I could start right away. Is that okay, Mom?"

She studied her son's face, surprised he didn't look gloomy or despondent about his fate. He actually seemed like he was looking forward to it. Was he lonely? Or did he just crave some company other than hers?

"Of course. I can make dinner for you both, if you'd like. Then you can head out."

Connor grinned. "Would love to jump on that, but I need an hour to work on my paper. I have this teacher I'm having a hard time impressing. I'll pick you up at six, Luke."

"Thanks."

Connor headed to the door, then swung back to motion to her son. "Don't forget to give your mom her present."

"Present?"

"Oh, right. Wait here!" He rushed out of the room.

Connor grinned. "Was your day as bad as mine? Hey, where are your glasses?"

She reached up and touched her naked nose. "Sat on them. My spare is upstairs."

"Damn, you did have a bad day."

She laughed. "Yeah, it was a doozy. I'm surprised you don't have a hot date tonight, though."

"Nah, they jack up the price for everything and there's no one special that's really worth it."

Ella rolled her eyes. "You're such a romantic."

"Yeah, what's your excuse? Why do you hate V day so much?"

The memory tore through her, but the pain was just a slight throb, a reminder that she hadn't been enough. "My husband left two years ago on Valentine's Day," she finally said. "He said I didn't inspire him anymore."

Silence fell.

Why had she told him that? Such a deeply personal fact of her life? Embarrassment made her cheeks hot but she forced a laugh. "He probably just wanted to save himself some money. He'd been buying me all sorts of trinkets because of guilt from his affair. Now, I realized he did me a favor."

He still didn't speak. Thank God, Luke came running back in and thrust a huge bouquet into her hands. Shock filled her. She gazed at the beautiful flowers, blood red with perfectly formed petals eliciting just a touch of scent. Her son had never bought her anything before. Her voice trembled. "Luke, these are beautiful! Thank you so much."

"Happy Valentine's Day, Mom," he said.

And then he walked into her arms without pause.

She hugged her son and the flowers close to her chest and lifted her gaze.

Connor watched them, ocean-blue eyes filled with an intense longing that stripped away the delicate barriers and dove deep into her soul. She knew in that instant, he'd been the one to get her the flowers. He'd been the one to suggest it to her son.

Her breath caught, and a swirling mass of hot energy sizzled between them, choking her with a want she'd never experienced before. Where had this come from? And why did it feel like it was growing each time she saw Connor Dunkle?

Fighting her rioting emotions, she closed her eyes to try and get back control.

When she opened them again, he was already gone.

Chapter Eight

"The Eskimos had fifty-two names for snow because it was important to them: there ought to be as many for love."—Margaret Atwood

"You were right about the flowers," Luke said.

Connor headed to his last stop of the night, maneuvering carefully on the roads even though his tires were stellar with their grip. He'd never had a kid in his truck before so he drove extra slow.

"I told you, women like to be appreciated. Especially Moms. Especially on Valentine's Day, even though it's not my favorite holiday."

"Mine either. Christmas is so much better."

He laughed. "Yeah, Christmas is pretty epic. We have one house left and then you've completed your parole time for the day. You did well."

Pride etched the boy's features. Funny, Connor figured the night would be torturous trying to entertain a ten-year-old, but Luke was good company. He owned a wicked sense of humor and worked hard without grumbling. Shoveling pathways and steps worked muscles most boys didn't have anymore because they mostly worked out by playing video games. Bet his grades were off the charts, too. He reminded him so much of Nate. "Is this your regular job?" Luke asked.

"No, I just do this as extra side work. I'm in construction. Right now, I'm working on the team that's building the Tappan Zee Bridge."

"Seriously? That's awesome. Do you go up on the crane?"

"Sometimes. Most of the time it's hard, repetitive type work in the extreme hot or cold. Sometimes it's real boring, but I like working with my hands and watching a structure rise from nothing."

"How come you're in my mom's class if you already have a job?"

He eased around the upcoming turn and cranked the heat a notch higher. "I want to get into management, and they require a degree. Don't make my mistake. Go to college after high school. It's harder when you're old like me and have to start over."

Luke seemed to mull over his words. "Mom says people do things when the time is right. Maybe you just weren't meant to go to college when you were younger."

Luke's simple acceptance of fate soothed him. Ella's words wrapped around him via her son's lips. He'd never forget her face when she told him about her ex leaving. A mixture of sadness and acceptance had radiated from her and made him want to pull her into his arms and comfort her. He couldn't imagine how hard it was to hear her husband tell her she wasn't wanted. The asshole had just walked out on a beautiful family and didn't seem to care about Luke. Her heart and trust was shattered, yet she seemed more whole than any other woman he'd known. She was truthful, and real and smart. Not to mention strong. She'd kept it all together and was raising a good kid.

The more he found out about her, the more he liked her. Underneath that drab exterior beat the heart of a very mighty woman. She'd looked different without her glasses. More touchable. More...vulnerable. If she only took more care with her appearance, she could probably meet a nice man who would be good for her and Luke. A conservative type, maybe. A man who was stable and employed, and appreciated all of her qualities.

Nate's girlfriend, Kennedy, owned a matchmaking agency called Kinnections. She'd teased him mercilessly about not setting him up until he went through social training to be more sensitive to women. Connor had just laughed it off. One thing he didn't need help with was finding dates. Women had always come easy to him, though he'd only fallen in love once. The memory still stung but it had been his own stupidity thinking he was good enough for more than great sex. He'd been thinking long-term future. She'd been thinking short-term orgasms. Eventually, she'd cheated on him and moved onward, not pausing to look back and see how she trampled his damn heart.

His fault.

But Ella could use some help and Kennedy had a magic touch when it came to makeovers. She'd completely transformed Nate and promptly fell in love with him. Could she do the same magic for Ella?

Connor pulled up to the house and parked. "Okay, dude, you're up. I'll plow the driveway and you work on the steps. Last call."

"Got it."

Luke slid out, grabbed his shovel from the back, and trudged through the growing mounds of snow. They both worked quickly and thoroughly and finally headed back home.

"Luke?"

"Yeah?"

"Have you decided what you're going to do when the Little Rascals show up?"

His statement had the desired effect. Luke grinned. "I like that. The Little Rascals."

"Thought you would."

Luke gave a long sigh. "I don't know. I just want them to leave me alone. I was stupid. I'm just sick of not having someone to hang with at school."

"Are there any guys you'd like to hang with?"

He nodded. "Yeah, there are two that seem tight and they're cool. But they kind of keep to themselves."

"I hear you. You're not going to want to hear this, but I'm going to say it anyway. They're not going to approach you. You need to man up and ask if you can hang with them. Either at lunch or recess."

The boy gnawed at his thumbnail. "I don't know. I'll look like an idiot if they say no."

"If they say no, it's really not a big deal. It's not like you're asking them on a date, dude. You just want to have a few conversations."

He laughed again. "Maybe. I'll see."

"What are they into?"

"Pokémon cards. Basketball, too, but we can't play outside until it gets nicer."

"You got any Pokémon cards?"

Luke snorted. "Of course. Got a whole binder full."

"That's your in. When you approach them, talk Pokémon. Usually you just need something to break the ice a bit." Connor mentally winced. Another cliché. Damn Ella and her crazy tyrannical English.

Luke tilted his head, obviously thinking over his suggestion. "Good idea."

"The weather's not going to be pretty the next couple of days. I'll talk to your mom, but are you up for helping me out?"

"Yeah, no problem. I'm alone every day until Mom comes home anyway. I do my homework and stuff but sometimes it gets boring."

"Same as me. My shifts start early. Other than Tuesdays and Thursdays, when I have your mom's class, I'm home in the afternoon. If you ever want to do homework together, just come over. And if you've ever read Virginia Woolf, come by with your notes."

Luke laughed. "Okay."

They drove back in comfortable silence, and Connor dropped him back off at the house. He watched him disappear inside and he parked the truck, his spirits light. Luke was just like his mother. After a while spent in his presence, it became easier to find ways to like him.

He settled in for the rest of the night with a smile on his face.

Chapter Nine

"Love is like the wild rose-briar; Friendship like the holly-tree. The holly is dark when the rose-briar blooms, but which will bloom most constantly?"—Emily Brontë

The next couple of weeks, Connor settled in to a comfortable rhythm.

Luke accompanied him when he needed to plow, and they got into a habit of stopping at the diner afterward for cheeseburgers. On Monday and Wednesdays, he showed up with his homework and hung out until Ella got home.

Connor was used to being solitary, so it surprised him how easily he fell into a new routine and began to look forward to spending time with Luke. Through him, Ella had softened and often invited him over to the house for dinner. As the grueling winter hurled its fury in various ice and snowstorms, they huddled inside for warm food, hot cocoa, and sometimes the occasional board game.

His paper began to take shape at a slow, grueling pace. Sometimes, he'd bitch about the convoluted style of feminine whining from her assignments, but now she just laughed and challenged him by offering up various facts and shared stories about their lives that were so vivid, he found himself reluctantly intrigued.

Connor wasn't sure when it happened, but he knew somehow, some way, they'd become friends.

He refused to analyze the reason or try to dig deeper. He was too afraid if their odd relationship was examined too closely, it would disintegrate under a strong wind and disappear forever.

He usually worked on Saturdays, but he found himself with an afternoon free and no motivation to take on an odd job or do homework. The snow had melted just enough to clear the roadways, and the upcoming March week promised sun and a good thaw. On impulse, he walked next door and rang the bell.

Luke answered, his face lighting up when he saw him. "Hi, Connor. Come on in."

He stepped inside and Ella came around the corner. Her hair was twisted up in a messy knot, and she held a broom in one hand, with a dirty rag in the other. She gave him an evil smile and crooked her finger at him.

"Ah, he's stepped into our lair, Luke. You know what that means, right?"

"It's a fate worse than the plank. Worse than the guillotine."

Connor glanced between them, grinning at their silliness. "You guys are seriously scaring me."

"Any brave soul who ventures forth in the Blake household has to clean!" Ella declared.

"I'm outta here."

Luke laughed and blocked the door. Ella held the mop out like the Wicked Witch about to cast a spell on him. "Too late, Dunkle. You get the bathroom."

"Forget it. I came to see if you guys wanted to go snow tubing, but since cleaning seems more fun, I'll go check with someone else."

"Snow tubing!" Luke jumped up and down. "Mom! Can we go?"

Ella wrinkled her nose. "But we didn't finish cleaning."

"Mom! Please, oh, please. I swear I'll finish later when we get home. Some of the guys at school were talking about it, oh, please."

Connor crossed his arms in front of his chest. "That's some mighty fine begging, Mom. But I don't want to break up you and Mr. Clean."

Ella made a face. "Cute. What do you need? Snow pants and boots?"

"Yep, that's it. We rent the tubes there. Up for it?"

"Mom?"

The whine was perfectly pitched and coincided with puppy dog eyes. Ella let out a breath. "How can I say no when I'm outvoted? Let's go."

Luke gave a whoop and raced up the stairs. "I'm gonna change!"

Ella looked down at her mop in mourning. "I guess no one ever died from dust bunnies, right?"

"If so, I would have suffered a horrible death years ago."

She punched his shoulder in a playful motion and touched her hair. "Ugh. Give me a few minutes to freshen up."

"Sure."

She came down in record-breaking speed, gliding down the stairs in black snow pants, a baggy sweatshirt, and snow boots. He was used to women who spent hours creating a palette on their face and a runway look for their wardrobe. Ella was comfortable in her own skin, didn't care what she wore, and owned both with a confidence that had originally puzzled him, but now he admired. Still, he much preferred her pale pink natural lips than the orange she sported. He wondered if he could steal it from her purse and help her lose it permanently.

They drove to the snow tubing park and hit sheer chaos. Kids swarmed the hills with giant black tubes, and a contraption that worked like a ski lift pulled them to the top of the hill. Screams and laughter cut through the air. The mountains shimmered in the distance, jagged white rock framing blinding blue sky. The air rushed deep and clean in his lungs as they trudged to the cabin to register and get tubes and got in line to wait.

"Mom, you're not going with us?"

She shook her head. Cheeks flushed from the cold, she laughed and slid her glasses back up her nose. "I'll pass on this one, guys. You two causing a spectacle is enough for me."

"A spectacle, huh?" he said. "Never pegged you for a snob, Ms. Blake, but I may need to rearrange my original opinion. When was the last time you did something completely undignified?"

She rolled her eyes at his deliberate language. Luke chuckled.

"Yeah, Mom, you should go. It'd be a riot to hear you screaming as you slide down the hill."

Her brows snapped down in a frown. "Are you both baiting me? I would not scream."

"Care to make a bet on that?" Connor drawled.

Her lips pursed and irritation simmered around her. He'd learned she was kind of a sore loser. When he won at Monopoly, she accused him of using the green real estate to drive them out of business. When he beat her at Bananagrams, a game similar to Scrabble, she claimed he'd used abbreviations and slang. When he found poop in the actual dictionary and reigned champion, she got all snarky and muttered under her breath the rest of the night. It was kind of cute.

"What bet?"

He pondered her question. "You go down the hill once without screaming and I'll take you both out to dinner. Your choice."

Luke whistled. "That's a good bet, Mom. You've been craving Italian for a while now but said that place was too expensive."

Connor raised a brow. "Care to take the bet?"

She glared at both of them, then stomped her feet. "This is the stupidest thing ever. I'm going to get wet and be miserable, but the lasagna will be worth it. Also the literal egg on your face."

Connor smiled slowly. "Nice cliché."

Her mouth fell open in shock.

"Save our place. I'll grab you a tube," he told her. Laughing the whole way, he got another one and when he rejoined them, they were almost to the top. The attendants were brisk and efficient, setting them up on the lift and showing them how to hold the tube as they were pulled along. When they reached the summit, they were each set up in their own row, with Luke all the way to the left and Ella on the right. Connor was in the middle.

They waited their turn and then the attendant gave them the thumbs-up signal.

Everyone pushed off at once.

Connor slid down the hill with decent speed, especially since his arms and legs were dangling over the tube, slowing him down. He spun in a full circle, the wind whipping at his face, stealing his breath, and laughter poured out of him as he reconnected with childhood memories of him and his brother spending a snowy day together.

Luke got up first. "That was awesome! I'm getting back in line right away."

"Okay, go ahead."

Luke rushed back to the line and Connor looked for Ella. Where was she? His heart started to pound furiously, and finally he spotted a tag of black to the far right of the hill. How had she gotten over there?

He bounded down the slight hill and found her spread out on the snowy ground, eyes closed, deadly still.

"Ella!"

He bent over her, cupping her cheeks, looking for any injuries. Her eyes suddenly snapped open, causing him to jerk back.

"Gotcha! I didn't scream once, Dunkle. You owe me a lasagna."

He stared at her in disbelief. "I thought you were hurt!"

She rose up and smiled slow. "I know. Now who let out an undignified scream? What'd you think, I got hurt from a little snow tube? I'm tougher than that. Where's Luke?"

He shook his head and stood up, reaching out his hand. "He's back in line. You know, people have gotten head injuries from this sport. Next time, have a little consideration."

She looked a bit chagrined. "Sorry. Geez, I didn't know you'd get so worried." She reached out and took his hand. In one perfect motion, Connor pretended to pull her up, then dropped her back so she tumbled into the snow.

His grin was evil. "Oops. My bad."

She glared at him, shaking snow out of her hair. "You're gonna pay for that."

"Bring it."

They stared each other down and then moved. In a flash, she went for him, but he pinned her down and they wrestled in the snow bank, rolling over and over until her giggles reached his ears and he finally stopped.

"Okay, okay, get off me. You win."

Her knot had loosened and thick inky black waves covered

her face. Slowly, he pushed them back from her cheeks and stared down at her, smiling. "You're a real pain in the ass, Blake."

She stuck out her tongue.

When he'd first met her, she struck him as the intense type. A real dry academic. Not much fun. He preferred the impulsive, easy, flirty type of women who didn't take themselves so seriously. But over the weeks, he'd discovered Ella's sense of fun was childish and pure at heart, like Luke's. Simple things gave her joy. Their gazes locked, and suddenly, everything changed.

The air charged. Simmered.

Sexual energy blasted to life. Crackled.

Raw arousal struck him hard. Squeezed.

She sucked in a breath. Hypnotized, he took in the lush pink mouth that had been rubbed free of lipstick. The gold-rimmed irises within eyes so dark and deep, a man could sink forever and never want to be pulled out. He leaned over. Her breath struck him with soft, breathy wisps.

"Ella?" he whispered.

Her lips parted. "Connor?"

They paused on the barrier, reluctant to take the tumble, frozen in place by the question asked of each other.

Connor made the only decision available because if he didn't kiss her in this moment, he'd spend the rest of his nights grieving the lost opportunity of a lifetime.

So he kissed her.

He swallowed her moan and tasted pure sweetness, an intoxicating swirl of purity and lust in one delicious twist. Her lips opened under his without hesitation, not only allowing entry but demanding. Her hands closed around his shoulders and she held on with a brutal force that rocketed his desire. Laid out on the snow, tucked away from the crowds, Connor kissed her like he'd never kissed another woman, and when he finally pulled away, he knew nothing would ever be the same again.

They stared at each other in pure shock.

"You guys okay?"

The deep voice cut through the fog. Connor jumped up, turning around to see one of the park attendants. He hoped his voice would work when he tried to use it. "Yeah, sorry. Had a bit of a wipeout. Thanks."

"No problem. Want me to take your tube?"

Ella stumbled to her feet, looking dazed. "Umm, yes, I don't need it anymore. Thanks."

"Sure." He took the tube and trudged away.

Ella averted her gaze. "I better go check on Luke."

"Ella?"

She shuddered. Wrapped her arms around her chest. "Yeah?"

He searched for the right words but didn't know what he really wanted to say. "I'm sorry."

She stiffened. "Don't be ridiculous. We were just caught up in a moment. It was silly. Let's forget it, okay?"

He tried to study her face but she turned and headed up the hill. As he followed, Connor wondered if he'd be able to forget it.

* * * *

She'd kissed Connor Dunkle.

Ella nodded and smiled as Luke chattered nonstop through dinner. He'd met two boys from school during snow tubing and spent some time with them in the arcade. Watching her son bloom from sullen to joyful filled her with such relief her muscles seemed to actually sag. The weeks spent with Connor had been good for him. He never complained about shoveling, and got into the habit of doing his homework next door with Connor. They'd gotten close, and a bond had developed between man and boy she'd never seen before.

Of course, it was dangerous.

Especially after the kiss.

Ella sipped her wine and picked at her salad. Luke was her main priority, and she didn't want him to be confused with the relationship between her and Connor. Somehow, they'd become good friends. He was also still technically her student. She wasn't about to screw anything up just because she had a physical weakness and was tempted by rock-hard muscles and stinging blue eyes. She'd need to forget the way his thighs had pinned her in the snow, parting her legs just enough so she could feel his erection through his jeans. She refused to think about the drugging, addictive taste of him on her lips, or the way his tongue had slid inside her mouth and taken charge with delicious, drugging thrusts.

No way. They had a good thing going, and she knew how Connor worked. Women fell into his path like they'd been hypnotized, helpless against the mix of gorgeous looks, physical stature, and melting charm. She wasn't the type of woman he dated or looked for in a mate. She had small boobs and dressed like a sparrow rather than a peacock. She had no idea how to flirt or play games. She had no desire to have a one-night affair and wreck their friendship. Pretending that kiss was anything but an impulse, quickly forgotten, would be disastrous.

The encounter proved one thing to her. She needed someone in her life. It was time. The image of the business card from Kinnections flashed in her mind, and Ella knew what she was going to do.

"I'm going to the bathroom," Luke announced.

"Okay, honey."

Her son left them alone. An awkward silence descended.

"Ella?"

She dragged in a breath and forced herself to look up. "Yeah?"

His blue eyes filled with worry. "Did I screw up? With us?"

She wondered what she'd do if he boldly stated he wanted her. Woman to man. Naked. When he kissed her, she'd experienced such an intense bolt of hunger, her body had wrested control of her mind and let her fly free. Maybe this was a sign it was time for her to begin searching for what she needed. His kiss proved she had her own needs. It had been two years since she had a date or sexual experience. Hadn't she sacrificed enough yet? She loved her son, but didn't she deserve to find love or companionship, too? Wasn't it her turn?

Ella forced a smile and shook her head. "No. We're friends, right? We're not going to let a kiss ruin that for all of us."

Relief flickered over his face. "Good. Wouldn't want to lose the best neighbor I ever had. Or Luke, of course. He's an incredible kid."

"Yeah. I'm kind of crazy about him."

"He seems to be happy. Making some friends."

They stared at one another for a bit. Again, the connection hummed between them. Ella cleared her throat. "So I made a decision. Remember when you offered to babysit for me?"

"Yeah?"

"I may need to take you up on that. I found a card for a matchmaking agency called Kinnections. I'm calling them to start the process."

"Did you say Kinnections?" he asked in disbelief.

"Yeah, why? Have you heard of them? They're located in Verily."

He shook his head and grinned. "My brother's girlfriend is an owner."

They were interrupted when the waitress came back and placed their dinners on the table. She was young, with pretty blonde hair, a short black skirt, and a gaze that focused solely on Connor. Ella bit back her irritation while she fluttered around him and completely ignored her. He shot the girl his standard, charming smile, and she practically sighed with pleasure.

"Thanks, darlin'. I appreciate you working so hard."

The girl boldly stared at him, cat green eyes hungrily roving over his body. "Don't mind working for a man who appreciates it."

"Well, I do appreciate it. Your pretty face brightened up my day."

Ella blanched at the awful line, but the girl smiled with pride. "Well, you can brighten my day anytime."

What? Oh, she was so going to lose it.

Ella cleared her throat. "Yes, thanks so much for doing your *job*. We're good." The waitress shot her a glare, then slunk away. Ella pointed her fork at him. "What's wrong with you? I don't care if you flirt with every female in a skirt, but why do you have to sound like you have zero intelligence? I mean, *darlin'*? You're not even Southern!"

He frowned. "I was just trying to lift her spirits. Waitressing is hard work."

She ground her teeth in frustration. "Then don't thank her for having a pretty little face! Thank her for working hard and anticipating our needs as customers. Ugh, it's like you dragged womankind back a few decades. How do you get away with this stuff?"

He gave a suffering sigh. "Now you sound like Nate and Kennedy. I never had complaints before, okay? Women seem to like it."

"Well, they shouldn't. And if they do, you're dating the wrong type of women," she muttered.

"Can we go back to our original subject? I can call Kennedy and tell her you'll be calling. She may even be able to give you a discount. I'm excited for you. They screen all their clients and match you with a guy who's right for you. It's thorough and safe."

She picked up her fork and dug into her lasagna. Did he have to sound so damn excited about her suddenly dating? "Sounds good."

He began eating his ravioli. "They do a consultation and a makeover, too. It's all included in the price."

A flash of pain cut through her. She'd never be a woman to inspire a man to rip off her clothes and tumble her on the ground. But she'd be damned if she'd settle for the dregs of his pity for the poor, single mom. Did he want her to get a makeover that bad? If he was so turned off by her appearance, had he kissed her out of obligation? To make her feel better about herself? Shame burned.

She tried to keep her voice light and teasing though she squirmed inside. "Didn't know you were so excited about hooking me up, Dunkle? Trying to keep me distracted for a bigger curve on your upcoming assignment?"

He grinned. "Nah, I know how that works now. No more pissing off my professor. I just think you deserve to be happy, Ella. You're, well, you're—" he stopped off, shaking his head. He rarely stumbled over words or compliments toward females, so she studied him with interest.

"I'm what?"

"You're an incredible woman," he said softly. "You deserve...everything."

She sucked in her breath. Raw emotion flooded her system, but she had no time to answer. Luke came racing back, shoveling spaghetti and meatballs in his mouth in between trading bad knock-knock jokes with Connor.

Ella told herself to forget his intimate words and the way he made her feel. He was right. It was time to move on.

It was time to join Kinnections.

Chapter Ten

"A woman, especially, if she have the misfortune of knowing anything, should conceal it as well as she can." –Jane Austen

Spring rolled in like a lamb, leaving the lion's roar far behind. The days turned sunny, and as the snow melted into oblivion, flowers and trees peeked their heads out, deciding it was safe to finally come out and play.

He'd cleared the weekend to work on his brother's shed and swung by to pick up Luke and Ella. He smiled as they trotted out and climbed in the truck. "I'm surprised you wanted to come with us," he said to Ella. He took in her loose jeans, rain boots, and hooded sweatshirt. Though it was warmer, they'd be working outside so he'd told them to dress warm.

"I wanted to meet your brother," she offered, buckling her seat belt. "Also Kennedy said to come and keep her company while you do manly things."

Luke grunted from the back. "That's right, Mom. Maybe you can make us lunch while we build the shed."

She rolled her eyes at his poking. "Wise guy. Turn on the HGTV channel and half of the contractors are women. Is this how I raised you to think of females? Or have you been hanging out with Connor too much?"

They laughed. Connor threw up his hands. "Hey, if you want to take over, I'll be happy to prepare a meal in the warm house."

"Point taken. I'll stay inside."

"Good choice."

He drove out to Verily, radio blaring loud, windows cranked halfway down. He was so used to being with them it was almost like his own family. He'd grown close to both of them, and other than the odd electricity that crackled between them, Connor settled into a comfortable routine of companionship.

He never thought about the kiss. Well, hardly ever. Sometimes, the memory snuck up in the night, taunting him with the brief flash of her body underneath his, the sweet taste of her lingering on his lips. He'd never been affected by a simple kiss, but Connor figured it was the typical male game of wanting what he couldn't have. He wasn't about to risk losing Ella and Luke over a physical reaction that would pass after one tumble. He'd done it again and again. The next morning, Connor rarely felt anything but the need to move on. He'd never hurt Ella like that by playing games. She'd become too precious.

He refused to delve further into his strong feelings for the two people next to him, choosing to do what he did best. Just enjoy the day, moment to moment.

He drove past the familiar white sign welcoming them to Verily, and headed down Main Street. Nate had been begging him to move here, but the rents were a bit pricier, and his current place was a shorter commute to work. Still, he loved the small Hudson River town. Quaint and artistic, shops lined the streets, lights strung over the large oak trees, and popular cafes set up tables and chairs for guests. They passed the used bookstore, the Barking Dog bakery, and Kinnections, the matchmaking agency owned by Kennedy and her two friends, Kate and Arilyn. The dog park was packed on a sunny afternoon, and he grinned at the crowds of people with leashes gathering for social time.

He reached Nate's house in a few minutes and pulled into the driveway. They'd moved out of their old apartment and bought a small cottage house with a spacious yard, quirky slanting red roof, and a wraparound porch. His brother came out with Kennedy at his side.

"Hey," Nate said in his standard greeting. He grinned and leaned in for a half hug. "Good to see you, man."

"You, too. Looking good, little brother. Growing your hair?"

Kennedy laughed and enveloped him in a bear hug. "No, he's refusing to see Bennie for a trim until he finishes this round of testing on his current prototype. He's living in the lab. Thank goodness you're here to force him to breathe some fresh air."

Connor hugged her back. His future sister-in-law—well, one day he hoped—was a vibrant, commanding woman who stole Nate's heart at first glance. Her looks were dazzling, from her caramel-colored hair, curvy body clad in designer clothes, and whiskey gold eyes. But she was so much more than knee-buckling good looks to Connor. She was a friend, supporter, and made his brother happy. She challenged them both on any bullshit, pushed them to their limits, and loved them unconditionally.

She was family.

"Gonna help us build this shed, Ken?" he teased. "Bet you have cute little pink work boots and a matching hammer."

She tossed her hair in dismissal. "As if. Now introduce me to this charming young man who's going to break a million hearts."

Luke flushed from the attention but stared at Kennedy like she was a movie star. "I'm Luke."

"Nice to meet you, Luke." She shook his hand. Nate followed. "I've heard great things about you. Thank you for helping us build a shed. Nate has so much equipment, we can't jam it in the house any longer. Hi, Ella! I'm so happy you came to keep me company."

They hugged. He didn't get much information, but it seemed she'd already had her consultation, counseling appointment, and was moving forward with securing a date via Kinnections. He trusted Kennedy would keep her safe and set her up with the right man.

His gut squeezed at the sudden thought she wouldn't really belong to him anymore. But of course, that was stupid. They were only friends, neighbors, and teacher/student. Ella had never been his in the first place.

He shook off the strange emotions and ruffled Luke's hair. "Okay, dude. Let's get to work."

Ella and Kennedy wished them luck and disappeared into the house.

The supplies had already been delivered and were spread out in the backyard. He'd marked out the ground on his last visit, and the plans had been carefully plotted and confirmed with the proper zoning authorities. He called them over and explained the drawings to Luke, going over safety rules and the jobs he'd be responsible for. The boy listened and took it all seriously, his face etched with excitement for his first official build.

"Luke, the first thing we do when we're getting ready will set the tone for the day. Know what it is?"

He shook his head. "What?"

Connor shot his brother a knowing look. "Take control of the music before your partner does. If you don't you'll end up getting tortured by Mozart or bad country songs. Power up my phone, young man."

Luke laughed and turned away.

Nate gave him the middle finger.

Yeah. It was going to be a great day.

* * * *

Ella sat at the high counter in the breakfast nook, her gaze sweeping over the house. "I love your place," she said, taking in the gorgeously designed pieces that made the rooms pop. From the canary yellow rug to the massive red vase filled with exotic dried blooms, her senses were filled with delight. Lush green plants scattered about, the furniture was comfortable, yet elegant, in rich fabrics of velvet, leather, and linen.

The kitchen gave off a cozy, but airy feel with bright white cabinets and polished gleaming tile, paired with a natural wood table and sturdy chairs with Monet-type cushions. "Did you used to study art?" she asked.

Kennedy laughed and leaned against the counter. "Lord, no. But I'm obsessed with beauty in all forms. I love when things come together to please individuals in a visual and spiritual sense." She wrinkled her nose. "Wow, that sounded pompous."

"No, I know exactly what you mean! You were the one who put the photographs up in Connor's place, weren't you?"

"Guilty as charged. Connor is wonderful but decor is not one of his strong suits. Like most men, I'd have to say."

"Agreed."

"Now, let me ask you a question and you promise to give me an honest answer."

Ella swallowed. Her heart pounded furiously, and she prayed

Kennedy didn't want to ask about her and Connor. About their relationship. She wanted to relax this afternoon and indulge in some girl chatter she'd been sorely lacking. She wanted fun and laughs and gossip, but not about her. "Of course." She held her breath.

"Do you really want coffee or can I just open up this bottle of wine? It's five o'clock somewhere."

Her shoulders slumped in relief. "Yes. No, I can do better than that. Hell, yes!"

Kennedy grinned and grabbed a corkscrew. "I knew I really liked you from the beginning. Are you excited for next week? It's makeover time."

She tapped her unpolished nail against the swirling gold granite. "I think. I'm nervous, though. I've always been a huge believer in appearances not being important."

"You sound exactly like Nate. I understand, but I don't agree. It's not about making you into someone you're not. It's about becoming a better you. Someone you like and can be comfortable with. I believe it's important to make a strong first impression and give yourself an opportunity to dive deeper. Make sense?"

Ella sighed. "I guess. Arilyn's counseling session was helpful, but I still have reservations about Luke adjusting to my dating. He's been so happy lately. I don't want to wreck anything."

Kennedy poured the Chardonnay into two glasses and slid one over to her. "I understand completely. But Luke also needs to see you taking care of yourself and being happy. You shouldn't have to deny that part of yourself in order to be a good mom. It's been two years, Ella. You're ready. We already found a fabulous match and Arilyn is working on getting a date set up."

She sipped her wine and tried hard not to think about Connor. "You're right. I'm definitely ready, and I'm excited to explore this new chapter."

Kennedy slid on a stool across from her and lifted her glass. "I know it's scary, but I promise you, it will be worth it. Sometimes we have to be brave enough to open up to someone new. Break out of our routine. Now, tell me about Connor."

She avoided her gaze. "What about him?"

Kennedy leaned in. "How bad are you torturing him in

class?"

Ella smiled slowly. "Really bad. Gave him an extra credit project. A little Woolf. A dash of Brontë. And a dose of Austen. Hopefully it will teach him a bit of how far women have come and how we don't deserve to be called 'darlin' or 'pretty little thing.'"

Her new friend laughed with delight. "Finally! Do you know how hard it was to break Nate of his habit of saying the most awful things to women? I had to electrocute him with a buzzer to re-form his habits."

"You didn't."

Kennedy sighed. "Yeah. I did. At least it all worked out." She took another sip of wine. "See, the thing about Connor is besides being gorgeous and a bit clueless, he's got a great big heart that's just waiting for someone to keep it safe. He protected Nate when their household fell apart. He took care of him, put him through college, and never thought twice about himself. A man like that is special, even if you have to dig a bit deeper to unearth it. That's a man who you can count on for the long haul. Once he commits, he's all in."

Fascinated, she thought over the past weeks. The way he treated her son with a loving care that rocked her soul. His insistence on taking her car for an oil change, or fixing the backed up sink instead of calling the plumber. She remembered the roses on Valentine's Day, and the hours he spent with them on a Saturday night playing board games. "Why does he continue to date women who mean nothing to him?" she finally asked.

"I think we all get hurt and hide in certain ways. His way was removing any depth from his relationships. Then he'll always be safe."

Ella stared thoughtfully into the golden liquid, swirling it around the edge of the glass. The words shot straight and true across the counter and fired a direct hit. Kennedy was right. It was almost as if he was comfortable slipping into a role he rarely questioned. He smiled, flirted, and kept things light. He seemed to do the same thing on all his dates. Did he not know anymore how to allow himself to really feel? More importantly, did he even want to try?

"You're good at therapy, too. How do you see so much?"

"I spent years in therapy myself. I had issues galore. Still do. I learned one thing watching endless relationships begin, fail, break, and triumph." Kennedy lifted her glass in a mock salute. "You just have to find the right crazy for you."

Ella laughed and raised her own glass. "To the crazy."

They clicked glasses. And drank.

* * * *

A few hours and a bottle of wine later, Nate trudged inside, pressing a kiss to the top of Kennedy's head. Her hand automatically entwined with her lover in a rehearsed dance that had seeped into memory. A pang of envy hit Ella as she watched them, but it was a beautiful pang because it reminded her that type of love was out there.

"How's it going, ladies?" He raised a brow at the empty bottle of wine. "Good, I see."

"Very good," Kennedy affirmed. "You guys need a break? I've got some brownies for Luke."

"Did you bake them?" Nate asked.

Kennedy gave an affronted humph. "Of course not! I bought them at the bakery."

"Thank God. Then he'll love them."

Ella laughed. "There hasn't been a brownie Luke hasn't liked. I'm surprised they're still at it."

Nate faced her. He was a handsome man, with a sexy goatee emphasizing his sharp features, and gorgeous brown eyes with swirls of green. He was shorter and leaner than Connor, but the resemblance was immediate in the thrust of the nose, arched brow, and brightness of their eyes. "Luke is a wonderful kid, Ella. You should be really proud. Not only is he respectful, but he's a hard worker. Seems to have Connor's talent for woodworking."

"Thank you. Connor's great with Luke. They seem to have bonded."

Nate nodded, his gaze a bit foggy, like an absent-minded professor. "And with you," he said. "I've never seen my brother so happy."

She jerked in her seat. Trying to cover up her emotion, she

jumped up. "Umm, I'm going to go check on them. Be right back."

"Take the side door," Kennedy said.

"Thanks." Ella headed down the hallway and out to the back deck, making her way down toward the newly framed shed. Her boots made no noise on the steps, and she heard the mingling of voices as she drew nearer. She was about to raise her voice and yell their names when she stopped cold, ears straining to hear more.

"Dad doesn't really care about me," her son was saying. Ella pressed her hand against her mouth, wishing she could teleport and kill her ex-husband for hurting Luke. "He's got this new woman now, and a new kid on the way. He doesn't need me anymore." His tone reflected an acceptance and bitterness a ten-year-old shouldn't have to know.

"That sucks, Luke. There's really nothing I can say to make it better either. I learned that myself when my own mother left me."

"What? Your mom left?" Luke asked in disbelief.

She heard the clanking of tools and then a deep sigh. "Yeah, it was pretty bad. I was only fourteen. She packed up her suitcases, and when I got home, she was gone. Never came back. Never called. It was like she decided she didn't want that type of life anymore so she left it behind. Along with me and Nate."

She blinked away the sting of tears and concentrated.

"What did you do? How—how did you get over it?"

"I didn't. But I needed to take care of my brother, and when my father began drinking and checked out, we were alone. Life went on. Even though I was sad and I missed my parents, I had Nate. I had friends. I had hope for a great big life I wasn't going to let anyone take from me. Does that make sense?"

Silence. Then a small voice. "Yeah. It does."

"Your dad may come back and ask for forgiveness later. He may not. But you have your mom, and with her on your side, you have more than a lot of kids today. Now, that's not going to make every day better, and you're still going to do stupid stuff like listening to the wrong boys or making huge mistakes. That's okay. You're a kid, you're supposed to screw up. The good news is your mom will be there to catch you every time. Just give her a break once in a while, okay? She likes that touchy feely stuff like hugs and it makes her happy."

Luke chuckled. She heard the shift of weight and another rattle behind the freshly formed shed wall. "Okay. I guess I can handle that."

"Cool. You did an awesome job, kid. Let's head back inside and see if we can wrestle up some sugar."

Ella backed slowly away, retreating into the shadows as they began to clean up.

Her hands shook, and her heart seemed to expand in her chest, breaking out of its limits and bursting in a frenzy of light prisms. She had done a terrible, awful, ridiculous thing.

She had fallen in love with Connor Dunkle.

Chapter Eleven

"I am not an angel,' I asserted; 'and I will not be one till I die: I will be myself. Mr. Rochester, you must neither expect nor exact anything celestial of me - for you will not get it, any more than I shall get it of you: which I do not at all anticipate."—Charlotte Brontë, Jane Eyre

Connor checked his watch and hurriedly snapped the book closed. Damn, he'd lost track of time. Shoving the book under a pile of papers, he told himself it was completely acceptable to think *Jane Eyre* did not suck. To his horror, he found it kind of hot. At least Brontë didn't ramble on nonstop about being stuck in a room as a metaphor for her life.

He'd never be a Woolf fan, no matter how hard Ella tried. But over the weeks working on the paper, and being forced to research the lives of the three authors she'd picked, he began to understand the limits placed on creative females. A man could break the rules and be called heroic. A woman was locked up in a mental institution or told to shut up.

Heavy stuff.

He quickly brushed his teeth, changed his shirt, and headed next door. Ella had her first big date set up by Kinnections and he was on his first official babysitting night. He figured they'd order a pizza and play some video games. Or maybe he'd let Luke rent the new Marvel movie out on Pay-Per-View. He loved a good kick-butt superhero movie.

He hadn't seen Ella since her makeover. Besides extra work shifts, he'd finally scored a meeting with management for an interview. With his solid reputation on the construction site and degree almost in hand, he'd exhibited confidence and felt good about his performance. All his hard work and preparation was finally paying off. He wondered if this was how Nate felt when he was hired at NASA. It was a heady feeling.

Connor didn't bother to knock. He let himself in and found Luke already playing his Wii. "Hey, dude. You up for pizza tonight?"

"Yeah! You up for me demolishing you in Super Smash Brothers tonight?"

He laughed. "You can certainly try. But I've been practicing. Where's your mom?"

"Upstairs getting ready. She even smells different. Perfume, I guess."

Unease trickled through him but he shrugged it off. He'd talked to Luke about his feelings seeing Ella dating, but the kid seemed solid. He hoped Kennedy had taken away the orange lipstick. It was easy for Connor to see past the surface and appreciate how amazing Ella was, but guys were still stuck on physical appearance. He hoped this guy treated her nicely and made her feel good about herself. She deserved it.

He headed to the kitchen to pour himself a glass of lemonade and turned around.

Then almost dropped the glass.

"How do I look?"

He stared. Speechless, his voice died in his throat and he could only look at the woman before him that was no longer Ella.

She was stunning.

Her hair had been cut and was finally out of the constricted bun. Glossy black waves tumbled over her shoulders and half covered one eye in a flirty manner. Where were her glasses? Instead, wide, dark eyes peered at him with a wariness he'd never seen before, almost as if she was vulnerable, waiting for his opinion. Without the thick frames, her eyes gleamed with gold, giving off an intensity that made shock waves tingle through him. Her face glowed in the low light, and her lips were full and lush, painted a deep, sexy red that contrasted dramatically with her dark hair and eyes.

But her body. Dear God. Her body...

A clingy red tank dipped low in the front and emphasized the full curves of her breasts. A trendy black jacket skimmed the lean lines of her body. Her skirt halted just short of her knee, showing off a tantalizing strip of bare skin before the leather of thigh high black boots began. His gaze dropped to her feet. The boots held a wicked heel that made him imagine all sorts of naughty things. A musky, earthy scent danced in the air and surrounded her, urging him to move closer and bury his nose against her skin.

Blistering heat surged through him. He was hard in seconds, aching to cross the room and touch her. This was not his Ella. This was some other woman bent on seduction and naughty games. What had Kennedy done to her?

She tugged at the jacket and clasped her arms nervously across her chest. The red tank slipped a bit lower, giving him a teasing glimpse of olive skin. "You don't like it. Oh, my God. Do I look like a slut? Kennedy told me to go in bold so I thought I'd take a chance. She helped me pick this out."

He tried to speak but he still hadn't found his voice. She waited, but when he was unable to utter a response, she gave a deep sigh and shook her head.

"Forget it. Just like a man to give no feedback. I'm not going to change. I spent a lot of money on this stupid outfit, and I can handle this. Listen, thanks for watching Luke tonight. I better go. I'm running late."

Finally, words emerged from his throat. His head spun like he'd gotten clobbered and little birdies were circling him. "You look, you look—great. Umm, maybe you'd be more comfortable in flats, though?"

She waved a manicured hand in the air. He caught the flash of scarlet red nails. "I practiced, I can handle it. Luke, sweetie, I love you. Listen to Connor and don't go to bed too late, okay?"

"Mom! You look beautiful!"

Her face lit up with pleasure. Why hadn't Connor told her that? Why was he acting so frikkin weird?

"Thanks, honey. That means a lot to me. Text me if there's any problem. See you later."

Her heels clicked on the floor and he followed. "Wait a minute. You're meeting him somewhere? Why isn't he picking you up? Don't you think that's kind of rude?"

Her red lips curved in a grin that was sexy as hell. "Come on,

Dunkle, you've never picked up any of your dates, have you?"

He blanched. "That's different!"

"No, it's not. I feel safer meeting him at the restaurant, anyway."

She opened the door but he kept talking. "Be careful. He'll probably invite you up for a drink, but that's code for him trying to make a move."

She gave him a naughty wink. "Oh, goody. Maybe I'll be later than I thought."

"Ella!"

"Kidding, just kidding. Geez, calm down, Dad. I have done this before, you know."

"If you feel uncomfortable, call me. I'll come pick you up."

"I have my car, remember? Have you been working too hard? You're losing it."

His palms began to sweat. He fought the overwhelming urge to beg her not to go and stay home with him. They'd do their usual and hang out in sweats and play games and argue over Woolf. What if this guy tried to touch her? Was he kidding himself? What guy alive on the face of the earth would not want to touch her looking like this?

"Ella—wait—I—"

"Sorry, I gotta go. Have fun and thanks for this!"

She banged the door closed and left.

He stared through the window and watched her get into her car. The fabric of her skirt slid up even more, revealing a delicious path of skin that led all the way up to heaven. He should've told her to change. No, he couldn't do that. She needed to boost her confidence. But holy shit, that outfit should be illegal.

"Connor! Come on, let's play!"

Shaking off the fog, he sat next to Luke and grabbed a controller. He had no idea what he was doing, and at this point, he wasn't going to relax until she came back through that door.

This was going to be a long night.

* * * *

Ella sighed and counted down the minutes till she kicked off her shoes.

Being sexy was a lot of work. She'd been out of practice for a while, so maybe her body needed more time to adjust. Her toes were pinched by the high heels, and the leather snugly clasping her leg was making her itch. Her hair kept sliding into her face until she wished she had a few bobby pins to jam it up and forget it. The contacts she'd put in caused her eyes to dry, and she couldn't wait to pop them out and put on her glasses. And as usual, her lipstick had slid off within the hour, along with the rest of her makeup.

She pulled to the curb and cut the engine. Luke should be asleep by now. Dinner had been a long, relaxing affair with good conversation and expensive wine. She liked Ed. He was a professional, divorced dad who seemed to get the challenges she faced. They'd traded pictures of their kids, talked Common Core education, and discussed popular fiction. He was a big reader and knew Woolf. He was impressed with her career. He was nice.

And he invited her up for a drink afterward.

Ella had a hard time not laughing as she imagined Connor's face. She'd declined, and instead they strolled to the used bookstore in town and spent a pleasant hour shopping and sipping a cappuccino.

Ed asked to see her again. She'd agreed. It was the most positive, life affirming date she'd ever had because it reminded her she was a woman. A sexual woman. A woman who enjoyed a man's company and conversation. A woman who would eventually enjoy sex if she could just get there.

The only problem was Connor Dunkle.

Ella stared into the darkness, hands tapping the steering wheel. She kept seeing his face throughout the date. The way he'd stared at her in shock and gotten that hungry gleam of lust in his eyes. For her. She could practically feel the energy zinging between them, and she'd fought the impulse to cross the room and kiss him. She dreamed of feeling his lips just one more time over hers and his hands stroking her skin. She dreamed of him slamming her against the wall and taking her like a man possessed, hungry to slip between her thighs and claim her.

She squeezed her legs together as arousal hit. Why did she keep doing this to herself? She had to accept Connor was only a friend. She may have done something stupid and fallen for him, but it was her secret to keep. This date was the first step of her moving on. She may not have wanted to attack Ed across the table, but he'd made her feel good. Like there was hope.

She grabbed her purse and went inside. The house was quiet and halfway dark, so she tiptoed into the living room to see if they'd fallen asleep on the couch in front of the television.

"Did you have a good time?"

She jumped and spun around. Connor leaned against the wall in front of her, holding a beer. "You scared me! Is Luke in bed?"

"Yeah. We watched *Antman*, ate pizza, and he went to sleep an hour ago." His gaze narrowed, raking over her figure. Goose bumps broke out on her arms. "Did you have a good time?" he repeated.

She swallowed and walked past him, laying down her purse. "Yes. It was good. Thanks for watching him. I owe you."

She waited for him to say good night and head home, but he remained standing, oddly silent. Her stomach clenched and she nervously walked around the house, straightening odds and ends. Her skin burned as if he'd touched her, and tension cranked in the air around them. What was going on?

"Aren't you going to give me the details?" he drawled.

She put two cups in the dishwasher and opened up the refrigerator to snatch a bottle of water. "We had a nice dinner. He was a nice guy. Nothing much left to tell."

"Did he kiss you?"

She choked on the water and coughed uncontrollably. Anger replaced her nerves. "What kind of question is that? It's none of your business. I don't ask about your dates."

"But we're friends, right? Don't friends share all the juicy details?"

She raised her chin and glared. "We're not that type of friends, Connor. You're also still technically my student. Look, I don't know what's going on here, but I think you better leave."

He put the beer down on the counter. "You're right. I should leave." He squeezed his eyes shut as if an inner battle was being waged. "I don't want to mess this up. I should go home and forget everything I want to say to you right now. I should forget everything I want to do."

She stilled. Poised on the edge of heart-stopping danger, Ella knew the only way to escape unscathed was to tell him to leave one more time. He'd obey, and the next time they saw each other, they'd be back to friends. Instead, she sealed her fate. "What things?"

His eyes flew open. She waited for him to walk away. Instead, he strode toward her. Her breath whooshed out of her lungs as he stopped inches away, his beautiful face tight with concentration. The burning blue of his eyes scorched her. "Bad things. I've been thinking about you all night. About another man touching you. I hated it. I don't want to leave, and I don't want anyone else touching you, Ella."

Her body trembled. The leashed fury of lust and want flicked at her, and a low groan rose to her lips, a groan of pure need. Warning bells clanged. She desperately tried to think of all the reasons this was not a good idea, but her brain shut down and her body roared for more. "This isn't a good idea."

"No. This is a terrible idea, but I'm not in control. So you need to stop me. Because all night while you were on your date, I thought of touching you. Kissing you." He paused. "Fucking you."

"Oh, God." She practically shook at his dirty words, growing wet between her thighs. She lifted her arms to push him away, but instead they lay against his hard chest. The muscles jumped beneath her touch. "Connor."

He lowered his head. His breath struck her lips. "I don't want to hurt you. I don't want to screw up the best relationship I've ever had with a woman. But I want you, Ella. I want to put my hands all over you, under you, in you. I want to give you so much pleasure you can only say my name over and over. I know I should walk away, for both of our sakes. So, stop me, sweetheart. Stop me right now."

Their eyes met and locked. Her arms slid up over his chest and around his neck, and she rose to her tiptoes and said the words. "I can't. I don't want you to stop," she said softly. "Take what you want."

His mouth slammed over hers.

It was as if the months not touching had built up between them and exploded in a firestorm. Their first kiss in the snow had been so sweet and slow, a preliminary dance of exploration and growing arousal.

This kiss was raw lust and blistering need in a completely uncivilized world. He devoured her mouth whole, his tongue staking his claim, and he lifted her up in one swoop and placed her on the kitchen counter. Swallowing her throaty moans, he pushed open her legs and stood between them, his fingers gently caressing her cheek as his mouth worked its dirty magic.

Drunk on the taste and feel of him, she slipped her hands under his T-shirt and hit silky hard muscles and a nest of dense hair. Digging her fingernails into his flesh, he nipped at her bottom lip and ripped off her jacket, his erection pressing against her in mouth-watering temptation.

Ella lost her mind under his sensual assault. There were no rules between them as they tugged off clothes and worshipped bare skin. He yanked down her bra and sucked on her hard nipples, and she bit her lip to keep from screaming in pleasure. Her skirt was pushed up to her hips, and his fingers hooked under the lace of her panties and dove into her wet heat.

Her legs squeezed around his hips as he pumped his fingers in and out of her pussy, licking her nipple, and then he brushed the tight bud of her clit and she jerked in his arms.

"You feel so damn good," he muttered in her ear. "Wet and hot and sweet. I should take you to bed, go slow—"

"Right here, right now." She arched up as he teased her clit, his thumb rubbing in slow circles, driving her further. "Do you have a condom?"

He bit her neck, licked the hurt. Her fingers stumbled on the zipper of his jeans, but it finally opened and she pushed the denim over his hips. His hard, massive length sprung free, and she thanked heavens the man didn't wear underwear.

"Yes, in my pocket. Oh, God, you're going to come, aren't you? Come now. Come for me."

He pressed against her clit and plunged his fingers deep,

curling just right.

She exploded, her hips jerking against him as she buried her mouth against his chest to muffle her scream. He cursed viciously and kept up the movements, wringing out her orgasm to a shattering conclusion.

He twisted his hands in her hair and kissed her fiercely. "Get the condom." Her voice came out husky, raspy. "I need you."

She squeezed his erection, working her fingers up and down his shaft until he threw back his head, eyes squeezed tight, his face carved in the lines of pure ecstasy. She drank in his expression, loving the pleasure she gave as her thumb skimmed the dripping tip and she increased the rhythm to a rapid pace, as he grew harder and longer under her touch.

He fumbled in his pocket and withdrew the condom. Ripping it open, she helped him sheathe himself, and then he pushed her back onto the counter and raised himself up, his arms resting on both sides of her body like a conqueror about to enjoy his spoils.

"I don't want to hurt you," he grit out. "I don't want to go fast."

She spread her legs wide and offered herself up. "Hurt me. Take me. Now."

He grasped her panties and tore. The material fell off, leaving her bare. He said her name, in a curse or a prayer, and surged inside her.

Ella gasped, embracing the raw edge of pain and pleasure as he filled her completely. Her body surrendered under his gentle hands, his rough thrusts that pushed her to the edge again, trembling under the force of earth-shattering tension and need.

She memorized every line of his face, every spark in his eyes. She gave him everything as he claimed her body and soul, and let herself fly with no other thought than to give in to the wracking waves of pleasure that claimed her body.

Gripping her hips and yanking her higher, he thrust even deeper, his fingers playing with her clit, and she whispered his name over and over as she came again.

"Yes, yes, fucking perfect. Fucking mine."

With a growl, he joined her, slamming his hips and taking her mouth in a deep, soul-stirring kiss.

Time paused. Their breathing slowed. Quiet fell.

Moving slowly, he removed and disposed of the condom, pulled up his jeans, and eased her gently to a sitting position. Ella watched in silence, not able to speak or think. He pulled down her skirt, eased up her jacket, and picked her up from the counter, walking into the living room.

Sitting down on the couch, he cuddled her on his lap and pulled the afghan over both of them. With a sigh, she laid her cheek against his chest, breathing in his scent. He stroked her hair and pressed his lips to the top of her head.

"I just want to hold you for a little while," he said quietly. "Is that okay?"

She held him tighter, snuggling into the warmth, and closed her eyes. "Yes."

Then she drifted to sleep.

Chapter Twelve

"Beauty was not everything. Beauty had this penalty — it came too readily, came too completely. It stilled life — froze it."—Virginia Woolf, To the Lighthouse

Connor stared at his test, trying to get his head in the game.

Cliché.

God, what had he done?

Her voice filled the classroom in a lilting melody that haunted him. She walked on soundless shoes, back and forth in front of the classroom, dressed in her usual attire. Long dark skirt. Black ballet-type slippers. A loose mid-sleeve sweater in a dull beige. Her hair was still up, but her bun wasn't as severe, and several silky locks escaped and pressed against her cheek. The glasses were back, sliding down her nose at regular intervals, and she used a scarlet-painted fingernail to jam them back in place. The orange lipstick was gone, replaced by a stained red that made it hard for him to concentrate on her words.

She was back to herself, but different. Everything had now changed. He knew how soft and silky her skin was underneath her clothes; knew the muscled strength of her legs as she wrapped them around his hips; knew how her tight, wet pussy clenched around him when he thrust inside her; knew the stinging bite of her teeth and the ripe fruit of her lips.

He'd spent all night imagining her kissing another guy. Imagining his friend, his Ella, belonging to someone else. He'd drank a beer and brooded, and soon he'd worked himself into such a state, when she came through the door he'd lost control.

He was wrecked. He couldn't stop thinking about that night, though three full days had passed without contact. He'd slipped away in the middle of the night, disentangling himself with her warm body. He thought about showing up at her door the next morning to talk. He thought about calling her. Instead, he took on back-to-back shifts, arriving home late, then spending hours on his homework.

He knew he'd see her today and planned to arrive early. Exchange a few words.

But he'd gotten caught in traffic and walked into class late. She hadn't even deigned to make a comment, keeping her gaze firmly averted and her focus on her lecture.

He was a monster. He'd slept with her and disappeared. She must despise him. This was the reason he didn't get involved with messy, raw emotions with women. This was the reason he stayed away from relationships and kept things light.

Nothing was light with Ella.

The big red C+ reflected his growing understanding of literature. What began as a boring, torturous class had evolved into a foray of thoughts and words that affected him. He'd finished *Jane Eyre*, tore through Brontë, and actually went back to find more of their work. They were nearing the end of the semester, and as long as he passed the final and turned in his extra credit paper, he'd graduate with honors.

Finally, she dismissed the class and he took the familiar path to her desk. He waited his turn while she spoke to some other students, and then the room emptied.

"What can I do for you today, Mr. Dunkle?"

He winced. Yeah, she was pissed. And she had every right to be. "Ella, I'm so sorry."

She studied him coldly. "This isn't the time nor the place. My classroom is reserved for academic questions. Is there a question you want to ask me, Mr. Dunkle?"

He jerked back, reminding himself she was right. He didn't want to get her in trouble. "No, Professor. I'm sorry to interrupt."

He walked out and did the only thing possible.

Waited until she was done.

He tracked her to her car and appeared in front of her. "Ella?"

She jumped, her hand at her throat. "You scared me! Why are

you stalking me?" She looked around nervously. "We're still on campus. You may not care, but I don't want to put my son or my job at risk."

"I understand. Open the car."

She glared, but finally pressed the button. They got in the car, and he turned toward her. "I'm sorry," he repeated.

"Another apology? You seem to be good at them. Unfortunately, I'm unsure of what you're apologizing for. Leaving me in the middle of the night? Staying away for three days? Avoiding Luke? Or having sex with me?"

He winced and pushed his fingers through his hair in frustration. "None of it. All of it. I screwed up bad. I panicked because I didn't know where this would leave us. You and Luke mean the world to me and I couldn't keep my hands off you the other night. You deserve to hate me. I hate myself."

His honesty must have hit the right chords because she let out a deep breath and met his gaze. "Look, I was confused, too, but I don't regret it." Vulnerability gleamed in her eyes. "Do you?"

"No."

She nodded. She seemed to struggle with her emotions. He waited for her to share her confusion and admit her feelings for him. Instead, she gave him a tight smile.

"Good. I don't want us to act weird or avoid each other. It was an amazing night, and we'll just move on. Deal?"

His gut lurched. Why did she seem so eager to forget how amazing they were together? She didn't even seem interested in talking about their relationship. The sex had been the best he ever experienced. The level of heat and hunger she exhibited and released in him was almost primitive. He'd never felt such a deep connection. But she was smiling like he was a stranger and she was trying to be polite.

Irritation tingled his nerve endings. "Yeah. Fine. Deal. How about I come over and see Luke tonight?"

"He actually has a sleepover tonight."

"On a school night?"

"Yes, I gave him special permission. He's working on a science project with his two friends and the mother called to see if they could stay. I like these two boys, and I've met with Cathy for coffee. I figured it was good for him, and he promised he'd FaceTime with me."

"That's great." He paused, his heart pounding ridiculously in his chest. "Maybe you want to go out to eat tonight? Talk a bit more?"

Her gaze dropped from his and she stuck the key in her ignition. "Thanks, but I can't."

"Why?"

She dragged in a breath. "I have a date tonight."

His head was suddenly taken over by a swarm of angry bees. "With the same guy?"

"No, a new guy. Kennedy felt this new man would be a great match, and we both ended up free this evening."

"Oh." She'd been crying his name as he thrust inside her and now she was going to dinner with another man. This was what he wanted, right? He'd been afraid she'd get too serious on him and ruin their friendship. Things were back on the right track.

Cliché.

"Great. Hope you have a good time." He reached for the door handle.

"Connor?"

"What?"

Her voice was whisper soft. "This is what you want, right? For us to move on with other people?"

Tension drew his body taut. His heart did a strange flip-flop, screaming for him to change the rules. Tell her he didn't want her to date anyone else. Admit he was scared but wanted to see where this could go.

"Yes. I think it's good for both of us."

She paused. "Okay."

"Have a good time tonight."

He left the car without another word, wondering why the hell he was so pissed off.

And what he could do about it.

* * * *

That night, he watched from behind his curtains as she left

on her date. Tonight, she wore silky black pants that clung to her magnificent ass, spiked heels, and a lacey black top that looked like it wasn't enough material to go out in public with.

He fumed and waited. Drank a beer and waited some more. Tried to do homework, watch television, or read a book.

And waited some more.

A few hours later, her car pulled up to the curb and she got out. He watched her head toward her apartment, then pause in front of his door. Connor held his breath, his palm pressed to the cool windowpane. She glanced over, as if sensing his presence. She turned, stopped, and closed her eyes as if in an inner battle with herself.

Come to me, he mentally urged. His body tensed, waiting for her next move. Waiting for her decision. *Come to me, Ella.*

Her lips parted and she mouthed a familiar curse word she loved but rarely uttered. Then headed toward him.

He met her halfway. Just opened the door, dragged her inside, and took her in his arms. She never hesitated, lifting her mouth for his kiss, the earthy, musky scent of her curling in his nostrils. He was ravenous, rock hard in seconds, and his brain repeated one word over and over again without pause.

Mine.

He possessed her mouth with all the pent-up arousal and frustration racing through his body. Without speaking, he lifted her and walked into his bedroom, laying her down on the navy blue comforter.

"I waited for you," he finally said. He took in the spill of her dark hair over his pillow, the rapid breath raising her breasts, the long lines of her legs spread open.

"I know," she said huskily.

"You are so damn beautiful."

She blinked, raised her arms, and he crawled on the bed. Clothes drifting off, he worshipped her, spreading her out, touching and tasting every precious inch of flesh. He buried his mouth between her legs and drank in her essence, his tongue swiping her hardened clit, gripping her writhing body and bringing her to orgasm while he drank in every spasm and demanded more, always more.

Fitting himself with a condom, he rolled and lifted her over him. She took him deep, rocking her hips to a wicked, eternal rhythm, her breasts spilling into his hands as he rubbed her tight nipples and let her set the pace.

When his orgasm came, the brutal pleasure shook him to the core, diving deep into places of his soul he never knew existed and giving it all over to her. He swallowed her screams as she shattered around him, and Connor held her tight afterward, knowing he may not be able to let her go again.

Chapter Thirteen

"A person can't have everything in this world; and it was a little unreasonable of her to expect it."—Kate Chopin, The Kiss

"I have to go."

A full moon hung ripe in the sky. She sat on the edge of the bed, looking out the slats of the blinds, realizing she couldn't do this anymore.

She had wanted to try. God, she wanted him that badly. She'd gone on that date, made polite conversation, laughed at his jokes, allowed his touch on her elbow as he guided her to the car, and thought about Connor Dunkle. Her date promised to call and she agreed to go out with him again, and then she drove home and knocked on Connor's door.

He'd been waiting for her. Somehow, deep inside, she'd known. She wanted to convince herself she'd be able to engage in a hot affair with her next-door neighbor and her friend. She swore she'd be able to keep it light, realizing he was the type of man who didn't look for long term and liked his easygoing, uncommitted lifestyle.

Instead, she'd fallen in love with him. And she wasn't going to pretend any longer.

"Don't go." He rolled over and rubbed her shoulders. Pressed a kiss to the nape of her neck. "Stay with me."

"Why?"

His grip tightened. "Because I want more time."

Ella took a deep breath and stood. She felt his gaze on her as she pulled on her clothes, and he kept silent until she faced him.

"How is this going to work, Connor?" she asked with a lightness she didn't feel. "Are we going to have sex each time I come home from a date? What's the term everyone uses? Fuck buddies?"

He flew up from the bed and stood before her, naked. His voice was a low growl of sound. "Don't you ever use that term about us," he bit out. "You're important to me."

"And you're important to me. But we've crossed over into new territory and I've been afraid to scare you off. I can't pretend I don't have these feelings for you while I date other men. So, I'm going to ask, what do you want?"

He blinked. Stared at her. "I want you."

She nodded. "In a committed, long-term relationship?" she asked calmly.

The look on his face told the truth. Sheer panic lit up those blue eyes, and he turned quickly away, as if to buy more time. "I thought—I thought we'd just take it slow. See how things go."

Her heart shriveled but Ella needed to see the whole thing to the end. She owed both of them the truth.

"I understand," she said softly. "I really do. But I can't play those types of games. See, I'm in love with you."

He flinched. Tore his fingers through his hair. Stared at her as if she'd sprouted wings and was about to fly off into the night like some alien creature. "What?"

She fought the pain and humiliation, raising her chin. "I love you. Crazy, right? I'll tell you this—I never expected to fall for a man like you. You were right when you told me I had made judgments. I thought you were a chauvinistic, egotistical, shallow man out for a good lay and a good time. Instead, I discovered you have a beautiful heart, and mind, and soul. You treat Luke like your own. You rose above odds so many others couldn't and made a life for you and your brother. You're kind and giving, loyal, and wicked smart. You're everything I've always dreamed of."

He shook his head as if trying to register her words. "Ella, I don't know what to say. I'm crazy about you, but we just started this, and it happened kind of fast, and I don't want to hurt Luke or you. I don't want to hurt anyone."

As she studied him, the light bulb exploded and shattered in tiny, jagged pieces. She pressed her hand to her mouth as a bitter, humorless laugh left her lips. Now she understood.

"My God, I get it. You only made a move because I changed my appearance. I wasn't enough for you physically before that, was I? You just liked who I became when I pretended to be like all the other women you date. I bet if I hadn't gone out with Ed, you would've never tried to kiss me or take me to bed. Suddenly, it was easier for you, wasn't it? Less of a risk."

"That's ridiculous. I don't know what you're talking about."

But the truth was revealed in his face, and anger bubbled up like lava, whipping her into a frenzy. "Oh, yes you do. As long as I was dressing plain and not up to your sexual standards, I was safe. Easy to stay away from, huh? But the moment you got tricked with what I could look like, you had to make a move. You haven't changed at all. And I was an idiot to think I was special to you."

He closed the distance and grabbed her arms with a fierceness that challenged her own. "You are special! Don't ever talk about yourself like that. I always thought you were beautiful."

"I call bullshit." She jerked away. "You know what you think is beautiful, Connor? This." She tugged at the form-fitting lace top. "Fancy clothes and sexy heels." She fisted her hair and shook the waves wildly. "Perfectly tousled hair and red lipstick and perfume that makes you think of sex. It's easier, isn't it? But guess what? It's all a mirage. One morning, or one day, or one year, you wake up and find this." She swept her hands over her body with emphasis. "You get glasses and sweats and messy hair and a bare face. You get just me, with no fancy trappings. You get real. And I was crazy to think you were ready for it."

Waves of anger and frustration emanated from his figure. "I don't know what I'm ready for!" he yelled. "I know I'm crazy about you and Luke and that my feelings have changed since I walked in your class that first day, and I'm not sure what to do about it. I don't give a shit about your appearance. Can't you see I'm nuts about you? I can get real!"

She wrapped her arms around her chest and shook her head. "No. I just know I can't do this with you. I'm looking for a relationship, not just sex. I'm looking for a man I can grow old with and who wants to be a father to my son. How's that for real?"

"You don't want to give me a chance here? Let me catch up. Think about how this will work and what I can offer you?"

She smiled sadly. "Your answer said enough, Connor. I have to go."

"What about us? What about Luke?"

Her heart ached but she forced herself to speak. "Luke adores you and I'd never say you can't see him. Just—just give me some time, okay? I think we need a break."

"I don't want to hurt you, Ella."

"I know," she said. "When you open yourself up to love someone, there's no way not to get hurt. You just have to decide if it's worth the pain."

Ella left him alone in his bedroom, wondering if he could hear the sound of her heart shattering.

* * * *

"You look like shit."

Connor lifted his beer mug and stared moodily at his brother. They'd agreed to meet at the pub downtown. Nate held his usual cocktail, a Darth Maultini, but Connor wasn't even in the mood to tease him about it.

The semester was coming to an end. Luke continued to come over to his house and do homework, but Connor made sure to cite work as an excuse to stay away from Ella. Class became a torturous session that tore him apart. He ached to touch her. Talk to her. Insist they were being ridiculous by not trying to be together.

But he realized, deep down, Ella was right.

He hadn't made a move until she walked in that kitchen transformed. When he looked back on their first kiss in the snow, he remembered keeping a lock-down on his hormones and emotions. He'd treated her more carefully, with more respect. The moment she came at him in a low-cut top and short skirt, and he thought of her kissing some guy, he'd lost his control. Somehow, it seemed safer to play with a sexually experienced, hot woman. He knew the rules.

God, he was such an ass.

"Yeah, it's been a tough few weeks. How's Kennedy?"

"Hard-headed as usual. She found her engagement ring and kind of freaked out."

He almost spit out his beer. "Dude, are you serious? You asked her to marry you?"

Nate waved a hand carelessly in the air. "I ask her to marry me all the time. The ring is for the formal asking I'm planning for her. Of course, she stumbled across it and majorly lost her mind. This may be the hardest woman in the world to pin down."

"Why can't you just leave things alone?" he asked in frustration. "You're both happy. Shacked up. Who needs marriage?"

Nate looked surprised. "I do. I love her. She wants to get married, too, but the woman is stubborn. Eventually I'll get her to agree. How's Ella?"

He grunted. "Fine."

"Luke?"

"Fine."

"How's school? Graduation is May, right?"

"Yep, I'm all set. As long as I pass Ella's class."

"And work? You still going for that big management position?"

"Yep. They offered me the job."

Nate laughed with delight. "Congratulations! Not that I'm surprised, but damn, I'm proud of you."

"Thanks."

He tried to force a happy smile, but he was too miserable. Nate stared at him hard, his green eyes seeing way too much, like he always did. He tapped a finger against the edge of the table in a steady rhythm. "You're in love with Ella, aren't you?"

Connor jerked back, splashing beer over the rim of his glass. "Holy shit, dude, why'd you ask me a question like that?"

His brother shrugged. "I could tell. You're a mess. Something happened between you two. Just tell me."

So Connor did. He told Nate the entire story from start to finish, and Ella's expectations, and his confusion, and dumped it all out in one long, messy stream of words. There was no one else he trusted more in the world than Nate. His brother took it all in with that quiet manner, just nodding here and there as he urged him to continue.

Finally, he fell silent. The cocktail waitress took that moment to slide by their table and smile cheerily. "Can I get you another round, gentlemen?"

He automatically switched into gear, giving her a big smile and wink. "We'll have anything you're giving, sweetheart."

She giggled and cocked her head in a flirty manner. "Oh, yeah? I may have to take you up on that offer later."

"I'll be waiting. For now, I think we're good."

With another sidelong look, she walked away with an extra swing of her hips that did nothing for him. When he turned back to his brother, Nate was looking at him in pure shock.

"You're unbelievable. That was the stupidest, most asinine pick-up line I ever heard. And she fell for it! You're the only guy I know who gets away with that behavior. No wonder you're such an ass. Women have been falling for you your whole life and you've never had to work hard to really keep one."

Connor's mouth fell open. "That's a shitty thing to say to me! I just poured out my heart and you're giving me a hard time because the waitress liked me?"

Nate dropped his face into his hands and groaned. "God, you're just like Kennedy. I swear, it's scary. You both have intimacy issues. You're both stuck on stupid images and your ideas of beauty. You're both terrified of being left alone and getting your heart broken. You both are driving me nuts."

Shock poured through him. "I'm not afraid of being left. I've always broken up with women, not the other way around. Is it wrong to accept the truth about myself? I'm not meant for long-term or serious relationships. I'm not built that way."

Nate looked up and stared at him with serious eyes. "Connor, I need you to listen to me, man. You were left in the most devastating way possible. Mom left you. Oh, you always talked about how hard it was on me, but you're the one who got stuck with all the crap. You watched Dad take off and had to raise me. You had to be the parent in the relationship, and you never got the answers of why. Then you got this stupid idea that you had no brains, like the intelligence was distributed only to one family member, and you limited yourself."

His stomach lurched at the mention of Mom. He hated thinking about it, but Nate held his attention and he knew it was important to listen.

"I think you built this whole image of yourself because it was easier. Women flocked to you, so you gave them what they expected, and along the way, you lost who you really are. Dude, you're graduating with honors from college. You work on the fucking Tappan Zee Bridge, you're a master in construction, and now management hired you for their team. I saw you with Luke. He adores you, and that doesn't surprise me in the least. You're great with kids, and you'd be the best father in the world."

Raw emotion cut at him like tiny paper cuts. He wanted to duck his head, walk away, and not deal with his brother's speech, but he kept still and let himself really hear his brother for the first time.

"Ella sees everything in you that we all see, except for you. The only reason you let yourself make a move on her wasn't because she suddenly appeared in a skirt and heels. It was because you finally gave yourself permission. You took a chance. But then you spooked and backed off and tried to make yourself think it was better this way. It's not, Connor. You love Ella. You love Luke. Just let yourself love them, man, and take a shot. What do you really have to lose? A life of loneliness? A life filled with shallow encounters that never scratch the surface? You're worth more than that."

As his brother's words washed over him, his body came to life. The shaking started deep inside and spread throughout his body until the most ridiculous thing began to happen.

Tears stung his eyes.

Oh, fuck no. Not here. He absolutely refused to cry like a pussy in front of his brother in a bar.

Instead, he rubbed his face, took another swig of beer, and cleared his throat. "Okay."

Nate nodded and sipped at his god-awful feminine cocktail. "Okay."

A mixture of peace and acceptance flowed through him. His

brother was right. He'd made a mistake, but it wasn't too late yet. He owed them both a chance to fix the wrongs and fight for something he wanted.

He sat with his brother in companionable silence and drank.

Chapter Fourteen

"...who shall measure the heat and violence of a poet's heart when caught and tangled in a woman's body?"—Virginia Woolf, A Room of One's Own

Ella clasped her hands on top of her desk and swept her gaze over the classroom. Students scribbled furiously, occasionally sneaking glances at the clock. The familiar sounds of low mutters, chairs creaking, and deep sighs echoed in the air. Final exams stressed everyone out, but she was positive she'd done her job and every single student would pass.

Even Connor Dunkle.

Her gaze settled on him for a heart-stopping instant. Those golden locks spilled over his forehead, and his brow was creased in concentration. He wrote in a frenzy, fingers gripped around his pen like a vise, concentration evident in the tight lines of his face.

It had been a week since their night together. Each day was painful, but Ella reminded herself it was better to heal now. At least Luke never got attached to the concept of them as a couple. At least she was the only casualty this time.

A sigh shuddered through her. After the anger passed, only a dull resignation settled in like a bad bruise. Connor had never pretended to be different. He hadn't promised her a future or even a tomorrow. Oh, she knew he cared about her, but he hadn't tumbled into love like she had. Eventually, she'd heal and hopefully they could remain friends. Maybe, with time, she'd be able to look into his face without craving to touch him.

Maybe not.

One by one, students finished their exam and dropped it off at her desk, gathered up their stuff and left. The end of the semester was always bittersweet. It reminded her of the passing of time, the growth of her students, and the hope she'd made a slight difference. Her love of literature was a part of her, and if she'd converted just one more person to recognize the beauty of the authors she taught, Ella considered it a life well lived.

"Time's up," she announced. Four students remained. She waited while they trudged over, dropping their papers, saying good-bye, and then leaving.

Connor remained behind.

Ella prayed he'd let her be. She was still too raw, like an oozing, open wound refusing to scab. Slowly, he unfurled his length from the chair and walked to her desk. Laid the exam in front of her. Then handed her a stack of papers neatly bound in a folder.

"I finished my extra credit project."

She nodded, her throat thick with emotion. "Congratulations. I'll grade it quickly and make sure I send the Registrar your grade so you can prepare for graduation. I have no doubt you did well on the final. You've been working hard."

"Ella. There's so much I want to say to you."

"Don't." Her voice broke and she let out a small laugh. "You don't, you don't need to say anything."

"I'm asking you to do one thing for me. Read my paper when you get home tonight. I need your feedback."

"Connor, I'm sure you did a great job."

"Read it. Tonight. Promise me?"

She gave a jerky nod, unable to speak. Those ocean-blue eyes raked over her face and down her body in a caress, blazing with intensity that made her shake. Then he was gone.

Ella buried her face in her hands. At least she didn't have to see him in class any longer. That would help.

She picked up the folder and skimmed through it. Neatly typed, with a full bibliography and references, it looked to be perfectly acceptable. She tossed it in the pile and got ready for her next class.

Hours later, she drove home, made dinner, and climbed into her pajamas. Luke had been in a good mood, chattering about school and his two new friends, and she savored his happiness, allowing it to fill her up and soothe her pain. He went upstairs to shower and get ready for bed, and Ella decided to make a cup of tea and curl up on the sofa with a book.

As she made her tea, her gaze fell on her briefcase. Why was Connor so insistent she read his paper tonight? Was he really worried she wouldn't pass him? A tingle of awareness flowed through her. With a sigh, she retrieved his paper, a red pen, and sat down with her tea. Better to read it now and let him know or he'd worry.

Time ticked. She flipped pages, jotting down notes and growing more impressed by the depth of the work. It was obvious he wasn't crazy about *To the Lighthouse*, but he seemed to embrace *Jane Eyre* and *Pride and Prejudice*. A smile rested on her lips. He was a closet romantic and didn't realize it. His overall insights to *A Room of One's Own* startled her with depth. He'd stripped away his usual mockery of whining women and connected with the isolation and dedication a woman writer had to face; the solitude and willingness to dive deep in order to unearth the emotions needed to bleed on the page.

A dull ache settled into her bones as she reached the end. God, she missed him. It was as if he was right here next to her while she read his voice on the page. Ella began to close the folder when her fingers skated over one last paper.

A letter.

She sucked in her breath. A letter handwritten to her, the personal scrawl filling up the page. She closed her eyes. Could she do this right now? Was she ready to hear things that would only hurt her deeper?

Ella began to read.

Dear Ella,

You were right. When we first met, it was easy to resist you. Besides being a pain in the ass, failing me in class, and finding out you were my new next-door neighbor, I wasn't truly prepared to think of you in any romantic way. When I bonded with Luke, I realized what a wonderful mother you were. When you insisted on pushing my limits in class, I realized what a wonderful teacher you were. When you challenged me to get real, I realized what a wonderful woman you were.

But you were also wrong. It wasn't your image, or clothes, or perfume that finally made me surrender to my need to touch you. I had been searching for you my entire life, but I didn't know it yet. Unfortunately, what I had been searching for I was also terrified of finding. It was easier to hide with shallow relationships and believe in a stereotype I'd been taught my entire life.

That I wasn't worth loving.

You taught me I am. You taught me to stop settling and relying on my surface qualities to skate through life without injury. You taught me there was something greater to fight for, but once again, my insecurities and fear allowed me to let you walk away.

I love the way you scrunch up your nose when you're irritated. I love the way you giggle when Luke tells those terrible knock-knock jokes, and I love your awful meatloaf you still insist on serving, and I love the way you defend the beauty of Virginia Woolf, and I love those ugly sweaters you wear, and the beautiful body and heart and soul that beats true beneath your clothes.

I love you, Ella Blake. I love your son. You're the only woman I want, and I'm going to spend the rest of my life convincing you I'm worth taking a second chance on.

Open your door.

Connor

She didn't hesitate. The decision had been made the moment his soul-stirring words lifted from the paper and arrowed straight through to her heart. She rose from the couch, walked across the room, and opened the door.

He stood before her clutching a bouquet of red roses.

"Will you be mine, Ella Blake?"

She gazed at his beloved face and the way his eyes told her the truth, gleaming in the depths of a bottomless ocean blue.

"I already was," she said simply.

She stepped into his arms and he kissed her, long and slow and sweet. When he lifted his head, Ella smiled.

"You officially passed my class. Congratulations."

He laughed and swung her up high, holding her close, and Ella realized they'd both found what they were searching for and more.

The End

Also from 1001 Dark Nights and Jennifer Probst, discover Somehow, Some Way.

About Jennifer Probst

Jennifer Probst is the *New York Times*, *USA Today*, and *Wall Street Journal* bestselling author of both sexy and erotic contemporary romance. She was thrilled her novel, *The Marriage Bargain*, was the #6 Bestselling Book on Amazon for 2012, and spent 26 weeks on the *New York Times.* Her work has been translated in over a dozen countries, sold over a million copies, and was dubbed a "romance phenom" by Kirkus Reviews. She makes her home in New York with her sons, husband, two rescue dogs, and a house that never seems to be clean. She loves hearing from all readers! Stop by her website at http://www.jenniferprobst.com for all her upcoming releases, news and street team information. Sign up for her newsletter at www.jenniferprobst.com/newsletter for a chance to win a gift card each month and receive exclusive material and giveaways.

Also from Jennifer Probst

The Billionaire Builders
Everywhere and Every Way

Searching for Series:
Searching for Someday
Searching for Perfect
Searching for Beautiful
Searching for Always
Searching for You

The Marriage to a Billionaire series:
The Marriage Bargain
The Marriage Trap
The Marriage Mistake
The Marriage Merger
The Books of Spells

Executive Seduction

All the Way

The Sex on the Beach Series:
Beyond Me
Chasing Me

The Hot in the Hamptons Series:
Summer Sins

The Steele Brother Series:
Catch Me
Play Me
Dare Me
Beg Me

Dante's Fire

Everywhere and Every Way

The Billionaire Builders
by Jennifer Probst
May 31, 2016

Hot on the heels of her beloved Marriage to a Billionaire novels, *New York Times* bestselling author Jennifer Probst nails it with the first in an all-new sexy romance series featuring red-hot contractor siblings who give the Property Brothers a run for their money!

Ever the responsible eldest brother, Caleb Pierce started working for his father's luxury contracting business at a young age, dreaming of one day sitting in the boss's chair. But his father's will throws a wrench in his plans by stipulating that Caleb share control of the family business with his two estranged brothers.

Things only get more complicated when demanding high-end home designer Morgan hires Caleb to build her a customized dream house that matches her specifications to a T—or she'll use her powerful connections to poison the Pierce brothers' reputation. Not one to ignore a challenge, Caleb vows to get the job done—if only he can stop getting distracted by his new client's perfect…amenities.

But there's more to icy Morgan than meets the eye. And Caleb's not the only one who knows how to use a stud-finder. In fact, Morgan is pretty sure she's found hers—and he looks quite enticing in a hard hat. As sparks fly between Morgan and Caleb despite his best intentions not to mix business and pleasure, will she finally warm up and help him lay the foundation for everlasting love?

* * * *

Prologue

Caleb Pierce craved a cold beer, air-conditioning, his dogs, and maybe a pretty brunette to warm his bed.

Instead, he got lukewarm water, choking heat, his head in an earsplitting vice, and a raging bitch testing his temper.

And it was only eight a.m.

"I told you a thousand times I wanted the bedroom for my mother off the garage." Lucy Weatherspoon jabbed her French-manicured finger at the framing and back at the plans they'd changed twelve times. "I need her to have privacy and her own entrance. If this is the garage, why is the bedroom off the other side?"

He reminded himself again that running your own company had its challenges. One of them was clients who thought building a house was like shopping at the mall. Sure, he was used to difficult clients, but Lucy tested even his patience. She spoke to him as if he was a bit dim-witted just because he wore jeans with holes in them and battered work boots and had dust covering every inch of his body. His gut had told him to turn down the damn job of building her dream house, but his stubborn father overruled him, calling her congressman husband and telling him Pierce Brothers would be fucking *thrilled* to take on the project. His father always did have a soft spot for power. Probably figured the politician would owe him a favor.

Yeah, Cal would rather have a horse head in his bed than deal with Congressman Weatherspoon's wife.

He wiped the sweat off his brow, noting the slight wrinkle of her nose telling him he smelled. For fun, he deliberately took a step closer to her. "Mrs. Weatherspoon, we went over this several times, and I had you sign off. Remember? Your mother's bedroom has to be on the other side of the house because you decided you wanted the billiard room to be accessed from the garage. Of course, I can add it to the second floor with a private entry, but we'd need to deal with a staircase or elevator."

"No. I want it on the ground floor. I don't remember signing off on this. Are you telling me I need to choose between my mother and the pool table room?"

He tried hard not to gnash his teeth. He'd already lost too much of the enamel, and they'd just broken ground on this job. "No. I'm saying if we put the bedroom on the other side of the house, it won't break the architectural lines, and you can have everything you want. Just. Like. We. Discussed."

She tapped her nude high-heeled foot, studying him as if trying to decipher whether he was a sarcastic asshole or just didn't understand how to talk to the natives. He gave his best dumb look, and finally she sighed. "Fine. I'll bend on this."

Oh, goody.

"But I changed my mind on the multilevel deck. I found this picture on Houzz and want you to recreate it." She shoved a glossy printout of some Arizona-inspired massive patio that was surrounded by a desert. And yep, just as he figured, it was from a spa hotel, which looked nothing like the lake-view property he was currently building on. Knowing it would look ridiculous on the elegant colonial that rivaled a Southern plantation, he forced himself to nod and pretend to study the picture.

"Yes, we can definitely discuss this. Since the deck won't affect my current framing, let's revisit when we begin designing the outside."

That placated her enough to get her to smile stiffly. "Very well. Oh, I'd better go. I'm late for the charity breakfast. I'll check in with you later, Caleb."

"Great." He nodded as she picked her way carefully over the building site and watched her pull away in her shiny black Mercedes. Cal shook his head and gulped down a long drink of water, then wiped his mouth with the back of his hand. Next time, he'd get his architect Brady to deal with her. He was good at charming an endless array of women when they drew up plans, but was never around to handle the temper tantrums on the actual job.

Then again, Brady had always been smarter than him.

Cal did a walk-through to check on his team. The pounding sounds of classic Aerosmith blared from an ancient radio that had nothing on those fancy iPods. It had been on hundreds of jobs with him, covered in grime, soaked with water, battered by falls, and never stopped working. Sure, when he ran, he liked those wireless contraptions, but Cal always felt as if he was born a few decades too late. To him, simple was better. Simple worked just fine, but the more houses he built, the more he was surrounded by requests for fancier equipment, for endless rooms that would never be used, and for him to clear land better left alone.

He nodded to Jason, who was currently finishing up the framing, and ran his hand over the wood, checking for stability and texture. His hands were an extension of all his senses, able to figure out weak spots hidden in rotted wood or irregular length. Of course, he wasn't as gifted as his youngest brother, Dalton, who'd been dubbed the Wood Whisperer. His middle brother, Tristan, only laughed and suggested wood be changed to *woody* to be more accurate. He'd always been the wiseass out of all of them.

Cal wiped the thought of his brothers out of his head, readjusted his hard hat, and continued his quick walk-through. In the past year, Pierce Brothers Construction had grown, but Cal refused to sacrifice quality over his father's constant need to be the biggest firm in the Northeast.

On cue, his phone shrieked, and he punched the button. "Yeah?"

"Cal? Something happened."

The usually calm voice of his assistant, Sydney, broke over the line. In that moment, he knew deep in his gut that everything would change: like the flash of knowledge before a car crash, or the sharp cut of pain before a loss penetrated the brain. Cal tightened his grip on the phone and waited. The heat of the morning pressed over him. The bright blue sky, streaked with clouds, blurred his vision. The sounds of Aerosmith, drills, and hammers filled his ears.

"Your father had a heart attack. He's at Haddington Memorial."

"Is he okay?"

Sydney paused. The silence told him everything he needed to know and dreaded to hear. "You need to get there quick."

"On my way."

Calling out quickly to his team, he ripped off his hat, jumped into his truck, and drove.

* * * *

A mass of machines beeped, and Cal tried not to focus on the tubes running into his father's body in an attempt to keep him alive. They'd tried to keep him out by siccing security on him and making a scene, but he refused to leave until they allowed him to stand beside his bed while they prepped him for surgery.

Christian Pierce was a hard, fierce man with a force that pushed through both opposition and people like a tank. At seventy years old, he'd only grown more grizzled, in both body and spirit, leaving fear and respect in his wake but little tenderness. Cal stared into his pale face while the machines moved up and down to keep breath in his lungs and reached out tentatively to take his father's hand.

"Get off me, for God's sake. I'm not dying. Not yet."

Cal jerked away. His father's eyes flew open. The familiar coffee-brown eyes held a hint of disdain at his son's weakness, even though they were red rimmed and weary. Cal shoved down the brief flare of pain and arranged his face to a neutral expression. "Good, because I want you to take over the Weatherspoons. They're a pain in my ass."

His father grunted. "I need some future political favors. Handle it." He practically spit at the nurse hovering and checking his vitals. "Stop poking me. When do I get out of here?"

The pretty blonde hesitated. Uh-oh. His father was the worst patient in the world, and he bit faster than a rattlesnake when cornered. Already, he looked set to viciously tear her to verbal pieces while she seemed to be gathering the right words to say.

Cal saved her by answering. "You're not. Doctor said you need surgery to unblock some valves. They're sending you now."

His father grunted. "Idiot doctor has been wanting me to go under the knife for years. He just wants to make money and shut me up. He's still bitching I overcharged him on materials for his house."

"You did."

"He can afford it."

Cal didn't argue. He knew the next five minutes were vital, before his father was wheeled into surgery. He'd already been told by the serious-faced Dr. Wang that it wouldn't be an easy surgery. Not with his father's previous heart damage from the last attack and the way he'd treated his body in the past few years. Christian liked his whiskey, his cigars, and his privacy. He thought eating healthy and walking on treadmills were for weaklings. When he was actually doing the construction part of the business, he'd been in better shape, but the last decade his father had faded to the office work and wheeling and dealing behind the scenes.

"I'm calling Tristan and Dalton. They need to know."

In seconds, his father raged at him in pure fury. "You will not. Touch that fucking phone and I'll wipe you out of my will."

Cal gave him a hard stare, refusing to flinch. "Go ahead. Been looking to work at Starbucks anyway."

"Don't mock me. I don't want to deal with their guilt or bullshit. I'll be fine, and we both know it."

"Dad, they have a right to know."

"They walked out on me. They have a right to know nothing." A thin stream of drool trickled from his mouth. Cal studied the slow trek, embarrassed his father couldn't control it. Losing bodily functions would be worse than death for his father. He needed to come out of this surgery in one whole piece, or he didn't know what would happen.

Ah, shit, he needed to call his brothers. His father made a mule look yogic. They might have had a falling-out, and not spoken for too long, but they were still family. The hell with it. He'd contact them as soon as his father went into surgery—it was the right thing to do.

Christian half rose from the pillow. "Don't even think about going behind my back, boy. I have ways of making your life hell beyond the grave, and if I wake up and they're here, I'll make sure you regret it."

Again, that brief flare of pain he had no right to feel. How long had he wished his father would show him a sliver of softness? Any type of warmer emotion? Instead, he'd traded those feelings for becoming a drill sergeant with his boys, the total opposite of the way Mom had been. Not that he wanted to think of her anymore. It did no good except scrape against raw wounds. Caleb wasn't a martyr, so he stuffed that shit back down for another lifetime.

"Whatever, old man. Save the fight for the surgery."

They were interrupted when the Dr. Wang came in with an easy smile. "Okay, gentlemen, this is it. We gotta wheel him into surgery. Say your good-byes."

Caleb froze and stared into his father's familiar face. Took in the sharp, roughened features, leathery skin, bushy silver brows. Those brown eyes still held a fierce spark of life. In that moment, Caleb decided to take a chance. If something happened in surgery, he didn't want to regret it for the rest of his life.

He leaned down to kiss his father on the cheek.

Christian slapped him back with a growl. "Cut it out. Grow some balls. I'll see you later."

The tiny touch of emotion flickered out and left a cold, empty vastness inside his belly. So stupid. He felt so stupid. "Sure. Good luck, Dad."

"Don't need no damn luck. Make sure you do what I say. I don't want to see your brothers."

They were the last words Caleb heard as his father was wheeled into a surgery that took over five hours to perform.

The next morning Christian Pierce was dead.

And then the nightmare really began.

Dance of Desire

By Christopher Rice

1001 Dark Nights

Acknowledgments

Once again, a huge thanks to both Liz Berry and M.J Rose for inviting me to be part of this special project. (And Steve Berry for being the instigator.) Another huge thanks to Jillian Stein for making romanceland a better place with her personality, humor and social media saavy.

Kimberly Guidroz and "Shy" Pam Jamison did a wonderful job of editing this one, as always. But Kim, in particular, deserves more thanks than one page can accommodate, for more reasons than I can list here. As always, Asha Hossain does a wonderful job with the Dark Nights covers. Two more big rounds of thanks to cover model Jamison Murphy and photographer Cathryn Farnsworth.

For her friendship and general support of my romantic endeavors, I will always be grateful for the fact that Lexi Blake lives and breathes and is so generous with her knowledge and talent. And in the case of this particular novella, I'm eternally indebted to Liliana Hart, who not only invited me to write a story set in the world of her MacKenzie Family, she allowed me to crossover some of its characters into DANCE OF DESIRE.

And I'd be remiss if I didn't also give shout outs to my good friends and general support network, Eric Shaw Quinn, Becket Ghiotto, Christina Barnett, Karen O'Brien and my mother. And of course, all my Texas relatives who inspired the finer parts of this story.

Prologue

Then

Amber resists, but finally opens her eyes.

Caleb really is kneeling next to her bed, whispering her name.

This isn't just another one of the sexy, grown-up dreams she's been having about the boy since summer started. Dreams in which he traces the curves of her body with his fingertips and gazes into her eyes with that serious expression that always makes him look so manly and handsome.

He's really here, his breath soft against her cheek as he whispers her name.

The smell of his cologne is as strong as all the other woodsy smells inside her father's lake house. A few hours ago, they'd both gone to bed at the same time. He in one room, she in another. So did he spritz himself before appearing at her bedside? The idea of him doing a little grooming before calling on her in the middle of the night makes her face feel tingly and hot.

The brand is probably Ralph Lauren Polo, but never would she ask because then he'll know just how much she likes it. Every whiff makes her envision the parts of his body that have become impossible to ignore, no matter how many times she tries to avert her eyes from his new biceps and his suddenly thick and powerful legs. That cologne is the aroma of his undeniable manhood. And the smell of it at her bedside makes her head spin.

They're only fifteen, but already the son of her father's best friend is over six feet tall, prompting her dad to cry more than once this trip, "Boy, you don't quit growin', you're going to be brushing the clouds by the time you're a man." That's the Caleb she's started to dream about, a powerful giant of a man, his back ridged with muscle, his solid arms powerful enough to lift her off her feet and make her feel like she's flying.

She whispers his name. But that's all she says. She doesn't want to scare him away.

Late night television drones in the living room downstairs. Her dad must have nodded off in front of the thing again.

Was that what Caleb was waiting for? For her father to fall asleep?

"It's happening," he says, taking her hand in his. "Come see!"

He tugs on her hand as she stumbles out of bed, stops long enough for her to slide her flip-flops on without releasing his grip. He waits patiently, making her feel even warmer inside.

Together they pad silently down the carpeted stairs, through the living room lit only by television flicker.

She was right; her father's out cold in his favorite recliner.

Caleb opens the sliding deck door, then once they're outside, kissed by warm air and surrounded by cricket song, he slides it shut behind them with barely a squeak. The whole time, he doesn't let go of her hand. Amber's not sure what's making her heart race—his persistent grip, or the sight of him so cheerful and excited in spite of all the trouble that's descended over his family that summer.

She doesn't know the whole story, but she's overheard some of her father's phone calls these past few days. He's used words like *detox* and *rehab* and *men who can't come back from over there*. She knows *over there* means Iraq, and she's pretty sure the man in question is Mr. Tim, Caleb's father, her dad's closest friend from the Marines. Things must've gotten bad lately. Her father plans these lake house trips weeks in advance, especially if Caleb and his dad are coming.

This trip was last minute. This time they only brought Caleb.

Whatever it is, Caleb's not talking about it.

He's not much of a talker in general and when he does open his mouth, it's usually to give soft-spoken lectures about stuff he's seen on science shows, like how volcanoes form and birds migrate. Sometimes the topic doesn't interest her that much. What interests her is how Caleb gazes into her eyes while he explains another nerdy factoid. It's like he needs for her to listen, needs for her to know what he likes. Needs for her to look into his eyes too. Just the other day, he placed one hand between her shoulder blades because he didn't want her to miss the sight of a duck skimming the lake's surface as it came in for a landing. She didn't want him to stop touching her so she just kept nodding and watching, as if landing ducks were the most interesting things ever.

They keep walking through the dark.

He's taking her to the lake.

Last spring her father replaced the steps leading down to the boathouse, and when the air is thick with humidity, like tonight, the waft of cedar comes off them in overpowering waves. The closer they get to the shore, the faster Caleb goes and the harder she has to work to keep him from pulling her off her feet.

Whatever he wants her to see, it'll be gone in a few minutes if they don't hurry.

When they reach the tip of the boathouse, he releases her hand. He's behind her suddenly, gripping her shoulder in one hand, pointing to the night sky with the other. A full moon, bursting with light, sends rivulets of ivory across the lake's black surface. This is exactly the scene he described to her earlier when they were pretending to sunbathe on the dock while sneaking looks at each other's half-naked bodies.

"What time was it last night when you saw the moon?" she'd asked him.

"Past midnight."

"But you only went to bed at eleven."

"I couldn't sleep."

They both knew what thoughts were keeping him awake, thoughts of his father's drinking and of how crazy his mother was going trying to rein it all in.

"Wake me up next time," she'd told him. *"I'll keep you company."*

Such simple words, but she'd felt like she was jumping off the edge of a cliff when she'd said them. Instead of answering, Caleb gave her a long look as he fiddled with the leg of his shorts. She'd silently cursed herself, called herself an idiot and worse.

Caleb was just a friend. Honestly, he wasn't even that, was he? Circumstances had thrown them together, that was all. He was the son of her father's best friend, so they were basically like distant cousins, only with no shared blood in their veins. Crazy of her to think there might be more there.

If her friends could see her now, they'd probably laugh at her; the same friends who'd swooned that day her father had picked her up from school with Caleb in the passenger seat of his truck, and Caleb, wearing a Stetson that was about a half-size too big for his head, had given them a cocky grin, looked right into her eyes and said, *Afternoon, pretty lady.* Not afternoon *pretty ladies,* even though she'd had about four other girls standing on the curb next to her when he'd said it.

Clearly she'd made way too much of that moment. Sometimes *afternoon* just meant, *afternoon* and *pretty lady* was what a guy called you when he was trying to look cool.

Or so she'd thought earlier that day. Before he took her up on her offer and woke her up in the middle of the night so they could look at the moon together.

Which they do.

Because it's beautiful.

When he lowers his right hand, the same hand with which he was just pointing to the night sky, her breath catches. Every muscle in her body tenses in anticipation.

Where will it land?

Her shoulder, it seems.

She forces herself to breathe.

Gently he turns her around. The tips of their noses are inches apart, breaths mingling in the moonlit darkness, his as rapid and shallow as her own. The knowledge that he's as nervous as she is comforts her.

"Need to kiss you," he says.

"Need to or want to?" she whispers.

"No difference when I'm lookin' in your eyes," he says.

When her mouth opens to say his name, he pulls her to him.

At first it's awkward and tentative. She's only ever kissed one boy, and now she has a terrible moment of wondering if this is really what everyone else has been talking about, this fumbling of lips and tongue tips and trying not to breathe right at the wrong time.

Then Caleb takes her chin in one hand, cups the side of her face in the other, centering them both.

His tongue slips between her lips. She relaxes, invites him in. Heat spreads from her scalp to the tips of her toes. Heat and a sense of having been suddenly connected to a man for the first time. Not just any man. Caleb. Strong, handsome, sure-to-be-a-giant-someday Caleb.

A phone rings in the distance.

They both ignore it

More rings. They stop.

Her father's high, barking cry pierces the night.

She wants to yank back from Caleb's kiss, but her mind fights with her desire. If Caleb is experiencing a similar struggle, she can't sense it. His kisses intensify, his arms around her now, gathering her T-shirt into his fists.

The house's sliding door squeals in its track. Her father's boots pound the cedar steps. Have they been caught?

"Caleb?" her father shouts. "Caleb? You out there, boy?"

She hears not anger but fear and sadness in her father's voice. He can't see them through the shadows.

"Yes, Mister Abel! I'm here."

"Come on up, son," her father says. "Something's happened…"

His face is hidden in the shadows, but his voice cracks with emotion.

"Sir?"

"It's your parents, Caleb. Something's happened to your parents."

1

Now

Even though she's spent the past few days crying at work, Amber Watson Claire has managed to avoid shedding a single tear in front of her boss. So far her breakdowns have all started the same way. She loses herself in some menial task for about fifteen minutes, then she suddenly, violently remembers it's been less than a week since she opened the door to the storeroom at Watson's, the bar her father built, and found her husband plowing one of his bartenders with the abandon of a porn star.

The tangle of their sweaty, clawing limbs amidst cases of beer and piles of flattened cardboard boxes is like a frame of film she can't excise from the reel no mater how many times she pulls it from the projector and goes after it with a pair of scissors.

She sees them screwing when she's sorting her boss's mail into three neat piles—bills, junk, and personal.

She sees them screwing when she's printing out the seating chart for the Women of Industry breakfast at the Prestonwood Country Club her boss is scheduled to host later that month.

Everywhere Amber looks she sees the crazed rutting of her husband and that vile home wrecker in those last few seconds before the woman saw her standing in the doorway and let out a small scream.

She's not sure why, but she's convinced that after one week from that horrible, life-changing moment, things will get better. Or at least easier, if not altogether easy.

One week! That's all she needs.

One week between the present and those horrible twenty minutes it took her husband to empty his side of the closet into some suitcases, shouting excuses for his cheating while she sobbed in the other room.

Couldn't she see it was all her fault? She was the one who was always riding his ass. About what exactly he didn't say; maybe she'd said *Please don't break our marriage vows* one too many times for his liking? She was the cold fish in bed. She was the one who never wanted to be touched. The first accusation had been a steaming crock of bullshit, the second and third, outrages on par with his cheating.

For months she'd quizzed her girlfriends on how to liven things up between the sheets. And she hadn't just come up with new ideas. She'd bought toys, ordered costumes, printed dirty stories off the Internet she thought he would like and offered to read them to him. But every time she'd made an attempt to warm the chill that had gripped their bedroom for a year, he'd dismissed her like she was some sex freak. *The only problem, Amber, is that you keep saying there's a problem*, he'd told her again and again and again.

And yet, the one who couldn't connect was him, it turned out, and he couldn't connect because he was plugging himself into another socket every day at work.

"Amber?"

Her boss's confident baritone ripping out of the house's intercom system never fails to make her jump. But a few weeks into the job, she had trained herself not to scream whenever it happened. When she cries out this time, it leaves her red-faced and ashamed.

A short silence follows. Her boss heard her little outburst. Great.

"Darling, can I see you in my office upstairs?" Belinda Baxter says. Her East Texas twang makes everything she says sound vaguely accusatory, even when she throws in a *darling*, a *honey*, or a *sweetheart.*

"Be right there," Amber croaks, clearing her throat.

"Great. But first, honey, can you go to the wet bar in the living room and fix a vodka martini? I think Henry moved all the liquor in from the pool house after the Neighborhood Council meeting."

"How many olives?" Amber asks.

"However many you'd like, sweetheart. The drink's for you, not for me. See you in a bit."

So much for hiding my tears, she thinks.

She doesn't even like vodka, but when your wealthy boss offers you a top-shelf cocktail in the middle of a workday, you don't say no. That's just a given, she's sure of it. Maybe it's even written somewhere in the handbook of personal assistants. If there is a handbook for personal assistants. So far she's learned everything about working for Belinda on the fly, and she's only made a few missteps here and there. That's to be expected when you get hired to organize the personal details of a multimillionaire's life not on the basis of your actual resume, but because you made a moving speech about your late father's efforts to combat PTSD at a fundraiser organized by said multimillionaire.

The job comes with plenty of stress, but she can't think of a more comforting work environment, a sprawling, contemporary mansion in one of the best neighborhoods in Dallas. Indeed, Belinda's home is so thoroughly covered in cream-colored carpet and upholstery, so thoroughly dotted with fragrant room diffusers, sometimes she feels like she works inside of a really expensive breath mint no one can bring themselves to take a bite out of.

And Belinda's office would put Oprah's to shame. A fifteen-foot ceiling complete with a chandelier that would barely fit in Amber's living room. Soaring bookshelves in between gold-framed maps of all the oil fields her family has managed in the sixty years since her great grandfather struck black gold on his cattle ranch outside Fort Worth.

As usual, Belinda sits amidst this splendor dressed like she just stumbled out of a spin class. A pink workout visor sits on her tight cap of steel gray curls. Her yoga pants slide down her legs as she rests her sandaled feet on the edge of her antique black and gold Louis XIV desk.

Belinda doesn't look up when she enters, just keeps flipping through a copy of *Texas Monthly* so fast it looks like she's afraid all the pages will stick together if she pauses to read any of them. She loves her boss's mix of big money and no bullshit. Hell, she even invented her own term for it—*brash casual.* When Belinda took a liking to the phrase the minute she heard it, Amber knew they'd have a good relationship. Maybe even a kind of friendship.

"How's that drink, honey?" Belinda asks without looking up from her magazine.

"Haven't tried it yet. I'm no bartender."

"Have a seat and take a sip." She drops her feet to the floor and sets the magazine to one side.

Seated, Amber says, "I've got the seating chart for the Women of Industry breakfast all printed out if you—"

"Yeah, yeah, later. Sip, honey. That's an order."

As she feels the burn, she fights the urge to take in a deep, gasping breath and loses.

"Good stuff, huh?" Belinda asks.

"I'm not much of a drinker."

"I can tell."

"Am I getting fired?"

"You think I waste good vodka on people I'm about to fire?"

"It doesn't seem like your style, no."

"I figured if you had a drink in you, you'd be more likely to tell me the truth when I asked you what was really going on at home."

"I've told you the truth. We're having problems."

"Like *he left dirty dishes in the sink* problems or *her name's Tiffany and she makes him feel like a real man 'cause she's too young and stupid to know what a real man is* problems."

"Her name's Mary and she's twenty-four."

"Son of a bitch!" Belinda hurls the copy of *Texas Monthly* to the floor. "*Scum!* I knew he was scum. You gonna get offended if I tell you I knew your husband was scum? Knew it since he walked through the front door at my damn Christmas party."

"Just please don't tell me he hit on one of your nieces."

"Oh, hell, no. He didn't need to. I just had to look at him. That's all."

"Look at him?"

"I know his type. Five years ago he was God's gift to women. Now he's over thirty and the chicken fried steak's leaving its mark and the music career ain't happening, so he's expecting the world to make him feel as good as it did when no one was judging him on the content of his character. That's all Little Miss Mary's about."

Amber downs half the martini. This time it doesn't burn so much.

"There you go, sweetie," Belinda says.

"Wait…his *music career*? When did Joel tell you about his music career?"

"Wouldn't shut up about it at my Christmas party, soon as you were out of earshot. Forgive me for saying so but it didn't take a detective to figure out that the main reason he talked your daddy into leaving him that bar is so he'd have a stage for him and his band to play on. What the hell are they called again? The Junky Toadstools?"

"The Blinking Jailbirds." Just saying the name of her husband's band now feels like coughing up a razorblade.

Hell, just saying the name of her husband feels like coughing up a razorblade.

"God, that's worse. They any good?"

"No," Amber answers truthfully for the first time in her entire life.

"Well, there's one small blessing in all of this. You won't have to listen to them murder cats anymore."

"It's not that easy. The situation with the bar is…complicated."

"Yeah. How's he been at actually running the bar?"

"Not so great."

"Maybe that'll work in your favor. One thing's for sure. *I'll* work in your favor if you need it."

"Thank you, Belinda," Amber whispers. She's afraid if she answers in a full voice, her gratitude over this offer of assistance will cause her to break down again.

"Finish your drink, darlin'."

She complies, then gulps much needed air. "Listen, Belinda, if I've been falling down on the job, I apologize. I just need a week to—"

"You haven't been falling down on the job. Don't be so damn hard on yourself. I just got sick of listening to you cry. That's all."

"Wait. When did… Oh my God, were you listening to me cry on the intercom?"

"Honestly, I was hoping to overhear a phone conversation, but you're really good about not doing cell phone calls at work."

It's called texting, Amber thinks.

"I'm a bigger fan of Cowboys games, to be frank, but I had to know what was troubling my precious personal assistant on whom I rely for pretty much everything in the world now… Oh, don't get all sad faced on me. I only did it about five or six times."

"It's your house."

"Answer a question for me," Belinda says.

"Okay."

"Are you sad or are you just angry?"

"Can't I be both?"

"Nope."

"Why not?"

"You're one more than you are the other. That's always how it goes when marriages end. Pick one. Just for the sake of this discussion."

"Well, I cry all day at work, so what do you think?"

"What do you do when you're home?" Belinda asks, sinking back in her chair, hands clasped against her stomach.

"Not much."

"Liar," Belinda says with a smile.

"I've got a dartboard. I put his picture on it. It sounds stupid, but it makes me feel better."

"You any good at darts?"

"I've gotten better."

"Congratulations."

"Thanks, but there are easier ways to become a better darts player."

"I'm sure," Belinda says with a grunt. She leans forward suddenly. The chair rolls forward a few inches, the ends of its arms thudding against the edge of the desk. But Belinda's a small enough woman that she's still got plenty of room in which to make dramatic hand gestures. "You're not crying over what you've lost, Amber. You're crying because you don't know what lies ahead. That's a big difference."

"I take it you have some experience with this?"

"Three experiences to be exact. The first one cheated. The second one drank until I threw him out. The third once starved me in the bedroom 'cause he was hoping *I'd* cheat and then he could try to get some of my money."

"I see," she says.

"I didn't cheat, by the way."

"I didn't ask," Amber says. "None of my business."

"Oh, enough of that now. We're gonna get *all* up in each other's business today, girl."

Amber flushes.

"Oh, no! Not like that, Amber. I haven't swum in the lady pond since college. Don't get me wrong. I've got plenty of friends who do, but… We're having a heart to heart. That's all I'm saying."

"So this is your *heart* that you're showing me today?"

"You thought otherwise?"

Amber just stares at her.

"Fine!" Belinda cries, shooting up from the chair. "I'm telling you how you feel! And I'm doing it because I'm older and wiser and more experienced than you are. There. You happy?"

"Happy isn't really a word I'd apply to my situation just now."

"Well, waste as much time on tears as you want, Amber. But I saw y'all together. There was about as much love between you two as a rattler and my front tires."

"Which one am I? The snake or your Bentley?"

Belinda laughs.

She leans against a bookshelf, studying Amber with an expression Amber can only describe as serious. In another moment, the arch grin is gone and replaced by a look that seems both intent and faraway. Belinda's mind had traveled to another place. She's wondering if she should take Amber there with her.

"I know it hurts like hell," her boss finally says. "You married that man because he was handsome and charming and full of big promises. But when it came down to it, he wasn't very much at all."

"I didn't need him to become some big country music star."

"Of course not. You needed him to be a good husband, and he couldn't even do that *before* he cheated. It's hard to say, so I'll say it for you. Nod if you know it's true. You'll have to admit it someday."

Amber nods.

It makes her head feel heavy and her neck feel like it's got a spike in it, but she nods because it's the truth and Belinda's right; nodding is easier than saying it out loud. And now, for the first time since her marriage ended, she's crying in front of her boss. There's no denying it. Joel has been a man of broken promises for their entire marriage, he was just good at distracting her from the last broken promise by making a new and even bigger promise over the pricey champagne he'd bought her as an amends. This time, however, champagne's not going to fix a damn thing.

"It may not seem like it, but this is your moment, Amber." Her hands come to rest on Amber's shoulders. "This is your moment to decide what you really want, who you really are. The thing about you, girl, is you give all of yourself to people. It's just your nature. Personally I love it because it makes you a great assistant, but it's not about me right now. It's about you. And this is about the fact that whether you believe it or not, you're in a much better place than you think you are."

"How's that?" Amber croaks.

"You thought Joel was just second-rate and he ended up being last place. So it's not like you tried for the brass ring and fell flat on your face. Hell, you don't even know what kind of ring you want yet. Gold, silver, brass? It's up to you, babe. They're all yours to try for. Yours to discover. And *I* am gonna send you someplace that will make the whole discovery process easier."

"Like a spa day?"

Belinda cackles. "Oh, honey. It's a lot more than a spa day."

"Rehab for divorced people?"

"Nope. You got any plans in the next few weeks?"

"You mean aside from making sure my hu—*Joel* doesn't get the bar?"

"Two days. That's how much you'll need. Two days to get away. I'll give you the time off soon as we get your…appointment set up." Belinda hesitates over these last three words, as if everyday business terms don't apply to whatever she's talking about without really talking about it.

"No offense, Belinda, but I'm not really a seminar person."

"It's not a seminar. It changed my life for the better, but it's not a seminar."

"Well...what is it?"

Amber's startled by the seriousness in Belinda's expression.

"It's an experience," she whispers. "And by the time it's over, you'll have a much better grasp on who you really are. On who you really want."

"This *experience*...does it have a name?"

"The Desire Exchange," her boss answers.

"A sex club?" she cries before she can measure her tone. "You're sending me to a sex club?"

"It's far more than that."

"How much more?"

"A million flat. That's the price of admission. Which I'm gonna cover for you along with any other expenses related to the trip."

"I don't understand," she says because *thank you* seems premature.

Sure, it's a lot of money, but what the hell is it *for*?

"And you won't until you're there. But I promise you, I swear on every penny I have, *no one* will hurt you and you won't be forced to do anything you don't want to do."

"And you can't tell me anything else?"

"Except for this. When you leave The Desire Exchange, you'll leave behind a version of yourself that's caused you nothing but confusion and pain. The same version of yourself that thought Joel Claire was a great catch."

Belinda's one of the chattiest and most gossipy people Amber has ever met. But on the subject of this Desire Exchange place, her typical wisecracks have been replaced by the kind of proclamations Amber would expect to hear out of a lawyer or a judge. Maybe it's the hefty price tag involved. If there's one thing her boss takes seriously, it's money. And maybe for that reason alone, Amber should just get over it and say yes, despite the fact that she'd have absolutely no idea what she was agreeing to.

But she drank the martini when Belinda asked her, why not just—

Because it's a sex club! a voice that sounds like her mother's cries. *There's a big difference between a sex club and a martini! Especially when the price of admission is four times the cost of her house.*

"I can tell you this, sweetheart," Belinda says, sounding nothing like Amber's mother. "This isn't about letting off steam or making up for lost time or getting your inner wild child out of your system. It's more than that. So much more than that."

The expression on her boss's face does it. The satisfied, glassy-eyed smile. Whatever this Desire Exchange is, it took a woman like Belinda, a woman who's been given every blessing one could ask for, and gave her something more, something better.

Why not give it a try?

Amber's been a good little girl most of her life. Barely any hookups in college; none sober, anyway. Always waiting for date three before she gave anything away. And what did she get for all that? Manipulated, lied to, and cheated on.

"Fine," she hears herself whisper.

Just one word, but it feels like total surrender.

"Excellent!" Belinda cries, back to her chipper, hands-clapping self. "Now I'll just—"

The first text tone startles them both. It's Amber's phone. She waves her hand in the air to keep Belinda talking. But then there's another and another and another, and by the time Amber stands up and slides her phone from her pocket, she's got four messages in all. Two from Julio, the manager at Watson's, and two from Annabelle, who oversees the kitchen.

They all say the same thing.

"What is it?" Belinda asks.

"It's my hus—Joel," she says. "It's Joel. He's trying to change the locks at the bar."

"Go," Belinda cries. "Go now!"

Amber's already flying down the stairs by the time Belinda shouts, "Call me if you need help!"

2

For its first three years of operation, Abel Watson's struggling country music bar occupied a single storefront between an ice cream parlor and a yarn store in a lonely strip mall. Amber was just a toddler then. Later, her dad would tell stories about how his bacon was saved when a nearby subdivision announced a massive expansion, and shortly thereafter, he found himself the owner of an upscale alternative to the Ft. Worth Stockyards, a place for wealthy Dallasites to line dance and listen to authentic country music without first spending forty minutes in the car.

Today, Watson's takes up three storefronts instead of one. The once dreary strip small is now a bustling shopping center studded with elegant restaurants, a ladies only gym, and a condo high-rise. The mall's wealthy patrons clearly aren't used to seeing physical confrontations outside of places like The Big Bend Bread Factory and Muriel's French Kitchen. That must be why several of them are frozen in place, a few paces from their parked cars, gawking at the standoff between Watson's entire lunchtime staff and Amber's husband.

The van for some locksmith company is parked a few yards away, right next to Joel's dusty pickup.

Dressed for work in his Western duds, Julio, Watson's manager of ten years, stands right in front of the entry door. He's about half the size of Amber's soon-to-be ex-husband, but his arms are splayed across the door behind him, his body tense and taut, as if he's prepared to launch himself at Joel the second the man gestures for the locksmith to step out of his van.

Annabelle, the kitchen manager who used to babysit Amber when she was a little girl, is right next to him, still in her apron, her back pressed to one quarter of the entrance, arms crossed tightly over her boat's prow of a chest. She's wearing her apron which means she was in the middle of work when Joel started whatever this nonsense is.

"Profanity's not going to be your best choice, here, alright Julio?" Joel is saying when she walks up. "Now if you'd all just step aside, we can avoid involving law enforcement. And that, my folks, means we can also avoid checking on the immigration status of any—"

"We're all legal!" Julio shouts. "And you'd know that if you weren't a lousy manager."

"Why's that, Julio?" Joel asks.

Annabelle says, "You have our papers on file, asshole!"

"Alright, so apparently the cursing just isn't going to stop which means I'm gonna have to put in a call to our friends at the Dallas Po—" He's in mid-dial when he sees her charging toward him down the sidewalk. "Goddammit to hell!" he shouts at the crowd. "Now who called Amber? That is just *not* appropriate! That is not appropriate at all."

"What are you doing?" she asks.

It's the closest they've been in days. Everyone on the curb seems to know it. They're being stared at like strippers outside a church on a Sunday.

"We're gonna need to have a pause while we work all this out," Joel says quietly. "That's all."

"A *pause*. What the hell does that mean?"

"He's not just changing the locks, Amber," Julio shouts. "He's shutting the place down."

Annabelle says, "He came in 'bout a half hour ago and told us all to go home. Locksmith pulled up about five minutes after that and he got all pissed because the guy was early. He wanted us all gone so we wouldn't know he was try—"

"For the last time! I am *not* shutting the place down," Joel barks. "I am stopping business temporarily while we sort everything out. That's all."

"That's *all*? You've got four acts booked this week alone," she says. "What are you going to tell their managers?"

"That the club's working out some issues related to ownership and we'll rebook as soon as they've been sorted out."

"Related to ownership?" she screams.

"It's just a business term, Amber."

"*Ownership*? Of my *father's* bar?"

"We're gonna figure this out. Would you just relax already?"

"Three of those shows you're canceling are sold out, Joel! That doesn't sound like good ownership to me."

"Yeah, well, I changed our refund policy."

"You can't—Watson's has been in business for *twenty-five* years. You don't have the right to shut this place down on a whim."

"A whim, huh? Is that what you call the end of our marriage?"

Discussing the end of her marriage right now in front of everyone would be an indignity worse than what he put her through a few days before.

"This club isn't about *us*, Joel. It's about the people who work here. It's about the music. It's about my father. He trusted you to—"

"To run it, exactly. And this is me running it. I own Watson's so I'll—"

"An LLC owns Watson's!"

"Yeah, and I'm the majority partner. Because that's how your father wanted it. Because he knew you and your mother didn't know a damn thing about how to run a business."

"My father gave you this place because you bullied him into it on his deathbed!"

It's the first time she's ever spoken this truth out loud. And she expects it to knock her soon-to-be ex-husband off his feet.

But Joel Claire, it turns out, is nothing if not resourceful.

"There!" he cries. "Did everyone hear my wife's acknowledgment that her father *gave* me this bar?"

"I heard her!"

The shrill cry has come from the direction of Joel's truck. Mary, the same woman she caught her husband fucking a few days ago, throws herself halfway out of the passenger side window of his pickup truck, wearing a big smile on her rosy-cheeked face.

In a low voice, Annabelle says, "Dogs should keep their heads inside cars. They might get hurt."

"I heard that too," Mary cries.

"Oh, yeah? Bowwow, *puta*!" Annabelle shouts back.

"You're fired!" Joel shouts at Annabelle.

"Uh huh, sure," Annabelle responds without moving an inch.

"Stop it, Joel," Amber says. "Whatever you're doing, just stop it!"

"I am, Amber," Joel whispers. "I'm putting a stop to everything until we figure out what we're gonna do."

"We're getting divorced," she whispers back. "That's what we're gonna *do*."

"I'm aware of that, sweetheart. I'm talking about the next verse of *my* song, not yours."

No thought to the years they've spent together. No thought for the plans they'd made for kids, for a life. Just a few days out from being caught red-handed with another woman and already her husband's thinking of the business, of money, of himself. She'd always made allowances for his ambition, had figured ambition was part of any exceptional man. But her husband, she can see now, isn't just ambitious; he's self-obsessed and greedy. The sight of him now, plotting his next career move with her father's life's work gripped in one fist, is a harder slap in the face than the sight of him fucking another woman.

"Jesus, Amber," Joel whispers at the sight of her tears. "Don't cry in front of them."

"Howdy, songbirds!" a familiar voice says from several feet behind her.

Amber hasn't laid eyes on him in four years, and even though she wouldn't have thought it possible, during that time Caleb has somehow grown taller and broader. He still walks with a casual, confident gait she'd be able to spot across a crowded arena, like he knows his sheer size is a better indication of his strength than any menacing pose could ever be. His Stetson's the right size now, unlike the ones he used to wear as a kid, and the brim shades the hard, etched features of a fully grown man, a man with a voice so deep it sounds like it's coming from some otherworldly place where he rules as king. His eyes are still so sparkling and blue she can't look into them without blushing. His jeans are scuffed and tattered, but his cowboy boots are brand new; so is his red and black plaid shirt. Not just new, spotless and freshly ironed.

Did he dress up a little for this surprise visit? Did he dress up for *her*?

"What are you doing here, Caleb?" Joel asks, his tone suddenly tense.

"Just got back in town last night. Thought I'd stop by the family business and have some lunch. But it doesn't look like lunch is being served."

"Who called him?" Joel shouts over one shoulder with real fear in his voice. No one answers. *"Who called him?"*

"Nobody called me, songbird," Caleb says. "Quiet down. You don't want to damage your signing voice there. Hey. You alright, Amber?"

"I…"

Her throat closes up. Maybe it's the shock of seeing Caleb for the first time in years. Maybe she just can't bring herself to spill her guts right there on the sidewalk, to paint the full picture of how awful Joel is being to her, to all of them.

"You know, well, uhm…" Joel says, with the nervous stutter of an elementary school student giving his first presentation in front of his classmates. "I'm sorry to say I've got to close the place for a week or two." Joel's voice seems to get a little shakier with each step Caleb takes toward him. "I'm not sure if you've heard but Amber and I…Well, we've decided to end our marriage."

Caleb freezes, expression hard as stone and impossible to read.

"I hadn't heard that, no."

There's now about three feet of space between Joel and the man she cannot bring herself to call her brother despite what the adoption papers might say.

"Well…" Joel says. "In light of that—I mean, given how much there's going to be to deal with, we just need to stop operating for a short while and then we'll be back—"

"How long's a while?" Caleb asks.

"Just a few weeks 'til we gets things sorted out. Now, with all due respect, this is a family matter so if you could ju—"

"I am family," Caleb says.

"On paper, maybe. But come on, now. We all know Abel was

just—"

"My father," Caleb says. "Abel Watson was the only real father I ever had."

"Sure, sure. Of course. But if you'd ju—"

"He cheated on her, Caleb!" Annabelle snaps. "She caught him in the back room last week with that girl over there in his truck. Now he's trying to take the bar so he can use it to promote his crappy band."

"Shut up, Annabelle!" Joel cries.

Caleb's entire body goes rigid. Amber's seen this change overtake him many times, mostly when they were teenagers and brawling became Caleb's preferred method for dealing with his grief for his parents. She knows just where to look for the telltale sign of the anger knotting itself through his soul; it's in the right corner of his powerful jaw. The tension there is suddenly so strong it sends that section of his jawbone into sharp relief. He has to tilt his head gently to one side to be rid of it, an oddly prim gesture for a guy on the verge of venting rage.

"That true, Amber?" Caleb asks.

"Yes. I caught 'em. It's true."

Joel takes a step toward Caleb. "Look, I don't mean to be blunt, *cowboy*, but this doesn't concern you, alright? And Amber and I don't need to litigate our marriage right here in front of—"

The punch is so silent and swift Amber's not sure where it landed. One minute Joel's standing, the next he's flat on his back. No blood comes from his nostrils. The hand Joel finally manages to bring to his face lands weakly on his jaw. As he wheezes, he blinks up at Caleb as if he's in genuine fear for his life.

"Try to get up," Caleb says quietly. "Just fucking try it. I dare you."

Joel doesn't get up.

Caleb steps off the sidewalk and starts for Joel's pickup truck.

"Drive away!" he calls to the terrified woman in the passenger seat.

"What?" Mary squeals. In her panic, she's pulled off one of her shoes and she's holding it beside her head like a makeshift baton.

"Roll up the window and drive away," Caleb says firmly.

"It's *his* truck!" Mary whines.

"Don't care," Caleb answers.

"Where am I supposed to go?" Mary asks.

"Somewhere Amber doesn't have to look at you. You got all of North Texas to choose from. Take your pick and get moving."

Mary crawls over the gearshift and into the driver's seat. Without taking her eyes off Caleb, she starts rolling up the window like a swarm of killer bees are heading straight for Joel's pickup. Caleb points at the parking lot's nearest exit.

The tires literally squeal as Joel's mistress abandons him.

As if he's just completed a task as simple as removing a kink from a garden house, Caleb turns and walks back toward the spot where Joel is still flat on his back, rubbing his bruised jaw with one hand.

"Got any brain damage there, songbird?" Caleb asks.

Joel wheezes.

"Okay. Good. 'Cause I'm gonna need you to take this all in, and it's complicated, so pay attention. You know that trust fund Abel set up to provide you with a cushion while you got started? The one that's got the proceeds of his retirement in it? The one you've been relying on for your marketing budget now for *four years*? Guess who's the trustee?"

Joel groans.

"Yeah, see, he didn't want to make me a partner in the LLC 'cause he didn't want you to think he didn't trust you. But just in case you *did* turn out to be a steaming stack of shit on a hot highway, he wanted a fail-safe in place. And that fail-safe's me, asshole."

"Whu—what do you…?" Joel tries.

"It means you do anything other than make a graceful exit—and by graceful, I mean you sign over your majority share back to Amber *tomorrow*—then your little slush fund's gone." Caleb snaps his fingers to indicate how quickly he'll make that happen. "And in your case, that means no radio spots, no T.V. spots, no nothing to promote any band you'd even think about bringing in here. Including *yours*. The Shitty Taillights, or whatever the hell they're called."

"The Blinking Jailbirds," Joel mutters in a lisping voice.

That's when Amber notices his bottom lip is swelling. "You can't...You can't do that. You—"

"I can and I will," Caleb says. "Four years now and you've got this place down to just above the red. Every other week you're switching out a menu item to something three times the cost. Paying shit-ass consultants thousands to find out what it would take to turn the place into a *wine bar.* You know damn well if you have to run this place off what you make from buffalo steaks and Corona, there won't be a dollar left to launch your music career. So sure, songbird. Go right ahead. Make a play. And I'll make sure you won't get a single band, manager, agent, or A&R guy anywhere within a hundred feet of you and this place."

She's more startled by the facts Caleb's just revealed in his speech than she was by the sight of her husband cheating on her.

Caleb, a *trustee*?

She's barely heard from him in four years, ever since her father died. Just a postcard here and there, usually with a line or two about whatever job he'd managed to land that month. Truck driver in the North Dakota oil fields. Ranch hand at some big spread up in Montana.

She figured he'd taken her father's death—*their* father, she reminds herself, against her will—harder than she had. She'd never imagined him playing any role at all in the business, not now, not ever. And yet, the whole time he'd been gone, the whole time he'd been riding the ranges, driving oil-filled trucks through the lonely highways of the Great Plains, Caleb had been reviewing paperwork and bank documents, using his position as trustee to monitor Joel's stewardship of her father's lifework.

Of course, he couldn't have learned all of what he'd just said from the bank. He'd probably stayed in touch with Julio and Annabelle too. The knowledge that for the past few years Caleb has been closer than she realized leaves her breathless. She's not sure if she likes the feeling.

Things seemed easier when Caleb was far away. For her heart, at least. For her head. But given how bad things are now, apparently it only seemed that way. In fact, now that he's back, it looks like things are going to get a lot better.

Joel struggles to his feet. The bruise on the left side of his jaw has doubled in size. When he goes to speak, his swollen lip seems to cause him so much sudden pain his sneer turns into a pained grimace.

"I don't need this place," he finally manages. "I don't need...*you two*!" He says the last words with such venom she's surprised when he doesn't follow them up by spitting at her feet. "You can have it. Take it. Run it *together*. Make it your special little project. I'm sure y'all will have a blast. Brother and sister, sitting in a tree—"

"Joel," she says before she can stop herself.

"Oh, come on. I've seen the way you look at him—"

"Joel," Caleb says this time. "There may be a saying about not punching the same man twice in one day, but I ain't ever heard it."

Joel gives them both a leering grin. When he starts to walk away, his first steps become stumbles.

Caleb moves out of his path, hands out and a polite smile on his face, like someone letting a drunk move past them in a crowded bar. Amber can hear sighs of relief from the staff when Joel gets a few yards from the curb and yanks his phone from his jeans pocket. But just then, he spins in place. She's surprised when he shouts a name other than her own.

"Hey, Annabelle," he shouts. "Since I finally got the chance to say this, your food? It's *shit*!"

"Oh, Mister Joel," Annabelle says with a broad grin. "That's 'cause I always added something special just for you."

Joel does his best impression of an idiot's laugh. But Annabelle keeps smiling and nodding, as if the memory of whatever she added to Joel's meals is a warm and happy thing that will sustain her for years to come.

His parting shot having missed its target, Joel stumbles off into the parking lot.

"So," Caleb says, "who wants some lunch?"

3

Watson's is so cavernous it feels to Amber like she and Caleb are the only ones inside. But Annabelle and her three cooks are busy making up for lost time in the kitchen while Julio and his servers frantically set up tables on the three levels of platforms surrounding the empty, sunken dance floor.

Nothing bums her out more than the sight of a dark stage, but apparently she's in the minority, because in a few minutes, the place will be packed with hungry regulars even though the only music will be coming from the jukebox.

Caleb walks up to the beer taps like he owns the place which, given what she learned a few moments before , he just might. He fills a pint glass with amber ale and sets it on the bar in front of her with a loud *thunk*.

"Thanks," she says. "But I had a martini at work."

"Hot damn!" he says. "I want your job."

"Not enough manual labor for you," she says. "And since when do you like martinis?"

"Since never. 'Sides, looks like I'm out of the job market now."

"How's that?"

"Gonna have my work cut out for me with this place."

"You're staying?" she asks.

Does this excite her or fill her with dread? She always feels a mixture of both when Caleb's around.

"Somebody's gotta run this place now that Joel's out of the picture."

"Caleb, I really appreciate what you did out there. Seriously, I do. But I'm not sure it was enough to get Joel out of the picture for good."

"You're not asking me to kill him, are you? Can I pat you down? You wearing a wire?"

"No!" she barks.

"No to which? The wire or the pat down?"

"I don't think Joel is through with us yet, is what I'm saying."

"Fine. Next time I'll aim for his stomach." He sinks his teeth into his lower lip, throws a mock punch into the air in front of him.

"Be serious. Please."

"Oh, I'm damn serious. He's not getting his hands on anything in this bar. Not the jukebox. Not the barstools. Not *nothing*. And I'm sticking around to make sure of it. Unless, you know, you think you can handle this place by yourself."

"I didn't say I didn't want you around."

"Didn't say you said that, sis."

"Please don't call me that!"

The words slip out before she can stop them, words she's stopped herself from saying again and again over the years whenever Caleb referred to her as his sister or called Abel his dad. They sound as dismissive and possessive as she feared they would. Like she's just some spoiled only child who doesn't want to share her father.

Explaining the far more complicated truth of the matter would fill her with shame. And besides, part of him *must* know.

Is that why he's staring at her now with the same intense gaze she used to dream about when they were teenagers?

He's certainly not doing that thing he usually does when he's hurt and trying to hide it; he doesn't cast his eyes to one side while he puckers his lips and looks for a task to distract himself with. Instead, he stares at her as if he's waiting for her to explain, waiting for her to take them back to the night on the boat dock before everything changed.

She can't look into those blue eyes for very long without the world feeling like it doesn't have an up or a down anymore. So she takes a sip of beer instead.

"I already called the bank while you were in the bathroom," he says. "No more automatic deposits into the operating fund. Not until we get this cleaned up. And I'm sorry to lay this on you this hard, Amber, but Joel won't give two shits about this place if there's nothing in that operating fund for him to spend on his band."

She doesn't need him to say the rest, that Joel doesn't care about *her* either. The only thing that makes this easier to accept is the dawning realization that Joel isn't really capable of caring about anyone except himself.

Good luck, Mary. Hope you used protection!

"So that's it?" she asks. "One call and the deposits stop?"

"They're not stopping. They're going into my checking account. I'll pay the bills myself until we kick Joel out of the LLC."

"You can do that? I mean, is that really how Dad set up the trust?"

"Yep," he answers.

"So this whole time you could have raided that trust fund with a phone call and instead you were driving trucks and working oil fields?"

"Not the whole time. A few years back I was a hand on a big spread outside Surrender, Montana. Didn't you get my postcards?"

Yeah, and who sends postcards anymore? she almost says. But she answers her own question instantly—*people who are afraid of e-mail because it gives them too much space to talk about forbidden feelings.*

"Still," she says.

"Abel trusted me to make the right call. The right call was giving you and Joel a shot. And giving you and Joel a shot meant giving Joel a shot at running this place. Also, it seemed like you loved him."

"You think I'm an idiot, don't you?" she says.

"I've never thought anything of the kind, Amber."

"You, Dad. You both knew. That's why you set up the trust like that. You both knew Joel was awful and you were just too afraid to say—"

"That's not true, Amber. We would've had doubts about anybody, *anybody* you were going to marry, especially someone who thought he was good enough to run the family business. If we'd had any idea what a shit Joel was going to turn out to be, we wouldn't have let him within ten feet of the house. Or you."

"I still feel like an idiot," she whispers.

"Well, that's a bunch of bull. You have to try for stuff, especially when it comes to marriage."

"Got a lot of experience in the marriage area, huh?"

Now Caleb does look away quickly.

When he turns his back to her and opens the nearest register, she realizes he's not hurt. He's hiding something.

"Wait a minute," she says. "Wait just a minute. You got *married*?"

She looks to the hands he's suddenly counting bills with. No ring.

"Did you really get married without telling us?" she asks.

"It was a spur of the moment thing."

"Like a Vegas spur of the moment thing?"

"No!"

"Are you still married?"

"No!"

"I can't believe you didn't tell me."

He shakes his head at the register, but he doesn't say anything.

She remembers the way he acted at her own wedding, how uncomfortable he looked inside the suit her father had bought for him just a few weeks before. He'd never been a big drinker, probably because of what alcohol had done to his father, but he'd shotgunned so many Coronas during the first twenty minutes of the reception, she'd been afraid he was going to embarrass himself. Instead, he ended up silent and sullen and rooted to a far corner of the reception hall where he ignored the flirtations of a dozen different women. Every few minutes, she'd caught him staring at her. And then there'd been his curt good-bye—a brief peck on the cheek for her, and for Joel, a hard clap on the back followed by the words, "You break her heart and I'll rip you to fucking shreds, dude." And then he was gone before either she or her new husband could remark that his parting words were the kind of thing an ex-boyfriend might say, not an adopted brother.

Maybe Caleb had wanted to spare her the same discomfort, the same storm of conflicted feelings, by not telling her about his spur of the moment wedding.

Maybe he was trying to spare her now by not giving her the details.

"I want details," Amber says.

"It was lonely work I was doing. She was transitioning away from someone else."

"You mean rebounding."

"Yeah. Sure. Rebounding. Whatever. We parted as friends. Maybe because we didn't have a bar to fight over."

"How'd you meet her?"

"I don't want to talk about her."

"Doesn't seem fair," she mumbles, sipping her beer.

"*What* doesn't seem fair?" he says, cocking one eyebrow and giving her a sidelong look while he counts bills.

"I don't know. Having the end of my whole marriage laid out on the sidewalk outside for you like road kill, and I just ask for a few details and suddenly you're like—"

"That is so like you, Amber."

"What? *What's* so like me?"

"That's what people call a false equivalency."

"False equivalency? That's not a Caleb expression. Where'd you learn that one? Your ex-wife? What was she? A college professor?"

"She was a scheduler I worked with up in North Dakota. They've barely got any pipeline up there so I was doing truck pickups from fracking platforms all day long. It started with radio talk and then moved on to dinner."

And then all those hard muscles of yours flexing as you bring yourself down onto the body of some strange woman and—

"And then marriage," she adds to distract herself from this image.

"Uh huh. But no baby carriage. And no white wedding I didn't invite you to either. So stop acting all butthurt and drink your beer. I'm here to save the day, remember?"

"Butthurt. Now *there's* a Caleb expression."

"Glad to see you haven't lost your mouth, sis," he says.

Done counting the money, he bumps the register drawer shut with one hip.

This time she doesn't ask him not to call her sis again. But she can see the challenge in his eyes. Did he use the term again on purpose? Does he want her to snap at him again for using it so that he can finally, after all these years, come right out and ask her why she really hates it when he refers to her as his sister?

"So here we are," Caleb finally says. "Pushing thirty and both divorced. Abel Watson was a helluva man but he sure didn't teach us how to stay married, did he?"

She knows he's kidding, but his words cut deep. The cocky grins fades from his expression as soon as he sees the look on her face.

"Hey," he says quietly. "That— Shit, that came out wrong. Sorry."

"It's fine," she whispers.

Amber allowed herself a few minutes of tears after they all filed back into the bar. But she'd been in the bathroom alone. Not sitting at the bar in front of Caleb.

He's resting one hand on top of hers, so gently she almost didn't notice at first. She stares at it. Tells herself to look up into his eyes because his eyes will tell her what this sudden touch actually means. But she can't. She just stares at his powerful, veined hand, hears her next words as if some other version of her has spoken them.

"When a man won't sleep with his wife, that's a problem, right? I mean, she should know something's wrong… Right?"

He removes his hand so quickly, she's left to wonder if he thinks that touching her in any way when she simply mentions sex might seal them together in some awkward or painful way.

"Maybe," Caleb says.

His Adam's apple bobs. He sucks in a quick breath through his nose and grips the counter on either side of him.

"We don't usually talk about sex stuff," he finally says with a startling blend of tension and hunger in his voice, the same way he'd tell a woman she was wearing a pretty dress even though he was really thinking of what she'd look like once he'd pulled her out of it.

"It's a simple question, Caleb."

"You're asking the wrong one."

"Am I?"

"You're asking if it's your fault. You're asking if you should take on the burden of a man like Joel. The answer's no. Scratch that. The answer's *hell* no. Kick his ass to the curb and get the hell out. But don't take responsibility for his failings. Not now, not ever. Feelings aren't a choice. Cheating is. If he was half a man, he would have come to you about the stuff that was making him want to cheat six months before he ever did it. If he were a *real* man, he would have copped to the fact that the stuff that was making him want to cheat probably didn't have a damn thing to do with you."

For the first time in years, she allows herself to gaze into Caleb's eyes, those beautiful, dazzling blue eyes. Her *brother's* blue eyes. And for the first time in a while, this knowledge doesn't dim her fantasies of what it would be like to taste his lips again, to rock forward into his powerful embrace.

She allows her mind to swim in the memory of that long ago night before everything changed, when the two of them were brought together by the promise of becoming something altogether different than what they are today.

Caleb stares right back. Has he gone back to the boat dock of her father's lake house?

Is he remembering what it felt like to gather her T-shirt into his fists in those last blissful moments before her father's cry pierced the dark?

It's no matter. Her father's voice returns just as it always does in moments like these, with the exact same tone he'd used with her that one time they were hiking and he overturned a log with a snake coiled under it.

Back away, girl, he'd say. *Back away, right now.*

Caleb's had his moments of aggression over the years, but he's no snake.

Still, the ghost of her father stands between them now. Her father's wishes. Her father's plans.

Her phone vibrates on the bar in front of her.

It's a text from Belinda asking if she's okay.

"I need to get back to work," she says.

"Not sure you should be driving right now," Caleb says.

"I bet. You're the one who just served me a beer even though I told you I had a martini at work."

"Is that why you want to get back? Your boss has better well drinks?"

"My boss doesn't serve well drinks."

"I forget. She's a fancy lady."

"She's got a fancy house. She's practically a cowgirl at heart. Kinda like your ex-wife, it sounds like."

"Uh huh. Julio'll get someone to drive you. Or I could drive you."

Alone in the car with Caleb. The thought makes her head spin. Amazing how many times in her life she's avoided being alone with him for more than ten or fifteen minutes. The effort became so commonplace when they were younger that it took Caleb leaving town for her to realize how much it had exhausted her.

"Belinda's got a driver," she says too quickly, like she's trying to protect herself from the fact that Caleb is just being a good guy.

"Suit yourself," he says.

"Thank you. For everything."

"Sure thing," he says.

"I'd give you a hug, but…"

"I'm behind the bar. Right. Don't worry about it."

She picks up her phone in one hand and gives him a weak wave with the other. A few paces from the bar, she turns. He hasn't moved an inch. He's staring at her with one hand resting on the counter next to the register.

"Where are you staying?" she asks.

"Old friend's letting me crash with him for a while."

"Where?"

"Denton."

"*Denton*? That's far!"

"Yeah, well, looks like I'll be looking for a place closer in now. Closer to this place, anyway."

"Keep me posted," she says.

"Sure thing, sis."

She steps through the entrance. On the sidewalk, she sucks in a deep, hungry breath of humid air.

She's not drunk. But Caleb's right. She shouldn't drive. And she wonders now if the real reason he put that beer in front of her was because he didn't want her to leave at all.

Then

Standing on the tip of the dock, Amber watches Caleb race up the cedar steps toward her dad. They're about to smack into each other when her dad seizes Caleb by his shoulders, halting him mid-stride.

Maybe she was wrong about the sadness in her father's voice a few seconds before.

Maybe he really is about to whoop Caleb within an inch of his life for giving her a kiss that made her forget her name. But violence isn't her father's style. At least not when she's around. But it is her father's style to pull the Band-Aid off in one swift motion. That's why it takes him a few seconds to deliver the awful news.

After promising to stay sober thirty days, Caleb's father snuck out to his local watering hole where his mom found him on his favorite barstool and literally dragged him out into the parking lot. The tussle that ensued might have ended uneventfully in any other environment, but on the side of a busy freeway it sent them both into the path of an eighteen-wheeler, killing them instantly.

She has never seen her father deliver news this terrible before. She's got no sense of what he's going to do now that the words are out.

A wail of pure anguish rips from Caleb, filled with more pain than any fifteen-year-old should be allowed to feel. Her father throws his arms around the boy, so tightly it looks as if he's afraid the news will literally drive Caleb apart. In that moment, her love for her dad grows roots nothing will be able to dig up.

She joins them, holding up the right side of Caleb's suddenly boneless body while her father holds up the left. The three of them struggle up the steps as Caleb's sobs rend her soul. But a part of her knows the crying is good and healthy, even if the cause is horrible. Caleb's releasing all the pain and anger he's kept bottled up for years now, and Amber and her father are right there to help him through it.

"Get him to bed," her dad whispers as soon as they're inside.

In the guest room, Caleb collapses onto the mussed comforter, curls into a fetal position, and starts to cry harder when she curls up behind him and drapes one arm over his side. She keeps her own tears as quiet as possible. That only seems right.

In the living room her father makes a frantic-sounding series of phone calls. She can only make out every few words. He's booking flights, it sounds like, or maybe he's just breaking the news to people. She's not sure.

Because they're spooning, she doesn't see him reach up to where her hand is resting against his chest. Instead, she feels his fingers close around hers and she returns his grip.

She has no words for him as powerful as simply being there with him, beside him in the dark. When staying silent becomes too much for her, she gently kisses the back of his neck. He gives her fingers a little squeeze in response.

The house is silent. She's not sure how much time has passed.

Suddenly her dad's silhouette blocks the light from the hallway. With careful steps he moves into the darkened bedroom. He sets a glass of water on Caleb's nightstand, grips the boy's shoulder, studies him through the shadows.

"Making arrangements to get you home, son," her dad says. "I'm going to go with you, get you through everything you need to do, 'kay?"

"Yes, sir," Caleb croaks.

"I need Amber for a minute. You going to be okay in here for a few?"

"Yes, sir."

She follows her father downstairs to the living room.

On the muted television, Dave Letterman cracks a joke and a faraway audience of people laugh silently. The sight seems obscene given what's happening, so she looks away from it quickly as if it's burned her eyes.

In a hushed whisper, her father says, "My buddy Dale Parsons is at his place on the other side of the lake and he flew his Cessna up. He'll fly us back to Dallas."

She's not surprised that her father is all business in this

moment. Her mother has explained it to her countless times—this is how her father loves people. He organizes; he manages. She figures he's avoiding eye contact because he doesn't want her to see that he's been crying.

"Okay," she whispers. "Should I get my things?"

"No, you're staying," he says quickly, as if this were an obvious fact she'd simply overlooked. "I know you hate being here alone so Miss Lita, Dale's wife, she's coming over to stay with you. You remember her, right? You met her at Fourth of July last year. Remember?"

"I remember," she says. But her own voice sounds far away suddenly. Something else is happening here, and she's not sure what. "Who's going to bring me back to Dallas?"

"I just spoke to your momma and she's going to cut her visit to her sister short and take Southwest in tomorrow. She'll probably be here by the afternoon. I'll leave the SUV up at the airport so y'all can drive it back to Dallas. No need for you to rush either. There's gonna be a lot he and I are going to have to deal with as soon as we get back. A whole helluvalot."

"Why can't I just go with y'all?"

"I don't think there's room on the plane."

She knows this isn't true. Dale Parsons flies his whole family up sometimes and they've got three kids. And her dad's choice of words is weird. *I don't think there's room.*

Why didn't he ask if there was room?

"Daddy…"

Suddenly her father grips her shoulders tightly. He's got an angry furrow to his brow. When he clears his throat, she realizes he's about to say words he's been practicing in his head for a few minutes now. "Amber, look. I know how you feel about the boy. I know what y'all were doing down there, but that needs to change now. You understand me? Caleb's gonna be in our lives now, but not in the way you want. And that's what's best for *him*. So you need to take all those feelings you're having for him and you need to change 'em. You need to turn 'em into something else. Something that's better for him. Do you understand me, girl? Are you hearing me right now?"

Better for him. Such simple words, and he said them in such a measured tone. But she's registered them the way she might register a slap to the face.

All her feelings for Caleb, all her dreams about him, all the longing looks she's given him that summer, her father could sense all of it. And he's judged her for it, judged her as bad. So bad, he thinks he has to put a stop to those feelings in the middle of this awful moment that will change their lives forever. He's determined to keep her and Caleb apart at the very moment when Caleb is most vulnerable.

She's always been a daddy's girl. The title's never bothered her in the slightest. Everyone agrees: her dad's a success in life and he's going to make her a success too. He's saved enough money for her to go to a good college. He's a war hero who will walk through fire for his fellow vets. Sure, he's controlling and overbearing, but the way he controls things, it all usually works out in the end. Right now, though, she wants to bat his hands from her shoulders. She wants to scream in frustration, and holding in that scream is making her jaw quiver. She can feel it.

"Amber," he says, an angry edge to his voice now. "Do you *hear* me?"

"Yes," she whispers. "I hear you, Daddy."

"Good," he whispers. Then he brings his hand to the side of her face, suddenly affectionate, suddenly relieved, like she's agreed to take medicine he's sure will save her life.

"I'm sorry, honey," he says. "I know it's not what you want. But it's like I always say, sometimes the road rises up to beat you instead of meet you." It's one of his favorite sayings, one he claims to have invented, and one he only uses when some grand plan of his has been defeated despite his best efforts. Saying it now has clearly sent regret coursing through him given how Mister Tim and Miss Abby were killed. "God in heaven," he whispers. "I'm gonna have to shelve that old saw after tonight."

A few seconds later, Miss Lita knocks on the glass door. When her father slides it open, she steps into the living room quietly, her eyes glassy from a combination of drowsiness and shock. It's clear she dressed in a hurry. Her thick ponytail is already coming free of its rubber band. When she sees the look on Amber's face, she curves an arm around her shoulders and steers her into the kitchen.

The neighbor's sudden tenderness frees the tears Amber's been fighting. She turns her back to the living room so her father won't see, but from the way the older woman is rubbing circles on her back, it's clear to all of them what Amber's doing.

"Where's Caleb?" Lita asks.

"In the guest bedroom," Amber whispers.

"Should we go sit with him?"

"No," Amber says, her voice a tremble. "No, we shouldn't."

4

Now

"Married?" Amber's mother says for the third time in three minutes.

"Yep," Amber answers.

She's been home for over an hour but she hasn't moved an inch from where she collapsed on the sofa right after stumbling through the front door. Reaching for the portable phone and dialing her mother's number took most of the energy she had left.

At some point, maybe a few hours from now, she'll get around to taking her shoes off. Maybe.

She can't remember a day in her life this exhausting that didn't involve moving or a six-hour plane flight or a spin class. But her mood has improved dramatically since lunchtime. That's for sure. Maybe it was coming home to discover Joel hadn't done anything shitty to the house. Maybe it's the familiar and comforting sound of her mother's voice.

Or maybe it's because Caleb's back…

"For how long?" her mother asks.

"Couldn't have been more than a year or two. He was only gone four and they're already divorced."

"Divorced or separated?"

"Not sure. He just said it was over. And there's no ring. I'm surprised he didn't tell you, at least."

"Oh, I'm not. He never had the kind of connection to me that he had to your dad."

"That's true, I guess."

"This business with Joel and the bar. You sure you don't want me to come?"

"God, why? So he can torture you too?"

"I'm serious, sweetheart. Say the word and I'll hop in the car."

Her mother was being charitable, to say the least. For her *a hop in the car* meant a drive of several hours, at least.

Her mom's life choices these past few years had given proof to her dad's old saying. *Try to make an ER nurse retire and she'll end up treating the sunset.*

Right after her husband's death, she'd been invited to spend some time in the Texas Hill Country by her old friend Amanda Crawford, a woman whose personal wealth rivaled Belinda's. Amanda's ten-room mansion perched on a hill just outside the town of Chapel Springs was the perfect vantage point from which to take in the surrounding paradise of rolling green hills, orchards, and rushing creeks terminating in swimming holes full of crystal-clear water.

The two women were as close as sisters, thanks to a fateful night fifteen years before when Amber's mom and some other nurses at Baylor Hospital saved the life of Amanda's husband after his ER visit landed him in the care of an idiot doctor who misdiagnosed his chest pains as a panic attack. Years later, Amanda's husband would succumb to the same heart condition Amber's mother had discovered that night, but if it hadn't been for her mother's quick thinking, Amanda would have had to bury her husband ten years too soon.

When her mother fell in love with Chapel Springs right off the bat, Amber wasn't the least bit surprised. But when she called a few days later to inform Amber she was moving there for good, Amber's jaw hit the floor.

Amanda Crawford's invite, it turned out, had been twofold.

The woman had just purchased an old ranch house she planned to transform into a luxury bed and breakfast and she'd invited the four nurses who had saved her husband's life that long ago night to join her in the endeavor. And all of them had accepted. Including Amber's mom. Never mind that The Haven Creek Inn wasn't due to open for another year and a half.

Four years later, Haven Creek, as locals called it, was considered one of the premiere travel destinations in all of Texas.

And it comforts Amber to think of her mother there now, safe, serene, surrounded by both beautiful country and the wonderful group of women who helped walk her through her grief over her husband's death.

"Stay put, momma," Amber says. "I think I'm gonna be okay."

"Caleb's got everything under control?"

"Something like that. Did you know all that stuff about the trust?"

"I knew your father and Caleb had a lot of conversations about it and they didn't include me. Like I said, the connection between those two…it was special. I tried not to intrude."

"And Joel?"

"What do you mean?" her mother asks.

"Did you have any doubts about him?"

"Amber, you *have* to stop doing this to yourself."

"Doing what?"

"Beating yourself up like this. Marriage is a roll of the dice and you never know how it's going to come out."

"But you can't win if you don't play?"

"If you want to be sarcastic, that's fine, I guess."

"I figure I'm allowed."

"Maybe for another few weeks."

"Remember that expression Daddy used to always say?"

"Which one?"

"Sometimes the road rises up to beat you instead of meet you."

"Oh, yeah. He stopped saying it after what happened to Caleb's parents."

"He only reserved it for the big things too. Not the everyday stuff. The big plans that went off the rails."

"I remember."

"Like a marriage. Think he'd use it now?"

"Well, he stopped using it altogether after Tim and Abby were killed, so no, I don't think he would. And this sounds suspiciously like you beating yourself up again so I'm not going to sign off on it."

"What about this thing I do with the dartboard? I took Joel's picture and I—"

"You told me about that already. That's fine."

"Okay. Good. Also, my boss is kinda sending me to a sex club," Amber adds.

"Hold, please," her mother says quietly.

"Uh huh," Amber answers, steeling herself for what's to come.

Her mother places one hand over the phone's mouthpiece and politely asks whoever's in the office with her to leave. Amber hears chair legs scrape wood floor, then her mother says, "A *what?*"

"A sex club. But it costs a lot of money. So I'm sure it's real nice."

"Your boss, Belinda Baxter, who has twice been on the cover of *Texas Monthly*, is sending you to a sex club?"

"I kinda had the same reaction when she said it."

"But you're going anyway."

"Yes…" At least, she thinks she is.

When Freddy, Belinda's driver, brought her home from Watson's earlier that day, Belinda had departed for a day full of lunch, fitness classes, shopping, probably a few stops off at some places that served fine wine in a comforting environment, and then some more shopping.

A note had been waiting for her on Belinda's desk. *Stick to the light list for the rest of the day,* it said, referring to the list of long-term household projects she was supposed to focus on in between managing Belinda's social calendar and travel schedule. *Will call you later tonight about TDE.*

"I figure it'll relax me," Amber says.

"A weekend out here at The Haven Creek Inn will relax you. We have two massage therapists now."

"It's probably not the same."

"Oh, I'm sure it's not the same, Amber. That's my point. If relaxation's what you're after, it can be achieved in other ways."

"Okay, fine! It's not just what I'm after."

"As long as you're admitting to it."

"Momma, it's been a year since that man kissed me on the mouth. I tried everything to get things going in the bedroom again. *Everything.* And he treated me like I was some kind of desperate, needy freak. And the whole time, he was—"

"I know, I know. You don't have to justify yourself to me, Amber."

"Well, I do if you're gonna get all judgy."

"I'm not being *judgy.* I'm just… This is a sensitive time for you, Amber, I just—I want you to be clear on what your motives are. Don't say you're just looking for a good time when in your heart you're looking for something else."

"Like *looooooooooove*?"

"Hello, fifteen-year-old Amber. Could you give the phone back to twenty-six-year-old Amber, please?"

"Oh, Momma. I appreciate what you're saying. I really do. But I have needs. And Belinda has never stayed at a hotel that doesn't have five stars, so that means whoever's gonna be tending to my needs at this place, they're gonna be *real* high end."

"Are you drunk?"

"Just a teensy bit."

"Is that why you're telling me all this stuff?" her mother asks.

"No. I'm going to be gone for a couple days coming up and I need someone to know where I'm going."

"Okay. When are you going?"

"I don't know yet."

"Okay… Where is this place?"

"I don't know that yet either."

"Well, alrighty then," her mother says with a sigh. "This has been very informative, Amber. Thank you."

"But when I do know, I'll tell you."

"And tell Caleb."

"Are you crazy? I'm not telling *Caleb* about any of this!"

"Why not? If something goes wrong, he's right there in town."

"It's none of his business!"

"Personally, I don't think it's any of *my* business either, but here you are, telling me all about it so…"

"'Cause I can't tell Caleb."

"I see."

"What? What do you see?"

How, in the midst of talking about Belinda Baxter's favorite sex club, did they wind up on the subject of Caleb? Is this how it's going to be now that her so-called brother is back in town? All Caleb, all the time, no matter how she tries to avoid focusing on him and his broad shoulders and the shift of his powerful legs in those ass-hugging jeans and those—

"Baby girl, I don't care if you go to this club. Hell, I don't care if you sleep with five guys in one night—*I need the room please, Nora. Just another minute, okay?*"

"Awesome," Amber whispers.

"All I care about is that you don't go looking in the wrong place for what you really want."

"That's kinda what the place is about, apparently."

There's a long pause before her mother says, "I don't understand."

"Belinda says they teach you about who you really are and what you really want. So who knows? Maybe I'll come away realizing this true love thing isn't for me after all."

"Yeah, you'll come away with a newfound love of handsome male hookers, in which case Belinda better give you a raise."

"Ouch, Momma."

"It may not sound like it, Amber, but I hope whatever this place is, you have a good time. And I hope that's *all* you have. Because that's really all you need right now. A very good time."

"Thanks, Momma."

"And Amber?"

"Yes, Momma."

"If you do have a good time, I don't want to hear another word about it."

"Deal!" Amber says brightly.

5

"Are you gay, dude?"

Caleb stares across the bar at his old friend, waiting for the guy to crack a smile.

Danny Patterson stares right back as if all he did was ask the time.

Apparently it was a serious question. Thank God nobody else inside Watson's heard it.

"No, I'm not gay," Caleb finally answers.

"You just never seemed that into Theresa is all."

"Well, we weren't in love. That's why we got divorced."

"I got that. So why marry her in the first place?"

"I don't know. Convenience?"

"Since when is marriage convenient? Especially if you don't love the person?"

We're not always supposed to be with the one we really love, Caleb thinks, but he doesn't say it because he knows Danny will just respond with more pushy questions.

Also, Danny hasn't shut up yet.

"Unless, you know, the dad's threatening your life 'cause you got the girl pregnant, in which case you do it 'cause staying alive is convenient. But…wait a minute! You didn't get Theresa pregnant, did you, 'cause I don't re—"

"Danny, you're twenty-three and you've been engaged three months. Quit lecturing me on marriage."

"Three or four sentences isn't really a lecture, if you ask me."

Which I didn't, Caleb thinks. *But you drove an hour out of your way to have a drink with me so I'm gonna be polite and not clean your clock today.*

People who watched too much daytime television liked to say

Danny Patterson was *on the spectrum.* But as far as Caleb was concerned, implying someone had Asperger's syndrome was just a fancy way of shaming them for not talking to you like you were their boss.

He'd first met Danny back when they were both working on the Proby Ranch outside Surrender, Montana. The kid was fresh out of high school then, so Caleb had blamed his 5-Hour Energy drink demeanor on the blissful ignorance of youth. But Danny's older now and a cop, and still he chatters away like a five-year-old who doesn't know when to stop bugging his parents during a long car ride.

"So," Danny said.

"So what, Danny?"

"Are you gay?"

"For the second time here, which I'm hoping will be the last. I'm not gay. Why are you asking me this?"

"'Cause women catch on fire the minute you walk into a room and you're still single."

"I'm a huge player."

"You're not. You hooked up with one girl in the time I knew you before you married Theresa."

"I'm not a fan of women on fire."

"You're evading, sir. A guy who looks like you…well, it's just not normal for you to fly solo for this long, Caleb."

"Unless I'm going full *Brokeback Mountain* in secret, you mean?"

"Pretty much. Yeah."

"Well, if this is your way of telling me you think I'm good looking, then thank you, Danny. And I'm sorry I'm not more excited about that information, but, see, the thing is, *I'm not gay.*"

"Eliza's got a gay brother and the dude's awesome. Good looking guy too."

"Son of a… Is this some kind of fix up?"

"What's wrong with that? What are you a homophobe or something?"

"What's wrong with it is that a good friend of mine is accusing me of lying about who I am. I'm not gay, Danny, and I'm not married to my ex-wife anymore 'cause we both moved on. It was a mutual decision, alright?"

"And you both moved on 'cause you were never in love with her to begin with and apparently she wasn't in love with you either. I guess that's supposed to make sense?"

"Danny, I'm fixin' to add some Drano to that Heineken if you don't shut up!"

"Just hate to see you alone is all," he says. He shakes his head with a faraway expression that says he's thinking about his new fiancée. Again. Because these days, he doesn't think about much else.

"I get it. You meet the love of your life and suddenly you're everybody's matchmaker. You're whipped, *dude*. That's all."

"Frat boys called it whipped. Grown-ups call it engaged."

"Sounds like something Eliza told you."

"It is," he says with a smile, as if his fiancée's corrections feel as good as her shoulder rubs.

"Serves you right for hooking up with one of your old teachers."

"Alright, now. Don't up the creep factor. You're sounding like one of the old gossips back home."

Danny's hearty slug suggests the gossips back in Surrender are bothering him more than he cares to admit. Caleb isn't surprised. In towns big and small, a ten-year age difference between lovers will make most people talk. But when the woman's the senior partner, people tend to freak out even more.

"Is it just talk or are y'all getting some real grief over it?" Caleb asks.

"Oh, just the usual busybodies, claiming we got together when I was a teenager and she was my teacher."

"Did you?"

"Hell, no. Back then, she pretty much wanted to chuck me out the window."

"Why's that?"

"'Cause I asked too many questions, apparently."

"You don't say."

"Only reason I give a damn is 'cause Eliza seems to give a damn, and after everything she's been through, I don't want her to have to give a damn about much besides being happy."

Caleb knows only part of the story, the part where Eliza's bastard ex got her involved with some nasty guys who didn't make it out of Surrender alive. There are about eighteen different versions of the story floating around Surrender. Every time he calls someone and tries to get the real scoop, he gets a totally different account. Whatever happened, Eliza and Danny survived without injury, and now they're in each other's lives for good. That's all that matters. More importantly, he'd rather get off the topic of their personal lives altogether before he has to answer any more questions about his own.

"Have you tried bringing her an apple every day? Maybe that'll cheer her up."

"Oh, that's real original, cowboy. How 'bout you sing me some of that old Van Halen song while you're at it?"

"Just trying to make light of the situation. Small towns can be tough."

"Yeah, well, Surrender's alright when the MacKenzies have your back!"

The way Danny says it, he makes Surrender's most beloved family sound like the mafia. They're anything but. Thomas, the doctor of the family, is the only MacKenzie Caleb had ever spent much time with, probably because he'd been willing to drive out to Proby at a moment's notice to treat even the first signs of an infection or a sprain among the ranch hands. If Thomas MacKenzie's generous spirit ran in the family, no wonder most of Surrender thinks he and his brothers hung the moon.

"Is that really why you came back to Dallas?" Danny says. "'Cause small towns can be tough?"

"Got family here," Caleb says. "Now I've got a family business, looks like."

"You never called this place your family business before."

"Danny, does Surrender have some intelligence agency that hires you to track down all the former ranch hands in the area and find out about their lives? 'Cause this is getting kinda intense, friend."

"Nah, I told you, Conference of Local Law Enforcement Agencies is at the Hyatt downtown this weekend and I'm representing my hometown." Danny taps one closed fist against his heart as if there's a shiny policeman's badge there.

"And you always like to kick off a conference by giving an old friend the third degree?"

Danny sips his beer and stares at Caleb.

"I was going to fix you up with Eliza's brother," he finally says.

"Danny!"

"Well, if it means anything, I lost the bet."

"The bet with who?"

"Eliza. I told her all about you and she's sure you're straight."

"She knows me better than you do, apparently."

"She also says your heart's on lockdown 'cause you already met the woman you want to give it to and you're convinced she won't take it."

Way better apparently.

"So who's the girl who got away?" Danny asks. "Is she married?"

If Annabelle hadn't picked just that moment to set an armful of invoices and order forms down on the bar with a loud *thunk*, Caleb might have faked a seizure.

"Here's everything you asked for," she says

"Whoa, you might want to get a filing system there," Danny says

Annabelle gives Danny a long stare, then turns it on Caleb.

"Who's the child with the mouth?" she asks Caleb.

"Old friend," he answers. "Just ignore him."

He reaches out with both arms so he can draw the mountain of lose paperwork closer to him without spreading it across the bar.

"Name's Danny Patterson, ma'am, and it just so happens I'm an officer of the law."

"In Dallas?" she asks.

"Nope. A beautiful little town in Montana called Surrender."

"Then shut up. You're out of your jurisdiction."

Danny gives Caleb a broad smile and says, "I always forget Texas is the not nice part of the South."

"And I'm the not nice part of Texas," Annabelle says. "So, Guy I Was Actually Talking To, this here's about six months worth of invoices and orders from my amazing former employer. As you'll be able to see, he forced us to use a cut-rate produce company even though every other batch they brought us was spoiled and also, he spent about seven thousand dollars on consultants to research"—she dug into the pile and read from the invoice in question—"the latest in jukebox technology. And by consultants, I mean members of his horrible band who Googled stuff about jukeboxes. Probably while hung over."

"I suppose I can't get you to file all of this stuff," Caleb asks.

"You can. For about forty dollars an hour."

"Oof," Danny says with a groan. "Pricey!"

"You know, normally, it takes people more than fifteen seconds to get on my nerves," she says.

"Oh, I don't believe that for a minute, Annabelle," Caleb says with a smile.

They just stare at each other while Danny looks back and forth between them like a kid expecting his parents to break out in a screaming match.

"I don't file, cowboy," Annabelle finally says. "I've got about a dozen chicken fried steaks that need to be battered before we open for dinner. But I'd be happy to take you back to the dish cabinet where he stuffed all the invoices for the past two years."

"Lord," Caleb groans.

"Nobody said being a knight in shining armor was easy," she says. Then, to Danny she adds, "Have a good one, Deputy Diaper. Enjoy those puppy dog eyes while you got 'em. I can already see the crow's feet starting."

"I love a woman who can make me feel small," Danny says after she's gone.

"You realize I'm calling you Deputy Diaper forever now?"

"Knew it the minute she said it."

"Want to do some filing?" Caleb asks.

"No, thanks. Knight in shining armor? She made it sound like you came home to rescue a lady, not a bar."

Don't look up. Don't let him see your eyes. He'll put two and two together and figure it out.

"Danny, unless you want to help me do some filing, you need to get gone."

"I love filing!"

"Danny, I was kidding. It was great to see you, buddy, but I need some time to pull things together here."

He's hurt Danny's feelings, and it makes him feel like crap. Truth is he's got all the time in the world to file these stupid invoices. Well, all the time in the world until tax day. But Danny's like a dog on a scent. Worse, he's following the trail right to a place Caleb needs to stay buried, and there's only one damn way Caleb can think of to stop him.

"Alright, well," his buddy says, sliding off his barstool. "Try to make some time to come down to the Hyatt this weekend so we can hang."

"Sure thing, buddy."

"And, you know, sorry if I asked too many questions or if I talk too much."

"Nah, man. It's work. That's all. Just gotta get back to work here."

"Sure. Sure. I get it. Good luck, you know…with all of it, I guess."

All of it. Including the stuff you won't talk to me about.

Caleb nods.

Danny nods.

Then he's out the door but not before giving Caleb a glimpse of his wounded smile.

He just stands there for a while, feeling like a royal shit.

He should have known this would be the hardest part. The questions. People noticing.

He didn't stay a loner for this long because he couldn't control himself; he'd never do something stupid where Amber was concerned. His self-discipline's always been good. Abel Watson, his only real father, is to thank for that. But his feelings and his anger about his feelings, those are another matter entirely. Making sure they stay hidden now that he's back in Dallas, that's going to be a lot harder than getting Watson's books in order.

Sometimes, when he'd had a few too many with the guys he'd worked with up in North Dakota, he'd mention the woman he couldn't have, the one it would never work with, even though he wanted it to. Desperately. And if anyone pressed for more details, he'd just tell them the woman in question, the one he never named, had gone off and married someone else, which had been true then.

It wasn't true now. And if he'd known that, he might never have come home.

This isn't just fear squeezing his chest. It's a kind of terror, the same terror he always feels when someone brushes the sand off that deep, buried place inside of himself.

In his memory, he's back on the side of a winding country road on that awful night when everything changed. Abel's shaking him by both shoulders and asking him what he'd do to have a family. A *real* family. And then there's darkness. Darkness and branches and a whole lot of other stuff he doesn't want to think about.

He doesn't drink after people. It's a rule. But panic attacks call for an exception to pretty much every rule, so he downs half of Danny's abandoned beer in several swallows.

It helps a little, but only a little.

Maybe I should have let Danny believe I was gay, he thinks.

If he'd had any gay friends, he'd have put the question to them. What's harder, being gay or in love with the woman the State of Texas considers to be your sister?

When his phone rings, it gives him the crazy sense that he's been caught.

It's the woman the State of Texas considers his mother.

"Miss Tina?"

"We're not having this conversation," she says immediately.

"Okay. You want me to hang up?"

"No, no. I just… What I'm about to tell you, you need to act like you heard it from someone else."

"When?" he asks.

"What?"

"*When* do I need to act like I heard it from someone else? Right now or later?"

"When you do something about it, that's when."

"I'm real confused right now, Miss Tina"

"Okay, well, let me unconfuse you. Amber's about to do something crazy and I need you to stop her."

6

"Heroin?" Belinda asks.

"*What*? No!" Amber answers.

"Okay. What about cocaine?"

"Oh my God. Never."

Brow furrowed, Belinda stares at Amber like she's a cop and Amber's a suspect who will crack at any second. But they're not in an interrogation room. They're in the dining room of Amber's house and Belinda's holding a wine glass, not a notepad.

Next to them the wall is studded with bright spots where they just took down every picture featuring Joel. Or even a tiny piece of Joel. Amber tried to contest the removal of a big sky sunset over Chapel Springs on the grounds she wasn't 100% sure the elbow in the bottom right corner actually belonged to her ex, but Belinda insisted.

"Are you sure you went to college?" Belinda asks.

"Yes, I'm sure."

"Not even one little bump at an office party?" Belinda asks.

"I didn't even know they were called bumps. And the only office parties I've been to are yours."

"That's not an answer, honey."

"Belinda, I do not sniff cocaine!"

"Alright, there's my answer. No one calls it *sniffing* cocaine."

"I thought you came over to talk about The Desire Exchange."

"I did, and to erase all evidence that Joel Claire ever set foot in this house."

"And I appreciate that, but why are you asking me about my drug history?"

"I just need to know if you have any allergies."

"To *cocaine?*"

"They're just gonna give you a little something to relax you while you're there."

"Belinda, I do not do drugs!"

"Oh, come on. You never smoked a joint?"

"Not one I liked. No."

"Well, as long as you keep an open mind, I guess."

"Why would I need to keep an open mind if they're gonna drug me?"

"You'll have to have an open mind to *take* the drug, sweetie."

"I have a headache," Amber groans.

"Want a Percocet?"

"No. I've had too much to drink today, thank you."

Amber can't remember the last time she's heard tires squealing on her quiet residential street. But that's exactly what she hears now. Tires squealing.

"So has someone else apparently," Belinda mutters.

Headlights swing across the front windows of her house, headlights belonging to a large pickup truck which pulls into her driveway so fast, the front bumper knocks over one of her trash cans.

"Is that him?" Belinda asks. "Is that Joel? If it is, get my purse."

"Why?"

"'Cause my gun's in it."

The shadow that strides past the front windows is over six feet tall. But it's missing its familiar cowboy hat.

"It's not Joel," Amber says quietly.

"Who is it?" Belinda calls after her as she heads for the front door.

She opens it. Caleb lowers his hand. It's curled into a tight fist and he had the side of it aimed at the door, not his knuckles. A polite knock wasn't his plan. His sandy blond hair is mussed. His broad chest is heaving with big, fearful breaths. If she hadn't just witnessed his hijinks with the truck, she would have assumed he ran clear across Dallas to get to her house.

Gone is the confident guy who struck down Joel that afternoon. He's forgotten whatever words he was practicing on the ride over, that much is clear. He looks fearful and boyish, and together, they make him look innocent. Over six-foot-four, chorded with muscle and somehow innocent. Dangerously innocent.

"Oh, my," Belinda says. "You weren't cheating too, were you?"

"Belinda, this is my brother. Caleb, this is my boss, Belinda Baxter."

There's a second or two of shocked silence before Belinda says, "You have a *brother*?"

"On paper," Amber says.

Caleb flinches. It sounded terrible, the way she said it. But she couldn't think of another way to make the obvious chemistry between them seem less dirty and wrong.

"I was afraid I wouldn't catch you before you left," Caleb says.

"Oh my God. Momma told you?"

"You told your *mother*?" Belinda cries.

"Please don't go," Caleb says.

The quiet authority of his request shoots through her bones. This isn't the sauntering Caleb who can deliver a precise punch powerful enough to knock a man off his feet. This is the Caleb of fifteen years ago—needy, hungry.

"Why not?" she asks before she can stop herself.

He stares into her eyes. His lips part but nothing comes out.

For a few seconds, the only two things in Amber's world are the two of them and the years of unspoken feelings between them.

"Miss Baxter, I don't mean to be rude, but do you think I can have a moment alone with Amber?"

"Of course," Belinda says, grabbing her Gucci purse off the foyer table. "I'll just, you know, take a walk into the middle of the nearest freeway now that Amber's mother thinks I'm a freak."

Caleb steps aside to let Belinda pass, gives the woman a polite nod. Once she's behind him, she gives Amber a look full of wide-eyed confusion. Then Caleb gently shuts the door with one hand. Now it's just the two of them, alone together for the first time in years.

"It's a terrible idea," he says.

"Why did she tell you?"

"Because she wants me to stop you."

"That's not true. I talked to her this afternoon and she told me she wanted me to go."

"Well, she must have changed her mind," he says.

"Well, I haven't changed mine."

"A sex club?" he bellows. "What are you? Crazy?"

"Since when are you so full of judgment? I've never seen you in church!"

"And I've never seen you in a sex club!"

"Have you been to that many? Who knows? I could have a whole secret life you don't even know about."

"I know who you are, Amber. I know *how* you are."

"And what does that mean?"

"Amber, you stayed a virgin until you were nineteen. That puts you in the, like, one percentile of girls in our high school."

"How do you know that? I never told you that!"

"I had my sources."

"You were keeping tabs on my virginity? That's rich. I thought you were too busy starting fistfights outside Valley View Mall so you didn't have to feel anything."

"And you were too busy tending to my wounds 'cause it gave you an excuse to look at my chest."

"Get out of my house!"

"Amber—"

"Get out!"

He bows his head. A lesser man would ignore her request, but he knows he's bound by it.

"I shouldn't have said that," Caleb whispers. "I'm sorry."

He turns to leave.

"You know, I forgave you a lot because you lost a lot. But don't you pretend for one second that you joined our family with a smile and a thank you and that was that. Those first few years, it was like living with a tornado. You were *impossible*! And you were nothing like the guy I'd..."

He turns away from the front door. "The guy you'd what?"

"All I'm saying is that even if I'd wanted to…"

"Wanted to what?"

He's closing the distance between them. Her head wants to run from him. Her soul wants to run to him. Her body's forced to split the difference. She's got no choice but to stand there while he advances on her, nostrils flaring, blue eyes blazing.

"Tell me why you really don't want me to go," she hears herself whisper. "Tell me why you—"

He takes her in his arms and rocks them into the wall, so suddenly she expects her head to knock against the wood, but one of his powerful hands cushions the back of her skull just in time.

His lips meet the nape of her neck, grazing, testing. It's hesitant, the kiss he gives her there, as if he's afraid she's an apparition that will vanish if he tries to take a real taste.

He gathers the hem of her shirt into his fist, knuckles grazing the skin of her stomach. She's trying to speak but the only things coming out of her are stuttering gasps. She's been rendered wordless by the feel of the forbidden, by the weight of the forbidden, by the power of the forbidden.

It's the first time they've touched since that night on the boat dock, if you don't include the light dabs of hydrogen peroxide she'd apply to the wounds he got fighting, usually while they sat together in the kitchen, her parents watching over them nervously. So many years living under the same roof and they never shared so much as a hug after that night, nothing that might risk the feel of his skin against her own.

And now this.

Now the intoxicating blend of the cologne he wore as a teenager mingling with the musky aroma of his belt and boots. Now the knowledge that he'd asked after her virginity years before, that the thought of her lying with another man had filled him with protective, jealous rage then just as it does now.

She feels boneless and moist. One of those feelings isn't an illusion.

If this is what it feels like to be bad, she thinks, *no wonder so many people get addicted.*

"Tell me," she whispers. "Tell me why you really don't want me to go."

"I am," he growls.

He presses their foreheads together, takes the sides of her face in both of his large, powerful hands. It's torture, this position. It's deliberate, she's sure. It keeps her from lifting her mouth to his. Keeps her from looking straight into his eyes. He's fighting it, still. Just as she's fought it for years.

She parts her lips, inviting him to kiss her.

"Please," he groans. "Just, please *don't* go."

"Caleb…" She reaches for his face.

She's reaching into open air.

The door slams.

He's gone.

By the time she realizes what's happened, the truck's engine has already started. His headlights swing across the front of the house.

"You son of a bitch," she whispers to no one. "Coward, bastard son of a *bitch*!"

But real anger, the kind of anger she feels toward Joel, can't make it to the surface through all the other emotions she's feeling.

She wasn't nuts. She wasn't some deluded freak who'd made too much out of one kiss twelve years before. He'd wanted her as badly as she'd wanted him, and he'd been just as tortured by it. They'd had all of the anger and fighting of siblings, but with none of the loyalty and companionship. To try for either of those things would have awakened desires her father had declared off limits. Still, every argument they'd had, every time they'd forced themselves to look away from each other, every frustrated attempt they'd made to connect since the night his parents died, had just been another step in one long dance of desire leading up to this very moment.

But what *was* this moment?

Where the hell are they now?

Would he disappear again? Maybe for ten years this time. Or twenty!

Her father—*their* father—was gone, so why is this still so hard?

Dazed, she walks in circles around the living room while these questions assail her. She's holding her phone in one hand, waiting for anything. A text. A call. An e-mail. Something from

Caleb that proves she didn't just imagine what happened.

Part of her wants to cry, but every time she starts, the smell of him, the feel of him, the sounds of desire and struggle that came from him turn her sadness into something more like exhilaration. Even the speed with which he left is proof that everything just changed. And maybe it will keep changing. And maybe changing means no more running and no more avoiding and no more shame.

Maybe.

But he still fucking left.

No text. No missed call.

What did he expect her to do? Chase him down the front walk, screaming his name?

The front door creaks. The truck hasn't come back so it can only be one person.

"Girl," Belinda says quietly.

Amber had completely forgotten her boss was lingering outside.

"When do we leave?" Amber asks.

"Uhm. Never."

"What?"

"You're not going, honey."

"Why? Because I told my mother?"

"Nope."

"Because Caleb doesn't want me to?"

"Nope."

"Then *why*, Belinda?"

"Because you don't need to find out what you want. You already know. He just stormed out of this house."

"He's my brother."

"On paper, you said. So what's that mean? Adopted?"

"Pretty much."

"Well, is he adopted or isn't he?"

"Yes. My parents adopted him when we were fifteen."

"I see… Well, people will talk, but they always talk, so who cares? And if you ever want to get married, you just dissolve the adoption before you—"

"Belinda, it's not that simple!"

"It is if you want it to be, Amber."

"Belinda. Come on, now. You promised me and I want to go. Seriously!"

"No, you don't, Amber. You want to avoid what you're feeling for this man *again.* And forgive me for saying it, but it's starting to look like the last time you avoided it, you wound up jumping into marriage with a cheating, lying bastard."

"Oh, come on! That is way too simplistic. You don't—"

"Honey, if you've got something that good knocking on your door here at home and you won't let him in, nothing they're going to show you at The Exchange is going to help you either."

"You don't even know him."

"I know how you two look at each other. And trust me, if there was someone in my life who looked at me like that, I'd never turn my back on him. Unless, you know, we were about to try a little—"

"He's the one who left."

"You told him to!"

When Amber shoots her an angry look, Belinda throws her hands in the air and says, "Oh, come on. You know I'm an eavesdropper. Stop acting all surprised every time I do it."

"I told him to tell me why. Why he didn't want me to go."

"And he did. Don't worry. I only watched part of it."

She sinks to the sofa, fully intending to sit, but she goes over backward the second her butt meets the cushions. Suddenly she's sprawled out just like she was when she arrived home earlier that day, her breaths feeling more like ideas than actual grabs for air.

"Shit!" Belinda says. "We missed one!"

Belinda takes a framed photo of Joel, in full fishing regalia, off the wall just above the mini-bar. She looks for a place to put it, doesn't find one that meets her needs and shoves it in her purse.

"I'll toss it out the window on the ride home," she says.

"Am I fired?" Belinda asks.

"No. Why do you always go to that place? Do you *want* to be fired?"

"No. I just want things to…change."

"Oh, honey. That's not your problem. They're changing all around you. What you want is for them to change on your own schedule, and trust me, that's never gonna happen. I got all the money in the damn world and even I can't slow time down. I mean, I can fill it with spa treatments, but that's not the same thing."

"What are we talking about?" she asks.

"Nothing. We're stalling. Like you've been stalling for, well, a good decade, it looks like."

"Fine. I'm not going to The Desire Exchange."

"Because you don't need to."

"I'll have to take your word for it, considering I still don't know what the place even is."

"And you never will. Because you, Amber Watson, already know good and well what you want. You're just afraid of it. And you're going to have to get over that fear all on your own. However, I'm happy to give you some time off to do it."

"No," Amber says. "I need to focus on something."

"Yes. And that something is you." Belinda starts for the front hallway. "I don't want to see you for five days. Take a drive down to Chapel Springs and see your momma. Maybe ask her why she thought it was a good idea to squeal on you to your *alleged* brother."

"What does that mean?" she asks, sitting up.

"Five days, Amber. Show up at my house before then, I'll take a shot at you. I swear to God."

"Wait. What did you mean about my mother?"

By the time she makes it to the front hallway, Belinda's already out the door.

"Does anyone else want to storm out of my house tonight?" Amber calls out. "Maybe one of the neighbors?"

A barking dog answers from next door.

She dials her mother's number.

Voicemail.

Fifteen minutes later, she dials it again.

Voicemail again.

She can't remember the last time her mother let her go to voicemail. Her mom hates going to the movies, maybe because the nearest theater is forty-five minutes away. She also covers so many positions at The Haven Creek Inn, she never turns off her ringer.

Amber would love to be worried about her mother; she really would.

But she's not.

Because her mom's hiding, that's all. And that's why Amber heads for her bedroom and starts stuffing her favorite weekend bag full of blue jeans, halter tops, and T-shirts. First thing in the morning, she's got a date with a few hundred miles of blacktop and a little town called Chapel Springs. And if her mother calls back before then, well…Amber's got voicemail too!

7

If only he hadn't touched her.

If he hadn't touched her, he could leave her in his rearview right now, along with Watson's, Dallas, and the entire State of Texas. Maybe he'll hit Colorado this time. Or Canada. Canada isn't that much farther, but maybe an international border was just what he needed to protect his heart.

But there's no way he can go that far now.

Because he'd touched her.

And it wasn't like he'd had to either.

There were other ways he could have kept her from going to some crazy sex club.

Like reasoning with her. Or teasing her. Or begging her.

Telling her how he really felt, that should have been the last option. The absolutely dead-last, nuclear apocalypse option. And touching her? Well, that was beyond the nuclear option. That was a "zombies are breaking down the front door and the only way out is through the nearest window" kind of option.

And yet he'd gone ahead and done it anyway, touched her like he was some idiot teenager who couldn't control his hormones. He'd also tasted her, inhaled her scent, felt her heat on his skin. Sensed that her hunger for him was equal to his own. Heard that hunger with his own two ears, a vibrating pulse under her every desperate breath as he'd held her in his arms.

And now it's all falling apart. Now he's flying down a Dallas freeway with all the windows in his truck rolled down because he's hoping the wind will drown out his crazy thoughts. He's been driving for hours now, aimless circles around the city. Sometimes he'll head in the direction of old landmarks, old places he used to visit, but as soon as he gets close, he forgets about them altogether and goes back to thinking of Amber. Amber's eyes. Amber's skin. Amber's anger. Amber's passion.

Bye, bye scrapbook, he thinks angrily.

Over the years, he'd come up with all sorts of ways to keep his feelings for her under control. But the thing he called the scrapbook had been the most effective.

Early on, after he'd moved in with the Watsons, he'd forced himself to think of her only in her most unflattering moments. Her furious expressions during dinner table fights after which Abel would send them both to their rooms; her shuffling walks to the coffee maker first thing in the morning, replete with hay bale hair and baggy pajamas. The times a cold or the flu turned her into a red-faced phlegm machine. Out of these awkward, everyday moments, he'd made a scrapbook which he opened whenever Amber, the wickedly smart doe-eyed girl he'd fallen in love with that long ago summer, threatened to tilt him off his axis.

The scrapbook had not been without its problems, however.

Every now and then he'd try sliding in an image of how awful she'd looked the night her appendix burst. But the cruelty of this, using one of her most painful moments to dampen the fires of his desire, shamed him into further confusion. Worse, it would often backfire, serving only to remind him of how he'd wanted to protect her in that moment. How he'd wanted to take her into his arms and carry her down the stairs once it was clear it wasn't just a stomachache, that she was truly and terribly sick. Instead, he'd shouted for Abel and Tina. When they'd burst into her room, he'd hung back, shaking and trying to hide tears, but refusing to break the rule they'd both set for each other, however silently.

No touching. No grazes. No brushes. No hugs. No kisses, even on the cheek.

The scrapbook is as good as burned now. Now, every time he thinks of her from here on out, he'll see the pale creamy skin of her throat bared, her lips parting for him, inviting him to taste. Fuck that. He'll see that smoldering intensity in her stare when she said *Tell me why you really don't want me to go.*

Sometimes he'd hoped that if they ever did make a move on each other, they'd realize instantly their desire was an illusion. Kind of like prison love, or some outdated teenage fantasy they'd held on to for too long even though it had lost its fire years before. They'd try to kiss each other again and crack up laughing because the whole thing would seem ridiculous.

Some days he hoped for this. Other days he feared it.

When he finally did make his move, everything was very real. All of it. Too damn real.

Danny Patterson answers his phone after the first ring. All Caleb has to say is that he needs to meet, and Danny's giving him directions to the hotel, right down to which escalator he should take to get to the lobby bar. Maybe it's the tone of Caleb's voice that does it.

Caleb pulls into the motor court at the Hyatt Regency, hands the keys to his truck to the first valet.

Dealey Plaza and the Sixth Floor Museum are just a couple blocks away. Caleb knows this because Abel took him there several times when he was a kid.

Inside the hotel, there's a soaring atrium with a sloped glass ceiling that allows you to look right up at the glittering orb that is Reunion Tower. Caleb knows this because Abel brought him here to see visiting friends when he was a kid.

And that's half the problem, isn't it? In Dallas, Abel is everywhere, because Abel loved Dallas as much as he'd loved his own children. *Both* of his children.

Danny's waiting at the top of the escalator, a beer in hand. He'd probably have one for Caleb too, but he knows Caleb barely drinks. Caleb prepares himself for some smartass comment about how wrecked he looks. Instead, Danny steers them to a table and chairs. Rowdy law enforcement types fill the bar. Men, mostly, patting each other on the back, sharing loud war stories about shootouts and crazy arrests. Glass elevators whisk people to their rooms on the floors above.

The place is loud as hell, but Caleb hears the racquet as if he's underwater. Underwater and struggling to breathe.

"I did something terrible," he finally says.

"You finally put the moves on the sister who isn't really your sister?"

"Are you kidding me? You knew the whole time?"

"Figured it would mean more if you said it," Danny says with a serious nod.

"*What* would mean more?"

"I'm just kidding. I left my room key at Watson's and when I called back, Annabelle answered and I got the story out of her."

"Which story? Wait! *Annabelle?* She hated you!"

"Nobody hates me. They just need time to…get used to me, that's all." Danny frowns and takes a sip of beer. "Do you hate me?" he asks, suddenly sounding twelve years old.

"You think I would have called you if I hated you? I'm having a breakdown here."

"You're not having a break*down.* You're having a break…*in.* Wait. That didn't come out right. What I'm trying to say is—"

"Just stop trying to say stuff and listen, Danny."

"Oh. I get to listen now. Does that mean you're actually going to talk about what's really going on with you?"

"In a minute. What did Annabelle tell you?"

"That you two were made for each other. That you were practically in love by the night your parents died and when Abel adopted you, it screwed you both up."

"Screwed us both up? Is that what she really said? If Abel hadn't adopted me, I woulda been homeless. Or living with my aunt in Oklahoma City while she turned tricks right in front of me in her trailer."

"So, homeless, basically," Danny says.

"Yeah," Caleb answers.

"But still."

"Still what?"

"I'm just repeating what Annabelle said!"

"Okay. Fine. What else did she say?"

"She said she'd call and give you updates on the bar 'cause they wanted you to come back. That they knew Amber's husband was a piece of dog shit, and she only married him so she wouldn't have to deal with how she felt about you."

"*Annabelle* said all this?"

"Yes, Caleb. Apparently you're the only one who had a hard time figuring any of this out."

"I didn't say I hadn't figured it out. I just don't know how to fix any of it."

"Same thing. Anyway. She also said there's only one thing keeping you apart."

"Yeah. She's my sister."

"No, Abel. She says both of you are in a boxing match with his ghost. Her words. Not mine. Says you both think if you got together you'd be crapping on his memory."

These words hit him like a sucker punch, and that's a good thing. A sucker punch is exactly what he needs to wake up.

"Wish I could say out of the mouths of babes, but these are her words, right?"

"Yeah, also, I'm, like, four years younger than you, dude."

Danny smiles.

"You're a good guy, you know that, Patterson?" he hears himself say. The words come out of him before he can measure them, but it's the night for following his instincts, apparently, and saying them out loud makes him feel good. "I give you a lot of grief, but you're a good guy."

"Aw, shut it."

"Seriously. I was a dick to you today at the bar, and here you are taking time out from your friends to listen to me whine."

"Listening to you whine ages me," Danny says with a broad grin. "That's a good thing, right?"

"Well, now you know why I've been such a loner."

Danny spits up beer. It takes Caleb a second to realize the guy's laughing at him.

Once he finishes coughing, Danny says, "Dude, you were never a loner. You were always having the other hands at Proby over for cookouts at your cabin. You'd organize all the trips into town. Second an injury looked like it was infected, you were on the phone to Thomas MacKenzie. The reason I went to see you today is 'cause pretty much everyone you met back in Montana wants to know how you're doing.

"You're not a loner, Caleb. A wanderer, maybe. But not a loner. Just 'cause you've been running from one woman your whole life doesn't mean you're not a people person. You're one of the biggest people people…or persons… Oh, hell, I don't know how to say it. But you know what I mean. You love people, is what I'm trying to say. That's why you're not going to be able to run from her for very much longer."

"Maybe it's not her I'm running from," he says.

"What's that mean?" Danny asks.

Even though it's not his intention, Caleb finds himself looking from happy couple to happy couple. Some of them are leaning in to each other, so close it looks like their eyeballs are about to touch. Whenever he's in a crowded place, his attention seems to go right to the nearest happy couple, and no matter how hard he fights the urge, his gaze lingers on them while the Goddess of Envy places her cold, invisible hands around his throat.

There were moments with Theresa. Moments when it seemed like maybe the two of them could pretend their way into being in love. Moments when, if you didn't know any better and you saw them together in a bar, you might have thought they were as happy and contended as most of the couples in the Hyatt's atrium bar looked to Caleb right now.

But for the most part, they were just lonely. Like him, Theresa had convinced herself that true love, the kind you saw in movies and read about in romance novels, was something the universe only offered to other people. People who had their shit together. People who didn't have so many wounds.

And that's what had held them together for a while. A shared belief that the right one, the one for them, had been placed permanently off limits, so why not make a go of the one who was in front of you? That, and their matching wounds.

Back then, if you'd asked Caleb why he couldn't be the one Amber loved, he would have told you it was her decision, her choice. After all, she's the one who'd gone and married someone else. What more proof did you need? Now he knew that was a lie, a lie he'd told himself so he could get comfortable with his decision to run.

Now he'd seen her desire for him, seen it right where it had been lying just beneath the surface for going on twelve years.

She wasn't the one standing in his way.

Abel was.

And therein lay the unavoidable contradiction that had defined Caleb's life—the man who had saved his life was also the one who had shamed him out of pursuing his heart's desire.

"Caleb," Danny says softly. "You still here, man?"

"The night my parents died, we'd just kissed. For the first time."

"You and Amber?"

"We'd been building toward it all summer. She was… When I'd look at her that summer, something would happen to me. It was like everything about her was more vivid. More *there*. And when she'd look at me, something would happen to me too. I could feel it in my chest."

"You were falling in love with her," Danny says

"I was fifteen."

"Yeah, you were fifteen and falling in love with her."

"But…"

"But, what?"

"I took her down to the boat dock with me so I could show her the moon. 'Cause I'd told her how beautiful it looked over the lake at night and she said she wanted me to show her. And 'cause…"

Motherfuck, he thinks as his vision blurs. *Goddamn motherfuck shit. Crying right here in the middle of the bar.*

"I knew my father was gonna die. And so did she. And she knew I couldn't sleep and she didn't want me to be alone when I was lying there awake in the other room, so I took her down to the boat dock and when I kissed her it was like… When I kissed her, it was like there'd never been a thing called pain. Like I didn't even know what the word meant. It was like… It was like she was the only thing that existed."

"She still exists, Caleb. And she's getting divorced."

"I'm not finished," he says, hating the gruff sound of his voice. But if he stops to apologize, he knows he'll lose his nerve. Knows he won't finish the story. And if he can't do anything else right tonight, at least he can do that, finish the damn story for the first time.

"Few minutes later, Abel got the call about my parents and he came and got us. I don't remember much after we got back to the house. Except her holding me. I remember that. I remember lying on the bed crying my eyes out. I remember her reaching up and taking my hand. I squeezed it, I think. I squeezed it 'cause even then I wanted her to know that she still existed for me. That she would always exist for me. And then…"

One time he was horseback riding in the mountains near Proby outside Surrender. His mind had wandered as he took in the gorgeous view. At the last possible second, he'd seen the horse's hooves perched at the edge of a hundred-foot drop. For a few minutes, he hadn't been able to do anything except quiver and stare into those aspen-fringed jaws of death. That's how he feels now.

"Next thing I remember, I was in the car. Abel was driving. But Amber wasn't there. He said he was driving me to the airport. That a friend of his had a plane and was going to fly us back to Dallas. And all I could say was, Where's Amber? I remember saying it over and over again. At first, he didn't say anything. Then he just pulled the car over, got out, and pulled me out of the passenger seat. We were in the middle of this dark stretch of woods where there wasn't anything for miles and he was just shaking me, shaking me and saying all kinds of angry things. He was so mad I couldn't tell at first that they were questions he was asking me.

"Did I want a real family or did I want to end up drunken white trash, dead on the side of the road like my father? Did I want to listen to my dick the way my father had listened to the bottle? 'Cause that's what it would mean to be with Amber. Amber was going to be my sister and if I fucked that up, I wouldn't have nothing, he said. No family, no home. *Nothing*."

Danny curses under his breath. Is he trying to contain his reaction because he doesn't want Caleb to stop telling his story? Caleb's not sure, so he keeps talking.

"And I just kept yelling at him over and over again, no matter what he said. Where's Amber? Where's Amber? And he drew back like he was going to hit me."

"Did he?"

"No. He drove off and left me there instead."

"For how long?"

"I don't know. I didn't have a watch on me. I thought I could find my way back to the lake house, but I was wrong and I ended up in the woods. Sun was rising by the time he found me. He was half out of his mind by then. Sobbing and crazy and begging for my forgiveness. And what choice did I have? Only other option was my aunt, and she probably would have left me on the side of the road and never come back. Or sold me to some freak for meth."

"Jesus, Caleb."

"He wasn't a bad man, Danny. He lost one of his best friends that night."

"Still."

"He worked so hard to try to keep his men together after they came back from Iraq. But my dad, he was the one Abel couldn't fix. It's not like he took his hand to me. My real dad did that plenty."

"He left you in the woods, man."

"He came back."

"After he scared the living shit out of you."

"I wasn't scared. I was something else."

"What?"

"Lost."

"And then you were what…found?"

"Something like that, yeah."

"Bullshit. He created the situation just so he could fix it. You wouldn't have been lost if he hadn't thrown you out of the car."

"He wasn't thinking like that. He was upset."

"You're talking like him because you're thinking like him, and if you're thinking like him it means there's a part of you that still believes what he said to you that night. You think if you go after Amber, you're going to end up a drunk like your father, dead on the side of the road. You really believe that, Caleb? You really think everything you want is dangerous just 'cause your dad was an alcoholic?"

He can't answer.

"How many things in life have you wanted and not gone for because of what Abel said to you that night?"

"Sometimes you decide that something else is more important."

"Like what? Moving? Again?"

"It's not that simple."

"Are you a drunk, Caleb? Do you wake up without knowing where you are? Do you lose track of your truck? Do you get in fights you can't remember starting? Wake up counting the minutes until your next beer?"

"No," Caleb whispers.

"Then you're not your father."

"Still…"

"Still, *what*? You're not your father, Caleb. And Amber isn't booze. Abel was wrong. He was wrong that night. Hell, lot of people would say what he did to you was downright abusive, but I'll leave that for you to decide. Point is, he didn't understand what a drunk really was, and he sure as hell didn't understand you."

"He was a good man who made a mistake," Caleb says. "And God knows, he made up for it later."

"Yeah, okay. I never met him so I can't say. But if twelve years later, you're not going after the love of your life because you're still buying into the bullshit he said to you that night, then the one making the mistake is you, buddy."

Caleb wishes he had something in front of him. If not a beer bottle, at least a glass or a bowl of chips. Something he could grip. Something that would make it easier to resist the urge to punch Danny in the face.

Danny stares right back at him. Baby-faced, for sure, but also cool as a cucumber under the pressure of Caleb's furious, unrelenting glare. The kid's not backing down. And so Caleb breathes through it. The anger, the desire to argue with his words and his fists. The desire to turn over the table.

Because Danny's right.

Abel's not standing in his way.

Amber's not standing in his way.

He's standing in his own way.

"It's almost one in the morning. My room's got two beds. You want to crash here tonight?"

"I'd like to drown you in that fountain is what I'd like to do."

"Good. That means you know I'm telling the truth."

8

Amber wakes from a dream of kissing Caleb to find her mouth full of bedsheets.

Her bedroom is dark save for the alarm clock, which tells her it's only three thirty in the morning.

This was the best she could do? Two hours of fevered dreaming that left her feeling jittery and wired, as if she hadn't slept at all and didn't really need to?

A text or call from either Caleb or her mother would have lit up her cell phone's display. Even though it's a dark patch on her nightstand, she grabs for it anyway, unlocks it just to be sure.

Nothing.

Well, if I *can't sleep!*

She dials her mother's home number.

How many voicemails has she left for the woman already?

Shouldn't she start the clock over now that she's had somewhat of a night's sleep, however terrible? Fifteen unreturned voicemails the night before, which would make this current call the first official call of—

"For the love of the baby Jesus, Amber, it's three thirty! Go to bed! You can yell at me in the morning!"

"It *is* morning!"

"Sunup, then!"

"How dare you rat me out to—"

Click.

Enraged, Amber throws the phone across the room.

For a terrifying instant, she's afraid it's going to smash into the opposite wall and break into several pieces. Instead, it lands on the foot of her bed with a weak *thump*, a reminder of why she never played softball.

All hopes of sleep dashed and the source of her current troubles unwilling to remain on the phone with her for longer than ten seconds, Amber sees only one option.

A brief, frenzied shower and two Diet Cokes later, she grabs the weekend bag she packed the night before and heads to her Sentra. She's got the driver's side door half open when she shuts it suddenly, heads back inside the house, grabs four Diet Cokes out of the fridge, gets back in her Sentra and speeds off in the direction of the freeway.

If she manages to drive straight through to Chapel Springs, she might catch her mother before her first cup of coffee. She speeds up, hoping to get there sooner. Too bad she didn't bring a pair of cymbals with her. Maybe she can stop and pick one up along the way.

An hour south of Dallas, her eyelids start to get heavy.

Are you kidding me? Now? Now I'm tired?

It's still dark out, which is why she doesn't notice the approaching thunderstorm until lightning forks on the horizon. Lightning. Her least favorite thing next to menstrual cramps and snakes.

Also, I'm tired. Really tried. And getting more tired. And even though this fact seems dramatically unfair, saying so over and over again to herself isn't making her any less tired.

A few minutes later, sheeting rain washes the windshield. The taillights in front of her become vague, bleeding suggestions. She's got another two and a half hours to Chapel Springs. Maybe three, if this weather keeps up.

If I were home in bed, I'd be wide awake and staring at the ceiling. But now I'm getting sleepy. So very, very sleepy.

Traffic slows to a crawl. Traffic! At four in the morning.

Unfair. All of it. So unfair. She just wants to get to her mother, that's all. All she wants to do is rant and yell and scream at her mother for breaking her confidence, thereby blowing the lid off a potful of feelings she's tried to keep at a low simmer for twelve years.

She's going to get herself killed if she doesn't pull over.

The motel she pulls into is the kind of place where people go to have one-night stands with men who love face masks and recreational chainsaws.

"Can I get a room until this storm lets up?" she asks when she goes into the front office.

The kid behind the front desk looks like a twelve-year-old playing a game of Let's Be A Motel Clerk. He's even slicked his hair into a perfect side part.

"We're not that kind of place," he says.

"Not what kind of place? Aren't you a motel?"

"Yes, but are you in some kind of trouble? Is somebody following you?"

"What are you? Twelve years old? I just want a room. I don't do lighting all that well, okay?" And then she catches sight of herself in the reflective glass behind the clerk and realizes she looks like she's been struck by it.

No wonder the kid seems terrified. Apparently she started thinking about something else when she was in the middle of drying her hair after her frenzied shower, because even after getting rained on, it still looks wild and teased, like she's a backup singer out of an 80's music video who's been run over by a car. Only now does she remember that she actually started to put makeup on before thinking *I don't need to be wearing makeup to strangle my mother*. Problem is, she didn't bother to take off any of the makeup she applied before changing her mind, and now half of her face is running with it, making her look a little like that dog that used to sell beer when she was a girl.

She's startled back to the present by a metallic thud.

The clerk drops a key on the desk in front of her.

"You may not believe this, ma'am, but I'm a Christian and as such I kinda feel like it's my duty to keep you off the road right now. You can have the room for free 'til sunup."

"Thank you. I guess."

"Also, I'm twenty-nine."

"Yeah, sorry."

Only when she's almost to the room does she realize the clerk didn't say anything about keeping her safe during a storm. He probably meant it was his duty to keep the road safe from her.

The room's actually not as bad as she feared.

And there's a phone.

A phone with a number her mother won't recognize on caller ID.

"I've got bail money," her mother answers, sounding bored. "Just tell me where you're holding her."

"How could you?" Amber cries.

"How could I what? Where are you?"

"I'm driving to Chapel Springs to murder you."

"You're going to murder me right now?" her mother asks.

"No, I was going to murder you once I got there."

"Are you still drunk?"

"Stop deflecting!"

"So you are still drunk."

"I am *not* still drunk. It's been hours since I've had a drink."

"Human hours or dog hours?"

"Now who's being sarcastic?"

"I am! Because it's five in the morning."

"I called you fifteen times and you didn't return one of my calls. Don't act like I'm being crazy for no reason."

"Okay. Fine. But we can agree that you're being crazy?"

"Sure. Fine. Alright."

There's a silence on the other end. Thunder rolls outside. She can just make out the rustling of her mother's comforter. She's sitting up in bed, a sure sign she's getting ready to talk some truth.

"So what did he do?" her mother finally asks.

"What did *who* do?"

"Caleb. What did he do when I told him?"

Amber's so caught off guard by her mother's directness and the resignation in her voice, she can't manage a response at first.

"Oh my God," she finally says. "Belinda was right. You told him for a reason. You were trying to make him jealous."

"Pretty much, yeah. Did it work?"

"I'm not going, if that's what you mean."

"To the sex club place thing?"

"It has a name, but who cares? No. I'm not going. So yeah, you got your way."

"Did *you*?"

"What does that mean, Momma?" But she knows exactly what she means, and the knowledge makes her voice sound shaky and weak.

"Honey," her mother says. "I'm just gonna cut right to the point because it's five in the morning and I don't actually know where you are and I'm just hoping it's someplace you're not about to get murdered or washed into a ditch. But twelve years ago your father made a decision about what would be best for Caleb and what would be best for you. He made it without consulting me or anyone else, but he made it with his heart and the absolute best of intentions, I can assure you. And you know what, Amber?"

"What?" she asks.

"He was wrong. He was dead as a doornail wrong. And if you accept how wrong he was, you will not besmirch his memory or his name."

I'm just tired, that's all, she thinks, tears blotting out her vision as she sinks to the foot of the bed. *I'm just tired and about to get divorced and stressed. That's why I'm crying. That's why I can't speak.*

"I'm going to tell you a story. I never told you before because as soon as Caleb grew up it stopped being my story to tell. And it was one of your daddy's greatest regrets. But the night Tim and Abby were killed, when you all were up at the lake house and he decided to leave you there and take Caleb back to Dallas, he lost control. He and Caleb were in the car on the way to the airport and Caleb wanted you to come and he wouldn't stop asking for you."

Amber's too startled by this information to even gasp. She'd always assumed Caleb's grief for his parents had effectively killed his desire for her. Had taken whatever he'd felt for her on the boat dock that night and sent it into exile. But he'd asked for her. Even in the midst of all that pain, he'd asked for her.

"Well, he threw a fit is what happened," her mother continues. "And your father pulled the car over and he shook him. He shook him and he said all sorts of terrible things. He told Caleb that our family was his last shot at ever having one. He told the boy that if he ever acted on his feelings for you, he'd lose that shot forever, that he'd be out on the street.

"And then he left him there. He drove off like he wasn't coming back. Of course, he had a change of heart instantly. He was out of his mind with grief over Tim and Abby, you see. But by the time he turned back Caleb was gone. The boy had tried walking back to the house, but he got lost and it took your father hours to find him.

"Darling, your father had to do things in the Marines he never wanted to talk about. Hard things. But I can assure you, he didn't regret any of them the way he regretted what he did to Caleb that night. He spent the rest of his life trying to make up for it. But he was convinced the only way you two could care for each other was if you were siblings, not lovers, and nothing I said ever changed his mind about that. He said brothers and sisters last forever, but teenagers fall out of love all the time. And Caleb couldn't afford to have you fall out of love with him or vice versa. 'Cause what Caleb needed more than anything was a family and you had to be part of that family, no matter what. And like it or not—and I didn't like it, not one bit— there was only one way your daddy knew how to make that happen. Unfortunately, it was the wrong way.

"I guess I always thought you two would just grow out of it. That one day, you'd both be grown-up enough that you'd see y'all were made for each other and that your father had just been delaying the inevitable. But it's not that easy, apparently. Even with Abel gone, it's still not that easy. I guess I understand. Sometimes, if we wear them long enough, chains can seem like clothes."

Her mother goes silent for a minute.

"You still there, darling?" she asks.

"Yes," Amber croaks through her tears.

"Aw, honey. It's easier to get over the mistakes of a bad man 'cause you can just dismiss the man. But the mistakes of a good man? Those are much harder to contend with."

Someone pounds against the door. Amber jumps and leaps to her feet.

"Darling?" her mother asks. "You alright?"

Amber peels back one corner of the curtain. The man outside is so tall he blocks out the overhead light. And he wears a dripping Stetson and a light jacket.

"He's here," Amber says in disbelief.

"Who's there?" her mother asks. "And where is *there?*"

"Caleb's here. I'm in a motel and Caleb's here."

"Well, that escalated quickly."

"It's not like that."

Another series of pounding knocks, followed by Caleb's voice bellowing her name.

"Okay, well, I guess if I'd wanted more of an explanation I could have returned one of your ten thousand calls."

"I should…"

"Yes, you should. You let that man inside, darling. You just go right ahead and let that man inside."

Amber stands there for a second listening to the dial tone, realizing that as soon as she puts the phone back in its cradle she'll be crossing a point of no return.

When she opens the door, he reaches up and pulls his hat off so she can see it's him. The gesture sends raindrops spraying from the hat's brim to the pavement beside him. How long was he out in the rain looking for her? How is it possible that he's here at all? There's fear in his big, beautiful blue eyes and his tense mouth suggests he's having trouble breathing.

"What the hell are you doing?" he asks.

"What are *you* doing?"

"Following you."

"Well, come inside."

When he steps across the threshold, he seems to fill the room. He sets his cowboy hat down next to the tiny boxy television. Then he begins to slide out of his jacket, one arm after the other, slowly, so as not to send raindrops spraying everywhere. And now there's just the sound of the rain pounding the roof and the occasional roll of thunder and the occasional flash of lightning as the man she's resisted for years greets her in an anonymous motel room.

He looks bigger than he's ever looked before. Maybe it's the room. Maybe it's how close they're standing. Maybe it's what they did to each other just a few hours before. Or maybe it's because she's seeing him as a teenager, a teenager clawing his way through dark woods, sobbing and grief stricken and desperate to find his way back to the only family he'll ever have.

"How long have you been following me?" she asks.

"I was parked outside your house. I was going to wait until you woke up but then you sped off so I followed you."

"Why didn't you call me? You knew I was awake once I was driving."

"I thought you were going there, that place. The sex club."

"I see."

"Are you?"

"She won't take me anymore."

"Your boss?"

"Yeah?"

"Why's that?"

Because of you, she thinks. *Because she knows I'm in love with you.*

"My mother…" The words leave her. She hasn't closed the door all the way. She moves to it, shuts it with a final-sounding click.

"Is she okay?" Caleb asks.

"She told me what Daddy did to you the night your parents died. She told me about the woods. And what he said to you…"

Caleb looks away as if he's been slapped. He's never done that before. Looked away from her with a turn of his head so pronounced it seems as if some loud noise in the bathroom has stolen his attention.

"He did something to me that night too," she says.

He looks back to her as quickly as he looked away.

"He took me aside and said I couldn't go with y'all back to Dallas. He said he knew what happened down on the dock and that things were going to have to change. Did you know? Did you know he said something to me too?"

"No," he whispers. "No, I just thought…"

"Just thought what?"

"I just thought…me being in your house, I thought it was too much for you, is all. And I thought you didn't want to be with someone whose parents had just died. I thought my sadness…I thought my sadness drove you away."

"Tell me that's not what you thought," she says, blinking back tears. "Please tell me that's not what you thought for *twelve* years."

"It's not your fault. We didn't tell each other anything.

Nothing real, anyway. So how could you have known?"

"'Cause you were afraid if we did anything other than fight all the time, that he'd throw you out on the street. Was that it?"

"Something like that. Yeah."

"How long were you in those woods, Caleb?"

"I don't know." His voice is hoarse. He makes no attempt to hide his tears. "But when I watched you marry Joel, a part of me felt like I'd never left 'em."

He's got her in his arms before she's closed the entire distance between them. He's so much bigger, so much stronger and more confident than the fifteen-year-old she kissed years before. And his embrace alone is intoxicating. The feel of his powerful hands stroking her back warms her entire body. His breaths rustle her hair, sending gooseflesh down her spine.

"Is it really going to be here?" she asks.

"Is what going to be here?"

"Our first real kiss is gonna be in this crappy motel room?"

"Second," he says.

"Still."

"Well…" he says, and then he releases her suddenly, and for a second she's terrified she's infuriated him by being too casual and sarcastic about a moment that could change them forever.

Caleb hurls the door open, but he only takes several strides before he turns to face her, arms thrown out, the heavy rain pelting his shirt and jeans, soaking his hair instantly.

"There's no full moon," he cries over a roll of thunder. "But I've waited this long, I could kiss you anywhere."

She runs to him, leaving the door open behind her.

There's no resistance. No fumbling. Their mouths meet instantly, then their tongues follow suit, and suddenly she's cradled in his powerful embrace, so powerful he's lifting her up onto the balls of her sneakers.

Several minutes go by before she even realizes she's soaked from head to toe, and even then she doesn't care. All her life she's been afraid of lightning. But not now, not here. It could strike several feet from where they're standing and still she wouldn't be able to pull herself away from this kiss, this kiss she's imagined countless times. And if lightning struck the two of them, then at least she'd die doing what she'd most wanted to do since she was a teenager.

Her hands come to rest against his chest. She realizes she's been pawing at the collar of his shirt, that the top few buttons have come undone, and there's his hard muscle, glistening with rain. And it's like a second glorious revelation. She doesn't just get to act on her love for him now, she gets to act on her lust too.

"See," Caleb says, voice gravely, "we don't always need a full moon."

"That thing you said…"

"What thing?"

"About kissing me anywhere. Was it a promise?"

"Let's go inside and see."

9

"Take it," she whispers as Caleb pushes her closer to the bed.

He gives her another desperate kiss, then grips her chin in one powerful hand.

"Take what?" he rasps.

"All of it," she says.

He kisses her again, drags the hem of her shirt up over her chest with both hands, then his fingers trace the edge of her breasts. His thumbs find her nipples and apply two pinpoints of pressure through the fabric of her bra. He rubs smaller circles, then bigger circles, then smaller. Then bigger. Smaller. Bigger.

"Take all of *what*, Amber?" He says this with the tone of a schoolteacher who knows the answer and is trying to get his pupil to say it.

"All of me," she says.

He gives her a slight shove. She bounces on the mattress. When his weight comes bearing down on her, she realizes what she's trying to do. She's never spoken to anyone like this in the bedroom before. She wants to unleash him with her words, to set him loose upon her body.

She doesn't want to work for it. She doesn't want to ride; she wants to be ridden. More importantly, she doesn't want to think. Doesn't want to hesitate or falter or do anything but let him taste every inch of her. She wants him to take her the way he's always wanted her, the way she's always *hoped* he wanted her, and when he does it, she wants him to blast all thoughts of other people's expectations from her mind.

If he were resisting, this approach would seem selfish on her part, childish even. But her commands have unleashed a torrent of growls and hungry kisses from the only man she's every truly craved.

His fingers claw at the button of her jeans.

The door swings open behind him. Rain swirls in the room.

No one fills the doorway. Caleb just failed to close the thing all the way during their lustful dance back into the room.

He leaps to his feet and shuts the door so hard with both hands, the building shakes.

"Fuck this door!" he shouts.

"Or fuck me instead," she says before she can think twice.

"Dirty girl," he growls, crawling onto her, hands braced on the mattress on either side of her, bending down to give her deep, lingering kisses. "Dirty, dirty girl," he growls.

"Not unless you make me..." She hesitates over her next words, wondering for a second if it's too much, if it might blow the whole thing. But when he unbuttons her pants and a flush of deliciously chilly air bathes the crotch of her panties, lust devours fear. In a hissing whisper, she says, "Not unless you make your little sister a dirty girl."

His eyes widen. He grips her chin in one hand, stares into her eyes, as if this label were a kind of challenge. Did she just blow it? The passion uniting them is more than just some suppressed incest fantasy, and maybe her wording was too careless and heated and rushed. Why bring up the labels her father forced on them both? To destroy them, that's why. To cast them into the fires of their newly released passion so they can be incinerated and replaced by something altogether different, altogether new. And maybe that's what she really means when she tells him to make her a dirty girl—change me. *Change us.*

He's kissing her like she's something altogether different, that's for sure. Then he licks his way up the side of her neck with the flat of his tongue while he palms the crotch of her panties gently with the heel of one hand, drawing figure eights that brush her clit at the top. She's clawing at the buttons of his shirt, pushing it back over his shoulders, chills racing through her at the feel of his bare, muscular skin beneath her fingers, beneath her palms, beneath her desperate, hungry grip.

There's so much of him. So much size, so much brawn. So much muscle and so much hunger. It feels like he's everywhere on her at once, the sheer size of him distracting her from the fact that he's just unfastened her bra and drawn it off her breasts with his teeth. Then he's suckling her neck until he finds a special spot that makes her legs rear up off the bed and wrap around his waist—a spot no other man has found. Then he's got one of her breasts in a powerful grip, squeezing it just enough that he gets the right angle on her nipple, which he tongues madly, then suckles, tongues madly, then suckles. And just when she feels consumed by this pleasure, just as he switches from one breast to the next, he peels the crotch of her panties back from her mound and fingers her folds, dazzling her clit for a few brief seconds before diving deeper into her wetness.

Awestruck, quivering, she watches as he pulls his mouth from her slick nipple, brings his fingers slathered with her juices to his nose and takes a deep smell. "There's my Amber," he whispers. He slides her fingers between his lips and sucks on them briefly. Tasting her. Savoring her. "There's my sweet Amber," he growls. Then it seems as if he can't decide between the lure of her pink, pebbling nipple or a deeper taste of the juices he just sampled as if they were divine nectar.

Breathless with suspense, she watches him. He senses this and his eyes cut to her. He smiles devilishly. He's got her right breast in one powerful grip and his other hand is rubbing lazy, cloying circles across her mound. "Let's see," he grumbles. "Decisions. So many tasty decisions." He flickers her nipple with his tongue.

But it's just a distraction.

In a flash, his still booted feet hit the floor. His hands grip her waist. He's got her jeans off in no time flat, and then her panties, and then, as if that weren't enough to make her skin catch fire, he grabs the back of her thighs, drawing her legs up and apart. And then he goes to work. And she screams. She literally screams.

No one's ever done it like this before. No one's ever devoured her with this outright abandon, this determination not to miss an inch. In his every move, in every flicker of his tongue, there is as much a desire to dominate as there is a desire to please. He even dips just below her folds, coming to the edge of a place no man has ever been. Each brush of this place causes her to let out a small cry, and each time she does, he locks eyes with her. The message is the same. No part of you is dirty. No part of us, of the way we've always felt for each other, is dirty. Not here. Not anymore.

His powerful hands slide under her butt, gripping her cheeks, lifting her off the bed so he can bend forward and get a better, more focused angle on her clit. She hears strange thuds before she realizes she's balled her hands into fists and she's striking the comforter on either side of her to keep from screaming.

Devoured. Consumed. Taken. Never before has she connected these words to the act of sex. Hell, she would have laughed at anyone who did. But they all describe exactly how she feels now. Caleb gives her clit a rest now and then so it doesn't go numb. He takes time to search her folds with his tongue and puckering lips, looking for new sensitive spots. The whole time he keeps his eyes locked with hers, searching for any evidence of new, unexpected pleasure in her expression.

It's not a certain spot that does her in. It's those eyes. Those eyes she spent so many years refusing to meet for fear of being drawn into dangerous temptation. Those eyes that stare into her own now. Those eyes that belong to Caleb, the man she was forced to call brother before she could claim him as her lover. Those eyes and his name, which escapes from her lips unbidden. Which she says again and again and again until the dam breaks and the hands she's balled into fists turn to claws and Caleb rears up, sucking harder.

He uses the arm he's braced under the small of her back to lift her further up off the bed. And as she cries out, he grunts sharply against her slick folds. She has some sense of what's happening, but part of her thinks it can't be true, and she can't exactly pause to investigate while in the grip of her own orgasm. But just the thought of it quickens the waves of pleasure coursing her limbs.

He's coming too, she thinks. *Is he really coming in his own Levi's?*

He pulls his mouth from her sex as if it were a struggle, stands erect suddenly. She's spent, boneless. For a few minutes the idea of moving seems an abstraction. Then she lifts her head and stares down at the foot of the bed. Caleb is just standing there, hair tousled and still rain slicked. The baffled expression on his face makes him look innocent, despite his God-like muscles. The bulge in his jeans is considerable. So is the wet spot.

"Son of a gun," he says. "Can't believe it."

"Seriously?" Amber asks.

She slides off the bed and hits her knees in front of him. He backs away, one hand going up to stop her as she reaches for the button on his jeans.

"No, no, no," he says, but he's laughing. "No. This is embarrassing."

"Don't be embarrassed. Show me your cock."

"This is the first time this has ever happened to me," he says. But he's moved his hands out of the way. "I swear."

She unbuttons his jeans. The idea that just the taste of her made him lose control like this is almost as gratifying as the orgasm that just pulsed through every cell of her body.

"Well, tonight's a first for a lot of things, isn't it?" she says.

Not once did she ever try to sneak a peek of him in the shower when they were growing up. The sight before her now is her thick, beautiful reward. The way his cock, still slick with his seed, peels away from his stomach once she pulls down his briefs makes it seem as if the thing is literally presenting itself to her. The only thing missing is a bow and a silver tray.

He laughs softly, still embarrassed. This display of vulnerability as he towers over her awakens as much desire in her as the ministrations of his skillful tongue. She closes one hand around the shaft. A small sigh escapes him. He's not laughing now. He's dead serious as he gazes down at her, fingers twining in her hair, biting his lower lip gently. He must feel exactly the way she did when he was deciding between suckling her breast or devouring her sex. She can feel the tension in his body, the desire to force her mouth onto him fighting with the desire to take in the sight of her, submissive and on her knees.

"You're a big boy, Caleb," Amber whispers.

"Oh, yeah. Well, you're a—"

Before whatever porn star line he was about to deliver can come out of his mouth, she takes his cock into her own. The sound that comes from his half groan, half cry, there's a tremble to it, the tremble of a strong, powerful man being shaken to his core. She's sure it's not just the physical sensations of his still sensitive cock sliding between her lips, but his surprise at having her suck his fresh seed from his shaft.

Both of his strong hands grip her head now. But he doesn't try to drive her; he's steadying himself, taking care not to pull her hair. There's a loud thud from above and she knows just what made the sound—his head slamming into the wall behind him.

Once she's cleaned him off, she pulls away. In response, he cups her face in both hands, even though his eyes are shut. He's drawing her gently to her feet. She's never done anything like this before. Never tasted the essence of another man in this way. Never wanted to before him. And the idea that she might have just destroyed his desire to kiss her pains her suddenly.

Too much, she thinks. *Too far. I went too fa—*

He kisses her tenderly, gently, at first. The way he holds her face as he does slays her thoughts and conquers her self-judgment and makes the motel room fall away.

"So long," he whispers. "I have waited so long for this, so long for you."

"I'm sorry if I—"

"No," he says, placing a finger to her lips. "No. There's no sorry here, not right now. That, what we just did, was nothing to be sorry for."

As to prove his point, he reaches down and before she realizes what's happening, he picks her up like a bride and carries her toward the bed. He lays her down gently, then settles down onto the mattress behind her, spooning against her, a reverse of the position into which they'd settled the night his parents died.

He rolls away from her. She hears his belt buckle clacking against the button of his jeans. When he spoons into her again, he's naked against her bare behind. The intimacy between them feels somehow sealed by this simple act. He's already spent. He doesn't seem to be demanding another go-around, and yet, he's disrobed just so she wouldn't feel more exposed than she currently does.

"The kid in the office said I had to be out by sunup."

"I paid him already," Caleb whispers.

"Seriously?"

"It's how I got him to tell me which room you were in."

"Good thing you're not an axe murderer."

"Good thing a night in the sack with me didn't rid you of your smart mouth."

"You got that right," she says.

"Good. I love your smart mouth."

"Do you?"

He reaches up, grips her chin gently and tilts her head back so he can look into her eyes.

"Do you know what I'm about to say?" he asks.

"That if we get anything from this bedspread you're gonna kill me?"

"No," he says with only a slight smile at her joke.

Whatever he's about to say, it's serious.

"You don't need to wait for me to say it, do you? I mean, you've waited long enough, haven't you?" he says.

"Caleb—"

"I love you, Amber Watson. I've always loved you. Even when I believed we could never be together, even when it hurt so bad to love you I couldn't see straight, I never stopped. I couldn't even try to make myself stop. It was true then, and it's true now. I'd rather spend the rest of my life feeling the pain of not having you, than spend one moment of it not loving you."

"You won't have to," she whispers. "You won't have to know what it's like to not have me ever again."

It feels as if someone else has spoken through her, but maybe that's what it feels like when you finally speak your truth. And when he kisses her, she feels like she's floating somewhere just above her body, but maybe that's what it feels like when you kiss the man you truly love.

"I love you, Caleb…"

And she stops.

She was about to echo his words. She was about to use his full name, just as he used her own, but now?

"Eckhart," he says. "My full name, my *birth* name, is Caleb Eckhart, and when I was fifteen years old, a good man named

Abel Watson allowed me to live with him and his wonderful family and so when he adopted me, I changed my name to Watson. But that time has passed now. There's something new on the horizon. New and better. So as soon as we're back in Dallas, I'll get myself to a lawyer and find out how to change my name back to Caleb Eckhart, and you and I will be able to slow dance in the middle of Watson's and won't a soul be able to say a damn word about it. If that's what you want, of course."

She smiles.

"Do you want me to, Miss Watson?"

"Yes," she answers. "Yes. Because I love you, Caleb Eckhart."

People really can kiss like this, she thinks. *Long. Slow. Forever.*

"Caleb," she says a few minutes later.

"Yes, Amber."

"Don't get me wrong. This has been one of the best nights of my life. But I'm really slee—"

10

A phone rings close to her head.

Amber's not sure where she is at first. She rolls over and recognizes the motel room's corded phone, the same one she used to call her mother. But it's not ringing. That would be her cell phone, which is on the opposite nightstand.

She rolls in the other direction, grabs her cell, glimpsing the clock on the display as she brings it to her ear.

It's three thirty. Again. It's the afternoon version of three thirty this time, and she's not sure if this should make her feel guilty or not.

For nine hours she slept. That's probably a good thing. But she's alone. And that's not good at all.

She sits up, panic tensing her limbs.

"Hello?" she croaks.

"I take it you've changed your mind about my imminent murder," her mother says.

Just then, Amber sees the spread of items on the dresser next to the T.V. At first she assumes the cowboy hat is Caleb's, but it's way too small, and it's not the same color as the one he wore that morning. As the daughter of a man who ran a country music bar, she knows her Stetsons. This one's a royal Western, flesh-colored with a slender black band. Caleb's partial to a black skyline, where the band blends in to the dark fabric and the upturn along the brim is more severe.

The reason this hat is different, she realizes, with a skip in her chest, *is because it's mine. He bought it for me!*

"You're not answering so I assume that means you still plan to murder me?"

"I am not," she says, rushing to the bathroom mirror so she

can see how she looks in her new duds.

Wow. Huge mistake. She still hasn't washed off her freak show makeup.

"Oh my God," she whispers. "Did we really have sex with me looking like this?"

"That was more than I needed to hear."

"Oh, cut it out. You were the instigator of this whole thing! Don't get all high and mighty now that you got your way!"

"I see," her mother says. "So crazy's getting replaced by sassy this afternoon. You are aware it's the afternoon, right?"

"I needed sleep."

"Where are you?"

"Some motel somewhere."

She returns to the dresser. Caleb's also left out a just purchased, folded pair of blue jeans—almost the right size, but not quite—and a T-shirt which, for a second or two, she's afraid has some dirty saying about riding cowboys written on it, but which turns out to be printed with the spare but lovely silhouette of a cowboy on horseback before a giant, setting sun.

Sweet.

There's also clean underwear and a fresh pair of socks and bottles of her favorite shampoo and body wash.

"Is Caleb with you?"

"I think so," she says. "I hope so."

She draws back the curtain, and there he is, sitting by the motel's woebegone swimming pool, a postcard of cowboy perfection with his hat tilting forward on his head while he—

"Caleb plays the *guitar*?" Amber asks.

"Lord, I hope not. All that strummin' and whining. Makes me want to drown myself in a creek."

"Momma. That's no way to talk about the guitar."

"Really, Amber? After your track record with musicians?"

"Is there a reason for this phone call other than to give me an apology you haven't given me yet?"

"Yes. Where are you?"

"I don't know. Some motel. We're about an hour outside of Dallas. I was on my way to you."

"To murder me. Yes, I remember."

"I'm still considering it."

"Yes, well, that's very interesting, baby girl. In the meantime, I'd like you to drive another two hours south because the pleasure of your company is being requested at The Haven Creek Inn."

"By who?"

"By your *mother*, thank you very much."

"And whose company is that exactly?"

"You and Caleb. Now I'm gonna get off the phone before you slip and tell me how big it is."

"*Momma*!"

"See you in a few hours, sweetheart."

She wants to join Caleb by the pool, but she also doesn't want to go out in public looking like a psychotic cowgirl who just survived the running of the bulls. She showers quickly with the products he just bought for her, each squirt of shampoo and body wash feeling like a kiss from the man who took the time to buy them for her.

Only once she's standing at the motel room door, clean and dressed, the cowboy hat he bought for her perched on her head, does the fear hit. Maybe he's sitting by himself outside because he's having second thoughts. The gifts could have been compensation prizes, not tokens of affection, and he could already be planning his next escape. He hasn't looked in her direction once. Is he rehearsing a little speech about how last night was a giant mistake?

Start walking, she tells herself.

By the time she's a few steps from the chain link gate, Caleb looks up from the guitar on his lap. As soon as his eyes meet hers, the fear vanishes. Everything about him seems relaxed and unguarded. Seeing her so close seems to brighten everything about him, from his smile to his eyes.

The storm's passed over completely, leaving behind towers of puffy clouds against a dome of blue. In broad daylight, the motel actually seems a little charming. The room numbers are all the same antique-style brass, the parking lot lines freshly painted. And the water in the pool looks clean, even if the pool itself is just a plain concrete rectangle fenced in by chain link.

"Thanks for the care package, sir," she says.

"You're welcome," he answers. "Hope you didn't think I was trying to brand you with all the cowboy paraphernalia. Nearest place I could find was a country western emporium, this being Texas and all. Although, I must say, you do look mighty cute in that hat."

"Thank you," she says. "So, guitar, huh?"

"Yeah, I've been taking lessons. Didn't want to come right out and say it, you know, given your history with a certain songbird."

"That's sweet. Thank you."

"You want to hear something?"

Uh oh.

"Sure, I guess."

"You guess? Well, that doesn't sound very enthusiastic."

"I am. I'm very enthusiastic. Play me a song, Caleb *Eckhart*."

With a big grin at the sound of his newly modified name, he gestures for her to take a seat on the lounger next to his. She does, wondering, *Is this going to be like one of those moments in a Nicholas Sparks movie?*

Caleb sucks in a deep breath. He grips the guitar's arm carefully, his chest rising and falling. He strums.

Something doesn't sound right.

He strums again and it sounds worse.

Oh, shit, Amber thinks, trying to freeze a plastic smile on her face.

"Aaaaamber," he says.

"Hello, Caleb!"

"Shhh. That's part of the song. It's about you."

"Oh. Okay. Sorry."

Caleb nods, takes another deep breath, and starts again.

This time, the strumming sounds even worse.

"Amber," he sings. "A-uhm-ber. She's like the mooooon."

Oh, shit, Amber thinks again.

He strums wildly, and if there's a connection between the notes he's singing and whatever he's doing to the guitar, only he can hear it. And she would like to stop hearing it. Very soon.

"She's like the moon, if the moon was hot and had breeeeeeeeasts."

"Put that thing down!"

Caleb cracks up laughing as he sets the guitar to one side. "I've never had one lesson in my life. Some guy left this out here and asked me to watch it while he went inside to take a call from his wife."

"Good, 'cause that was God-awful."

"But you really are like the moon if the moon had bre—"

"Shut up," she says.

He pats one thigh. "First have a seat right here, *sis*!"

A bolt of heat shoots up her spine. As she settles onto his lap, the hard muscles in his thighs flex. He curves an arm around her back. They're an hour's drive from anything she'd call home, but still, to be this intimate with him right out in the open makes her feel flushed and light-headed and a little giggly. In its own way, it's more intoxicating than much of what he did to her body earlier that morning.

"Now you really do need to stop calling me that," she whispers with a sly grin.

"You didn't seem to have a problem with the whole forbidden passion routine last night," he says.

"This morning, you mean."

"Details," he says.

"That's 'cause I was doing away with it."

"Us being brother and sister, you mean?"

"Yep."

"How's that?"

"Well, you know. By turning it into a little role-play game, it stops being a real label. I mean, people can role-play pretty much anything they want. Cops. Fireman. Cowboys. It usually means they're not actually any of those things."

"I am a cowboy," he says.

"That's true. But for the most part."

"I see. So role-play. Was that something they were going do out at Belinda's sex club?"

"If you call it that to anybody else, you'll probably get me fired."

"Sorry. Lips are sealed. Promise. I will, however, be willing to consider opening them for other more important activities." He gives her a gentle bite just above her collarbone, more like a light pinch of his teeth. She grips the back of his head, fights the urge to drive his mouth further down where it can nibble on her breast.

"The point is that's not what we are anymore, right?" she asks.

"That's right," he says. "That's very, very right. We did away with all kinds of things last night. Things that weren't working for either of us."

He rests his head against her chest. She's breathing deeply for the first time in days. Or weeks. Or months. Years, even.

"And today, at almost four o'clock in the afternoon, we're starting something altogether new," he says.

"Exactly," she answers. "New."

They hold each other for a while as the trucks blow past them on the highway.

"Can we start it by getting out of this motel?" Amber finally says. "I've kinda had enough of this place."

"Ah, really. I'm always gonna have a special feeling for it, you know, considering." He sits up suddenly. "What's it even called?"

"Something shameful, I'm sure."

Caleb spots the sign. "The Showtime Inn. Ha!"

"A shameful name for a shameful place," she says.

"Nothing shameful about what *we* did," he says, looking up at her.

He reaches up and smoothes her bangs back from her forehead.

"I was only kidding," she says.

"I wasn't."

"Kidding about the motel, I mean."

"And not last night?"

"This morning, you mean."

"Details, details," he says with a grin.

She bends forward. He closes the remaining distance so they can kiss. "The details were important," she says. "I liked the details. Very much."

Footsteps slap the pavement nearby. A guy's heading toward the pool clad in swim trunks and a tank top, probably the owner of the guitar Caleb just used to fool her. He smiles at them both, a smile Caleb returns. Then Caleb grabs the back of her neck quickly and brings her ear to his lips. In a hoarse whisper, he says, "My favorite detail was when I found the spot right below your clit that made you whimper like a little kitten, and I sucked on it till you clawed the bed on either side of you like you thought I was going to tongue fuck you into outer space. What was *your* favorite detail, my little cowgirl?"

The guy's two feet away by the time Caleb finishes this filthy declaration. Her breath lodged in her throat, Amber straightens and gives the guy a broad smile. She sat up so quickly her cowboy hat almost came off, but she rights it just in time. Caleb's whispers have sent shivers of pleasure throughout her body.

"Thanks, partner," the stranger says as he picks up his guitar. "Hope you fooled her like you wanted to."

"I see," Amber says.

"Y'all make a cute couple," their visitor says with a smile, then he heads off back in the direction of his room, guitar in hand.

Because they've never heard these words before, said with such innocence and so free of drama, the two of them just sit for a while, soaking them in.

"So," Caleb finally says. "Where to?"

"Our presence has been requested at The Haven Creek Inn in Chapel Springs."

"Cool. I've never been."

"Really?" she asks.

"Nope."

"Well, it's certainly a day for firsts, isn't it?"

"Yeah," he says with a boyish grin. "When's seconds?"

"Bad boy," she says, then plants a kiss on his lips.

"So we heading out now?"

"I guess, yeah."

"You guess? What's troubling you?"

"I think we should head straight there. She sounded pretty eager. Maybe 'cause I threatened to murder her last night."

"Forgive me if I seem confused, but when someone threatens to murder me, I'm usually not in a rush to have them over to the house."

"You know what I mean. Last night we had words. I think she wants to make up for it."

"This morning, you mean."

"Exactly."

"Alright, well, still doesn't explain the long face."

"I just don't want to take separate cars, that's all," she says. "You and me, we've been taking separate cars our whole lives practically because I was so afraid to be alone with you. And now all I want is to be alone with you. So I don't know where we'll leave my car, but fact is, I want to ride with you and I'm not going if I can't."

Her pouty expression earns her a belly laugh from Caleb.

"Well, that's a lucky coincidence, miss, 'cause I don't feel like going if you don't ride with me either. And while we're speaking the truth, I don't feel much like letting go of you once we get there neither."

"Unless," she says.

"Unless what?" he asks, expression falling.

"Unless you try playing the guitar again, in which case I might run for the hills and never come back."

"Well, I'll just have to catch you then!"

She's not quite sure how he does it, but in an instant, he's standing and he's got her in both arms and she's got no choice but to wrap her legs around him to keep from falling. And just like that, he's carrying her across the parking lot and back to their room.

"Or you could just never let me go," she whispers into his ear as he walks. "That way, you don't have to risk me running in the first place."

"Sounds good to me, darlin'."

11

It's amazing what you can learn about someone after two hours alone together in the car, Amber realizes.

Like the fact Caleb's actually a smooth and focused driver, his antics in her driveway the night before not withstanding. Or that he likes country music way more than she realized, and when he sings along with it, he sounds a heck of a lot better than he did during his little comedy routine by the motel's pool.

She also feels blessed he's such a country fan because for the first time in her life, the love songs they're listening to seem written just for her. She doesn't find herself thinking things like, "Well, that's just lovely Miss Hill! But let's hear about a *real* marriage!" And when Chase Rice asks her to climb to the top of the water tower so they can kick it with the stars for an hour, it sounds like the invitation is sincere.

The troubles and pain of the last few days don't just feel miles away. Rather, with Caleb's free arm draped across her shoulders and a blazing big sky sunset off to the west, anything seems possible.

Do you have to have love to feel this way, she wonders, or is this how most people feel when they finally walk through the fires of a fear that's lain in their path for most of their lives? Love certainly helps, that's for sure.

Once it was clear her marriage was in a nosedive, she'd had fantasies of getting in the car and just driving and driving until she wound up in her own version of Chapel Springs, some suitable, peaceful refuge from a life defined by fear and hasty choices. But the trip she and Caleb were on now was of a different nature. They weren't driving away from something; they were driving toward her mother and The Haven Creek Inn, and the very real fact that people who cared about them both had wanted the two of them to get together long before they were willing to take the leap.

Some of those people, anyway.

Rather than stew over what her father might think of this new development, Amber slides out from under Caleb's arm so she can take his free hand in her own and hold it to her chest. He returns her grip, but his expression seems distant, more distant than someone watching the road.

"Listen," he says suddenly.

Uh oh.

"What?" she answers.

"This place Belinda was going to send you to," he says.

"Yeah?"

"Did you really want to go? I mean, I'm asking because you told me about what things were like with Joel, how he went cold on you in the bedroom, and then I kinda barged in and did my thing and… I just don't want to feel like I took something away from you. Something you needed before…"

"Are you asking if I needed to sow my wild oats?"

"Kinda. Yeah."

"So did it seem like there was something missing this morning? Did it seem like I was distracted while you—how did you put it? Tongue fucked me into outer space?"

He grins at the road and bites his lower lip and tightens his grip on her hand. He likes it when she talks dirty. She makes a note of that. Good thing the feeling's mutual.

"Is that a trick question?" he asks.

"Nope. Did I seem distracted?"

"You did not. You did not seem distracted."

"Well, there's your answer then."

"Still, I don't want to feel like I shamed you out of doing something you needed to do just 'cause the thought of you with other men made me want to break the door down."

"Well, if we're being honest here, the thought of you breaking the door down to keep me from being with another man kinda makes me want to do a repeat of this morning right here in your truck."

"Well, we can certainly add that to the list," he says.

"Good."

"You're asking me if you're enough, aren't you?" Amber says.

Caleb tilts his head from side to side as if he's considering her question, then he says, "Yeah. I kinda am, I guess."

"Well, I think that's sweet."

"Sweet?" he asks, grimacing.

"Yes. I think it's sweet that the most beautiful man I've ever met in my entire life, probably the only man I've ever really loved, just a few hours after giving me the best orgasm of my entire existence, is asking me if he's enough. It speaks well of your character. I don't want your head to get so big your Stetson won't fit."

"Sassy," he says, and gives her left thigh a hard, loud slap. "Sassy girl, Amber Watson."

"That's me!"

"But you're not answering my question."

"Well, the funny thing was, about five seconds before you pulled into my driveway last night I was about to throw in the towel on the whole idea."

"Why's that?"

"Well, for starters, Belinda wouldn't tell me anything about it. Honestly, I still don't know anything about it. I know it has a name, The Desire Exchange. I know that they were going to try to give me some kinda drug to relax while I was there, which I had *no* intention of taking. And I know we were supposed to be gone for two days. But that's it."

"But you said yes?"

"I said yes at first 'cause when Belinda talked about the place, she got this look in her eyes, like… I don't even know how to describe it. But I thought, here's one of the richest women I know, who could have pretty much anything she wants, and when she talks about this place, I don't know, it was almost religious."

"Huh," Caleb grunts.

"But she's the one who said I shouldn't go. And she said it after she saw the way we looked at each other. She said I didn't need the place or what they had to offer. She said what I needed was right there in front of me and his name was Caleb."

"Caleb Eckhart," he says quietly.

"Yep," she answers.

He smiles, brings her hand to his mouth and gives her fingers a gentle kiss.

They've passed through Austin. The rolling green landscape of the Texas Hill Country spreads out before them now, painted with oranges and deep reds by the westward leaning sun.

"There was one other thing," Amber says.

"What?"

"There was an application process and for part of it, I was going to have to write down my deepest sexual fantasy. Those were Belinda's words. *Deepest* sexual fantasy. The one I was afraid to tell anyone."

"You just have one?" Caleb asks.

"Dirty boy."

"Dirty girl," he answers.

They both stare at the beautiful countryside in silence for a few minutes.

"You can tell me, you know," he finally says. "Your fantasy, I mean. Doesn't matter how deep or how dark."

"Yeah? And then what?"

"I'll do my best to make it real. That's what."

He takes his eyes off the road just long enough to give her a devilish wink. Between this simple gesture and the promise he just made, her breath catches and her cheeks flame and her heart skips a beat. Maybe a few beats, she can't really be sure.

Why the hell not? she thinks. But as soon as she goes to speak, a cold weight settles down over her chest. A day before the fantasy would have seemed fairly tame, as sex fantasies go. Now, not so much. Caleb might not consider it so tame considering it involves being lost in the woods.

"Amber?"

"I'm working on it," she says.

"No rush," he says. "Maybe writing it down'll be easier, when you're ready."

"Maybe so."

Her heart's racing. If she doesn't tell him now, she'll feel like she's withholding something of value. But will the fantasy still work for her now, given the awful story she just learned of what her dad did to Caleb the night his parents died? The thought of Caleb forcing himself to act out some sort of sex scene that might stir such a painful memory, just because he's desperate to make it work with her, fills her with anxiety. For so long now, she's felt like little more than the victim of her husband's betrayals. She never felt like she was even capable of hurting Joel; that's how little the man seemed to care for her. But now, all of a sudden, she's responsible for someone else's heart.

"Hey," Caleb says, "did I push a little too hard there?"

"No," she answers.

"Prove it," he says, curving his arm around her shoulders, pulling her body into his as he drives confidently with one hand.

A few minutes later, the gates to The Haven Creek Inn come into view.

12

The Haven Creek Inn sits on a large hill that dominates the property's eighty acres of live oaks, sloping green lawns, and winding hiking trails. The main building, a two-story L-shaped structure of roughhewn stone, is perched on the hill's crown, the rocking-chair studded porches on its first and second floors commanding gorgeous views of the expansive landscape to the west.

Her mom asked them to meet her at the newest guest cottage, so Caleb drives past the inn's main building, past the half-circle of smaller guest cottages that dot the hill's gentle slope, past even the large, rectangular swimming pool framed by a smoother version of the roughhewn stone used in the main building.

In the early evening dark, Amber can see flickering candles lining the serpentine front walkway of the newest guest cottage. Each glowing candle bag is cut with the inn's logo, a half-moon partially shaded by tree branches. None of the cottages they pass on the way had string lights laced through the gutters of their shiny metal roofs as this one does. Her mother must have added this glittering touch just for her as well.

Just for *them,* she realizes.

And there's her mother, standing on the front porch, dressed in a white polo shirt bearing the inn's logo, the same shirt she always wears when she's on the job. She's flanked by two of her closet friends in the world.

Because she's only four foot nine, most people mistake Nora Donner for a small child from a distance. She's pushing sixty, but she has a child's energy level combined with a desperate desire to please. Some call her codependent, others simply call her kind. Amber's in the latter camp, and her mother goes back and forth between the two, which is probably why she and Nora have been close friends for years.

To her mom's left stands Amanda Crawford, the woman who had made The Haven Creek Inn a reality. She's Nora's polar opposite; a tall, slender gazelle to Nora's energetic pixie. The multimillionaire is also possessed of a classic beauty she maintains through an unassailable combination of good genes, good nutrition and, when necessary, the scalpel of a talented Austin surgeon with whom she sometimes spends romantic weekends she refuses to discuss.

Caleb kills the truck's engine. For a minute, the two of them just sit there, staring at the beautiful scene before them.

"Wow," Caleb finally says.

The hill country to the west spreads out before the cabin's decks like a vast, green sea. In the absence of city lights, a riot of stars is unveiling itself throughout the night sky. Now that they've parked, Amber can see more string lights wrapped around the trunks of the live oaks that watch over the cottage like sentries.

And that's when the tears start.

"Hey," Caleb says quietly, drawing her close with one arm. "Hey, you alright?"

"Yeah," she manages, wiping quickly at tears with the back of her hand. "It's just really beautiful, is all."

"I guess she really wanted us to visit," he says.

"Together. She really wanted us to visit together. That's the thing."

And then Caleb seems to get it. That every candle, and each string light, and the cottage itself, are all her mother's way of trying to make up for twelve years of misunderstanding and confusion and thwarted desire.

"Y'all going to get out of that truck?" her mother finally calls. "Amanda's gotta get home before her manicure melts."

"Tina," Amanda says, voice smooth as silk, "I do wish you would stop using my beauty against me."

"We better get out of the truck," Caleb says.

"Sounds like a plan."

Amber's halfway up the front walk when her mother says, "I don't see a gun so it looks like I'm going to be okay, ladies."

"Hug your daughter, Tina," Nora cries.

And so she does. And when Amber tightens her embrace, her mother tightens hers as well. They've been about the same height ever since Amber graduated high school. But her mother's got a lean, wiry frame from the laps she swims every morning. Her mane of salt and pepper hair is healthy and thick, but it's also threatening to come loose from its ponytail, so Amber adjusts her mom's scrunchee even as they hug. By the time they've parted, her mom's hair is back together again.

Tina stares into her daughter's eyes with newfound seriousness. "See," she says. "There are some things your mother's big mouth is good for."

"Thank you," Amber whispers.

"Don't mention it," she says, smoothing hair from Amber's face. "Just stay a while."

Caleb's introducing himself politely to Amanda and Nora, both of whom have moved so close to the guy it looks like they're about to manhandle him. When Amber steps up onto the porch, Amanda works to pull her stare from the towering hulk of a man in front of her. Then she places one hand on his shoulder gently as she steps past him. As soon as she makes eye contact with Amber, she wags her hand in the air as if the man were literally hot to the touch.

"Darling," Amanda says once she has Amber in her arms. "How you went twelve years without laying a hand on that hunk of burning love is simply beyond my ability to comprehend."

"Well, it was pretty weird, Amanda. I can tell you that."

"Uh huh. Whatever. Notice we gave you the cabin furthest from the inn. So have at him, sweetheart. Only ones eavesdropping are the birds. And the bees!" She gives Amber a light peck on the cheek. "Lord. I need to go book myself a massage. Y'all have fun now, ya hear."

Nora waits for Amber on the top step of the cottage's front porch, which makes her and Amber almost the same height. Almost. The tiny woman throws her arms out in front of her, shifting her weight back and forth between both feet. As always, Nora Donner's happiness is a force that cannot be contained.

"Oh, what do you say kiddo?" Nora cries as they hug. "*What* do you *say*?"

"Oh, you know, just getting divorced and hooking up with the man who used to be my brother. That's all."

Nora cackles.

"Well, we're so happy for you," Nora says, pulling away but holding Amber's hands in hers. "We are. We are. We really are. I mean, you know, Joel was just..." Nora pauses as if she's considering whether or not to add mint or rosemary to a glass of lemonade. "Well, he was just such a piece of shit, that's all. I wish there was a nicer way to say it. But there really isn't now, is there?"

"No. There isn't. He really was a piece of shit. In fact, I was just with him yesterday, and he still is."

"I'm so sorry, honey." Nora takes her hand and leads her to the far side of the porch. "Now listen..."

"Nora!" her mother calls out when she sees the two of them alone together. By then the tiny woman's already reached under her polo shirt and removed a glossy trade paperback she's been hiding inside the waistband of her jeans for Amber doesn't know how long. "Now if there's something about Joel that didn't seem quite right, something that seemed off in a way that was perhaps, nonhuman, I want you to read this book and tell me if any of it makes sense to you. You know, on a personal level."

The cover art features a tiny black silhouette of a man surrounded by swirls of star-filled cosmos that partially conceal a giant pair of black inverted teardrop eyes. The book's title is *The Stars Are Upon Us.*

"Now don't read it late at night because it might frighten you. But what it makes clear, darling, is that the infestation is already underway. They're already at the highest levels of government. There's evidence they're crossbreeding us. It's got pictures, see, in the insert in the middle. Pictures of the hybrid children. And honestly, I was thinking about Joel's facial structure and comparing it to some of these drawings and I think it's very possible he could be a hyb—"

"Nora, get that alien nonsense away from my daughter! She's on vacation!"

"Now your mother thinks this is nonsense," Nora explains gently. "But what I'm trying to say is don't blame yourself if you end up being taken advantage of by one of them. They're everywhere, you see. And they don't think and feel the way we do. It's not about Republican versus Democrat, sweetheart. This is about us versus the stars!" Nora points an index finger skyward and nods solemnly.

"That's really sweet of you, Nora, but I don't think Joel was an alien. I just think he was an asshole."

"Even so, read the book. It's very important."

"Nora Donner, men in white coats will be the least of your problems if you don't stop with that this instant!"

"Your mother likes to threaten me because she can't bear the truth," Nora says gently.

"I understand. Thanks for the book."

Nora gives her a peck on the cheek and more of that big smile, that smile Amber can never get enough of. Then, like a chastised dog, she walks into her best friend's outstretched arms, which curl vise-like around her upper back and begin guiding her away from the cottage.

Amanda has just pulled up next to Caleb's truck in one of those golf carts the staff uses to get around the property.

"Dinner service starts at six," Tina calls back over one shoulder.

"Please," Amanda purrs. "We're not going to see those two for hours. Days, even."

"Oh, you hush!" Tina hisses.

She and Caleb stand together on the porch like new homeowners, watching the golf cart speed off uphill.

"What was Nora going on about?"

She hands him the book. "She thinks you might be an alien."

"A good alien or a bad alien?"

"I'll have to thoroughly examine your body to be sure."

"Sounds like a plan," Caleb says with a grin.

He takes her by the waist and leads her into the cottage. On the console table inside the front door is a map of the property, across the top of which someone, presumably Nora, has drawn a giant smiley face next to the word, *Welcome*! Most of the cabin is decorated in creams and light browns, with sliding glass doors that lead to an expansive deck offering views of the sunset's last, dying rays. In the bathroom, the Jacuzzi tub is flush up against a plate glass window that looks out over treetops.

"Can we do my alien examination in this tub?" he asks.

"Sounds like a plan."

He takes her in his arms. Their lips are inches apart. "That's turning into a refrain with you this evening."

"What can I say? You're just bursting with good plans."

He kisses her, gently at first, then harder. Then he's holding her so tightly he's lifting her up onto the balls of her feet, and she realizes this is going to be one of those things he does that drives her wild. One of the many things he does that drives her wild.

"Easy, big boy," she says when they both come up for air. "We plan on taking a bath in that thing we better start filling it up now."

"Why? It'll only take a few minutes."

"Clearly, cowboy, you have little to no experience with Jacuzzi tubs."

"Oh, don't be silly."

Twenty minutes later, or as she'd prefer to think of it, three and a half make-out sessions later, they're sitting on the edge of a half-full tub, watching the water line rise gradually even though the faucet's gushing.

"Damn," he says. "You weren't kidding."

"Toldja."

"Alright, well, it gives me time to prepare something."

"What?"

"You'll see. I want you naked and in that tub by the time I come back."

"Is that an order?"

He grins, rises off the edge of the tub. He grips the back of her neck gently, then firmly. When she doesn't wince or ask him to stop, he tilts her head so she's staring up into those blue eyes she's spent so many years not looking into.

"Would you like it to be an order, little lady?" he asks in a deep, gruff voice.

Shivers dance down her thighs. The heat in her belly is poised to spread throughout her body. Images from the fantasy she still hasn't shared with him swirl across her vision before she blinks them back.

"That feels like a yes," he says.

He tightens his grip a little more. She gasps.

"I think I'm getting closer to that fantasy you don't want to tell me about. Am I right?"

He tightens his grip a little more.

"Am I, little lady?"

"Yes," she whispers.

He releases her suddenly, takes a few steps backward, and says, "Good. Then get those clothes off and get in the tub. I'll be with you in a minute."

On his way out of the bathroom, he dims the light.

Technically she's alone, but the act of undressing feels deliciously naughty given she knows who she's doing it for.

She leaves the faucet running as she sinks down into the warm water. A few minutes later, Caleb walks into the bathroom wearing a cowboy hat and nothing else. Their first lovemaking was so frenzied and rushed, she didn't have the time to study his body. Now she can clearly see every ridge of muscle, the light tattoo of old scars from his years of hard labor, and the heft of his cock and balls, which swing as he walks. Surrounded by the opulent bathroom's marble and polished stone, he looks like he walked right out of the dark woods and into her most secret chamber.

Only once he's settling into the tub across from her does she realize that his nudity was also meant as a distraction. In his right hand, he holds several sheets of hotel stationary and a slender coffee table book he lifted from the living room. And a pen.

In a neat pile, he sets all three items into the space between the window and the edge of the tub. Then, with a beaming smile, he slides them toward her with one arm. Before she has time to respond, he finds her wet, eager folds under the surface with one big toe and begins prodding at them gently but insistently.

"What could possibly be in that head of yours that you think I'd be too afraid to try?" he asks.

"Caleb…"

"Alright, well, if it'll make you feel safer, I'll add some ground rules. For me, I mean."

"Go ahead," she says.

"No other people. Although I'll be happy to play more than one role, if you like. Oh, and I won't draw any blood. Not 'cause I'm judgmental but because I don't trust myself to handle that kind of situation in a way that'll keep you safe. I'm just not experienced in that manner is all, and I'm not confident I'd be able to keep you safe."

"Caleb Eckhart, what kind of girl do you think I am?" she asks, batting her eyelashes.

"What I think, Amber Watson, is that with me, you're allowed to be any kind of girl you want."

The expression on her face is the one he wanted to see because he smiles warm, sinks further down into the tub, his big toe finding and then gently grazing her nub.

She picks up the pen, but the sight of the empty page terrifies her.

"Maybe if it wasn't the stationary for my *mother's* hotel."

"Come on now," he says gently, and just then his big toe finds her clit and begins rubbing lazy, gentle circles around it. "Just turn the paper over if it bothers you."

His voice is something between a growl and a purr. Between its lustful timber and the job he's doing on her under the water, she can barely see straight enough to keep the pen steady.

"Do you want me to stop?" he asks.

"My writing assignment or your big toe?"

"Either? Both?"

"Just promise me something."

"Sure."

"I don't want you doing it if it's not something you want to do," she says.

He nods solemnly, but she can tell he's sure there's not a chance in hell he won't want to do it, no matter what it is.

"You promise me?" she asks.

"I promise," he says.

"Okay," she says. "Now quit it with your foot so I can concentrate."

He jerks his foot back so suddenly it sloshes the water in the tub, which causes both of them to crack up for several minutes. Once they manage to calm down, once she takes a deep breath and finds herself staring again at the blank, empty page, she finds the courage to say, "Why is this so important to you, Caleb?"

"Because after what you went through with songbird, I don't want you to be afraid to ask me for anything."

And just like that, she's writing. She's writing without regard for how he'll react when he reads it. The fantasy isn't really all that outlandish or kinky. Girlfriends of hers have shared far stranger ones with her over cocktails. But this one involves dark woods, woods as dark as the ones Caleb got lost in on that long ago night. True, it also involves being found. Hard. Still, it seems like a cruel trick of fate, the fact that her most private, unrealized sexual fantasy could trigger one of Caleb's most painful memories. But maybe she's overthinking it.

By the time she's done, she's filled two pages with her hurried block printing.

Her heart hammering, she slides the coffee table book and the pages back across the edge of the tub toward Caleb, who dabs his hands dry on a nearby towel and picks up the pages gently and carefully, as if they were made of old, thin parchment.

She watches his face as he reads, watches the tense set of his jaw, the focus apparent in his dazzling blue eyes. Watches him suck in a deep breath through his nostrils when he gets to a certain line—she has no idea which one, but she's got a few guesses. Is it stirring painful memories for him or something else?

Look down and see, genius, she realizes.

The head of his majestic, swollen cock just pierces the water's surface.

"Oh, Amber," he growls, still reading. "Amber Louise Watson."

It's been forever since anyone's used her middle name. This must be serious.

"What?" she asks.

He sets the pages aside.

"Get ready, baby," he says. "We are *so* doing this!"

13

Are we really going to do this?

Amber's lost count of how many times she's asked herself this question in the past thirty minutes. It would have made more sense to ask Caleb back when they were still plotting out the details. But she's on her own now, making her way through the woods just below the cottage, bound for the spot Caleb marked on the map Nora left in their room.

When she'd asked him how he'd ensure their privacy, he'd told her not to worry, that he'd take care of that part. That he'd take care of everything. All she had to do was trust him.

They'd agreed on two safe words. Slow down was *leaf*; full stop was *Chevron*. But still, the thought of him asking Nora or—oh, dear Lord, no—her mother to keep one of the hiking trials clear just so the two of them could do some outdoor role-play leaves her flush with shame.

The wrong kind of shame.

Of course, he'd probably try some sort of cover story. But it wouldn't matter, because neither Nora nor her mother would believe it for a second.

Her flashlight beam bounces across the old, capped wellhead he marked on the map. Rustic benches sit on either side. A dense canopy of interlocking oak branches filters the night sky above. If she keeps walking, she'll hit woods too dense to move through without a machete. Now she realizes why Caleb picked this particular location. It's the dead end of a hiking trail, a long distance from the inn's main building, but closer to their cottage if things go wrong.

She's here. She's got everything she needs—the blanket, the box of condoms, the flashlight, and the T-shirt they've already tested out on her wrists. She can turn the shirt into a makeshift pair of cotton handcuffs, easy to escape if she gets cold feet, just tight enough to give the illusion she's actually restrained.

She spreads the blanket out in front of her, parallel to one side of the bench and its curved metal armrest.

This is the part of the script about which she's the most nervous.

Once she turns the flashlight beam off, she's got ten minutes.

Once she turns the flashlight beam off, she's committed.

Unless, of course, she decides to use one of her safe words once they've started. But the ten things she has to do before the scenario starts—that's what they've agreed to call it, apparently. The scenario!—those have to be perfect! Otherwise, the whole thing will turn into either a colossal joke or a huge embarrassment. Or both.

God save me, she prays silently. *Save me from feeling like an idiot. The other stuff? I might be beyond hope in that regard.*

She kills the flashlight.

She slides out of her panties and kicks them to one side.

She drops to her knees on the blanket, and then, just as she practiced back in the cabin, she laces the T-shirt around the bench's armrest until she's tied it loosely around her hands. She tugs gently with both wrists until the cotton's tight enough to give the illusion she's handcuffed.

Then she waits.

She waits as the cool night air kisses the cheeks of her ass and everything in between.

She waits as the fear—of wildlife, of discovery, of mortification—turns into a feeling of exhilaration. A feeling of taking all of the rules and limitations and lectures she's endured all her life, all the finger-wagging nonsense abut what good girls are and what good girls have to do, and blowing them into the air like they were nothing but a handful of sand.

Footsteps approach, cracking twigs. Fast at first, then slower. Then Caleb lets out a long, slow whistle.

"Well, well, well, well, *welllllll*," Caleb says. Only for now, he's not Caleb. He's just some random cowboy who emerged from the dark woods to find her half naked and tied to a bench. And he's playing up the accent too, just like she asked. "What have we *here*?

Lord!"

"Sir, could you untie me please?" she asks.

Her voice sounds like someone else's. She's speaking words she's imagined countless times while pleasuring herself with a showerhead or her fingers, all while her husband slept in the other room. Or lied to her about staying late at work so he could bang his mistress.

"Untie you?" he asks, feigning shock. "Are you tied up, ma'am? Is that what you are?" He reaches down and tugs at the makeshift handcuffs. Pretends as if they're locked in place. "Well, you most certainly are, aren't you? Now how in the heck did a pretty little thing like you get tied up out here in these dark woods?"

"It was my husband…"

"Your *husband* did this?"

"Yes and then he left me here. We were playing a game and he freaked out and he left me."

"A game, huh? What kind of game? The kind of game where you gotta turn this pretty ass to the woods?" A light touch. Feather light. Torture light. Just a graze of his finger from the very top of the crack of her ass up into the small of her back.

Oh, God, he's good at this. He's. So. Damn. Good. At—

"And, uh, whose idea was this little game?" he asks.

"Mine," she answers, sounding as sheepish as she can. Which isn't all that hard. Because she's in this, gripped by it. Feeling the boundaries between the scene and reality blur into a kind of blinding heat.

"I see. So it wasn't your husband's idea?"

"No. He said he was into it, but he freaked out. And he called me all kinds of names and ran away."

"Really?" There's concern in his voice now, and a bit of protective anger. "What kind of names?"

"He said I was disgusting. He called me a filthy, dirty whore."

"And then he just left you?"

"Yes, sir. He just left me."

"With no way to get free," he says as if he's realizing the implications of this for the first time. The implications for *him*.

She hasn't looked at him once since he crouched down next

to her. She knows if she looks at him, her juices will start to flow. And it's way too soon for her to do or say or look at the things that will induce a moist inclination toward surrender. That's his job. If he follows the script. If he plays his part.

So far, he's doing an Oscar-worthy job.

"Sir," she whispers. "Please. If you could just untie me so I can get home to my husband."

"So why are you in such a rush to get home to your husband when he called you all those rotten names and left you out here in the woods all by yourself?"

"I just… Please, sir."

"Yeah. I don't know."

"Don't know what, sir?"

"Well, it just doesn't make much sense, is all."

"What doesn't make sense, sir?"

He traces several fingers along the crack of her ass, then down, ever so lightly across her mound. A quick, furtive, stolen motion that still manages to touch the most intimate part of her. "When you find a pretty little pussy like this out in the woods, you don't just take it straight home," he growls.

Home run, she thinks. *Home fucking run.* They've been improvising the rest of the dialogue but this is the exact line she wrote out for him earlier that night, the line that's electrified her fantasies for years. A line that makes her feel both degraded and celebrated, captured and set free. And his tone, his delivery. Both were perfect! But all she says is, "Sir, please. You have to take me home."

Or fuck me. Right here. Right now. I can't wait.

"Tell you what, little lady. I'll make a deal with you."

"Okay," she manages.

"You're gonna let me put my hands all over this body of yours. And if that pussy of yours stays dry, or if those cute little nipples stay soft under my fingertips, I'll take you home to your husband. But if you're a dirty slut just like your husband says, and you get all hot just from the feel of my touch, well, then, honey, I'm going to fuck you right out here in these woods. Does that sound like a deal?"

"Yes, sir. On one condition."

"What's that?"

"You can't touch my..."

"Your what, honey?"

"My clit, sir."

"Okay. Sounds fair. I won't touch your pretty clit, but I'll touch the rest of you. Every last inch of you. Does that sound fair?"

"Yes, sir. But only with your fingers."

"Well, alright, then," he says, lips to her ear. "Sounds like a deal. Let's get started."

He sinks down onto the blanket behind her, the denim of his jeans scratching the skin of her ass. He reaches around her and under her T-shirt, cups her bare breasts as if the sheer weight of them were a pleasure in and of itself. Grazes her nipples with his fingers.

"Bet you want to lose, don't you, little lady?" he rasps into her ear. "Maybe if I win, I won't fuck you out here. Maybe I'll take you back to my cabin. With my buddies."

"Buddies?"

"Yeah. Maybe I'll take you back to my cabin and me and my buddies will take turns on you."

Yeah, uhm, I didn't write a word about your buddies.

"Leaf."

"Maybe I'll take you back to my cabin and make my buddies watch while I have my way with you."

Much better.

"Whatever you say, sir."

"That's right. If I win, you do *whatever* I say. That's the deal."

He bends forward so he can dip one hand all the way down to her mound. He keeps his word, avoiding her clit, running his fingers gently down her folds instead.

"I don't know, honey," he drawls. "Feeling pretty hot down here."

"Is it?"

"Yeah. Sure is. Now we made a deal, isn't that right, honey?"

He's using his palm now, rubbing it across her folds, back and forth, stopping just shy of her swollen, aching nub. Teasing it so well she's aching for him to touch it.

"Yes, sir. We made a deal."

"So if I free these hands of yours, you're not gonna try to run away on me now, are you?"

"No, sir. I'm not going to try to run."

"Good." He rips the T-shirt away from the bench's armrest. "Because I'm going to have to examine you up close now to see how you're responding to my little test here."

Suddenly she's on her back and he's lying on the blanket beside her. He's pulled her T-shirt up and over her breasts. Now she feels even more exposed to the night, to *him*. And this time, when his fingers pass over her folds, there's no ignoring the wetness there, even though she'd like him to. Even thought she'd love to draw out this teasing for another hour. Hours, even.

"Oh," he says with a start. "Oh, my. You've got a wet pussy here, girl."

"Do I?"

"Yes, ma'am. A nice, hot, wet pussy. For the life of me, I just can't figure out how a man would leave a pussy this hot and wet all the way out here in these woods. But I guess I shouldn't complain. Because now it's all mine. Ain't that right, little lady?"

His desire for her, real and authentic and unscripted, makes his voice shake. She stares up at him for the first time since they started. He's got his Stetson on and his light leather jacket and his Levi's. Being practically stark naked and under his control while he's still fully dressed only makes her hotter and wetter.

"And since we had a deal," he says as he tugs her T-shirt up over her head. "It looks like it's time to pay up."

He fingers the box of condoms she dropped on the blanket when she first got there.

"I've got your husband to thank for a lot of things, don't I?" he says, then tears the condom wrapper open with his teeth.

"How about you stop talking about my husband and take what's yours?"

"Yeah," he says, sliding out of his jacket and unbuttoning his plaid shirt. "Well, he was right about one thing."

He unbuttons his jeans, frees his cock, slides the condom on with one hand. His tone is calm and collected but his speed is all horny, desperate teenager. The combination of the two makes her feel as if she's the one who's got him under control, not the other way around.

"You really are a filthy little girl," he growls.

He closes one hand gently around her throat. With the other, he drags the head of his cock back and forth over her folds, then in a slow circle over her clit.

He's free to touch it now that she lost.

Won. I won. I so won.

"But right now, you're *my* filthy little girl."

Slowly, he pushes inside her. As he drives himself deeper, his lips hover inches above hers. There's wonder in his expression, the joy at being inside of her for the first time. Not inside the character she was playing seconds before. Inside of her. Amber Watson.

He's so big. So much bigger than any man she's been with. But he's taking his time, thank God. Kissing her neck the way he did in her front hallway the night before. Palming her breasts the way he did in the motel room that morning. It's like his desire demands that he tend to every inch of her in any way he can. Stroking, teasing, tasting, gazing.

He's also dropping the role, becoming himself once again now that they're joined in a way they've never been before.

"You like that?" he rasps. "You like getting fucked by a stranger in the woods?"

She wraps her legs around his waist and squeezes. His eyes pop open. He seems unsure of what she's doing until she starts to sit up. This gives him no choice but to rock backward onto his haunches under her shifting weight. She's still impaled, but sitting up now, clutching the sides of his face in her hands.

"You're not a stranger, not anymore," she says, even though they never planned to drop the fantasy like this. "You're Caleb." She kisses his cheek, the line of his jaw. "Be Caleb." She pulls back, grips his face again. "Fuck me like Caleb wants to fuck me. Like you've always wanted to fuck me."

A groan escapes him, the sound of the role dropping away, the sound of the man who's wanted her for years melting into her, driving himself into her, tasting her nipples as he thrusts with his powerful hips. His Stetson slides off the back of his head and thuds softly to the blanket behind him. The cool night kisses her everywhere now, except in those spots where the heat from his hands and his lips and his powerful arms set her skin aflame.

"Amber." It's a plea, full of equal parts pleasure and resistance.

"Yes, baby."

"Amber…I…"

"Yes."

She grabs the side of his face. His thrusts intensify. His eyes shoot open as he stares up into hers. There's that plea again. He's seeking permission to let loose inside of her. "Anything," he gasps. "I will be *anything* for you."

"Be the man who comes inside me," she whispers.

That does it.

His jaw goes slack, his mouth a near perfect *O*. The waves of his climax pulse through his hard, powerful body as he drives himself deep inside her with a frenzy of hard thrusts. His bellows become shudders. He wraps his arms around her, holding her against him as tightly as he can, which in their current position, places his face just above her breasts.

Well, I got mine last night, I guess, she thinks.

Suddenly, he tilts her backward, one arm curved around her lower back for support.

Once he's laid her down on the blanket, he reaches down, grips the base of the condom and pulls himself gently from her folds.

As he kneads and massages her thighs, his fingers drive waves of pleasure up into her sex. Before Caleb, every man she'd been with had rolled off her as soon as he'd peaked. Now, without pausing to free himself from his condom, he goes to work on her with his tongue. It's slow and languid but also perfect. Not the divine oral assault he'd subjected her to that morning. Something different and more careful. Having come allows him to pursue her pleasure in an unhurried way.

"Waited so long for this," he whispers. "Waited so damn long for you, for this."

In the past, her orgasms have been long, slow builds. Sometimes too long and too slow. This one comes on sudden as lightning, triggered by the power of his tongue and his whispers working in tandem. She grips the back of his head. Pleasure curls her toes and makes her hips feel liquid. He refuses to release her clit from his sucking lips even as she lets out gasping, stuttering cries. She bucks against him, fights the urge to flail her limbs, and still he doesn't relent.

She's not sure which way is up or down until he settles down next to her and takes her in his strong arms.

It takes her a while to remember how to breathe.

"Well," he finally says, lifting his head up off the blanket so he can look into her eyes. "How'd I do?" he asks with a broad, goofy grin.

"Damn," she whispers.

"You only had to use the safe word once. Pretty successful, if you ask me."

"Yeah, and it was the *light* safe word. Not the, you know, red alert."

"True."

"You don't really want to share me with your buddies, do you?"

"I'd sooner rip their damn faces off. Forgive me. I'd never acted before. I got kinda carried away."

"Okay. Good."

"I mean, I was just trying anything 'cause I couldn't wait for you to get wet. Hell, I would have put on a goddamn Kermit the Frog costume if I'd thought it—"

"Okay, okay. That's enough. Thank you."

"Seriously, though. Were you happy with my performance?"

"Baby, happy's not the word."

"Good." He kisses her gently on the tip of her nose. "I like it when you call me baby."

"Do you? I'll call you baby anytime you want."

"Good. Do it again."

"Baby," she whispers.

"Now do it while you give me a kiss," he whispers.

"Baby," she whispers and kisses him on the cheek.

"Awesome. Now do it while you lick my balls."

"*Shut up, jackass!*" she cries through her uncontrollable

laughter.

He's laughing as hard as she is. When she goes to slap him across his chest, he grabs for her hand and the ensuing tussle lands them in a new position, spooning like lovers snuggled up together in bed.

"I guess we'll have to do one of your fantasies soon," she says. "It's only fair, right?"

"Aw, you don't have to worry about me." Her back is to him, but she can hear him trying to suppress a smile. "I'm easy. My biggest turn-ons are wine and conversation."

"Are you always a sass mouth after you get laid?"

"Also, stuffed animals. Love me some stuffed animals."

"Alright, well, I'll make a note of that."

"Seriously, though. I don't have any big fantasies."

"Interesting. I'll remember that."

"Although…"

"Oh, boy. Here we go. What's it gonna be? French maid or schoolgirl?"

"Well, I was gonna say now's a terrible time to ask me this question."

"Why's that?"

"Because I can't think of a better fantasy than being with you now, just like this."

She rolls over so she can see his expression. He's not being sarcastic, not in the slightest. In fact, he looks a little nervous to have answered so directly.

"Do you have any idea what you did for me tonight?" she asks. "Do you have any idea the shame you lifted from me, from my body, from my heart? And the fact that you were the one doing it, the man I've always wanted. The man I've always loved…I mean, I can't even…"

"Of course I do, darlin'. Why do you think I did it?"

She snuggles up against his chest because for some crazy reason, it feels like this position will allow her to hold his words more closely to her heart.

After a while he says, "I do kinda have a thing for librarians, though."

"Good," she answers. "That's an easy costume."

14

The Haven Creek Inn only serves breakfast and dinner, so when Amber and Caleb walk into the dining hall at half past noon, they've got the place all to themselves. Except for her mom, who's setting one of the corner tables just for them.

The chandeliers are made out of antlers, a long painting on one wall replicates the view outside, and there's a wall of glass doors looking out over a stone patio and the steps leading down to the swimming pool. All told, the building's big enough to accommodate a wedding party of around one hundred people, more if you open all the doors.

When her mother sees them, she sets down her water pitcher and gives them a warm smile.

"And how are we today this *very* late morning, Mister Watson and Miss..." She remembers they already have the same last name and coughs to hide her embarrassment.

"Don't worry, Momma. He's getting a lawyer when we get back to Dallas so he can change his last name back to Eckhart."

"Oh," her mother says. "Okay."

A strange blend of emotions, most of them dark, it looks like, passes through her mother's stare.

Caught, her mom looks away and gestures for them to sit.

"I'll go see if your pancakes are ready."

"What was that about?" Amber asks.

"The name thing's kinda weird for now. Don't worry. I'll fix it."

A few minutes later, her mother's back, a plate in each hand. Lemon ricotta pancakes, served on the inn's signature blue toile china, pads of butter sliding off them like skiers in melting snow.

Too bad her mother's refusing to look either one of them in the eye.

"Momma, what?"

"Nothing. Y'all enjoy your pancakes."

She turns to leave.

"Momma!"

Amber points to the empty chair. Her mother flounces down into it. It's Caleb to whom she suddenly gives her full attention.

"I want this trip to be special for you both, I really do. And I hate to mention anything that touches upon that *jerk*. But what you said just now, Caleb, about changing your name?"

"Yes, ma'am," he answers.

"I don't have a problem with it. I really don't. But...these things with the trust and the bar..."

Amber's heart drops. Her cheeks flame.

Why didn't she think of this before?

"You and Abel," her mother continues, "y'all made all these arrangements that Amber and I didn't know anything about. And according to what she told me the other day on the phone, they're our first line of defense against Joel if he tries to make trouble in the LLC. So tell me, if you go changing your name right now, I mean, before we get this all sorted out. Is that gonna cause problems for Watson's? For everyone who works there?"

"Oh my God," Amber whispers.

"Oh, honey, don't get upset. It's just a technicality. But maybe for a little while, until we get Joel out of the picture, nobody changes their names, okay? And I hate to say it, but that also means nobody nullifies any adoptions either."

"It's fine," Amber finally manages. But her performance is a lousy one, so she tries again. "We'll figure it out. It's fine. Let's just eat." *Second verse, wore than the first*, she thinks. Because it's more than a name, and it's more than a piece of paper and they all know it, and that's why the three of them just sit for a while.

"It's not fine," Caleb says.

When she looks up at him, he doesn't seem angry, just calm and resolute.

"And it's not a problem," he says.

"What do you mean?" her mother asks.

"The trust documents don't list me as his heir. Yeah, I'm the trustee, but as an individual, not a family member. A simple name change won't affect that as long as it's properly filed. And nothing about the documents we drew up stipulates that a family member has to be the trustee."

"Really?" her mother says, stunned. "Abel agreed to that?"

"Not at first. But I managed to sell him on it."

"How?" her mother asks.

"I told him if this was really going to be a fail-safe in case Joel turned out to make a mess of Watson's, he should keep it as separate from family as possible. He thought I was worrying about a technicality and I pointed out that putting language in there about me being his son was just about emotions, not the law. As long as I was named as the trustee, I'd be able to keep tabs on Joel and shut down his promotions budget if I so chose. Didn't matter whether I was Abel's son or some guy he just met on the street. Unless I went and nullified the adoption, what did it matter whether or not the documents listed me as an heir?"

"And that's what you really wanted, wasn't it?" her mother asks. "The option to nullify the adoption at some point."

Caleb tightens his grip on Amber's hand. "Guess so. I've never been big on hope before these past few days. But I guess I had a shred of it in me back then."

"And what did he say?" Amber asks. "What did he say when you asked him to just list you by name and not as his son?"

"Not much. He was pretty sick by then and we were rushing to put the documents together while we still had time. I remember he just shook his head and kinda laughed and said some old saying that I'd never heard him say before."

"What old saying?" her mother asks, sitting forward suddenly, her voice tight as a drawstring.

"I think he said… Sometimes the road rises up to meet you instead of beat you."

Her mother's hands fly to her mouth.

Amber hears herself suck in a breath, and then suddenly she's blinking back tears.

"He knew," her mother whispers. "He knew what you really wanted."

"What do you mean?" he asks.

"It wasn't just an old saying," Amber manages. "He used to say it all the time but he stopped the night your parents died 'cause he thought it would be insensitive given how they'd died. He always said it when he didn't get his way."

"No," her mother says, shaking her head. "It was more than that. He first heard it in the Marines. He didn't just say it when he didn't get his way. He said it when he'd lost a battle of some sort. Something big. Something he'd been working on for years. Something like keeping you two apart."

"Oh, Momma," Amber says.

"He knew," her mother says through tears. "He knew why you wanted the trust written that way and he didn't stop you."

As she rises to her feet, her mother holds out one hand as if her tears are something outside of herself she can literally hold at bay. But the best she can manage is to turn herself toward the glass doors, her back to them as she cries into her hands.

Once she catches her breath, she finally says, "Goddamn, but that man could be a stubborn son of a gun. But every now and then he knew how to lose with grace."

Amber rises, takes her mother in her arms. They stare out at the sunlit treetops and the piled high clouds blowing across the blue sky.

"But I miss that bullheaded bastard, I really do," her mother finally says.

"Me too," Amber answers.

Clearing her throat, her mother turns quickly and kisses Amber on the forehead.

As she stands over Caleb, one hand resting on his shoulder as if she were anointing him with a new title, her mother says. "Promise me you'll change your name back as soon as you get to Dallas, Caleb. Promise me you'll walk right through the door Abel left open for you. Then we'll be the family we were truly meant to be."

She bends down and kisses him on the forehead too.

"Now eat your pancakes before they get cold."

Amber watches her mother hurry from the room.

"Should I follow her?" she asks Caleb. "I feel like I should follow her."

"I think when your mother wants your attention she knows how to get it."

"That's right, I guess."

He pats her empty chair with his hand. But it's his mouthful of delicious, molten pancake that really convinces her to take a seat. Once she does, and once he's managed to swallow, he raises his water glass.

"Bad luck to toast with water," she says.

"Fine," he says and picks up one of the tiny flower vases studded with sprigs of lavender. He clears his throat until she picks up one of the other ones in kind. "A toast."

"To who?"

"To *those birds*! Who do you think?"

"Alright, easy, cowboy. It's been an emotional morning."

"Fine," he says, then he clears his throat, lowers and then raises the lavender again as if he's rebooting. "A toast."

"A toast," she says. "With lavender."

"And sass, as is to be expected with the two of us."

"Indeed. What are we toasting?"

"Well, I can only speak for myself. I'm saying good-bye to the sister I never wanted and hello to the woman I've always loved."

"And I'm saying, I love you too. But you knew that already."

"It's nice to be reminded."

"Don't worry. I'll never let you forget it."

Epilogue

"Given that I'm losing my favorite assistant, I'm not really sure why I should consider this a celebration," Belinda Baxter says, then she scoops a handful of beer nuts into her mouth and chews angrily while surveying the crowd inside Watson's.

The bar's as packed as Amber's ever seen it, the kind of turnout they usually see for a concert or a record release party for some band that's gone gold. But this is a private event. For the most part, the guests are employees, both present and former, their friends and family, and pretty much every living relative Amber has in the states of Texas, Oklahoma, and Louisiana.

And they're all celebrating one simple fact. Just that afternoon, Joel Claire sold his majority stake in the LLC that owns Watson's back to Amber and her mother, and in turn, she and her mother signed over a majority share to the bar's new owner, Caleb Eckhart.

Belinda, on the other hand, has decided to turn tonight's festivities into a wake for her favorite personal assistant.

"I'm sorry you're choosing to see only the darkness, Belinda," Amber says. "But if I remember correctly, when I first told you I was going to take over the books for this place, you had a much different reaction."

"I don't know what you're talking about, miss."

"I believe you said something along the lines of, 'If I had a boyfriend that hot, I'd be riding him everyday at work too.'"

"That may be true, but you should still allow me my feelings. It's only fair. You know I had to hire two women and a gay guy to replace you. And the gay guy didn't even look twice at my shoe collection. He wants to work with my *cars*. I swear, I never should have encouraged you to look out for your best interests."

Her former employer's glass of Merlot looks distinctly out of place amidst the beer bottles and rock glasses scattered along the rest of the bar. But at least Belinda's made an attempt to dress for the venue. She's wearing a shiny jacket with Western tassels. Puffy and shiny and not exactly cowgirl material and…are those entwined C's on the lapel, almost hidden by a jeweled broach shaped like a horseshoe?

"I didn't know Chanel made anything with Western fringe," Amber says.

"They don't. I had one of my new girls add it this morning."

Just then, Belinda's face falls. She fortifies herself with a quick slug of wine.

Amber follows the direction of Belinda's gaze to…her *mother*? Really? What on earth does Belinda have against her mother? Is she still embarrassed by all that Desire Exchange silliness? It's not possible. The two women have been in the same room several times since then and neither has said a word about it.

Is it Nora? She's walking right next to her mom, wearing one of those thousand-watt smiles, and maybe, Amber wonders, trying to scope out any alien/human hybrid children who might be hiding among the attendees?

It's Amanda Crawford!

The woman's dressed in a flowy cocktail dress that screams, *I'm too rich to be here!* She's also wearing a stony, furious expression that matches Belinda's. The closer they get, the more Amanda raises her Louis Vuitton purse in front of her as if it were a shield meant to withstand both bullets, knives, and the furious glares of women like Belinda. So far, her mom and Nora are oblivious to the currents of icy tension passing between the two overdressed multimillionaires.

Nora gives Amber a huge hug. But her mother just gives her a perfunctory kiss on the cheek. The two of them spent most of the day together in lawyer's offices finalizing the paperwork of her ex-husband's departure from the business. And that's good. Because Amber doesn't want to be bothered with a lot of greetings right now. She wants to know why Belinda and Amanda are staring at each other like cornered rattlers.

"So I take it you two know each other?" Amber finally says.

"We do," Belinda says.

"Indeed," Amanda says. "We do."

"It's nice to see you standing up, Amanda," Belinda says.

"Oh. Don't be silly. You're just enjoying one of those rare moments of seeing someone other than yourself."

"Oh, dear," Nora says under her breath.

"Uhm," her mother says. "Should we, maybe, clear the air here? Is something going on that we don't know about?"

"All the ceiling fans in the world couldn't clear the air when *this* one's in the room," Belinda snarls, then she takes her wine glass and departs into the crowd.

"Whoa," Amber says.

"I'm sorry," Amanda says. "Was some creature just speaking or did one of you have Mexican for lunch?"

And then Amanda's gone too.

"What on Earth was *that*?" her mother cries.

"I have no idea," Amber says.

"Well, I think they're upset with each other for some reason and they don't want to say why," Nora says.

"You think, Nora?" her mother answers. "Get yourself a beer. I'm driving."

Amber's mother takes Belinda's suddenly empty barstool.

Nora heads off to get the attention of one of the overworked bartenders.

"If I never talk to another lawyer again, it'll be too soon," her mother says.

"I second that," Amber says. "But we did it. That's all that matters. We did it."

"You can say that again," her mother says.

"I will. A whole bunch."

"Also, I've got a present for you, sweetie," her mother says. But she's scanning the crowd, not reaching into her purse or revealing some gift bag she might have been hiding behind her back.

"I'm ready," she says.

"An old friend of mine from Baylor knows little Mary's aunt."

"Wait. *Mary* Mary?"

"Yes, Joel's Mary. Well, it turns out she's not Joel's Mary anymore. She already jumped ship for the drummer in some band that can actually get a gig. Joel apparently did a whole night of singing sad karaoke at some bar in Irving before they kicked him out."

"Well, God bless 'em," Amber says, toasting the air in front of her with her beer bottle. "God bless 'em both."

One of the bands they've hired for the evening has been tuning up on stage for the last several minutes. But it's Caleb who now takes the microphone. He clears his throat a few times.

"Alright, everyone. If I could just have your attention."

There's some whoops and applause from the crowd, but he quiets them with a wave of his hand.

"Now, I'm not sure if all y'all heard but as of today, Watson's is under new management."

The reaction inside is touchdown-at-a-Cowboys-game loud. And it goes on for several minutes as people clap and scream and war whoop.

"Wow," Amber cries to her mother. "They really hated Joel."

"Or they just love Caleb as much as you do," her mother shouts back.

When the applause and the screaming finally die down, Caleb's got a big smile on his face, but all he does is nod his head and touch the brim of his hat as if someone complimented him on his jeans. "Thank you. I appreciate it. And I can guarantee you, we're gonna keep this place on track so it lasts another twenty-five, or hell, let's make it *fifty* years being just the kind of place Abel Watson intended it to be."

More applause. And then people start shouting other intervals of time. One hundred years, three hundred. It's like a badly organized auction before Caleb silences it with a winning grin and an outstretched arm.

"Now, some of you may know my history with the Watson family is a long one. And if it hadn't been for them, I'm not quite sure where I would have ended up. Certainly not here with all you fine people, making my head swell with all your rowdiness and attention. But I did something else this week. Something important. And I need to tell y'all about it, regardless of what you're gonna think or what your opinions may be.

"See, a long time ago my parents died, and Abel Watson decided the best way he could take care of me was if he welcomed me into his family. So he adopted me. And that adoption probably saved my life. Today, though, things are a little bit different. You see, years ago… Well, let me put it this way. You ever know the minute you lay eyes on someone that they're the one for you? I mean, you ever hear someone's voice and think, that's the voice I want to wake up to for the rest of my life even if she's yelling at my lazy ass to get out of bed and get to work."

Peals of laughter and a few whoops of agreement come up from the crowd. But Amber's heart is in her throat as he continues. This is the moment she's feared almost as much as losing him—the moment when they stop ducking questions about whether or not their relationship has changed.

She expected him to make some sort of speech, and they'd agreed that tonight they'd stop hiding. But she's not sure if she's ready for him to be this specific and detailed. At least not in front of this many people. People who might already be judging them silently; people who will now have the chance to judge them out loud.

"Well, that's how I felt the first time I laid eyes on Amber Watson," he says.

The roar that comes up from the crowd is almost as loud as the one that greeted his announcement Watson's was under new management. And just like that, all her feelings of anxiety lift, carried away by the full-voiced joy and support of people who've only wanted the best for her.

He waits for it to die down again, then he says, "So, when I tell you that I went and had my adoption nullified, it's not because Abel Watson wasn't a good man and it's not because the Watsons aren't the most important people in my life and always will be. It's because years ago, before my parents died and before Abel took me in, Amber and I realized we were fated to be something else for each other. And every day since then, we've just been delaying the inevitable. And that's why I'd like to remind her that I love her. That's why I'd like me and her to be the first official dance of the new Watson's."

"Wipe your face, honey," her mother says.

"What?" Amber says. "I didn't wear any makeup 'cause I knew he'd do this."

Her mother reaches into her purse and hands her a tissue. Amber walks through the crowd, cheering faces on all sides of her, and then, once she's a few feet away, Caleb jumps off the edge of the stage and lands on the dance floor, arm out, ready to take her for a spin.

"Toldja I'd give you this dance, Amber Watson," he says once she's close enough to hear him.

"You sure did, Caleb Eckhart. You sure did."

"You ready, baby."

"So ready," she says.

He takes her outstretched hand and grips her waist. She panics for a moment when she realizes she doesn't know if they're about to waltz or two-step or what. But once the music starts none of that matters. The only dance that matters is one she does with him.

* * * *

Also from 1001 Dark Nights and Christopher Rice, discover The Flame, The Surrender Gate, Kiss the Flame, and Desire & Ice.

About Christopher Rice

New York Times bestselling author Christopher Rice's first foray into erotic romance, *THE FLAME*, earned accolades from some of the genre's most beloved authors. "Sensual, passionate and intelligent," wrote Lexi Blake, "it's everything an erotic romance should be." J. Kenner called it "absolutely delicious," Cherise Sinclair hailed it as "beautifully lyrical" and Lorelei James announced, "I look forward to reading more!" He went on to publish two more installments in The Desire Exchange Series, *THE SURRENDER GATE* and *KISS THE FLAME*. Prior to his erotic romance debut, Christopher published four *New York Times* bestselling thrillers before the age of 30, received a Lambda Literary Award and was declared one of People Magazine's Sexiest Men Alive. His supernatural thrillers, *THE HEAVENS RISE and THE VINES*, were both nominated for Bram Stoker Awards. Aside from authoring eight works of dark suspense, Christopher is also the co-host and executive producer of THE DINNER PARTY SHOW WITH CHRISTOPHER RICE & ERIC SHAW QUINN, all the episodes of which can be downloaded and streamed at www.TheDinnerPartyShow.com and from iTunes. Subscribe to The Dinner Party Show's You Tube channel to receive the newest content.

Also from Christopher Rice

Thrillers
A DENSITY OF SOULS
THE SNOW GARDEN
LIGHT BEFORE DAY
BLIND FALL
THE MOONLIT EARTH

Supernatural Thrillers
THE HEAVENS RISE
THE VINES

Paranormal Romance
THE FLAME: A Desire Exchange Novella
THE SURRENDER GATE: A Desire Exchange Novel
KISS THE FLAME: A Desire Exchange Novella

Contemporary Romance
DANCE OF DESIRE
DESIRE & ICE: A MacKenzie Family Novella

Desire & Ice

A MacKenzie Family Novella
By Christopher Rice
Now Available

I'm so thrilled and grateful New York Times bestseller Liliana Hart allowed me to reference characters from her MacKenzie Family stories here in DANCE OF DESIRE. If you'd like to find out how Caleb's buddy Danny Patterson got together with his new fiancée, buy DESIRE & ICE: A MacKenzie Family Novella, now available from all retailers. Here's a taste!

* * * *

She'd just give him one little kiss. Something to warm them, distract them and tide them over until they could be alone with all these explosive new feelings.

The next thing she knew she was on her back, their mouths locked, tongues finding their mutual rhythm. The thoughts flying through her head told her this was stupid, wrong. So what if he wasn't her student anymore, hadn't been for years.

They were still trapped. They should be watching the door, the window. They should be doing anything other than discovering they kissed like they were born to kiss each other. He broke suddenly, gazing into her eyes, shaking his head slowly as if he as if he were as dazed by this sudden burst of passion as she was.

"I think…" he tried, but lost his words.

"What do you think, Danny?"

"I think if we just keep our eyes on the door, we'll be fine."

"Okay."

Was he putting the brakes on? She wasn't sure. It was the most sensible thing to do, that was for sure. He slid off her and sat up, back against the wall, eyes on the door. She did the same. But he curved an arm around her back and brought her body sideways against his. It was awkward at first, but then he positioned her so that she was lying halfway across his lap.

"Now that I'm watching the door," he said, unbuttoning the top few buttons of her blouse, "I think we'll be fine."

"Oh, yeah?"

He brought his fingers to his mouth, moistened them with his tongue, then dipped them between the folds of her shirt. Slowly, he wedged them under the cup of her bra. When he found her nipple underneath, he said, "Yeah. Just fine."

In an instant, her body was flush with goose bumps.

Eyes on the door, his gun within reach, he circled her nipple with his moistened fingers. His precision and restraint combined to make her wet in other places as well. She'd seen the passion in his eyes, a youthful crush that had matured into a man's desire. But now, he was willing to delay his own gratification so that he could protect her and pleasure her at the same time.

"Let me give you a little help there," she whispered."

Sign up for the 1001 Dark Nights Newsletter
and be entered to win a Tiffany Key necklace.

There's a contest every month!

Go to www.1001DarkNights.com to subscribe.

As a bonus, all subscribers will receive a free
1001 Dark Nights story
The First Night
by Lexi Blake & M.J. Rose

Discover 1001 Dark Nights Collection Four

ROCK CHICK REAWAKENING by Kristen Ashley
A Rock Chick Novella

ADORING INK by Carrie Ann Ryan
A Montgomery Ink Novella

SWEET RIVALRY by K. Bromberg

SHADE'S LADY by Joanna Wylde
A Reapers MC Novella

RAZR by Larissa Ione
A Demonica Underworld Novella

ARRANGED by Lexi Blake
A Masters and Mercenaries Novella

TANGLED by Rebecca Zanetti
A Dark Protectors Novella

HOLD ME by J. Kenner
A Stark Ever After Novella

SOMEHOW, SOME WAY by Jennifer Probst
A Billionaire Builders Novella

TOO CLOSE TO CALL by Tessa Bailey
A Romancing the Clarksons Novella

HUNTED by Elisabeth Naughton
An Eternal Guardians Novella

EYES ON YOU by Laura Kaye
A Blasphemy Novella

BLADE by Alexandra Ivy/Laura Wright
A Bayou Heat Novella

DRAGON BURN by Donna Grant
A Dark Kings Novella

TRIPPED OUT by Lorelei James
A Blacktop Cowboys® Novella

STUD FINDER by Lauren Blakely

MIDNIGHT UNLEASHED by Lara Adrian
A Midnight Breed Novella

HALLOW BE THE HAUNT by Heather Graham
A Krewe of Hunters Novella

DIRTY FILTHY FIX by Laurelin Paige
A Fixed Novella

THE BED MATE by Kendall Ryan
A Room Mate Novella

NIGHT GAMES by CD Reiss
A Games Novella

NO RESERVATIONS by Kristen Proby
A Fusion Novella

DAWN OF SURRENDER by Liliana Hart
A MacKenzie Family Novella

Go to www.1001DarkNights.com for more information.

Discover 1001 Dark Nights Collection One

FOREVER WICKED by Shayla Black
CRIMSON TWILIGHT by Heather Graham
CAPTURED IN SURRENDER by Liliana Hart
SILENT BITE: A SCANGUARDS WEDDING by Tina Folsom
DUNGEON GAMES by Lexi Blake
AZAGOTH by Larissa Ione
NEED YOU NOW by Lisa Renee Jones
SHOW ME, BABY by Cherise Sinclair
ROPED IN by Lorelei James
TEMPTED BY MIDNIGHT by Lara Adrian
THE FLAME by Christopher Rice
CARESS OF DARKNESS by Julie Kenner

Also from 1001 Dark Nights:

TAME ME by J. Kenner

Go to www.1001DarkNights.com for more information.

Discover 1001 Dark Nights Collection Two

WICKED WOLF by Carrie Ann Ryan
WHEN IRISH EYES ARE HAUNTING by Heather Graham
EASY WITH YOU by Kristen Proby
MASTER OF FREEDOM by Cherise Sinclair
CARESS OF PLEASURE by Julie Kenner
ADORED by Lexi Blake
HADES by Larissa Ione
RAVAGED by Elisabeth Naughton
DREAM OF YOU by Jennifer L. Armentrout
STRIPPED DOWN by Lorelei James
RAGE/KILLIAN by Alexandra Ivy/Laura Wright
DRAGON KING by Donna Grant
PURE WICKED by Shayla Black
HARD AS STEEL by Laura Kaye
STROKE OF MIDNIGHT by Lara Adrian
ALL HALLOWS EVE by Heather Graham
KISS THE FLAME by Christopher Rice
DARING HER LOVE by Melissa Foster
TEASED by Rebecca Zanetti
THE PROMISE OF SURRENDER by Liliana Hart

Also from 1001 Dark Nights:

THE SURRENDER GATE By Christopher Rice
SERVICING THE TARGET By Cherise Sinclair

Go to www.1001DarkNights.com for more information.

Discover 1001 Dark Nights Collection Three

HIDDEN INK by Carrie Ann Ryan
BLOOD ON THE BAYOU by Heather Graham
SEARCHING FOR MINE by Jennifer Probst
DANCE OF DESIRE by Christopher Rice
ROUGH RHYTHM by Tessa Bailey
DEVOTED by Lexi Blake
Z by Larissa Ione
FALLING UNDER YOU by Laurelin Paige
EASY FOR KEEPS by Kristen Proby
UNCHAINED by Elisabeth Naughton
HARD TO SERVE by Laura Kaye
DRAGON FEVER by Donna Grant
KAYDEN/SIMON by Alexandra Ivy/Laura Wright
STRUNG UP by Lorelei James
MIDNIGHT UNTAMED by Lara Adrian
TRICKED by Rebecca Zanetti
DIRTY WICKED by Shayla Black
THE ONLY ONE by Lauren Blakely
SWEET SURRENDER by Liliana Hart

Go to www.1001DarkNights.com for more information.

On behalf of 1001 Dark Nights,

Liz Berry and M.J. Rose would like to thank ~

Steve Berry
Doug Scofield
Kim Guidroz
Jillian Stein
InkSlinger PR
Dan Slater
Asha Hossain
Chris Graham
Pamela Jamison
Jessica Johns
Dylan Stockton
Richard Blake
BookTrib After Dark
The Dinner Party Show
and Simon Lipskar

Made in the USA
Middletown, DE
04 September 2021